The Unleashing of Ren Crown

Anne Zoelle

ISBN-13: 978-0-9858613-8-4

ISBN-10: 098586138x

Books in the Series:

The Awakening of Ren Crown
The Protection of Ren Crown
The Rise of Ren Crown
The Unleashing of Ren Crown
The Destiny of Ren Crown – Coming in 2017

DEDICATION

To Matt, S, Mom, and Dad.

CONTENTS

ACKNOWLEDGMENTS

Special thanks to Maureen, Matt, Barbara, Poppy, and Sara.

And to S.

Chapter One

VISITS FROM OLD FRIENDS

MACHINES HUMMED steadily and wisps of light licked the air as Doctor Greyskull wrapped another thread of magic around my ribcage, fixing the fractures inside. Viewing screens teaming with spells were arrayed all around the room showing other rooms in Medical, areas around campus, the current telecast of the combat competition, and news reports on the Department and Excelsine.

Greyskull had called up each in succession; vainly trying to keep me perched in place while he worked.

I fidgeted, view wavering, as another flurry of mental communications ran rampant through my brain from all of the delinquents—the *Bandits,* as Patrick kept calling us now—with status reports, updates, or requests for reassurance that everyone in our group was safe.

I was still trying to incorporate the frequency simulator Trick, Saf, and the others had made for me. As an auditory process, it wasn't easy for me, but the benefit of knowing everyone was safe was worth the pain.

A flurry of replies came back—*"Safe!" "We did it." "Bandits United!" "When are you getting out?" "How's Olivia?"* mixed together in my head.

"Miss Crown," Greyskull said in a beleaguered voice, and I realized I had twitched again at hearing my friends' replies, ruining Greyskull's carefully placed healing string.

I cringed and gave my friends a mental "be back soon," then swiped my finger over my armband to turn off the communications.

"I know, yes. I just need to sit still for fifteen more minutes. Fifteen minutes. No time! Anyone can do that. I can do that! And, you can call me Ren," I tacked unnecessarily onto the end.

"Just until everything settles, Ren." He gave the magic a little twist, completing a complicated knot, and I released a breath I didn't know I'd been holding. I *did* feel better.

Chapter One

"On top of not being completely well at the start of your *outing* today," he continued, "during your trip you endured quite a few negative magic impacts."

There was a gentle rebuke in his words.

"Everything turned out okay," I said lightly. It was still something of a surprise. I had gone to rescue Olivia knowing that there was a chance I might not be coming back.

He cast a gently chastising glance up at me, then continued his delicate work. "Phillip and Miss Price are home, and that is something to be celebrated. It is to be determined how well everything else turned out." He pulled a new string of magic through a gash in my side in a quick series of motions, patching it. "And you can call me Grey."

"Really?"

"No." But he was smiling.

I relaxed a little. The "to be determined" pieces, as he deemed them, hadn't been my focus. And I'd learned few things ever went *well*. I always got the job done, in the end, though—even if I did end up in Medical every time.

I reached into my pocket and touched the marble resting there. I rolled it between my fingers. It contained a trace amount of the Third Layer's magic. Magic *I* had put inside.

I was capable of extraordinary things.

I could fix this world.

"And in the three-way tie for first—Alexander Dare!" declared the announcer from the combat competition broadcast on one of the screens to my left. "Amazing turnabout this past day. Fraught with seesawing standings. After destroying the competition for days, no one thought it possible that he still had a chance—not after the Dare scion missed the swords competition this afternoon and looked to be indisposed for the remainder of the events. But he recovered just in the nick of time to enter the Freespar field, and the media mages are *still* talking about what it was, exactly, that he used on the field at the end to stay in the competition. If I didn't know better, I'd say it almost looked like a piece of Origin Magic."

"How interesting," Greyskull murmured without looking up.

I swallowed, but said nothing in response. I hadn't given Axer anything. But then, if he wanted my magic, he didn't need my consent.

The announcer kept talking. "Speaking of earlier events, a record fifty contestants entered the medical tent a few hours ago, beset by the same flu enchantment that disabled Alexander Dare. Freespar was delayed for an hour in order to treat the participants, and though a number of groups are calling foul on the delay, the action was magically supported by no less than three quarters of the competitors. Truly a remarkable cross-layer diplomatic win this week in the sports world."

So that's how he'd gotten away from the competition. A flu enchantment. Probably with his "body" lying on a cot conveniently next to Ramirez's.

A fortunate event for Constantine, Olivia, and me. Constantine and I had gone to Corpus Sun to rescue Olivia knowing the risks—knowing we might not come back. That Axer, and whoever he had brought with him, had contributed to us getting out alive was certain, and I was grateful.

We had almost toted Raphael back to campus with us, though, wearing Marsgrove's skin.

"Would you have known?" I asked Greyskull, knowing he would make the connection to what I was thinking. "Would Raphael have been successful in coming here?"

"Likely, at least for the amount of time he'd need to implement whatever he planned. He knows Phillip, and hides himself well, especially from me." Greyskull didn't look up. "Though he will have far more difficulty doing so in the future."

A tattoo swirled in an infinity pattern on the back of his hand.

I watched it move sinuously across his knuckles. "Because of the tattoo?"

"Because of the tattoo," he confirmed, nodding.

I recalled the euphoric look of joy that had appeared on Raphael's face after the tattoo hit him. It had been a magic Raphael had been totally unprepared for. "What did it do?"

Greyskull continued to weave his healing spells, but his eyes were slightly unfocused, like he was internally gazing into the distance. "It was meant to remind him of things forgotten. Emotion can be the most powerful weapon one has."

I had certainly found that to be true.

"He used the tattoo against Kaine," I said. "It made Kaine scream."

Greyskull smiled unpleasantly. "Happiness is a potent sword against someone who lives solely on pain."

I examined the slight bend of his head as he worked. I thought about the yearbook and the feeling of kinship reaching up from each of its pages. Every choice the doctor made in this war was fraught with possible pain—his friendships pulling him in opposite directions.

"Are *you* okay?" I studied him closely.

"I am still where I choose to be." He smiled, directing the healing tattoo into my skin. "Your concern is noted, though."

There was enough playfulness in that response that I didn't want to ask the other question foremost on my mind. However, it couldn't be left unsaid.

3

Chapter One

"Will you...be targeted by Raphael now, for helping me?"

Greyskull fiddled with another of his tattoos before setting it on the back of my hand. I couldn't read his expression.

"I gave you something that I hoped would ultimately help him as well."

Compassion welled within me. I couldn't side with Raphael, but I understood Greyskull. I could see the hope that he didn't want to let go of.

"The power of friendship?" I said lightly.

"Perhaps. Never forget that there is a line, though, Miss Crown—Ren. That sometimes the most loyal thing you can do for your friends is to tell them they are wrong, or to help set them on a new path, even though they might hate you for it. Sometimes loyalty is in *not* towing the line. Or so I've been told." He smiled ruefully. "I will deal with any consequences from my actions. That is all each of us can do, in the end."

I rubbed my finger against my pocket, over the marble inside.

"I'm going to fix the world," I said, somewhat absently, looking at the screen in the corner that was cycling through replays of the destruction of Corpus Sun, the abnormal layer shifts currently affecting the region, the last year of terrorist activities, and the news conference being held by the Department's public relations head.

"I will watch it burn as you do," Greyskull said, just as absently, as if we were discussing preparations for a summer storm.

"Do you think that's what it will take?" I asked, watching a mushroom cloud of magic destroying a Second Layer city in a replay on the screen. "Burning?"

"Sometimes you can repair the walls of a home. Shore everything up—rewire, patch, and paint. But sometimes the entire foundation needs to be rebuilt. People have a bad habit of determining which is needed, based on factors apart from the actual timbers."

I tapped a finger mulling over his words.

I could fix this world.

"I will add," Greyskull said in an easy and calm voice, "that perhaps you might want to wait a few days before making any major decisions. The world is still running, much the same as it was the day before, whatever the Department wishes in the midst of its scrambling. Perhaps you might consider...being a student?"

I pierced him with a look of horror. "I'm a woman of action. Such choices would damage my reputation, Skeletor."

"My name is from a distinguished line of healing mages who practiced the mental arts, I'll have you know," he said placidly, while deliberately spinning the tattoo he was manipulating on my skin.

"Ow, ow, ow!" His manipulation didn't really hurt; it was more the way someone might repeatedly activate my funny bone or the weird spot under my kneecap—sending my leg into spasms.

"Okay, okay, settle down. You know you are the only hero for me." I rubbed my leg, and tried to hide my grin. "Don't you have healer's oaths—do no harm, and all that?"

"Mages are tricksters in all things. Better to trust no one," he said gravely, unable to hide the twitch of his lips, though he, too, tried.

"I'll certainly trust your word on that," I said, just as sincerely.

"You are wise beyond your fourteen years."

"And you are witty beyond your forty."

He shook his head. "My wintered eyes weep."

With his intensity, physique, and tattoos, Greyskull physically looked like he participated in a Fight Club after hours, but as a doctor, he always projected patience and kindness when he healed a student. It was an interesting juxtaposition.

I patted his hand affectionately. "Your eyes are like dark chocolate chips of sadness."

He produced a sandwich from the ether. "Don't eat them."

"No promises." I snatched the food, suddenly realizing I was starving. It had been a while since Constantine and I had eaten.

I let Greyskull work undisturbed while I ate and watched the screens monitoring Olivia's and Constantine's rooms.

Olivia was still out cold in hers.

Constantine's long body was reclined against a mass of pillows, like a sultan in his posh tent, and he was staring at the ceiling of his room while manipulating small bits of magic between his fingertips. Plotting something. Always.

A heavy field of healing magic surrounded his midsection.

I forced the last bite of sandwich into my mouth, relaxation failing me.

Greyskull had prioritized our injuries immediately, and had deemed Constantine's stomach wound—containing necrotizing components from Kaine's shadows—the worst of the lot, even above Olivia's mind-alteration.

I'd been allowed to hover and help Greyskull tend Constantine's wound, then secure Olivia in her own room, before being bustled into a third room for my examination.

I wiped my hands slowly against each other, gaze fixed on the wound. "Constantine will be okay?"

Greyskull tipped his head, and a tattoo rose and circled his neck, then disappeared beneath his shirt. He seemed to understand that I was looking for reassurance. "If you hadn't used the lotus bloom along with your connection to him, your friend's fate would have been different."

"But he'll be okay?" I probed, sinking the nails of both hands into the underside of the chair.

Chapter One

"Your friend will recover fully, especially with the group dynamics you have all stumbled into. The lotus held the shadows in a type of stasis, and we eradicated the seeds before they were able to do their intended damage. If left to serve their purpose, the shadows kill or...alter the victim. Kaine's shadows corrupt."

There was bleakness in the statement. And when it came to Greyskull, that almost assuredly meant the words tied back to Raphael.

"Shadow magic doesn't have to be evil." Greyskull delicately tied together two ends of my magic that had been hanging in burnt tatters for the past week, his fingers rock steady even through his bitter sadness. "But Kaine has few positive emotions. It makes his spells especially twisted."

"Raphael was with Kaine, fighting him, when they disappeared. Do you think...?"

Greyskull's lips tightened. "I don't know."

The two men were wherever the portal pad had spit them out—maybe in a shadowed limbo state created by the combined magic of a Shadow Mage and a man who had Origin Magic at his disposal and protection magic in his blood.

I wondered what a hybrid of Kaine's and Raphael's differing brands of insanity would look like.

I shivered.

Greyskull's lips tightened further, seeming to understand my unspoken imagining.

"Happier thoughts, Ren," Greyskull murmured.

I concentrated on the news feed on the left screen—the one giving manic reports on everything from the explosion in Corpus Sun and resulting layer shifts, to the hastily called commission examining the Department, to the All-Layer Combat Competition results.

"Yes," the announcer said. "The decision is in... A panel has decided that the unprecedented situation of having three combatants tied for first place—one Second Layer mage, one Third, and one Fourth—will be resolved thusly: They will not be competing in additional tie-breaking events, but will celebrate unity across layers as co-winners. They will start their victory tour after the closing ceremony events tomorrow night."

The combat mages from Excelsine had done extremely well. Nicholas Dare had absolutely dominated the distance categories. Axer's five-man squad had earned at least one first in their individual specialties as well as the team event, and each had placed in the top thirty overall competitors. A truly excellent showing for one school.

Bellacia had to be *swimming* in delight. Her broadcast outing the Department's illegal detainment of Phillip Marsgrove and the praetorians' accidental trapping of Helen Price's daughter in "hell" was on everyone's spelled lips, and Bellacia's correspondents had been in exactly the right places to gather each piece of news first. She'd had advanced knowledge of what might happen and she'd strategically placed her people.

She deserved the accolades for it.

I stroked my armband, where the recording device had been stashed. The destruction of Corpus Sun was receiving only a quarter of the attention it deserved amidst the other frenzied news broadcasts. It was just another minor data point in a long list of revenge inspired incidents by the Department's forces against the Third Layer.

News not nearly as interesting as what the government had been engaged in in their own layer.

Another thank you for Bellacia to add to my growing list. I had no doubt that she planned to collect on all of them, too.

Motion at the corridor window caught my attention, and I winced at the people plodding slowly down the hall, their gazes fixed on me until they could no longer crane their necks any farther.

Greyskull, attuned as he was to me while swimming in my magic, caught the flinch of my body and followed my gaze, eyes narrowing on the hall. The glass frosted over immediately.

"Thanks," I said.

"Take heart. People get used to spectacle, Miss Crown, and then it becomes boring."

Patrick's words about me after Bloody Tuesday echoed in my head. *"Leper and God, Crown."*

I touched the marble in my pocket again, and looked back at Olivia's screen, seeking solace in the current safety of my friends.

Olivia's eyes popped open.

I leaned forward abruptly, eyes narrowing, and Greyskull's gaze again followed mine.

He frowned and let go of a minor healing string in order to call up a deeper set of Olivia's vitals. "She shouldn't be out of the initial coma. No less the secondary measures." He swiped a hand in the air and a series of blue lines appeared. "Odd," he murmured.

Tension tightened further, uncomfortably digging into my gut. "You said a healing coma would last for days, if the person holding the magic wished it," I said.

In the aftermath of Bloody Tuesday, Greyskull had made it seem like a fantastically bad notion for me to undergo a healing coma, stating that if the Department got hold of the ownership of the coma spell things would rapidly spiral out of my control.

The kind of "out of my control" that ended in a collar.

And now, here was Olivia waking up from something that should have had her laid out for days.

"I don't like it," I said tightly. The coma had been placed to prevent Olivia from employing the spell implanted in her by Raphael.

I had to hold onto the edges of the chair, curling my fingers into the undersurface, in order to stem the vibrations of my body trying to rise.

"Nor do I," he said. A wave of his hand brought three charts into view. They shone blue and green in the air. He looked through them quickly. "Her vitals are stable, but her magic here." He pointed to the back section of her brain. "Highly elevated. Agitated. Something activated the system that flushes outside magic from the body."

I frowned, and freed from some of Greyskull's magic, I flipped the view on one of the monitoring screens from Olivia's room to the hall. No one was standing outside her room. There was just the normal amount of traffic traversing the corridor.

I switched back to her room view. Nothing seemed out of place.

I looked back at Greyskull, who frowned, but shook his head. "She's not doing anything harmful. We must spend four more minutes here, then the magic will release and you can check your roommate to your heart's content."

I remembered the way that Olivia had abruptly awakened when I'd drawn close to her in Corpus Sun. Maybe it was just a thing.

"What could happen in four minutes, right?" I asked, trying to relax.

"Naught but a pinch of time," Greyskull agreed, picking up the magic string he had set aside. Olivia's monitor zoomed nearer at his silent command so that we could both keep a closer watch. He tied the string to another in the healing web he was stitching.

I took a deep breath and let it out.

Olivia's gaze zeroed in on me abruptly, staring right at the enchanted bug in her room that I was looking through. My breath caught on my exhale.

"Can she see—?"

Olivia's gaze sliced toward her door and she pulled her legs beneath her, rising on her knees.

"Something's wrong." Heedless of patient courtesy, I reached out and switched to the hall view again, breaking one of Greyskull's careful stitches.

There was someone just coming into view. Who...? All breath in my diaphragm whooshed out as my gut clenched and I surged forward.

Helen Price strode fully into frame, heading straight for Olivia's room.

"Miss Crown! Ren!" Greyskull made a grab for me.

"No, no, no, no—" I started ripping away the healing magic hindering me as I tried to lunge toward the door.

Greyskull grabbed me, and immediately secured my arms to my sides with magic. *"Security,"* came a shout, inside my *brain*, stunning me into motionlessness for a moment. It sounded like Greyskull was speaking out loud, but his lips weren't moving. *"Corridor E2WA immediately. Escort Mrs. Price from the premises. She has no authority to be here."*

I understood in some deep recess of my mind that Greyskull had shared his end of a frequency communication, and was letting me listen to what he was mentally ordering. I also understood he was doing it for my benefit, and in order to keep me under control, but I couldn't look away from the feed where Olivia's mother was drawing closer to her room. I started struggling again, blindly pushing at the magic binding me.

"No, I do not understand," he responded to someone. *"What directive? From whom? Belay th—Stand by fo—I need you here. Unacceptable, Provost Joh—All doors, lock. Head access only. Administrator Stone, no I will not back down, this is my facility and I have direct c—"*

His shared frequencies were becoming mentally entangled as he tried to respond simultaneously to multiple people. The edges of each interrupted thought curled in my brain like mist blown by a breath on a cold morning, eventually lost in the ether. The stunning nature of the mental share finally receded enough that I stopped trying to keep any track of what he was saying, and put all of my focus into fighting to get free.

"Ren, cease. I can't—No, Provo—"

I stilled as Helen's hand hit the handle of Olivia's door. And something about that must have registered with Greyskull, because suddenly there was silence in my head, as he, too, focused entirely on Olivia's mother's hand.

I'd heard Greyskull give an overriding lock command on the whole ward. Olivia's room had already been made inaccessible to anyone but those healers to whom Greyskull had given explicit permission. An overriding lock should cancel everyone but the head of the ward—Greyskull.

The door was locked. Helen couldn't open it. She'd just have to stand there, ranting. That could be dealt with.

On the feed, Helen smiled. There was something very wrong with her eyes and she pulled a finger over her heart in a spelled line.

Blind panic surged in reaction to whatever I unconsciously recognized, reptilian instinct activated, and my magic shoved at Greyskull's. His magic unraveled around me and I managed two stuttered steps forward.

Greyskull grabbed me, freezing me again. "Answer," he yelled. Something had to be wrong with his mental voice if he was speaking audibly. "Fitz? Ng? Phillip? Anyone? *Answer.* Miss Price? *Olivia,* I need you to *answer.*"

But in the feed, Olivia was completely focused on the door.

Helen Price smoothed back her perfectly coiffed blonde hair, removed a pin from beneath the strands, and touched it to the handle of the door.

Chapter One

The lock to Olivia's room clicked open, and in that second, my world collapsed.

Chapter Two

TWO FOR THE PRICE OF ONE

MEDICAL STAFF RAN down the corridor from both directions as Helen entered the room, then slammed the door behind her, touching the same pin to the inside handle as she did. The first responder grabbed the handle and gave an ineffectual turn.

Inside the room, Helen's fingers gave another practiced motion, and our surveillance feed started to fade along with my tunneling vision.

I threw off Greyskull's magic holding me in place, heard the binding strands shatter on the floor, and leaped toward where the feed was fading. I gripped the air in both hands, and *yanked*.

Magic answered my terror immediately and the air around us whistled in a light grinding sound, as if the particles were pushing against each other, creating friction.

The feed ripped back into existence, no more than a second passing, with Helen striding forward toward the bed.

Helen's voice was sharp. "Here you are, you worthle—"

Olivia leaped from the bed, and in the same motion she extended her hand and a medical scalpel flew into her palm. She swung it forward and only Helen's quick reactive jerk backward stopped her beheading. A red line swiped across her clavicle and Helen's hands came up with her magic as her shields immediately responded to the death threat.

Olivia took a blast to the left of her chest, but she just let the motion turn her body sideways as she continued forward, undeterred, even as pain creased the edges of her eyes.

I slammed my hand against the wall, and the barrier started to melt under my fingers. The air buzzed around me. I had to get in there.

A hand wrapped around the back of my neck, squeezing, and all the magic that I had started to channel stopped. The melting wall cooled around my hand, imprisoning it.

Chapter Two

"Do *not*," Greyskull hissed.

I could feel all the hooks and healing spells he had been layering in me for the past fifty minutes, grip around my reaching magic, cutting it off ruthlessly and absolutely. This constriction was *far* different than the binds I had successfully thrown off.

"Let me go," I choked out. He wasn't squeezing my arms anymore, he didn't need to. He had me completely in his power just by connecting with his healing spells.

"You will seal your own doom, Miss Crown. *Two minutes*."

"I don't care about my own doom!"

"You *need* to."

"I won't—"

"Save your magic, Miss Crown. *Less* than two minutes now."

Two minutes could be a lifetime. Could *mean* a lifetime.

I abruptly dropped my magic to a docile state, then set tendrils seeking holes in Greyskull's control.

"I know what you are doing, Ren," Greyskull said as idly as he was able, while visually focused on the feed of the two women battling in blurs of motion. He was no longer trying to contact anyone. Whatever Helen had done had wiped out communications in our area.

"And it might work, eventually," he said. "You have the power for it. But not in the time you need. You will only expend both our resources— resources that we will *need* in two minutes."

For all my power, I was once again under the control of someone I had trusted. And there was nothing that I could do but watch my roommate, whom I had just rescued, fight for her life while trying to murder her mother.

"Please," I implored.

"Less than two minutes, Miss Crown." His free fingers were playing over the wall and zigzags of magic were zipping everywhere, forming grids and constructs that under any other circumstances would have been fascinating. "We will have time to rectify anything that happens to Olivia. Let me do my job. Part of that is making sure the students under my protection do not show themselves to the world after *just* buying themselves some time to hide."

Every time a new wound appeared on Olivia, Greyskull switched something in his construct, gaze never leaving the fight, cataloging every movement and hit, and making split second calculations of how he would fix each wound.

I watched his magic work—the depth and certainty of it.

"Okay." I took a deep breath, and drew back the magic I had sent to worm around his. "Okay."

He nodded, but didn't physically release me. I deserved that mistrust.

The web around me was constructed of healing magic, and I needed never to forget what it was capable of. Resurrection, rejuvenation, remediation. Destruction, termination, purification. Destroying bad magic, bad tissue, bacteria...

When targeting other things, healing spells could be just as deadly as any blade.

Watching the feed, I would never misjudge the damage a magical scalpel could do. It didn't just slice. It sealed, cauterized, butterflied, numbed, and petrified.

And Olivia was accessing every one of its secrets.

A crimson line opened across the upper sleeve of Helen's white blouse. Helen hissed, but got in a blow to Olivia's midsection. Olivia bent forward, but never stopped her motion, thrusting the scalpel up into Helen's shoulder. Olivia twisted the blade and flame burned on the steel, cauterizing a second wound.

Helen shrieked and knocked Olivia away with her good arm. Olivia withdrew the blade with the motion, and with a quick flip of her wrist, she lunged back at her mother. The heel of the handle hit Helen's good shoulder, petrifying her whole limb.

The first inkling of fear lit in Helen's eyes.

"You will *cease*," Helen roared. She tried to remove something from her pocket with the hand she could still partially use—some trinket intent on harm, surely—but Olivia's relentless attacks pushed her back into a defensive position.

A bloodcurdling giggle escaped Olivia's lips, as her limbs, in a flurry of motion, attacked her mother with the fury of a thousand freed thralls. Like someone who had nothing to lose.

I could see it in her eyes—that whatever spells Raphael had placed upon her, she couldn't quit. She had no resistance to do so, no matter what injuries she personally sustained. And she was sustaining many. The berserker nature of her attack—not caring in the *least* about the damage she sustained—left Olivia wide open for retaliation and injury.

Though completely on the defensive, Helen's impressive shields were fighting back—a slice here, a percussive blast there. But Helen was losing. Olivia, kept in line throughout her childhood by her mother's emotional abuse, had more than likely never provided Helen Price any type of challenge. So the extremely *unexpected* nature of the attack was likely contributing to Olivia prevailing, at present.

Arterial spray splattered the wall.

"The Department will have been alerted of that mortal wound," Greyskull said grimly. "One minute."

Chapter Two

Helen roughly healed the fatal wound, but paid for the moment with a slice across her abdomen. However, now clearly fighting for her life, her shields seemed to triple with the knowledge—beginning to deflect, by triple power, each attack she received.

And Olivia...

Olivia began to look less like a Valkyrie and more a ragged mass of injuries and flailing hands, as the enchantment upon her cared nothing about strategic planning or healing wounds. If Helen's shields managed to inflict even one mortal blow, as they were now gearing up for, it was going to be over.

Olivia.

There was a bloom of emotion, suddenly, in the threads that connected us. A bitter brew from her of regret, fierce love, resignation, and the dark exultation of long-awaited *revenge*.

I sent back as many positive emotions as I could. *Hold on.*

"Can't you do something?" I pleaded to Greyskull, my words stumbling over each other. "Knock them out? Make the room swallow them? *Anything. Please?*"

"Price did something when she walked into the room. Disruptor. Every available senior member on staff right now is trying to enter that room. And Olivia isn't responding to my commands. *Rafi, what did you do?*" he whispered, voice strained as he simultaneously handled a hundred communications, the healing web he was readying in blow-by-blow motions, and his own turmoil. "Thirty seconds."

"Administration override?" I replied numbly. The combat mages were gone, our security forces were in flux, and no students were answering my frantic mental calls, not even the Justice Squad. But I expected Marsgrove, at least, to be present and wielding the powerful magic that I had come to expect from him.

"Whatever Price has is overriding everything. We will be making protocol and security changes after this." His voice was heavy with promise. "I'm going to free you Ren, so I can try something else, but you *must* wait for the time to end. The magic *will* knock you out, if you don't. That means, if you can't wait, you will be unable to help your roommate in any way, *do you understand?*"

I nodded and coiled my fight response tighter within myself. I would control myself and get to Olivia. There would still be nine minutes to resurrect her as long as I kept *control.*

Greyskull let me go and we simultaneously strode to the door. His hand hovered over the magic latches. "Steady."

The screen was now on the door, Greyskull having projected it there to give us the most knowledge with the least delay once the timer reached zero.

His fingers were drawing runes on the wall and at the completion of one drawing, both Olivia and Helen stumbled. Greyskull's eyes were scrunched in concentration, his tattooed muscles straining with some inner effort. Two tattoos suddenly shot down each arm and into the wall.

In the feed, the women both jerked as small bolts of black shot from the wall and wrapped around their wrists. Their wrists pulled toward opposite walls, even as they struggled against the magic trying to manacle them, even as they both ineffectively swiped at each other—Olivia far more singularly driven in her state of insanity than Helen, who was actively fighting two opponents.

Helen, now somewhat freed from Olivia's assault, made a complicated motion toward Olivia with her free, but still damaged, hand. "You. Will. *Stop.*"

Olivia stumbled, knees giving out, then pushed through the obvious, crippling pain. She sliced her free arm through the air and Helen recoiled as if *her* string had been cut.

"What have you done?" Helen hissed.

"Your bonds have been replaced, Mother."

"Your little pet of a roommate will be *dealt* with. Easily managed."

Olivia smiled darkly, then reached out as far as she could, skin pulling from under her manacle in the motion, and threw the scalpel into her mother's still useful bicep. Helen's bicep sealed itself to her torso, leaving her with one completed frozen arm and the other with movement only from the elbow down. Neither had tried to use any other body part to focus their magic, and Olivia *definitely* would have, considering the spell, so I wondered if the restriction had something to do with Helen and whatever devices she had activated. Non-combat mages sometimes used devices to better control outside fights, so they could focus on fewer offensive maneuvers.

"Continue to think that," Olivia spat. "And I didn't say one person had replaced the bonds. You are *done*. And *I* will make you pay for *everything*."

Helen awkwardly shoved her half-free hand into her pocket, and pulled out a device. She grimaced in pain, and her glinting eyes narrowed. The manacle abruptly released her.

She clumsily shoved the device into her frozen hand and opened her free palm. "Ungrateful, wretch. I still have control of your life force."

Greyskull went motionless next to me, his breath catching in shock, terrifying me.

Helen squeezed her palm closed and Olivia screamed.

Time stood still then abruptly raced forward, as the last second on the timer disappeared and our room's magic shattered.

Chapter Two

Greyskull yanked open our door and we simultaneously vaulted into the hall at full sprint.

"Move!" Greyskull yelled at the crowd hovering in front of Olivia's door.

They parted immediately, people jerking back. Greyskull slid into the opened space and started dismantling the magic on the door with quick, looping motions.

"Someone will pay for this," he said tightly.

On the other side of the door, Olivia's shrieks grew in volume.

Everything went red for me, bleeding into swirling black-and-white patterns across my interior vision.

A phoenix tattoo with eyes glinting in gold materialized on Greyskull's arm, staring directly at me. I had seen it winding around before. It had made me think of Raphael.

I grabbed his arm, around the tattoo, and sent a package of imagery and magic directly into the connection. Greyskull jerked in shock, but he wasn't a complete badass for nothing—he grabbed hold of the mental package and slammed our combined magic against the wall. The tattoo burned like liquid nitrogen beneath my palm, then shot up his arm, through his shoulder, down his other arm and straight into the stone.

A shrill whistle split the air, and people in the corridor threw their palms against their ears.

In the room, a stone and metal hand reached out of the wall, swept down, and broke both of Helen's hands on the downward stroke. The device fell to the floor, then was crushed beneath the stone and metal fist. All of the previously undermined spells of the medical ward abruptly re-engaged, and Helen flew back to the wall, her pulverized hands secured to the stone at unnatural angles.

More importantly, Olivia stopped screaming. The swirling patterns in my vision subsided.

"It would have been nice to study that device," Greyskull mused, unable to completely hide his abject relief that it was no longer working.

"We'll reverse engineer it," I said, staring coldly inside, no doubt in my voice. I had access to the brightest minds in devices, communications, and disruption, friends who would be eager to do it.

I had more than one project for them.

"You *are* a little scary," Greyskull said mildly.

"I know," I answered without inflection.

Assured of Helen's captivity now, I only had eyes for the other person in the room. Olivia was slumped against the wall, breathing harshly. She was sluggishly, painfully trying to move, still trying to fulfill the terms of the spell Raphael had placed on her—to get to, and *end*, her mother.

* Two for the Price of One *

If she broke loose right now, I'd likely not stop her.

With a moment to breathe and the Medical ward spells renewed, neither Greyskull nor I attempted to enter the room, nor did I let go of his arm as our chests lifted in tandem with the exertion of adrenaline and fear. The hall was silent behind us, the staff waiting to see what their boss would do.

I followed Greyskull's gaze to Helen Price, who was staring back at him through the window. The dark smile that spread across her features was unnerving. She didn't look away from him, and no fear or pain was present on her face.

Never breaking eye contact with the madwoman in the room, Doctor Greyskull said to the hall at large, "Stand guard. Miss Crown and I will enter. Everyone else wait out here until Dean Marsgrove arrives."

I could feel the flurry of silent communication his words caused. Everyone in the hall was wondering why Doctor Greyskull would enter— with a student no less—and no other backup.

"The situation is secured. Councilor Price is going nowhere. And there is still a healing field on the room," he explained calmly. "Miss Crown is already coded into the field as Miss Price's roommate. I will leave her to deal with our patient while I sort out everything else. I don't want to change anything else in the field until I know what has been done to it. Understood?"

There were a few slow nods.

The healing field wasn't his only reason for the two of us entering alone, maybe not even the *main* reason, but his directive was accepted without argument—or at least without verbal argument. The staff seemed to have implicit trust in him.

I'd reflect on all of that later. Right now, I needed to be prepared. Greyskull was expecting something to happen inside the room, and Helen's expression only cemented that.

"They will not be able to move," he said to me, still not breaking eye contact with the psychotic woman inside. "I have complete control of the magic inside again. Take your readings, but don't touch either of them physically yet, understand?"

I nodded, my gaze focusing on Olivia, who looked torn, anxious, and bitter, struggling to pull herself from her bindings so that she could recommence her attack. My focus switched to Helen, who was standing absolutely still, but her gaze followed everything, reading our lips and assessing the magic being used.

Greyskull opened the door and motioned for me to slip inside.

As soon as I entered, I threw magic outward like a glimmering scatter plot, then set the glimmers to work collecting sensory data, reflections, and the remnants of the magic that lingered.

Chapter Two

Greyskull sent the pieces of the broken device sliding into a box in the corner, then pulled forth the healing construct he had built. He fit it over Olivia like shimmering body armor.

I tensely walked to the box. The magic of the container beckoned, receptive, willing me to add and share its ownership. I directed the magic I was collecting to the box before the magic reflections could dissipate and no longer be of use.

We'd figure out the spells in the device and make sure none of them could be used here again.

Finished with the task, I hovered next to Olivia, waiting for Greyskull to finish knitting her up. She was still straining at her bonds, conflict in her eyes. I managed a tight smile as Greyskull shook his head and reactivated her healing coma, levitating her into a relaxed position on the bed.

But Olivia was fighting the magic of her forced sleep. I exchanged a grim glance with Greyskull. She wouldn't stay under for long. We were going to have to figure out another way to deal with Raphael's spell.

Greyskull resealed the wards on the room, gave a nod toward Olivia's form, and I immediately put my hands on her arm. Some of the fight left her as warmth and connection spiraled to her, through my fingers. I breathed out a shaky sigh, trying to ignore the less positive emotions coming from her, and the conflict she was projecting.

"Councilor Price, now that I'm in the room, if you try anything more, you will not survive," Greyskull said calmly. Even his tattoos were calm and steady. It prickled the hair on the back of my neck, though, seeing them so unmoving. Held on a dagger's edge, as opposed to the free and almost playful way they normally moved about.

Only the retention tattoos on the wall pointed to a more agitated mental state, as they slithered in barely restrained anger away from Helen.

Greyskull released Helen from where she was bound.

I gripped Olivia's arm protectively, then forced my grip to relax. I couldn't afford to wake her. But Helen wouldn't *touch* her.

Helen pivoted, putting her back to the corridor window where half of the staff still stood. She awkwardly held up a freed arm like a broken puppet. One shattered hand dangled uselessly at the end.

"Ganix Greyskull, I will charge you with everything I possibly can for this barbarity." The only healing magic she had done on herself was to unseal her arms from her body. She was a ragged canvas of black, navy, and crimson. Even Greyskull's restraint tattoo had left a dark bruise on her arm.

"Illegal use of a holding spell," she said. "Illegal tattoo. Illegal stain. Using a spell against an officer of the law. And this—" She indicated her broken and shattered fingers, which she still wasn't bothering to heal. "What an interesting piece of magic that was. I don't think I have quite enough data to label it yet, but let's put it under Origin magic *assist*, for now."

"You *do* let your delusions drive you, Councilor," he said calmly. "You always have."

She smiled unpleasantly. "Your wretched vow chaining you to this facility and its students is the only thing that has kept you from our justice. What allows me to sleep at night is knowing that in the end, your vow will be your undoing."

"Such an impediment for you, that vow," he mused, whipcord muscles at tattooed ease, arms loosely crossed against his chest. "For it to disturb your guiltless sleep."

"For a time." She smiled. "But that vow will transfer to the new head of Excelsine, to *us*. And then what will you do, Ganix?"

"I will do whatever I must." He stroked a finger along his forearm with intensity and dark commitment. "Though the Department doesn't look to be in any position to run Excelsine, at present, Councilor. So your threats are even less interesting than usual."

"A temporary setback. Decidedly not permanent. And there's *such* a list of things that I've been waiting to try. What would it be like to test the abilities of dear old friends against their old confidantes? He screamed for you, you know?" She mused. "Long hours of it when we made him well aware that you'd never come."

Greyskull's control never slipped, but his eyes promised pain and death. His body held steady and ready, his rage leashed and focused, but I shivered at the look in his eyes.

"Such interesting connections between a healer, a protector, a maker, and a warrior," she mused. "Phillip always did have the best tools, shields, and healing abilities on the battlefield. Too bad he has none of the gall. Who knew that the protector would be the fiercest of the lot?"

"You are a stupid woman." It slipped out of me. That someone would think the protector was not the fiercest person on a field of battle was ignorant, at best. "Though I'm not surprised."

Helen Price didn't have a protective bone in her body.

One eyebrow rose, but she didn't look away from Greyskull. "It...is speaking to me."

Greyskull didn't say anything but I could feel him telling me to stand down.

I clamped my lips tightly together and looked down at my roommate. I had gotten lucky in the birth lottery. Olivia had not. But that could be rectified.

I concentrated on the vibrant connections between us and channeled more energy into her instead of vitriol toward her mother. I would make it so that Olivia had the family she deserved.

"A wise decision, little monster," Helen said in a tone that made me want to *end* her. "Now, Ganix, you will turn yourself and *it*"—she motioned at me—"over to the Department judicature immediately and perhaps I will be lenient with you. Whatever has been done to my daughter is beyond repair."

"Your request is denied," Greyskull said calmly. "It has been well documented in the media what happened to your daughter. Your troops locked her into a situation from which she couldn't escape. Anything she does today constitutes no willingness on her part. She isn't in her right state of mind. It appears she blames her trauma over the past few days on the people who harmed her." He tapped a finger. "The best thing is for her to be away from anyone associated with...torture."

Helen's cutting smile was too sharp. "Such words. You are such a useless man, outside of the connections we can exploit through you. And yet, when we get you, you will rue the day you Awakened. As if you were the rarest of the rare. As if you were an Origin Mage," she tacked on at the end, as if it was on a whim instead of pointed and deliberate.

The door opened. "You can stop there, Councilor."

I jerked my gaze upward as the door slammed shut and the wards resealed.

"Phillip." Helen turned abruptly on her heel. "Imagine seeing you here in the *bowels* underground, especially after your little vacation." She examined him with a razor-sharp gaze. "You look ill, Phillip. Perhaps retirement is in your future."

Marsgrove looked *haggard*.

"Your concern is touching, Councilor. Being held illegally and tortured was quite an incentive to the contrary. My tenure here will continue with increased *energy*."

I winced.

"Tortured?" She laughed. "You are mistaken. Your faculties departed. You were merely placed under a spell. Nothing you say can be construed as anything except false memory, as has been proven in the Tribunal of Fasteroy." She made a dismissive motion. "Now, as to the head of your medical staff, I want immediate—"

"Shut up, Helen, and get off my campus."

She smiled. It was both tight and overly serene, giving her a frightening mien.

She still hadn't healed a single injury—and basic first aid was available to anyone in the medical ward, administered by the rooms themselves, if the person hooked into the wards. Yet she stood calmly, with two shattered hands, multiple lacerations and contusions, and a hastily sealed mortal wound taken during the battle, and she simply allowed the blood to drip slowly down her skin.

It was more than a little unnerving.

"I have every right to visit my daughter, my heir, who is still under my control both by primogeniture and magic. You have simplified my plan by coming here. I will be removing her from this institution directly now."

My heart stopped. My magic, however, did not.

Greyskull was immediately at my side, his fingers pressing against the back of my neck. I hadn't even seen him move.

The motions did not go unnoticed by Helen, however. "Can't control your rabid pet, Ganix? How unsurprising and unimportant. We will control her just fine. The feral looks like she will not bear to be parted from my dear broken heir, so I'll just bring her along as well, shall I, so she can *feel* what I can do under my own roof."

As my body stiffened at Helen's threat, Grey's fingers pressed into my skin in warning. He hadn't touched any spells yet, but with all of his attention on me—knowing full well that Marsgrove could take down Helen —I knew Greyskull would have me down before my intention to channel magic fully formed.

I gave Helen a dead-eyed stare and tried to communicate through sight alone that if she tried to remove Olivia from school, Helen would die permanently and I would go to prison. It was that simple.

Her eyes narrowed on me.

"You aren't taking Olivia," Marsgrove said, voice unnaturally cool and controlled.

"That's *interesting* that you think that, Phillip," Helen said, turning to him. "As Olivia is under administrative review, and still completely under my control."

Administrative review? I swallowed nervously. Part of the contract magic we had instituted before Bloody Tuesday was that Olivia and I would be held accountable for all of the offenses that happened during a Red Status Alert. I had been expelled, but Marsgrove had reinstated my student status in front of everyone of import in the Second Layer when the Department had tried to take me.

In hindsight, it seemed obvious that part of the reason Marsgrove had been grabbed by the Department was that he had shown too powerful and rebellious a hand when he had issued my reinstatement in the aftermath of Bloody Tuesday's battle. Stavros had as much as said so when he spoke of drawn battle lines.

I looked at Marsgrove. I had no doubt that he had understood the ramifications and had made the choice anyway. I relaxed a fraction. He had made his position clear. And while Marsgrove might not normally be on my side, he was on *Olivia's*.

Still, the absolute impact of what might have happened—if Olivia had been expelled like I had—caused my hand to shake against her skin. Administrative review was bad, but it still meant the student was *enrolled*. If she had been expelled, her mother and the Department could have extracted her before Marsgrove had made it back to campus. The only reason we'd been able to bring her to Medical was that Greyskull had used the campus contract magic that placed those experiencing life-threatening injuries under his jurisdiction. As far as I knew, Greyskull still had her listed in the "life threatened" category.

If before the battle, I hadn't had Patrick switch the percentages so that I took more of the burden of the contract magic, Olivia and I both would have been expelled. And Olivia would now be at the mercy of her mother and the Department.

I sent a sliver of thanks to Patrick, along the thread that had started vibrating more clearly as the lingering effects of Helen's device faded.

"I will be removing her from this school this very moment. Do note it, Phillip." Helen snapped her eyelids shut, her fingers unable to do it for her, and waited for the contract magic to snap into place.

My eyes hardened as I looked at her and I prepared to duck and roll from under Greyskull's fingers. It *would* be over my dead body that she removed Olivia.

Greyskull could resurrect me as many times as it took to prove it.

"What is interesting is that you think she is still under your control," Marsgrove said calmly, when nothing happened.

My gaze jerked to him. And, strangely, Greyskull released me, as if I no longer posed a threat.

"Pardon me?" Helen said in clipped tones, looking between Olivia and Marsgrove with reopened eyes, clearly expecting something to be happening.

"Olivia submitted articles for emancipation two weeks ago, to be under the jurisdiction of the school until she is twenty-two." He smiled. "I signed the papers not ten minutes past."

"Absolutely not. I forbid it," she said viciously.

I found I didn't mind Marsgrove's superior smirk at all when it was aimed at his cousin instead of me.

Helen drew herself up and gave a thin smile. "Those papers will never hold up."

"After today's display, there is no tribunal in the layer that will hold up your right," Marsgrove said bluntly. "Life force hooks are considered barbaric and antediluvian. And the population has been trying to outlaw them for years. You should know—you've obstructed the legislation many times under the 'right of tradition' defense. Under the '*No one actually <u>uses</u> it, dear boy,*' defense. '*It is just there for primogeniture protection,*'" he mimicked.

"You have become a stain on this institution and our family, Phillip. And there is only one thing to do with stains." She smiled sharply beneath eyes dead of emotion.

"There are two dozen witnesses who will testify that you just tried to crush your daughter's life force." He waved toward the corridor. "You are the one needing to be *cleansed*."

"Will they also testify she attempted to murder me?"

"She was completely restrained when you used the hooks in vengeance, Helen, so *no*."

"We shall see during the Tribunal hearings, won't we?" She hummed, her mind already leaping forward.

"Olivia has put together quite a well-reasoned emancipation defense. I think it will go very poorly for you to seek the Tribunal under any premise. Of course, this releases you from any further monetary commitment to her education or her welfare, which was a previous concern. But that issue has been addressed. There is precedent, of course. If you require resource aids, take a look at articles five and eight of the char—"

"A Band-Aid. Really, I expect better," Helen said, smiling sharply. "It will hardly reach the courts anyway. And if it does..."

Her face did something complicated.

"Oh. Whatever have I done?" She looked distraught for a moment—an emotion so feigned that it was revolting—and tapped her head with the bent knuckle of a shattered finger. A spell glistened.

"It appears I've been poisoned. Oh, my. Perhaps it was by that Leandred boy." Her gaze swung to me and it was dark and anticipatory. "He's shown an affinity for mind magic and dark spells in the past few months. We have it well documented."

I tightened my hold on Olivia.

"Yes, I do believe that is where we will start our investigation." She hummed, watching me. "Stuart Leandred has been pushing so hard in the past year to get the life force hooks demolished. What an underhanded way to get that legislation passed—by using his son to undermine the opposing side, one-by-one, forcing them to use the spells in ill ways. It's practically Canoverian."

My translator offered me the choice of the translated version of Canoverian—substituting Machiavellian, the version of what my First-Layer-educated mind understood.

"Stuart has been increasingly incapable of making sound decisions," she said slowly, as if thinking it through, broken knuckle tapping her lower lip in a macabre way. "His son seems just as unstable. Perhaps due to having those life force hooks used on him—one has to speculate about what happened in that family after dear Ophelia died saving the child. Yes, I do believe Roald Bailey has a number of recordings supporting the assertion of his son's malevolent aims."

Her damaged arm dropped, and pleasure and triumph bloomed across her bruise-mottled features. "I will be getting my own revenge as well, of course. How dare they do this to me," she drawled, face not changing its cold, self-satisfied expression.

"You are getting sloppy, Helen," Marsgrove said.

She laughed lightly. "The recording enchantments you are trying to gather will never hold up, Phillip," she added. "Though, please *do* try to replay anything that has happened here today. The public *should* know the truth."

Marsgrove's eyes narrowed.

"You don't think I carried only one trinket here?" She shook her head. "I'm not the one getting *sloppy*."

Marsgrove smiled. "I see a significant slide in both your popularity and responsibilities occurring very soon, Councilor. I'm surprised that you aren't at the review. You are being tagged at this very moment for removal from your position and chair. Don't be surprised when you have neither in the morning."

She smiled, and tapped a gnarled finger against her thigh. I could see her cagey brain working overtime. "However, I am still on the Council at this moment, Phillip. And this *student*, Olivia Price, attacked me, a member of the Council. Therefore, she is under the immediate jurisdiction of the Department. I don't need to take her off this campus as an heir. A prisoner works just fine. Do keep up."

The fingers of my free hand curled into my palm. "If you try to take her, I will kill you," I said.

"Miss Crown." Marsgrove sounded as if he was hanging onto everything by a thread.

"It is speaking again." Helen shuddered. "But it *is* good to know what monsters will do."

I swallowed down my next response. Saying anything at all had been a mistake. I didn't need Marsgrove or Greyskull to tell me again.

"And I will keep those words in mind, little demon," she said, facing me. "Monsters should receive the full attention of exterminators and hunters."

"That's enough," Greyskull ordered.

That switched Helen's attention back to him. "I can see the focus of the spell upon Olivia, Ganix Greyskull. You think your spells will hold her?"

She laughed as Olivia twitched beneath my hand, proving her words.

"She won't last the day. And this one," she said, lip curled unpleasantly as she turned to survey me. "She will not last a week."

"That's what you said last week, and yet here we are," Marsgrove said calmly.

She laughed unpleasantly. "She has given us an unpleasant jolt today in public relations, but these things fade. They always do. The public might be outraged today. But next week? It will be mere indignation. And in a month?" She laughed. "The long game is not in her favor. Look at her."

She cast a broken, gnarled hand in my direction. "She is death. Destruction. The end of our world."

I swallowed.

"Maybe it is time for a new world," Marsgrove said.

"Treason," she replied mildly. "Did you enjoy your time in captivity, Phillip? I think there is a special place for you in the pits upon your next visit."

Phillip smiled, thoughtfully. "You are going to die an agonizing death, Helen, and no one will mourn you. You will be a footnote on the wrong side of history, not even important enough for a place on the page."

She smiled sharply. "And you, Phillip, will be a blotted stain on the parchment."

Magic rushed over her in a nearly transparent wave. She clenched, then straightened, perfectly healthy fingers. Her features were once more unbroken and sharp as she casually examined her hands for flaws. "I do think it is time to speak to Grandfather."

"You do that," he said. "Give him my utmost."

"I'll give him plenty, you can be certain."

"As for your claim of attack, Olivia's trauma has been well-documented. It is already making the rounds that you were the aggressor and instigator in an attack on a traumatized student. Prohibited entry onto campus. Illegal entry into a closed Medical room. You are slipping, Helen."

"You will rue this move, Phillip." She smiled widely, and it was terrifying.

"I'm not five anymore, frightened of an ailing, old man. And I'm certainly not that same five-year-old watching my back on the cliffs, fearing the shove from you, the bored university student home for a break."

"You should be."

"No. You were a great fear once, Helen, but you ceased to scare me a long time ago. Monsters only live behind closed doors or in darkened spaces. And your little basement? Just fills me with resolve." Magic appeared in his palm. "Only your impact on the world frightens me now, and soon that will be nothing more than a spare footnote."

Helen didn't move, but something glinted in her eyes for a second.

Chapter Two

Stavros. Stavros glinted in her eyes, like a caged tiger, savage and angry, restless and pacing.

She motioned toward the box in the corner, calling it to her.

"I'm afraid not," Marsgrove said, without an ounce of remorse, as the box stopped moving almost immediately. "Anything that is brought on campus is now under the direct purview of the administration. We retain all rights to *anything* brought to campus in the next hundred hours." He smiled pleasantly. "Do remember that when planning your next move."

Helen coldly looked at each of us before her gaze went to her daughter, lying magically comatose on the bed. Olivia twitched, and Helen smiled.

"Then let the games begin, Phillip."

Chapter Three

THE STATE OF AFFAIRS

AT MARSGROVE'S DIRECTIVE, Helen was escorted off campus by five fierce-looking members of the administrative understaff while Greyskull and I tended to Olivia's wounds.

"You *will* close campus for the night," Marsgrove said to whomever he was speaking, "or I will be sending an appeal to the bo... Good."

He ended the call and tapped a finger on the wall. With complexion sallow and bearing slumped, Marsgrove looked terrible again.

"Wake her," he said, striding toward the bed.

"Not yet." Greyskull calmly met Marsgrove halfway and motioned with his hand.

Marsgrove's palms curled into fists.

I wanted to object as well. However, nothing Greyskull had done so far had been to Olivia's detriment. I could be patient. And the tension building in the room was hypnotizing.

"Phillip." Greyskull motioned again.

I thought Marsgrove was going to refuse, but then he held out his hands, palms up. Greyskull approached each like they were circuit boards. He peered into the crevices and traced one of the lines on Marsgrove's right palm, then another. Greyskull pushed magic along the creases with each movement, up into Marsgrove's wrist, then zipping along his arm.

In his other hand, Greyskull withdrew pestilent magic through the fingernails on Marsgrove's left hand—a far more sluggish process.

Greyskull removed a piece of deadened gray magic and flung it into the disposal grate.

"Do you want to tell me what happened?" Greyskull asked.

"Do you?"

"Perhaps your loosened tongue will loosen mine."

27

Chapter Three

"I can make a guess, from eyewitness reports, Grey."

"Can you?"

"And I can see one missing. What did you do?" Marsgrove clinically, but carefully, looked over Greyskull, seeing things that I could not.

"A rhetorical question, as you already have the answer, Phillip." Greyskull studied the arcing energy, not meeting his friend's eyes.

"For years you've sat on the sidelines... And now?" Marsgrove's voice was oddly intent under the weariness.

"I have not moved my position."

"Haven't you?" Marsgrove asked, voice tightening with unidentified emotion.

Greyskull didn't say anything for a moment, steadily pulling rotten enchantments from Marsgrove's blood and magic while pumping in fresh infusions on the other side. "My position is the same," he finally said. "What you observe is a reaction to the addition of new players and a shifting board."

"There's no dishonor in admitting your views were mistaken," Marsgrove said. He winced a moment later.

I rubbed my knee in sympathy. *Never mess with someone healing you.*

"There is no admission," Greyskull said, his voice calm, but edged in steel. "I regret nothing. Past or present. Do well to remember your own vows."

"Both Kaine and Rafi are off grid," Marsgrove said, after a small silence where both seemed to agree that a slight shift of topic was in order. "Even Stavros doesn't know where Kaine is. When it happened, Stavros..." Marsgrove grimaced. "Went still."

"Stavros was with you?" I could hear the slightest vibration in Greyskull's voice, though it didn't show in his ever-steady hands.

With Marsgrove, in the Department's basement—the basement the government claimed didn't exist.

"All in my imagination, of course. Figments, since no one can ever be too sure under the cocktail they are *required* to pump into the cells, Fasteroy's Defense, *blah, blah, blah*..."

"But he was *there*?" Greyskull asked more intently.

Marsgrove shook his head. "Just a minion with very steady hands wearing his face. I wasn't yet *softened up* enough for an actual visit."

Greyskull's hands remained steady as he worked, and with each motion, Marsgrove's color improved—the pallor left, his cheeks brightened, the creases in his face smoothed.

Magical healing was fast, but this...this was incredible. It was like watching a flower bloom in frame-by-frame acceleration. A growth that usually spanned a few days' time took ten minutes. Greyskull was using a network that was already in place, running healing magic through well-used paths.

"Bone crush spell, blood void enchantment, shadow collar filaments," Greyskull listed them off as he worked. "Typical. I wish they hadn't healed the bones. I hate how they do it."

"You know how it is—they can't have someone exit looking like they've been tortured, even as they claim the wounds are self-inflicted, *blah, blah, blah.*" The ugly tones in Marsgrove's voice were barbed, and almost self-deprecating.

Greyskull reached up with one hand and a tattoo slipped from his thumb into Marsgrove's temple. It was similar to the tattoo he had given me.

Like an overly inflated balloon that had been leaked of its most pressing bloat, Marsgrove relaxed.

"Why did you do it?" Marsgrove's voice was softer—like he knew that the only way he could ask again was in appeal.

Greyskull didn't say anything for a moment. "Ren thought you were being held with Miss Price."

Marsgrove just looked tired now, his color nearly normal. "Kaine took his opportunity when I left myself open on a swing against Rafi. Kaine switched targets immediately. I should have taken Lassiter to guard my back, even though I know he's been selling Rafi enhanced weapons. I know better than to fight Rafi with Kaine nearby. Kaine is nothing if not an opportunist. And Rafi... He smiled as Kaine shadowbound me, before he disappeared again."

Greyskull's expression pained me on an intrinsic level—pain and regret and damage. I could feel his emotions like a ghostly echo as a consequence of performing so much magic together in such a short time. I nearly reached out for him.

"You were *there*, in the dream," I said to Marsgrove, wanting to defend Greyskull and his choice. "Olivia tried to cover you."

Marsgrove finally looked at me. "Rafi saw me taken. He knew I wasn't going to resurface to negate a deception. And he knows which illusions to spin, especially on you. The two of you are quite similar."

I took a moment to control my response. "That's not fair," I said quietly. "Just because you don't like me—"

"You are both inherently motivated to protect others. Seeing someone you love put another's safety above her own would have motivated you to save her even faster, hoping to prevent her sacrifice. You wouldn't have even realized it. Raphael knows you. It makes you even more dangerous and vulnerable."

"Like symbiotic poisonous fish?" I asked bleakly.

Chapter Three

"He got to you first. When you Awakened. There's nothing that can be done about that now," Marsgrove said. He closed his eyes and I felt a measure of guilt at how exhausted he looked, even with all of the very visible healing Greyskull had done. "Listen—"

"No. It's... It's fine." I sent a small tendril of relief to him, something so small that he wouldn't even feel it. With Greyskull touching him it was even easier—he might even think it was something Greyskull was doing...

Marsgrove's eyes popped opened.

...or maybe not.

"You sent magic to me days ago."

"Yes," I reluctantly admitted.

Marsgrove said nothing for a few moments, then, "Thank you. It...helped."

I swallowed. "You're welcome." I pulled my lips between my teeth, then let them free. "I would like for us not to be enemies."

We had had a pretty rocky start. But with Olivia's guardianship now under Excelsine jurisdiction, *Marsgrove* was going to have a massive amount of control over her fate. I didn't want to give him any reason to separate us.

I had been at Marsgrove's whim since the day after my Awakening—with my control cuff, getting incarcerated at his house, being blocked on campus. If he was going to go to bat for Olivia, though, then I wanted to be on decent terms with him.

Marsgrove examined me for long moments, then inclined his head. "Helen's next move will be to send someone from the Department—one of the assessors—to do a review. Helen is not stupid. She didn't have time to evaluate the precise nature of the enchantment on Olivia, but she would have seen the mark of a compulsion spell. She's used them often enough," he said grimly. "And with the way Olivia reacted coming out of the Midlands—your entire exit was publicly broadcast—Helen, if she hasn't already, will put two and two together about Raphael and the focus of the spell."

"Helen can't come back though, right?"

"No. But she will be counting on Olivia attacking the assessor in the same way. Perhaps with less...enjoyment...but with the same uncontrollable zeal. And they'll make sure to have an untampered record of it—with witnesses, maybe even Provost Johnson. They will gain a public record of Olivia's instability and threat to public safety, which will force the university to turn her over. We have one hundred hours to fix her."

I relaxed. A hundred hours was an eternity these days. I was used to working with *two*.

Marsgrove looked at me strangely.

Maybe a hundred hours wasn't something I was supposed to relax about? I fidgeted and cleared my throat. "Can we wake Olivia, now?"

Greyskull nodded and touched his forefingers to her forehead.

She immediately jackknifed upward on the bed. Her hands splayed out, as if she were going to call a weapon, but then she grabbed my arm, the one attached to her wrist.

Her gaze latched onto mine. "You came for me."

"Of course," I said, pulling her into a hug.

"You came for me. You came for me." It was a litany.

"Of course," I murmured into her shoulder. "I will always come for you."

A small hitch of breath, then, "I know. I *know*."

"Good," I soothed. "Come on. Let's take a look at you. Doctor Greyskull needs to make sure you can still do basic addition and recite legal briefs. And that you still have a taste for cardboard breakfasts."

I tried to pull back enough so that Greyskull could do his thing, but she tightened her hold.

"I can't control the compulsion," she whispered against my shoulder.

I stroked her back, wishing I could see her face. Though, I didn't need to see her in order to feel the conflicted emotions rushing through her.

"We know," I said softly, gaze catching Marsgrove's over Olivia's shoulder. "And we are going to fix it. That's why we need to take a look."

Marsgrove's gaze was darting between the two of us, and something slid into place on his face. Some realization or resolve. A resignation not dissimilar to the one he'd sported in the Midlands when Axer had revealed his hand in support of me.

"I tried to kill her," Olivia uttered, like a guilty secret.

"I can't say that you have too many people feeling sad about that. Still, we can't have you going on a murder spree," I said as cheerfully as I could manage while pulling away slowly.

One of her hands reached down and gripped something in her lap. The butterfly I had given her had somehow, miraculously, made it through five days with Raphael, the brawl in Corpus Sun, and the battle with her mother.

I touched a wing and the paper gave a small shudder of relief, like cracked earth finally absorbing a touch of moisture. It spoke to how Olivia had used it during her captivity—wringing every drop from it. I let a little of my magic seep in, refilling it. The papered creature would never work the same again—its life cycle was complete—but it could be a security blanket, an object that would let its owner know that safety was real.

Her safety, however, *wasn't* real.

"I'm sorry," I whispered.

Olivia grabbed my wrist. "You gave me something when I needed it. You gave *yourself*."

Chapter Three

But it was like the dam inside me had blown wide. "I should have put in something that prevented you from being taken. Or from being able to port to me. I should have done better." I wiped a shaking hand over my eyes. "I put that magic in there *for you*, but I had thought it would be used for your *safety*, not for your *sacrifice*."

She straightened. "I made that choice."

I grabbed her shoulders. "I don't want you sacrificing yourself for me, Liv."

"I'm *glad*. But *I* make my choices," she said fiercely.

Her mother, the life hooks, the way that Olivia had acted like a burned soldier when I first moved in with her versus the way she had grabbed her own personal authority, become a general and whipped Plan Fifty-two into place to help someone she loved...

Anguish and fierce pride collided. My overwhelming need to protect vied with the intense joy I could see reflected in her face. With Helen Price as a mother, making one's own choices would be important.

Already gripping her shoulders, I grabbed her to me in another hug, which she fiercely returned.

No, I would not make her choices, or anyone else's, but I could make the world *safer*. A stray bit of mind yarn linked with another. I could make the choices of loved ones *easier*.

"Something worrisome is happening in that brain of yours," she murmured into my hair.

I cleared my thoughts, sweeping them into a bucket where they could ruminate and form tangible threads to revisit and expand upon later.

"I worried, you know," I said lightly, pulling back, my emotions neatly relabeling themselves now that I understood Olivia's own.

"I know. Idiot." Her voice went soft and fond.

Greyskull cleared his throat, and I startled, having forgotten the two men were still in the room.

Olivia looked at Marsgrove, her gaze quickly sizing him up, her warmth disappearing behind a cool businesslike demeanor. "You look better, Cousin."

"The miracles of modern magical medicine."

There was a tension there, as if the floor between them was made of eggshells.

"I had wondered, whether you were a figment of my imagination or a hole in my memory," she said distantly. "As you were suddenly there when Ren came."

His mouth drew itself in grim lines. "What happened after you disappeared from campus?"

She absently tapped her fingers on my arm, her gaze distant. "Likely, not much you don't already know. I was held elsewhere at first, then we holed up in Corpus Sun for three days ago. Verisetti sent a message to Ren, and the idiot took the bait."

"*Hey!*"

Olivia gave me a withering look. "As I'm alive instead of dead, I am choosing not to question your idiocy in this matter, however, from a rational standpoint, you shouldn't have come."

She squeezed my arm before I could respond, the gesture softening her words.

She turned back to Marsgrove. "Verisetti's plan seemed to be twofold. To get Ren out of the Second Layer, and to gain control of her again. I had no idea he planned to masquerade as you, though."

Marsgrove and Greyskull exchanged glances.

"Rafi always has backup plans," Greyskull said. "He had control of the town and its wards, so he would have known it was only Ren and Mr. Leandred that were there, but he knows Ren's ties to the Dare scion. He would have made provisions for that. And for other variables, like you being followed. It's likely he counted on Ren being followed by the Department too."

"Kaine, Tarei, Stavros, and the others would have seen Raphael wearing Marsgrove's face, though," I said, frowning. "And known it wasn't really Marsgrove because they had locked Marsgrove away."

Greyskull shook his head. "The illusion shows what he wants others to see. Just like the illusions students weave every day, however without the lawful restrictions we have in place to protect people from being taken advantage of. He is skilled at impersonation and had plenty of time to create and set a strong enough enchantment to support his goals. Think of the spell on Miss Price and modify it for this purpose. Any Department-related individual sees one thing, all others see something else. He could have made it so that anyone with an attachment to you would have seen something different and specific to his purpose—maybe whatever you saw. Whether he could have held it together on campus with the strict restrictions against him in place is another matter. He'd probably have needed access to your magic, Ren. Or a large enough distraction." He indicated Olivia with a nod of his head. "What else occurred?"

Olivia and I quickly relayed the events, stitching our stories together. Finding Raphael-the-doll, watching him "blow up" the praetorians, releasing Olivia and "Marsgrove," the retrieval by "unknown parties" blowing us to the ground level, the fight—with some verbal dancing to ensure we didn't say Axer's name, the reveal of Raphael-as-Marsgrove, Greyskull's tattoo, the disappearance into my portal pad by both Raphael and a barely living Kaine, and the standoff with Tarei and Stavros.

Chapter Three

From that point on, they had both seen the recording that Bellacia had broadcast of my performance.

An "Oscar worthy" performance, if desperation and blood splatter were all the rage this season.

When we finished, Marsgrove nodded. "Rafi's first plan would have been to get Crown, Olivia, and Leandred to a port spot in town. With only the three of you and the element of surprise, he could have stunned you all. Failing that, his backup plan to accompany you to campus, then work a plan here, almost worked. Everyone was concerned with Olivia. Rafi would have been able to do a number of things, and probably take Crown right from campus. He will have another plan now."

"What about Kaine? They disappeared together, still fighting."

Marsgrove looked grim. "We shall see. Failing anything further, though, Rafi still has Olivia primed as a living bomb."

We all looked at Olivia.

"We need to speak of particular things, Cousin. Verisetti doesn't like silence," she said grimly. "He shared a number of items that I'd like to presume are fiction or insane fantasy. We need to discuss the thing that I said I wouldn't speak of to anyone else," Olivia said pointedly to Marsgrove.

Omega Genesis. Months ago they'd made the deal, that Olivia would tell Marsgrove, and only Marsgrove, whatever she knew in exchange for not turning me into the authorities for three months. That period of time was drawing to a close.

"No," Marsgrove said succinctly.

"That will not do, Phillip, and I think you know it." Olivia's dissatisfaction with her older cousin was in her gaze.

"The public can't handle such a revelation, Olivia."

"They will get it eventually. I read the same periodicals as you do. Although I think them bottom feeders, the Baileys are close to uncovering it," Olivia said.

"Then the world will find out when the Baileys do. You will get no relief from your end of the deal we struck."

I tried to read Greyskull's expression to see what he thought of their coded exchange, but he was tucked over his tools, shoulders tight.

"Then you will give me an extension of the clause stating that you cannot give Ren to the authorities," Olivia said. "Or else I will find the loophole."

Marsgrove's lips pinched. "Consider it done. I'm not too happy with the authorities in the Second Layer right now."

I opened my mouth to ask about Omega Genesis, but Greyskull held up a hand. "Let's take a look at Miss Price, shall we?"

Greyskull didn't dive inside her like he had with me. Instead, he spurred and gently prodded. He tapped his temple, and magic flitted across his vision. I was becoming much more used to seeing this type of magical lens, so it no longer startled me. The more time I spent surrounded by magic, the easier it was to see it in all its different forms.

Something flitted past my vision. Something black-and-white and circular.

And sometimes... Sometimes seeing magic was becoming way too easy.

Marsgrove fitted a pair of goggles over his eyes and watched at Greyskull's side.

"Careful!" Marsgrove spat almost immediately.

"Thank you, Phillip. It is as if I am not the medical practitioner here," Greyskull said acerbically.

"The barb—"

"I do know what one looks like."

"And that second hook—"

"Yes," Greyskull responded, voice clipped. "Standard these days."

Marsgrove remained silent for a moment, but the agitation in his body was loud in the otherwise quiet room. "And do you approve of that standard, Grey?"

"You know I do not."

"Then—"

"Phillip."

Marsgrove grimaced, but didn't finish his statement.

They were like brothers who could not speak of the sibling neither could agree on.

After a few more tense minutes, Greyskull pulled his hand back slowly, then wiped a thin trickle of blood from his nose using a sanitary wave of magic. He fluttered his hand again and I could see magic settle on him like a restorative balm, healing an invisible injury.

"Rafi might not have anticipated seeing my magic in Corpus Sun, but he anticipated that I would be the one to treat Miss Price, if she got away."

Greyskull didn't sound upset, but that same constricting look was present on his face every time he talked about his missing friend. I wondered when the feeling of loss would cease for him.

He moved a rod slowly around Olivia's head, like he was dowsing for an ailment. "The spell isn't permanent. I'd say two weeks more?"

"Unacceptable. There are only three weeks left in term. I will attend classes Monday," Olivia said.

"I can't treat it by Monday, Miss Price."

"I will not miss class." Olivia shoved the rod aside and turned to her cousin. "Phillip, remove it."

Chapter Three

Marsgrove withheld a flinch, by the barest measure. "There are barbs specifically against me in the enchantment, Olivia. Even more than the standard set he employs."

It was unsurprising. Out of anyone, Raphael would plan first against Stavros, who he hated, and second against Marsgrove, who had dedicated himself to taking out Raphael.

"Fine," Olivia said. "Ren, do it."

I shrugged and stuck out my hand. I was starting to recognize healing magic, and the warm buzz from our earlier success was returning. I could stand getting barbed. I'd dealt with worse things. All I needed to do was find Raphael's spell and terminate it.

Two shouts sounded, and I saw Greyskull and Marsgrove lurching toward us in slow motion as I touched Olivia.

A swirling, whirling vortex of sight and sound clasped my mind.

Then silence.

Chapter Four

DREAMS OF CONSEQUENCE

A GLASSY SHEEN warbled into view in waves of blue and white. Soft rippling undulations of liquid and endless streams of gossamer flowed. I felt like John Everett Millais' *Ophelia* floating in the pond, diaphanous wings of fabric spreading around me.

Except, I wasn't floating—I was *under the surface.*

Bubbles exploded around me in a panicked exhale that I couldn't afford to lose.

I tried to lift my arms to pull myself upward, but the weight of my sleeves—miles of fabric floating and sinuously pulling through the water in juxtaposition to my jerking movements—bound me with each motion, like cling wrap constricting a ham.

A golden laugh penetrated the glinting waves like a too bright ray of sunlight.

I was going to drown.

No, *no!*

The fabric of my sepulchral dress bound one hand against my chest. I twisted. The distance to the surface was farther than it had ever been. I was sinking, sinking away, and my lungs started to burn.

Sunlit rays played over lights of all colors beaming down upon me—a kaleidoscope of hues writhing with my movements, but constant in their light. The colors started to merge into one large, penetrating beam of white.

As the last vestige of breath expelled from me in a rolling hack of bubbles, I desperately found and yanked the bright thread of blue.

A hand plunged into the waves and wrapped around my arm, dragging me upward.

Lips breaking the surface, I gasped for breath, aspirating. Images tilted crazily in my view—watery blue sky, kaleidoscopic patterns, twinkling stars, dark hair, a broad shoulder.

Chapter Four

An arm wrapped around me, hand at the small of my back. My savior held me just above the brim of the water. "Shhh."

Hands cradled my cheeks and fingers pushed into my hair behind my ears. My gaze twirled another few endless rounds before finally resting on eyes a particular shade of blue.

"It's okay. Just breathe," he said.

I knew that voice. I knew those blue eyes.

"That's right. Breathe." He cradled my face. "What were you doing?" he whispered.

I couldn't answer. Pins and needles flayed me.

His gaze drifted left, and a strange expression crossed his features— something blank and focused, revelatory and troubled, all at the same time. He reached out and cupped a handful of water.

"Oh, Ren." He shut his eyes and let out a distressed huff of his own. "Why now." It strangely wasn't a question. "I had hoped..." He sighed.

The waves were moving around me again, but differently this time. Like someone was pushing them toward a whirlpool, gathering them into a jar.

Something about the idea was as concerning as the drowning and I started to struggle.

"It's okay." He pressed me against his shoulder, his hand gently cupping the back of my head. I could no longer see his beautiful face. "Just...just close your eyes, Ren. Everything will be fine."

The ebbing waves moved around me in peaceful motions. The buzzing in my head grew louder, and my panic grew stronger. His warm shoulder turned hot.

"Almost there," he soothed.

"Where?" I croaked.

"Everywhere," he murmured into my hair.

Then there was blackness.

~*~

The ceiling came into view as I slowly opened my eyes.

"*Ren.*"

I looked to my right and the dream slipped away like goose down in a breeze.

Olivia was pressed as far away from me as she could get while still *hovering.* On one hand, her terror was extremely concerning; on the other, she looked amazingly better than she had a minute ago—her skin far more peach than salt.

Olivia was staring at my arms. I followed her gaze, to where streams of magic surged through the air, connecting me to the walls of the room, the ceiling, the bed, the floor—suspending me by tubes of magic.

Surprise made me jerk, then relax as a tiny slice of imagining came back to me. This completely explained the underwater sleeve and feeling of being bound. I gave a rusty half-laugh and the dream slipped away completely. I was *awake*.

"What happened?" I had to clear my creaking voice in order to get the entire two words out.

"I happened," she said, her voice stressed and high.

"Oh, hey, it's okay." I tried to move.

"No! Let them do their work."

I pulled my wrist in, trying to examine what the streams—which had tightened at my movement—were doing. "What's happening?"

"You are on magic support."

"That sounds...bad?" *On par with a medical coma? I* did some mental calculations. "How did Doctor Greyskull get me hooked up so quickly?"

"Fifteen hours have passed, Ren."

Okay. That was...definitely bad. I had experienced plenty of blackouts as a result of black magic spells first term, and Guard Rock had fretted more than once over my prone form when I'd knocked myself unconscious with one of my necromancy rituals, but I had never come close to being out for fifteen hours.

An awkward glance confirmed we were alone in the room.

"So...the fix didn't go so well?" I asked her.

"*No.*"

"Well, we'll figure out something."

"You aren't *touching* me."

"I am showered and delightful, I'll have you know." Or, at least, I had been fifteen hours ago. A spell connected to the healing wards in Medical had done a really fine job of scrubbing me before I'd been treated.

"*Ren.*" Her voice was anguished.

"What?" I asked, refusing to take the emotional bait, though there was something weird in my brain that said that I should be concerned. That dream. Something... I shook off the weirdness as I examined her distress. I needed to fix her suffering first. "The first try at the spell didn't work. Pssh. The first try never works."

"It isn't funny!"

I slowly worked my way into a sitting position, the streams of healing magic shifted and lengthened with my careful movements.

"It's a little funny. I look like a magic squid that has been licking too many iced flagpoles. But this whole magic support thing is great," I said, flexing my muscles and feeling closer to full strength. "Definitely a boon to be used when the Department is locked out of campus and unable to breathe down my neck."

Chapter Four

"You nearly *died*, Ren."

"Nah." I waved my hand and a counter appeared with a glowing number two. I pointed at the death marker. "See. I'm still on my third life. Heck, I was probably far more dead when Axer healed me back at the start of all this."

Something about that recollection made me squint. There was something...

"Not *funny.*"

I shook off the oddness, again, and reached for Olivia.

"Don't touch me!"

I rolled my eyes and grabbed her arm. Her eyes shut tightly. After a few moments, when nothing untoward happened, she cracked an eye.

"Intent, Liv," I said. "Since I am not seeking to undo the enchantment with this touch, no harm done. Come on, you are the born mage, here."

When I'd first been learning magic, it had been startling to discover how much intention mattered.

Olivia looked away. "None of it matters if you are hurt."

I softened. Olivia was still getting used to caring, and it meant a lot that she'd forgotten a rigid tenet of magic in her panic for me.

"Well, in hindsight, it was a pretty stupid move on my part to try and undo the spell, if *Greyskull* wasn't going to make the attempt," I said, considering the streams of magic that were still tubing in and out of me.

I knew *why* I had done it, of course—because Olivia had asked me to. Best not to say that in her current state, though.

"But, I'm all fixed up now," I continued. "And we can try again in—"

Painful barbs shot through my fingers. I quickly released her before the spell could grab a firm hold of my intention to try again. Raphael and his touchy spells. Intent, indeed.

"In *never*," Olivia finished for me.

I looked at the magic in question, shaking out my fingers to divert the lingering pain. "Why did Raphael let me touch you at all?" I wondered. "He could have put in enchantments against it."

"It's more painful," she explained tightly, "for you to think you *should* be able to fix the spell and not be able to."

Truth. I tightened my fingers. "We will figure something out," I promised.

"There's no way you are working on this spell," she said in a low voice.

"Out of the question."

"I'd rather sit in Medical for two weeks," she said harshly.

"Liv—"

"Look at you," she demanded. "You look worse than when you came back from Corpus Sun. Do you know what *magic support* means?"

"I assume it's like life support, but for, you know, magic."

"The spell attempted to *drain* you. Verisetti probably *planned* it that way, with a container ready in hand."

Pausing, I looked around, slowly, and with mounting dread. "Where did my magic go? Is everyone okay?"

Olivia bit her lip. "Everyone is *fine*. Doctor Greyskull moved...quickly. He caught it and recycled it back into you. You lost the first draw, though." She looked away.

"Where did the first draw go?"

"No one knows." She pressed her lips together.

Concern rose. "Is campus all ri—?"

"Unaffected. Phillip...checked."

Raphael was likely giddy somewhere with a filled container in hand, then. "How did he siphon it from a distance?"

"Phillip is checking that, too," she said grimly.

I stared down at the tubes. If losing the first draw resulted in all of this, I wondered what losing all of my magic might do. When Raphael had taken my Awakening magic, my body hadn't yet incorporated it—so my body hadn't *known* to miss it. He had left me with enough to cause chaos, enough for my growing mind to use and become accustomed to, enough for seeds to regrow.

I didn't want to think of his taking as a gift. One that had allowed me to grow into my powers.

Oblivious to my internal struggle, Olivia looked even grimmer, "If Doctor Greyskull hadn't already been working on you and mapping your magic... It still took him a few seconds to stop the drain. Any more and—"

"And I'd be a crepe?"

Olivia tightened her hands into fists. "It's my fault. I made you try to fix me," she spit out.

"Eh." I settled back against cushions that I called into existence using the room's allotted magic. "I was a willing participant. Wanting the spell gone is a mutual desire."

"No," she said tightly. "I was *selfish*. I *knew* why they both refused to touch the spells. It was not out of fear for themselves. And I told you to do it *anyway*, knowing that you wouldn't consider an alternative."

It's true, that maybe I should have stopped and considered the consequences. However, I could dwell on that later. Olivia had obviously been left to wallow in misery for fifteen hours.

I called forth another pillow and dented the middle in studied nonchalance. "Are you saying I'm easily led?"

"By those you love, *yes*."

I crossed my arms on the pillow. "As someone reassured me not that long ago, I pick well."

"Pick well?" Her voice rose. "You pick people like *me*. And *Leandred*."

"And you are both fantastic."

"We are just short of *evil*, Ren!"

I gave her a look filled with fake pity. "Your supervillain status has, unfortunately, taken a bit of a hit recently. You are going to have to work harder next term."

"Ren, that is not funny," she hissed.

"Ren, Miss Price," Greyskull said, walking into the room. He didn't look surprised to see me awake, and I wondered how many patient monitors he had swirling in his head at all times.

He didn't look surprised, but whipcord tension pulled the muscles in his face, defining his cheekbones further.

"Is campus okay?" I asked, gripping the pillow. "Where's Marsgrove?"

"Campus is fine, and Phillip is...working." The lines of his body snapped out with a flick of his hand. Whatever Marsgrove was working on was a main cause of Greyskull's tension. "Phillip is off campus, testing Councilor Price's threat concerning the recording enchantment. Price laces her spells with the same paranoia that Rafi did. Likely stole the practice from him when she was testing him like a lab rat."

Tension coiled tightly in the room.

"I'm sorry," Olivia blurted out.

Greyskull closed his eyes, regret painting his features, then a small wave of his hand increased the calming spells. I stopped gripping the pillow so tightly, though I knew it was a false relief.

"Your apologies for encouraging Miss Crown to detach Raphael's spell were accepted already, Miss Price," he said, and between one blink of an eye and another he was the kind doctor he usually portrayed. "I believe that you will not be making the decision again to have Miss Crown attempt to disable the enchantment?"

Olivia shook her head tightly.

"Excellent. Then there is nothing further that requires apology from you," he said firmly. He started unhooking the magic around me. The streams slowly disappeared into tiny crystals set strategically into the walls.

Olivia stared at him for long moments. "Your motives are suspicious, if not your actions."

He smiled. "Yes. But you can believe in the vows I've made." Magic glimmered in the air and Olivia reached out and cradled the cloud in both hands, absorbing the contracts.

"I will look for loopholes," she warned.

"You will join the thousands who have," he said lightly. "Until then, we have work to do."

He unhooked the last of my tubes and the outside magic dissipated, leaving me feeling strangely bereft for two heartbeats of time before my magic kicked back in to start regenerating on its own.

"The assessor made an appointment Wednesday morning, the minute after the deadline deactivates," Greyskull said.

Suddenly those hundred hours seemed truncated. Fifteen hours sooner. "Can't we argue and get it scheduled for after term?"

"Wednesday? You're sure they won't send someone tomorrow?" Olivia's voice was filled with the type of distant pathos that came from always knowing that her mother was going to go against her best interests.

"They can't risk an assessor's tools getting into our hands. And I *will* take them, if they are brought early."

Olivia grabbed a scalpel and lunged toward the door, making me jerk back in shock. She was halfway to the door when the blade magically slipped from her hand into Greyskull's, leaving her gripping the air. She didn't stop, calling another tool to hand. That, too, appeared in the doctor's palm. With a quick flick of his wrist, Olivia zoomed back toward the bed and fell into an unnatural sleep on top of the covers.

I stared at her prone form. I had temporarily forgotten, in the discussion of guilt and acknowledgment, what we were actively dealing with.

"How many times?" I woodenly asked. It had been fifteen hours that I'd been out cold.

"How many times has Miss Price tried to attack someone walking by the room? This is number seventy-three," he said casually, pulling an extra ward across the door and blanking the view to the corridor. "And I restricted physical and communication access to Medical thirteen hours ago as well as putting visual and physical wards on the door to seal it from the outside. Interesting, that Miss Price keeps breaking the visual ward first."

"Who walked past?" I forced my voice to be calm, but it was difficult.

"A student returning to his room after a procedure."

"Who was it?"

"It matters little. There are hundreds more of them. Department-related mages are a penny a dozen here."

I stared at him, lips tight.

"There is nothing that can be done about that." Greyskull's voice was calm. "Miss Price wants to attend classes, but I don't think trailing her, anticipating the disarming of her, and forcing her to her fall asleep until the magic releases is going to work for her or anyone else. And there is nothing you can do at the moment." His gaze bored into me, too intensely for a second, then relaxed into his normal tranquil state. "I have been steadily mapping the spell. *We* will try again tomorrow afternoon."

"But—"

Chapter Four

"Do you want an inflated repetition of what happened fifteen hours ago, Miss Crown? Except perhaps next time, the spell will not inactivate the power of your magic as it slips away."

"No," I said tightly.

"You have to practice caution then. You can't just change things when you want and as you see fit."

We'd see about that. But my mind and body were starting to feel the full effects of the spell and yesterday's events, the adrenaline from reawakening dissipating.

"So, rooming," I said, changing the subject. "We stayed here last night, obviously. Are we repeating that tonight?"

Greyskull woke Olivia, and put a hand to her shoulder as she jackknifed upward.

"Yes. It is best if you don't leave the ward tonight. And as long as you are in the medical ward, you don't have to meet the various room requirements that are tethering you administratively."

"Doctor Greyskull—"

"You can call me Grey when we are without eavesdroppers."

I blinked. He'd said it before jokingly, but this time he was serious.

"You too, Miss Price."

"It's inappropriate," Olivia said stiffly, trying to regain her dignity after her seventy-third attempt to murder someone.

Greyskull tapped the purloined scalpel against his palm, his gaze far off. "Yes. But it's better. Familiarity will tether me to you in ways that will be harder to break."

I swallowed. "You held me," I said as calmly as I was able. "Earlier. Yesterday, I mean." I had lost nearly a day. "Against my will when I tried to get to Olivia through the wall."

"Yes," Greyskull—*Grey*—said. "Cutting through the fabric of magic to get to your roommate is not what you want to have on record with the eyes of the world on you."

It had all ended up okay, though. Olivia was alive. Helen—not that I cared about her state of life—was alive. Still...

I looked at where he had increased the calming spells. "I don't like to be controlled."

"Few do. But if you aren't in control of yourself, someone else needs to be."

He didn't say it unkindly. I swallowed my residual anger so I could sort through it later. I knew he had a point.

"How did you hold me? It was stronger than when..." I shook my head. No good would come of mentioning names. "A number of people have tried, and the ones who have succeeded used something extra." Either extra magic at their disposal, a specific talent, or a device that allowed them to overcome me.

"Your shields." He looked at the top of my head. "They...contain some of my magic. Most of Rafi's early work does. It allows me a measure of control, if I hook into them."

I nodded; relieved that there was an explanation I could work with. Marsgrove had told me, when he'd given the shield set to me, that Raphael would have more control over me with the shields.

Marsgrove's first mistake had been in assuming that I'd never be free of my prison to have that tested.

That Grey had contributed to my shields made a lot of sense. He had always healed me quickly. Stevens probably had her fingers in there as well. She, too, had influence over me that was far stronger than most. And there was no way Marsgrove would have given me something that didn't have some sort of backdoor control for him to activate.

I had blamed the administration magic for his ease in making me sit in a chair, or listen, but that wasn't necessarily the root.

"Shields, like most opportunistic magic, are a well-debated topic," Grey said. "If they are created by a professional, you are susceptible to their magic, but you also get the protection benefits from a trade master."

Not much choice: Get professional shields and be protected from everyone but the maker, or make your own and be less protected from everyone.

"Damned if you do; damned if you don't?"

He lifted his chin in acknowledgment. "All trades have their pros and cons. Mages find their own edges. Their own specialties. Damage can be done with creativity, and advantage can be pulled from any specialization."

I supposed for cooks, using a frying pan with hot oil in it and slicing it through the air worked to hurt and cut just as well as anything would. Or poisoning one's customers, then hitting a latent switch hours or days later before the poison dissipated.

"And with that lovely visual," he said. "I will leave you for an hour."

"What are we going to tell the others?" I asked, my gaze focusing on Olivia, who was steadily staring back.

I ran a finger along my armband, letting the streams push forward without opening them. Like looking at an inbox or chat window, but not yet engaging or opening the thousand messages inside. They were all clamoring on my muted comms—making the communications streams bulge with magic, encouraging me to answer. Some of the people on the other end of those communications were physically closer now, too. I could feel a few of them loitering in the corridors nearby, itching to enter. The physical ward on the door made it impossible to see where they were, but they could be just on the other side.

"Whatever it is, decide quickly," Greyskull said. "Patience is not their strong suit. Mr. O'Leary is attempting to break through the wards on the door again, even after I gave him quite an unpleasant shock fourteen hours ago."

Greyskull touched the wall, and I heard cursing on the other side of the door.

Greyskull raised a brow. "Your sidekicks seem to have an overabundance of time on their hands, at the moment. Perhaps you might make use of it?"

With that, he opened the door, and nearly a dozen faces peered inside.

Chapter Five

FRIENDLY RETURNS

THE DELINQUENTS spilled into the room, and Greyskull slipped into the hall. Patrick was full of boisterous cheer and sharp penetrating eyes, while Asafa was all warm, good-natured ribbing. The others who had been part of the plan, but not in the inner circle, kept a more respectful distance—Kita and Lifen hung back, their calmer personalities in evidence, while Dagfinn chewed a nail and Loudon looked amused, but slightly bored.

Mike and Will gave Olivia friendly arm squeezes as Asafa and Patrick chattered and Neph checked me over.

"We will be *speaking*," Neph said in a terse whisper, then she turned, suddenly brimming with calm and welcome again, and enveloped Olivia in an embrace. Neph's hugs were the best.

She returned to my side, and sent soothing, yet slightly censorious, magic into my skin. She was angry about the events in the last few days, and she was letting me know it.

Meanwhile, Delia...

Delia extended something to Olivia. "Good to see you, Price."

The two of them stared at each other for long moments, then Olivia's fingers curled around whatever Delia had given her. "You too," she said, a little stiltedly, unused to exchanging any pleasant words with Delia.

Some unidentifiable tension released at that, and everyone bustled in closer.

Olivia looked at all of them. "Thank you," she said softly.

Everyone beamed.

And with that, some of the steel that had been missing from Olivia returned. She narrowed her eyes, confidence strengthening her posture, fulfilling the queenship that Patrick and Asafa were always pushing on her.

"Now who is going to tell me *what* you were all thinking?" Olivia demanded.

Thumbs and pointer fingers whipped out as everyone pointed at me.

"No, I already know Ren wasn't thinking," Olivia said. "Let's try again."

She looked at each face, her mouth tightening when she didn't find anyone she felt capable of rational thought or enough care among them— Lifen and Kita had plenty of rationality, but didn't much care if I went off on a bender. The other frequent delinquents, including Will and Delia, were children of chaos.

Olivia zoned in on Mike and Neph, eyes narrowing further as she singled out Neph specifically. "You do whatever Ren wants, but how did she convince you to stay behind?"

Neph's mouth tightened and she crossed her arms, dropping the magical IV drip she'd had going with me. "We will be revisiting both of those items."

"So." I clapped sweaty hands together. "We are all back. Three cheers!"

"Ren, you aren't changing the subject," Olivia demanded.

"I'm trying?"

"We did it, though, yeah?" Dagfinn looked around, pleased. "Pulled one off on the world."

Far more manic smiles were exchanged. Dagfinn grinned and tucked his hands into his pockets.

"You seem...calmer," Olivia said to him, her voice filled with suspicion.

There was a bit of smugness in Dagfinn's smile. "Calmness befits a barely average college student. Which I am."

"Crown wiped his existence," Trick explained, with a flippant motion of his hand. "All the remnants of his tricks."

Dagfinn frowned at him, removing his hands from his pockets to check something. "Not cool, man, if we didn't have the devices on—"

"Yet, we do," Patrick said without missing a beat, his cool reply almost offhand.

"I am guarding anonymity with an iron hand, O'Leary." He fiddled with something. "*Retired. Retired from all things*," Dagfinn stressed.

"Retired? And what do you mean, *wiped* his existence?" Olivia asked, turning from Dagfinn to Patrick.

"Crown is shit at bargaining," Loudon said blithely from the side of the room, his fingers curling around one of the medical devices on the counter. I had a feeling the medical ward would never see it again.

"Is she now." It looked like it took a lot for Olivia to pull that tight smile into place. "Ren, what did you do?"

"I just did some...things. There was opportunity. Lots of opportunities. So easy! Seriously, they got the short end of the bargaining stick!"

Loudon and Lifen snorted and even Will gave me a look of disbelief.

"Then the vine! I just set it loose. And, wow, was it hungry. Though I don't think it ate anyone here. Wait, should I check that?" I darted a quick look around. "No, we would have known. Right? So, seriously, not that big of a deal. And it's gone now!"

"Is that why the Midlands are less hazy?" Will squinted.

"You mean the vine that was eating people in Corpus Sun?" Olivia demanded.

"Yes, that one. The one that is no longer *here*," I said earnestly. "Someone opened a cloak and took it. Or it ate them by jumping into their cloak. Either way, the cloak and the vine are *not here*."

"The *Caliverias Vine*?"

"Maybe? Is that a magic vine? It was a magic vine. A...carnivorous magic vine? I swear I didn't know it ate people. Before. I don't know if Aaa... I'm not to blame for that part."

With hindsight, based on Marsgrove's reaction to the vine, what he'd said to Axer, and my experiences with the vine afterward, I had a feeling that Axer would be in some major legal trouble, should it become known he was the one who had brought it to campus.

Olivia opened her mouth and her lips made little motions for a few moments before actual sound emerged. She turned away from me.

"How did she survive?" she demanded of the room at large. "What have you people been *doing* here?"

"Oh, it's been *excellent*."

"Completely magnificent."

"You should see what we got out of Crown."

"So many bargains."

"Indentured for *life*," came the flurry of responses.

"Welcome back, Olivia," Neph said drolly. "I don't think I have to express how much I missed you."

"Speaking of bargains and devices," I said, my voice a little high. I desperately needed a distraction. With a curl of my wrist, I pulled the warded box in the corner toward me. "We have something we'd love some help with."

The others shuffled forward, immediately interested. It spoke volumes, that a group of smart, jaded scholars assumed it would truly be something of interest. Warmth filled me.

Patrick started laughing in unholy glee upon seeing the carcass of Helen's device.

"I knew they had one," Dagfinn swore, using a sliver of air to separate one broken piece from another. "I'll need forty-eight hours with this and a Magiscope." He directed the second request to Trick, as if Patrick was to be the supplier of said Magiscope.

Chapter Five

"I thought you were retiring."

"...I can retire Tuesday."

"There's a jammer in there," Will said, peering inside. "Locked together with a field override."

Nothing on the broken device was physically touched, each person using slivers of air to move pieces an inch or two.

"The reflections are yours, Crown?" Kita asked, fingers hovering over one of the mind clouds.

"Yes, I tried to grab all the sensory details I could."

Kita nodded, opening one and flipping through the images, smells, sounds, and magic reflections. "Excellent collection. There's manipulation magic here." She pointed to a light cloud of pink. "And a dulling field—both will have attachment points, but might not be discernible in the hardware. I'm sure we'll find others, too."

Patrick looked at Olivia, his eyes piercing again. "This is what caused the communication outage seventeen hours ago."

Olivia nodded, her displeased gaze still locked on me. I gave her an innocent shrug and beaming smile.

"What happened? During the outage?" he asked.

Olivia's expression shut down, and I gave Patrick a frantic head shake.

Patrick's gaze darkened. I could see Saf nodding to something—a mental communication from Trick, likely—as Saf continued examining the box with the others. Patrick wiped the dark expression from his face, and resumed his normal mask.

I dearly hoped the Second Layer mafia was going to have words with Helen Price.

"We've got some scrubbing to do before we can get to the components," Patrick said, looking down, fingers dragging along his chin. "Usually I'd hit up Bryant. But we can't trust him on this one. Crown, your magic is already all over this. The doctor's, too. Best bet is one of you. Think he'd scrub for us?"

Patrick's gaze was sharp and probing. "Scrubbing" a government device —removing the proprietary and security protections—was illegal. And this wasn't a device that had gotten "lost." The Department knew exactly where it was.

I thought Greyskull would be *delighted* to do it, though.

"I'll ask. He needs to have it safely removed from his ward, after all," I said. "And if it *happens* to get lost for a little while in transit to Administration, I think he will have appropriate apologies ready."

Patrick's lips curled into a smirk, the kind of smirk that only a troublemaker, acknowledging a man who had electrocuted him twice in the last fifteen hours, for trying to break in, could have. "Yeah, always liked him."

"Think he can lose it for a week? It'll probably take a few months to reverse engineer, but we need a week to record everything," Kita said, her organized mind already engaging the rest of them in the plan she was putting together. "It's for the good of the company, after all," she said hurriedly, "if we decode and reverse it."

Group dynamics were slowly changing, but there was still an uneasy transition happening with many of the people in the room, between doing things "for oneself" and "working as a team." Rationalizing that it was for the good of the company was a step in that process.

Half of the people in the room had formed an advanced gaming company a few weeks ago, once they realized they had access to Origin art and a team of clever and willing participants who could create something incredible together.

As I'd told Greyskull, I had access to the brightest minds when it came to devices, communications, and disruption, and they were always eager to take a look at anything new and interesting.

The willingness of those currently in the room to help the highly illegal plans we'd implemented Saturday—to save one of our own—was a decided mark in favor of the team concept, though.

"So, the outage can be explained by this." Loudon motioned toward the shattered device, oblivious to the byplay that had already occurred. "How did it get here? Why was it here? What happened?"

He winced immediately, his gaze going to Patrick for what must have been a communicated, mental command. Loudon's shoulders drew into an apologetic, sheepish shrug.

Olivia looked around the room and gave her own edged smile. "Indeed. To start with, we know that none of you are working for the Department."

Relief swept through me. She had decided to share what happened.

"Not that anyone would think O'Leary would be," Olivia added sardonically.

"They carry none of the benefits to which I've become accustomed," Patrick said, though his eyes were sharp, filing away all of the little details to form a bigger picture faster.

She gave him a look that likely carried far too little of the distaste she was aiming for. "Benefits like taking advantage of my roommate while I was away?"

"Well, we can't morally function without you, I guess. You'll just have to stop getting kidnapped," Patrick said.

"What happened, Olivia?" Mike's voice was soft, deep, and calming as he interrupted the byplay. "We want to help."

Olivia looked at him and reclined further on her pillows. "I know you do." Her voice carried a wealth of meaning. "I was out of it for extended parts, though. Ren should tell it."

Given permission, I gave a succinct version of the events concerning Helen Price and Raphael's spell.

"There was also a pin she used to open and lock the door," I said, concluding the tale of Olivia's mother's visit with a description of the pin.

Kita was already nodding, her pity for Olivia barely hidden underneath determination. "We use something similar in raids. They jam the magic, override it for a moment. Greyskull set these wards up, though?" she asked, looking at the wards around the room. "Our pins wouldn't work here. Department R&D, however..." She spread her hands. "They'd be able to make something like that. They hire the best of the best. I've had friends recruited upon graduation."

"And then you never see those friends again unless they want something you are working on," Loudon said, with an unpleasant twist of his lips.

Kita shrugged, jaded look in place. "Pretty much."

"Once you go into the Department..." Loudon swirled a finger in the air. "You don't come back out the same."

"They don't want the two of us, Ludes," Patrick said. "We'd get the trip to Human Bomb Squad or Termination." Trick mimicked a noose cracking his neck. "Oh, I mean, *accidental* hiking fall. Off a cliff. That appears in the middle of the city. Suddenly. And I'm not wearing my hiking boots."

"The Department wouldn't kill you," Loudon said, pushing back blond curls. "They'd have a crime war on their hands. Your father scares even *me*."

Patrick waved the idea away, gaze both jaded and manic. "Accidental hiking fall, man. Or, better yet, terminal use of a terminal. Video games will kill you. Saf, check for death traps when we get back to the room. That's totally the route I'd go, if I was planning it. Sneaky. They could be anywhere."

Saf sighed and touched Olivia's arm. "Feeling better?"

"My mother tried to kill me yesterday. But I also tried to kill her. Those are better than my usual odds."

Every eye turned to Olivia. She was never so flippant about her mother. But it was as if talking about the subject had opened the doors completely.

She gave a grim smile. "I *will* be emancipated. It will not be pretty. And it will be very obvious soon that something is wrong with me. Pretending otherwise will not help."

Trick's smile bloomed brightest. "Good on you, Queenie. Living up to that title."

Saf's was warmer and saner than his roommate's. "First things first. Let's look at the spell."

I grabbed his arm. "Yeah... That's the other part of why we haven't been in touch."

Olivia told them about my fifteen-hour beauty sleep.

"It might not go as poorly for one of you," I said to the room at large. "But even Greyskull and Marsgrove are proceeding with caution."

Looks were exchanged that clearly indicated the others were wise to more than just the fact that two powerful mages were cautious.

Yearbooks were easily accessible. Learning who Raphael had been friends with wouldn't be hard to deduce—especially not with news organizations like Bellacia Bailey's covering the story.

"Nasty piece of magic, Price," Lifen said. She was wearing goggles and staring at something encircling Olivia's body. "Highly intricate and foul. I've done three stints on the Neut. Squad, but this enchantment is not one I would touch. You should talk to Mistress Sidonai."

"The head of the Neutralizer Squad?" Loudon whistled. "Good luck, Price. It was nice knowing you."

Strangely, Neph tensed at the mention of Mistress Sidonai. I was missing something.

"Is there something wrong with her?" I asked.

Patrick leered. "There's nothing wrong with her."

Lifen removed her goggles. "The spell is beyond my current abilities, I'll admit it."

"We could take turns trying to remove it," Trick suggested. "Wear it down. Revive each other in an 8-point lipse."

"No one here, other than Neph and Lifen, has anything other than the normal, first aid ability with healing spells," Kita said dryly. "And, no offense, Crown, but you would probably fry us all. No thanks."

First aid ability in the magical world was more advanced than that of the non-magical—most people could bring people back to *life* in the magical world—but there were *far* more ailments and enchantments, and they needed to be reversed precisely. Magic was a living thing that morphed far too quickly if not neutralized.

"We work on the disruptor; Price works on the emancipation; Crown works on the spell," Kita said. "One problem at a time."

"Where's Leandred?" Patrick asked. "He hasn't been around."

I checked my threads to him. Like the others, I had felt him brush my mind when I'd awakened from my spelled sleep.

"A few rooms over," I said, wondering why Patrick wanted to know.

Saf nodded. "He completed the contract."

There were a few exchanged looks—and exchanged munits—from one person to another.

"Did you bet against him doing so?" I asked, staring at the money slipping into different pockets. "Even with the contract he signed? Did you think he left campus?"

"Good odds on it," Patrick said unrepentantly. "Slippery one, Leandred. If anyone can figure out a way around contract terms, he's your horse."

Well, other than the equine part, I couldn't counter that.

~*~

No one wanted to leave, so it was mutually decided that everyone would stick around to watch the closing ceremony for the All Layer Combat Competition.

Jammed into the room together, a pleasant hum thrummed through the wards. Trick, Saf, and Dagfinn had called forth numerous enchantments so that screens and holograms were arrayed over every inch of the room, making it seem like we were simultaneously in the middle of the ceremony, mass gatherings in Dorm One, Seven, and Nineteen, and a slew of rooms around campus, depending on what received the most "energy" via the combined frequencies on campus.

The closing ceremony for the All Layer Combat Competition was full of pomp and circumstance. And, I learned, plenty of conflict.

"Those daft baggages, thinking they can gain an upper hand," one of Excelsine's more popular student broadcasters said on one of the many simultaneous casts being shared around campus. In our room and from our perspective, he appeared in a full color hologram to be leaning back in his recliner. I vaguely recognized him from one of my classes.

It had taken me a few minutes to get used to this viewing format. We could see the student broadcaster, but since our viewing was "private," he couldn't see us. He was out there in a thousand rooms right now, sitting alongside others, sharing his views.

"Look at that costume. It's an outrage!"

What he was looking at and discussing was part of the broadcast magic, and it popped up in front of him—a hologram within a hologram. I looked at the combat mage being discussed by the broadcaster and a bevy of other commenters, who had joined him in the view set.

The ensemble the combat mage in the hologram was wearing would be beautiful if it were just...simplified. He wore a heavy hauberk and a cape with dense splotches of black or maybe dark red? Blood? The splotches covered an intricately carved light mail made up of silver threads. The kind of light mail that I had seen in the combat competitions.

In muttered tones, Delia had a lot to say to Lifen about the design. When we had been working on the cloaks, Delia and Lifen had worked together to create the type of metallic thread that was used in the light mail. Instead of chain mail, it was a threaded mail that molded like a second skin and could follow the body's movements.

There was a large crest on a helmet that didn't really look like it would aid anyone in battle. And the man's boots were covered in spikes.

The entire outfit looked a little over the top, I conceded, but I wasn't sure about the outrage part.

Neph leaned over. "It's a traditional Elanzi ceremonial outfit. Fourth Layer mages. They slaughtered many of the Second Layer troops who were attempting "diplomatic relations" in the Fourth Layer two decades ago."

"Ah."

"It's an insult," the sportscaster shouted. "Don't invite them back! Ban them from competing!"

And that was the crux of another question.

I had thought it weird at first when I heard people use the terms Second Layer Combat Competition and the All Layer Combat Competition interchangeably.

When I'd asked, I'd received an *earful* about it.

"About 65% of the All Layer Combat Competition participants are Second Layer mages. 25% are Third Layer, and the remaining 10% are from the Fourth and Fifth."

A quick search of my encyclopedia indicated that with the diversity of beings in the Fourth Layer, it wasn't considered "sporting" to engage them in controlled combat and therefore there were strict rules about who could enter the competition.

"Take werewolves, for instance. They only win in melee," Mike said, enthused as ever about talking about blood and sports. "Or sneak attacks. They are great to have on a squad working in real world situations, but mages can easily put them down in a competition where your opponent is completely identified and at the opposite end of a battle square." He drew an imaginary square in the air. "Most beings don't stand a chance in open field battle against mages. However, in forests and between obstacles, mages are at a distinct disadvantage. But in open fields? Yeah. Slaughter."

"Group dynamics. Packs. Lots of pack dynamics in Fourth Layer societies," Will added. "While mages frequently fight in teams, there is still a lone man at the top type of dynamic. It's a very Second Layer notion of superiority, whereas, the beings in the Fourth Layer are more about the group and group fighting. Take Freespar for instance. You'd think it would benefit the Fourth Layer fighters, and it would if it was one group against a single mage or a single group, but it's open battle fighting with hundreds of different opponents all casting at comrades. Fourth Layer beings *freak*. They've succumbed to blood madness in Freespar. Lots of fighting and permanent death. Hence—" Will made a slicing motion across his throat. "No participation."

"Even the human hybrids?" I asked. Werewolves had been covered, but there were plenty of others—all of the monsters from First Layer stories, as well as plenty that I'd never even heard of.

"Even feldragons." Loudon shuddered. "And feldragons can repel most magic, but they have a few distinct disadvantages that competition grade combat mages can easily exploit in one-on-one battle."

I had to look up feldragons. I got a pretty great visual of a lethal-looking beast that was both feline and dragon, and that could morph into human form.

"Except for their berserker," Will said. "But berserkers can't enter. It's in the charter."

"Speaking of, did you hear—?"

"Yes." Loudon looked at me, askance. "I don't believe it a coincidence."

"What?" I asked, at his look. Berserker?

Loudon shook his head, tapping his pen in an off-rhythm against the table. "Just rumors."

I sat for a moment, trying to decide whether to pursue the line of questioning, but decided to go back to the topic at hand.

"So...it's a mage competition."

"Yes. Which the Second Layer rules. Hence, the colloquial *Second Layer Combat Competition*."

"But the Third Layer? They are a mage layer. They should have more participants, shouldn't they?"

Though, when I thought further about what I had learned in Layer Politics 101, the size of the Outlaw Territories, the dwindling countable populations, the lack of schools...

"The Third Layer—well, you know how it is there. There are lots of combatants from the Third Layer, and they do really well in the more survivalist categories, for good reason. But they just don't have the same practice facilities." Will shrugged. "It's like anything. Like science. You can overcome not having state of the art equipment, but sophisticated tools make everything *easier*. Proper tools and training give you an advantage."

"And, quite frankly, they don't want to be counted," Delia said, eyeliner heavy and gaze unamused. "The Second Layer tries to conduct a census every year."

Will nodded. "And every year there is a huge uproar in the accounting. There's a huge discrepancy in population numbers. The authorities doubt that there are so few people living there. Most think that they are deliberately concealing numbers and are planning something. Something big. Revolutionary."

I thought of the Ophidians. They hadn't looked like revolutionaries. They had looked like survivalists. But then, Professor Harrow had lectured that revolution frequently started at the tipping point of survival.

* Friendly Returns *

That led me back to the present, as the participants paraded *en masse* around the stadium in a direct reflection of the First Layer's Olympic ceremony.

"So, they are going to present the awards, then it's over?"

"Well, there is the letting of blood, then, yeah, pretty much."

I stared at him. "The letting of blood?"

"Each participant gives a drop, then it is combined and poured into The Well of Giving. It's supposed to help the Layer that wins the event, but also gives sustenance to the others. A sort of pledge of good faith."

Were the participants okay with that? They must be. It was apparently a predefined part of the games.

"Is there some sort of contract magic that can be forced upon them later?"

"Sure," Mike said. "It's a feudal contract. We'll help and protect you; you'll help us, blah, blah, blah."

And I could see it now. Even though participants like the Elanzi were very obviously disdainful of the officials who stepped forward to hand them their awards, when it came time to awarding Axer, the light in their eyes changed. Gazes grew charged. And it was the officials' faces that showed the strain of handing over an award.

The officials celebrated Axer at the same time they were frightened of him. Frightened of the *possibilities* that he presented.

And what he could do.

How many of those people gathered on the combat field right now had been under the cloaks helping us in the Third Layer? Helping because Axer Dare had requested their aid? Had they fulfilled the terms of a contract held over them by the winner of the previous year's competition? Or had them followed him because of the leadership he naturally exuded?

Were their focused gazes solely showing the mutual respect of one person at the top of their field to another?

Or was there something far more dangerous going on?

~*~

Greyskull shooed everyone out an hour later and Olivia immediately started arguing about returning to our room and attending classes the next day. She hadn't had an episode the entire time we'd watched the competition—the entire time our friends had been present—and she seemed to think this pointed to her being cured.

"You *might* be able to—" Greyskull's voice tapered off as the visual ward on the door slipped again and a student who we had long ago identified as a Junior Department stooge walked by.

Olivia calmly uncrossed her legs from the bed, and grabbed a knife.

57

Chapter Five

Greyskull immediately put her back under.

He looked at whatever the magic was showing him, and sighed. "Or not."

"I'm not leaving her," I said staunchly.

"No. She can't be left alone," Greyskull conceded. "She does far better when your group dynamics ground her. But you have far too many tugs on your magic at the moment, and the ward magic is sensing that you are healed enough to leave."

With Olivia back on campus, I had no less than four roommate connections, and five different rooms contributing to and pulling on me— three in the dorms and two in Medical.

Greyskull rubbed his chin. "You will need to serve a few hours with Miss Bailey tomorrow. But under the circumstances, I think I have a solution that might be best for tonight."

He levitated Olivia, and with a quick flip of his other wrist opened the wall on my left to another room in the ward.

The occupant inside the other room took a look at all of us—gaze traveling from one stationary or levitating body to another and sighed.

Chapter Six

CONSTANT PROTECTION

GREYSKULL WAS GONE. Olivia was out cold. And Constantine wasn't *listening*.

"Helen Price is hardly a concern," Constantine said dismissively, after my third attempt to make him aware of her threats.

I followed as he moved around the room that Greyskull had expanded to include three beds and healing threads instead of one. Olivia was resting in one, Greyskull having decided to let her wake on her own.

"But—"

"We can kill her, of course. I'm not opposed."

I'd caught him up—most of it mentally during the closing ceremony—on everything I could remember from the last twenty hours. It was different experiencing his full sensory reaction, though. The internal and auditory-only reaction from our mental communication had left out the peripheral emotions he usually sought to hide—the emotions that were keys to unlocking what he *really* felt.

He hadn't reacted well to hearing about the life-force hook—freezing and closing himself off completely for a moment—even with one being used on someone like Olivia, who he barely tolerated. In retrospect, I wished I had waited to tell him in person. There were all sorts of twisted bits he was trying to hide, and I couldn't help him, if I didn't *know*.

On the other side of the equation, the idea that the government or the Baileys might come *after* him, barely fazed him.

"Helen Price is going to frame you. And your father," I stressed, uneasily tacking on the last. Constantine never reacted well to anything to do with Stuart Leandred.

He smiled. It was not one of his nicer ones. "Good. I'd like to see her try."

"She said your father has been trying to get the life-force hooks banned."

Constantine laughed so unpleasantly that all of the hair on my arms stood on end. I rubbed the insides of my elbows. "He has been quite outspoken on the issue for the past, oh, what has it been now—seven years."

The threads beneath my fingertips vibrated. The Salietrex massacre had been eight years ago. What had happened in between the two to change his mind? "And before seven years ago?" I asked cautiously.

"He was far more *realistic* with his views of the world. Have you not investigated, darling?" His posture was indolent, but his eyes were sharp. Always so sharp.

I shook my head. I'd felt no pressing need to investigate his father over the other things I'd needed to do. "I will catch up one of these days," I promised.

He smiled and ran the back of a finger down my cheek. "Please do not. He was an industrialist. A ruthless one. Made his fortune in all sorts of unsavory things. Marrying my mother—the darling of polite society—was the best thing he ever did." His finger curved under my chin. "She softened the edges of his empire. Made it easier for him to find agreement with all the politicians and businessmen that he needed. Doubled his fortune and added a sheen of respectability. There was never a hostess as fine as Sashia Mayr Leandred."

His finger slipped away. "After she died, his aims changed, then changed again. Now he works for all the things she loved—especially for peace between nations and layers, completely against the weapons he sold in the past and the illicit deals he brokered. And all the connections she made for him now support him wholly, as do many of his shaded connections from his past. He has billions of munits and all the *right* friends. He is one of the most powerful individuals in the Second Layer."

The Stuart Leandred I had met had seemed genuine. This story supported my impression of him—a person who had seen the light and changed himself so that he might be allowed to stand eternally within its rays.

A change like that seemed positive, not the type of thing to cause pure hatred, and while Constantine could be mercurial, Constantine's seething hatred of his father was not.

There was another story sandwiched between years' seven and eight.

I touched his hands, turning them face-up in my palms. The deep, slicing canyons that had been there yesterday were mostly healed. Only angry lines remained to show the remnants of the episode.

Before leaving, Greyskull had looked at the room wards, in what had seemed like exasperation, then said that Constantine's wounds should be fully healed by morning.

Holding his hands in mine, I pulled my thumbs over the wound marks. I had done the same thing yesterday, when they'd been raw and angry, trying to numb them as best as I could. Axer had patched most of the damage with a sweep of his hand as we ran through Corpus Sun, but it had been a quick healing meant to seal the damage, rather than fix it.

There had been no time for anything else. Running for our lives had precluded fixing any non-life threatening injuries.

The episode that had created the wounds had only taken about thirty seconds, but had been undeniable—Constantine had risked his own life for that of his roommate.

"You saved Axer."

"He's loathsome, but useful," Constantine said dismissively.

The wire Constantine had been hanging onto had cut deeply as it slipped through his hands when he caught Axer. The initial wounds had become damaged even more, the further the two had slipped down the line —Axer doubling Constantine's weight on the raw wire.

"No." I shook my head slowly. "You caught him instinctively. And you could have gotten rid of him by letting him go, but you didn't."

Holding onto him had been a *conscious* choice. The catch could have been easily explained away by the way roommates instinctively sought to protect their own interests. But Constantine had made a conscious choice by holding onto him. Dangling there, over a vortex that would surely have killed them both, he had made eye contact with me.

He had made a conscious *choice.*

I could feel the scars beneath my thumbs, almost burning in response to the line of questioning.

"A waste of resources and pain," he said. "Had I dropped him, he would probably have *bounced* right into your arms. There is no portal to Hell that wouldn't spit him back out," he said viciously.

"Why do you hate him?" I asked softly. I ran my thumbs down the scars again, sending magic along them.

He shuddered. "It matters not. I saved him for you, not for me."

I thought maybe it had been for both of us, but didn't say so. "Thank you."

He captured my thumbs under his on top of his palms, and leaned forward. "As if I could damage the faith you have in me."

Something zinged through me. A magic of some kind.

"It can be more than just me who holds that faith," I said quietly.

He let go and walked over to his bag, tapping his fingers against his thighs, as if trying to figure out what to do with them—which was beyond strange. "I'm more interested in what you are planning to do with that little bauble you brought back."

"After we cure Olivia, we are going to fix the world," I said lightly, as I followed him, running one thumb over the palm of my other hand where it still tingled.

"Overconfidence is my flaw, darling, not yours."

I leaned forward. "In Corpus Sun—we weren't doing too poorly, even before the others arrived. And we'll be even more prepared next time. We traveled across the Third Layer, which even toughened explorers lament. Yes, we had the Ophidians for companions, and I think that they'd take us again, but even without them, we could figure it out, between us. We can do *anything*."

Something almost wistful passed across his face, before he reached into the bag. "I'm disturbed that I find your comments alarming."

I put a hand out and called his ribbon, pulling it from a pile on a chair across the room. I handed it to him so he could pull it through his fingers. He stared at it, then at me. Something very complicated was happening on his face again.

"We all made it back," I pointed out. "Mostly whole."

I didn't know why he was looking at me like that or sending that jumbled mass of emotions through our connection, so I poked out. He raised an eyebrow—he could feel what I was doing—but didn't stop me. The normal seething mass of emotion that never seemed to be directed at me was still there. But the elements that *were* directed toward me contained humor, disbelief, fondness, resignation, possessiveness, and a weird jumbled mass that I couldn't identify—but it wasn't negative.

Well, all of that seemed fine. I gave his threads the equivalent of a mental pat and stopped poking, and just let the connection rest there, pulsing between us. He was no longer trying to block or hide it, and I considered that a win.

"The state of our return is not the part I find alarming," he said.

"Oh, come on, you are always like, 'You have to own it, darling,'" I said, forcing my voice into a lower register. "And, 'You need to make others your minions.'"

I made a motion with my hands as if I were the one stroking the ribbon —which still hung limply in his hand—then looked at the blank space between my fingers. "A white Persian cat would better complete the image, you know. You could hold it in the crook of your arm. Maybe breed one to shoot lightning from its eyes."

"Cats shed."

"I bet magic cats don't shed. Or that there is some fur-collecting enchantment." I pictured little cat hairs zipping through the air and into a wall grate. I contemplated the grate in the room before turning back to him.

His eyes were closed as if he were holding onto his sanity by a thread. "I'm going to bed. If I find out Price has killed us in our sleep, I'm holding you responsible."

I followed him. "You are stressed. What do you really find alarming?" I prodded. It seemed open and shut—we could fix the world. Look at what we had already accomplished.

Everything was turning up roses.

Okay, so Olivia was here, in Medical, ready to execute anyone remotely government-related and the Third Layer was experiencing aberrant layer shifts due to us blowing one of the towns, and the Second Layer government was freaking out... But everything else? Great!

We had Olivia back. We even had Marsgrove back. We were breathing free, awesome air. None of us had died in the fight between a military death squad bent on capturing us and terrorists being terrorists.

Roses!

Constantine's thumb pressed into my temple suddenly, and his fingers wrapped around the back of my head, holding me in place. I could see magic sifting behind his eyes. They narrowed. "There is nothing *wrong* with you..." The way he trailed off indicated that this shouldn't be reassuring.

I sent all sorts of manically happy thoughts toward him, the exchange heightened by our direct contact.

"Ugh." He let his hand drop. "I can't take that much optimism. Maybe that's it."

"It's your kryptonite."

His gaze dropped to my hand as it patted him. Complicated emotions whipped through him again. "No, my biggest weakness is turning out to be something else entirely."

"A conscience?" I steered him toward his bed. He *did* look exhausted, all of a sudden. "I hear they are returnable."

A tiny smile lifted the edge of his mouth. "The fine print gave me forty-five days."

I hitched myself up onto the foot of his hospital bed, back against the wall, and remotely checked Olivia's vitals again—all fine—while Constantine fiddled with something on the small nightstand.

I picked at the hem of my shirt. After a moment, I asked softly, "You don't think we can do it? All of us working together?"

He paused, then continued his manipulations without looking at me. "Fix that blasted layer? Yes. Over the course of the next thirty years with plenty of political buy-in, yes. Will you be patient enough for that result? No."

And there it was again. That resignation. That strange *maturity*. Like he understood that I was going to do it anyway and that he was going to help, even though he thought the idea stupid.

I would have bet money on predicting the responses of each of my friends to me saying I wanted to fix part of the world. Constantine was defying my script.

Constantine was a "watch the world burn" type of mage. The bigger destruction, the better.

But...

"You didn't kill Raphael."

He froze, just for a moment, then the *feeling* of resignation doubled. "Sometimes there are moments when the realization of a goal changes."

"You no longer wish to kill him?" I asked doubtfully.

"I wish him a long, painful death. And if the axe and hood are handed to me, I will hasten him to it."

"Then...?"

"I'm going to bed." His clothes abruptly changed into loose pants but no shirt.

"Is it because we are discussing feelings?"

"Yes."

I tried to hide my smile.

"Also because I had a hole hand-carved into my stomach and still feel like shivitty carnage."

My smile dropped completely and I inched closer, nearly reaching out a hand to touch the bare skin which looked perfectly unblemished. "I thought we fixed the wound completely. Isn't that why you are still in isolation?" Pseudo-isolation now.

"My body is still panicking, though, and I couldn't sleep last night with that lovely little near-miss dirt nap you took. Only sleep reorders and soothes bodily panic." He eyed me deliberately. "Real sleep. Something you should avail yourself of some time."

"You don't feel strange? Poisoned?" I asked urgently, wanting to make *sure*.

"Whatever you did yesterday prevented Kaine's shadows from burrowing too deeply. Greyskull purged the remnants."

I shuddered. "I don't like Kaine's magic."

"Few do. Archelon Kaine was one of the most feared mages in the Second Layer, mere days ago."

"And now?"

"Well, that depends on if he is dead—hopeful thoughts—and on who is doing the fearing. There are other terrifying mages to choose from now," he said with a pointedly amused look.

"That's not funny."

"It's hilarious. Now *sleep*."

I bit down on my tongue to keep from arguing. Constantine needed to sleep. I needed to *let* him.

"I will," I said.

But I didn't want to sleep, not yet. What if Raphael and Kaine had formed into a super *super*villain—now one man instead of two—and they pulled me through the dreamglass?

Constantine was watching me through narrowed eyes. He must have felt my fear. "I can use one of those sleep spells on you, too, you know." He'd used one on Olivia, stopping her from murdering everyone Department-inclined when we'd exited the Midlands.

"Your sleep spells aren't going to stop everyone from gawking horribly tomorrow," I said lightly, as if that was what I was worried about.

"Accept their tribute as your divine right."

"Funny."

"Ren—"

"No. Don't worry. I'll sleep."

He muttered something that might have been *"Right"* and turned off the light. I opened my palm with the bauble inside and set its calmly swirling patterns to reflect on the ceiling like gentle northern lights.

It seemed so simple. I could see the streams—*right there*—the streams that could fix all our problems.

Silence stretched.

"I made a promise," he said into the air, answering a question that remained unasked.

"I know," I responded, as if he'd said the sun would rise tomorrow. I had never doubted Constantine's promises. Not since I'd gotten to know him. I didn't try to hide the thought.

"Come here." There were all sorts of strange tones in his voice and colors running through the threads.

I followed the motion of his fingers in the gently flaring green and purple lights, leaning over him so he could press one against my forehead.

I could feel a small phoenix spreading its wings over my mind.

Something slid around my neck.

When I opened my eyes, I was looking directly at him. There were bruised circles under his eyes, but dark satisfaction bled through his irises and our connection threads.

I touched the black ribbon which was now loosely secured about my neck.

"One thing at a time," he said. "Sleep."

~*~

Water...so much water.

Chapter Six

"Ren."

My eyes opened and the dreamglass unfolded. Used to a lot more color and life, the dream was strangely barren with its milky sheen extending in all directions—like I was in a bubble of the liquid.

"Ren." I focused on the person crouched over me. Ultramarine eyes were searching my face, hunting for something.

"What are you doing?" I croaked and stuck out my elbow to try and maneuver myself upright, suddenly dry like any weirdly shifting dream.

A complicated series of expressions crossed Axer's face—but I could see mostly relief. "You are okay."

Bloodshed and recollections of death suddenly danced across the dreamglass with Department faces I had seen on campus and in the news. Olivia and Helen's fight recreated itself across the panels and I made myself look away.

"Verisetti's work." His tone was distasteful, but not surprised, as he watched the reflections—like he already knew. He held out his hand and called one of the memories into his palm.

"I must compliment him on his perfidiousness," he mused as he looked at something specifically inside. "I would never have considered placing a hook there."

Hope took me, brightening the dreamglass. "Can you do anything about it? Put the spell in a container?" I asked. Dare's magic was pretty stupendous.

He shook his head. "I can take away her magic, but the spell isn't part of her magic. Verisetti's spell is on top of it, overlaying hers."

"If you took her magic, her magic could regenerate without—"

He shook his head again. "The spell will still be there. Only, without her magic, it will directly attack her organs, her brain, her heart, looking for a conduit that is enough like magic to work. Like a parasite rampaging through the host when its food source is gone."

I grimaced at the image. "Does that happen with all spells?"

"Most spells simply end when the magic in them is removed. More powerful spells have safeguards worked in so that they go dormant for a period of time if something damages the host."

I thought back to when Axer had died. After I had revived him, he had renewed his shields and enchantments manually.

"So..."

"So, it is very likely that the spell will wither on its own—it just needs time. If your roommate has to go through a spell removal process, though, you want a surgeon, not a bulldozer."

"The assessor is coming Wednesday. Greyskull is working on a plan." Tattooed thoughts of him swirled through the air, forming and dissipating with runic and patterned complications.

Dare's eyes tracked each one. He captured one in his hand and opened it, splitting the tattoo cloud as if it were a corporeal box he could peer inside.

"The spell won't wither by Wednesday. The belief is all over Greyskull's magic. And after seeing your memories, I agree."

He released the tattoo, and it flitted off into the ether of the dream.

"But Wednesday is a long time from now." He looked at my jumbled thoughts. "And I'm sure your roommate agrees—there's no one I'd rather have coming to save the day in an overly dramatic way than you."

I looked at him in astonishment. "That's rich."

He grinned.

But the flashing memories on the walls of the fight between Olivia and her mom sobered me. "But what if—"

He tipped my chin up. "Then you'll think of something."

He let go of me as my heartrate started to do something erratic. He splayed his fingertips against the ground and color shot out from them in all directions.

"Wait until I show you what one of the competitors did in the competition using art magic." Memories started to form on the walls—his, now, instead of mine—and colored paths led into each. "Not as mind-bending as you in a battle room, but you'll love it."

I smiled and stepped onto the crimson path of the first memory. I barely noticed the dry pond I left behind.

Chapter Seven

DUTY & ENGAGEMENT

I WOKE feeling optimistic.

I watched the time blink into existence on the ceiling tile I was staring at —magic answering my mental question. Constantine's bed was empty. Olivia still looked dead to the world.

I immediately checked her vitals, then looked around trying to determine what had awakened me. Justice Toad beeped silently on the nightstand.

Report for duty. Half of Leo Falling.

Thirty minutes from now, and not a call I could ignore.

I stretched my sore muscles, then rose. There were a lot of aches and pains that hadn't shown themselves before my body had shut down its defenses in sleep. I sorted through my clothes and sent out a quick call of my own.

Neph showed up ten minutes later.

"Thanks for staying with Liv until I get back," I said with a quick smile as I gathered things into my bag. "I should be back in time for class. Doctor Greyskull said he'd take care of watching her during LayPol," I said, giving the student abbreviation of the class name.

Neph and I had Layer Politics at 10:30—and politics class was sure to be stupidly exciting today.

I shoved a pad of paper from the nightstand into her hands, then hugged her. "I promised Isaiah I'd take double shifts. Thank you for doing this."

"Of course," Neph said absently as we parted. I looked up to see what was wrong, but her eyes were focused on my neck, where my shirt had slipped to the side. Her gaze was dark and intent.

I touched the ribbon. I had forgotten it was there. I reached around for the tie, but the ends had sealed together. I felt for a clasp, but there was none, it had formed into a single strand without beginning or end.

I tried to lengthen it, to pull it over my head, to tug it free, but the ribbon wasn't working for me the way it did under Constantine's touch.

Neph's solemn gaze met mine, but there was something strangely amused in the back of her eyes. The initial dark intent was completely gone from her gaze, so whatever she had at first suspected had been proven false, and she was now just amused by whatever she had deduced.

I shrugged. It was a ribbon choker. Whatever. I'd figure out how to remove it later.

"I don't know where Con is," I said. "He doesn't have class this early on Mondays, and if I'd known he was going to leave, I would have asked him to stay. But he's gone and Olivia *has* to stay in here if anyone Department related walks past."

"Of course. It will be done."

I hugged her, knowing that it *would* be done—Neph had mysterious ways.

"Oh, hey, I can't believe I almost forgot." From a secure pouch in my bag, I gently fished out the control device that I had secured from Keiren Oakley before heading to Corpus Sun. The device he had claimed to be "a one-way ticket to your muse's brains getting liquefied."

"I've been holding onto this like it was a bomb since I grabbed it from Oakley—may he rot," I said grimly. It was entirely possible he *was* rotting depending on what Bellacia had done to him.

I tried to hand the device to Neph. *Gingerly.*

She inched away from it, saying, "No."

Frowning, I didn't continue to push it toward her, but I didn't set it down either. I just held it in limbo between us. "You should take it."

"No. You keep it."

"I don't want to keep it," I said frankly. "What if I accidentally push it?"

She smiled. "Your intentions matter."

My shoulders drooped. "Oh, thank magic. You have no idea how carefully I held this thing before securing it." I turned it over in my hand, far less gingerly. "So, what does it do, then?"

"It's a conduit. Used for behavior."

I grimaced. "Like a shock collar for a dog?"

"We don't speak of such things," she said, a little stiffly.

I touched her arm. "I'm sorry."

"I know you meant nothing by it." Her soothing vibes wrapped around me. "My anger is not for you."

I turned it over in my hand again, examining the seams where magic had secured the pieces. When I'd been researching leashes, I had come across material on conduit devices. "It can't make you do things expressly; it just acts as punishment and reward?"

"Correct."

But pain and pleasure, especially when used together, were tools to control others. Punishment and reward, behavior modification—people could word it however they wanted. "Are these normal in the community?"

"Sometimes."

I frowned. "Wait, something you told me when Oakley was speaking..."

When I'd mentally asked Neph if someone had put something on her, she'd said, *"Just the control spells at my sanctioning...only accessible by the head of the community."*

The head of the muse community had some questions to answer.

"Neph, did the muses sell you out?"

The more I thought about it, lost in the violent recollections of Saturday, the more I realized that this was something that would need to be dealt with.

Neph looked tired. "No. They just saw an opportunity, I'm sure. Just...keep it. Better for you to have it. I'd be required to turn it in."

My mouth opened and closed, but no sound emerged for a moment. "But—"

Justice Toad beeped.

"Go, Ren," Neph prodded gently.

A mist of calm euphoria traveled through me and I barely remembered what we'd been discussing, even though something inside me told me I *really* needed to. I tucked the thing I'd been holding back into my bag and blinked, trying to remember what I had been doing. I had been going somewhere?

"Justice Squad," Neph said gently, a strange sliver of guilt in her voice.

Justice Squad, right.

I waved to Neph, leaving her in charge of Olivia's safety.

The feeds said that campus was still closed below Eighteenth Circle, but campus proper and the travel systems were all accessible again. Rumor on the feeds was that the mountain would be completely open again by the end of the week, including all arches off campus.

I...didn't know how to feel about it. Excited? Apprehensive? I'd never been able to wander off campus freely. I'd been restricted by Marsgrove, then I'd caused a series of incidents that had closed campus to everyone. It would be a first for me to have the choice to leave or not.

Closing campus had created an unexpected security issue, and opening campus had its own security downside. I could only speculate on what new safety measures might be implemented.

With a minute to spare I entered the Justice Squad meeting room.

Isaiah stared at the ribbon circling my neck for a long moment just like

Neph had, then looked up at me and shook his head slowly. "You know what? I'm going to say nothing. What matters is that you are here, healthy, and ready to help."

I fiddled with the ribbon, mystified by the attention paid to it. "Thank you again for the time off, Isaiah. Yesterday, well, it was a good thing that you agreed to Monday. I'm ready for double shifts."

It had been the promise I'd had to make to get Saturday's rescue off the ground. I had promised to fulfill my quota and I would. Neph had Olivia's back, and we had plenty of time to remove the spell before Wednesday. Everything would be fine.

"I just finished the schedule." He flicked a hand and a schedule of magic zoomed through the air into Justice Toad. "You are on from nine to ten, then again after lunch. Then one more shift tonight."

I nodded, swallowing panic and mentally rearranging my hours. There was still plenty of time to work on Olivia's spell. My second class was Individualized Architecture and Design, an independent study with Will, so I had the flexibility to manage it. Since we had been juggling our workload all term, I knew I could arrange to do the work Thursday, after the debacle that was sure to be Wednesday was concluded.

And vault time with Constantine, the other item on my Monday schedule, was time that would be useful, but could also be canceled.

I nodded again, trying to convince myself that there was plenty of time left to cure Olivia. Plenty. And I reminded myself that I wasn't alone in this. There was going to be help. Greyskull, who knew infinitely more than I did. And Marsgrove and Neph. And the head of the Neutralizer Squad, if we needed her. We had plenty of time.

"Expect grief calls," Isaiah said, sending updates to my tablet with flicks of his fingers across a screen in the air. "They haven't let up, though there are fewer calls and they *are* getting better and more focused. With the combat competition and the increased split in media chatter, students have other focal points. Some people have been bottling it up too long, though. They are the ones who will be seeking extra help today—with what they see as an attempt at *normal*."

Emotion tugged at my heart. I knew exactly how that felt—to see life going on and not to *understand*. *How could life continue when one's heart was broken?*

Steady resolve overtook me. I could help. I *would* help.

Isaiah seemed to sense something of my shifting emotions, because he looked over and his expression softened further, then took on a resolve of its own. "The goodwill groups are trying to figure out what can be planned each weekend to give the student body something specific to focus on and something to look forward to. There's talk of holding an event of some kind, in addition to the spring dance on the equinox. Maybe an activity on the full moon in two days. Or a healing ritual on campus—something that gets everyone together—or some sort of festival that is not Shift related. The Layer Shift Festival is going to create its own turmoil."

"Okay." I nodded and looked at Isaiah expectantly.

He looked at the ceiling, as if seeking divine help. "There is a lot of focus on *you* to determine a direction, Ren. And the squad would like to assist you."

"Great. I think working in teams is a really great direction and I'd be happy to hel—" His words finally sank in. "Wait, what?"

He smiled. "It's been pretty well established on campus that you want to help. There are entire groups that have the art and medical mages running mad trying to duplicate your creations. They've done a pretty good job so far."

When we'd emerged from the Midlands yesterday, I had seen the blonde girl I had resurrected on Bloody Tuesday in the rose line at the front of the crowd. A row of them standing on the Ninth Circle in solidarity and support.

I really needed to learn her name.

"Just be ready for those types of inquiries while you are out. Though..." His eyes drifted down to the ribbon around my neck again. Whatever that look meant he shook it off a moment later. "You make things interesting, Crown. Good luck"

As other squad members entered the break room complaining about the number of calls and classes starting again, pulling Isaiah's attention toward them, I decided to log into the system fifteen minutes early.

I could hear Draeger's voice in my head saying, *Go off and do justice! Toad Justice!*

~*~

The first two calls were delinquencies. I knew both offenders. The sheepish looks on their faces and their responses—"Just testing to see if there are any new restrictions"—earned them both aid duty beefing up the spells for the grief response team, as well as for cleaning the main warding complex. They had been thrilled with the challenge of the first and the objective of the second.

I relaxed into handling delinquencies and grief calls.

Unfortunately, my third call was to Bolton Haynes, a boy behind numerous false calls designed to get me to his door in order to proposition me.

I braced myself as the usual smile split his face from ear to ear upon seeing me.

"It's all over the frequencies; someone saw you with your tablet. And I couldn't resist—" His gaze dropped to my neck, and elation turned to horror. Freakish, terrified horror.

Violent cursing followed.

"*No.* Holy... *Mistake.*" He reached toward me, then pulled his hands in so fast that it was as if the air had combusted and burned his fingertips. He scuttled backward. "I won't do it again. I *swear.*"

"What?" I let my finger drift away from Justice Toad's "kill" setting.

The button would only transform the offending mage into an amphibian, not kill, of course, but I liked to call it the kill setting. However, Haynes already looked terrified.

"I swear I wasn't going to do anything," he wheezed, but his eyes were solely focused on my neck, as if someone had hit his optic nerves with a freezing spell.

I reached up to touch the ribbon. The first two callers had focused on it, too, but like Isaiah and Neph, they'd said nothing. *Constantine, what did you do?* I mentally sent the question to him.

A faint feeling of satisfaction tingled along our connection.

But Bolton Haynes was gasping, words tripping over each other. "I saw you with him, but no one thought, I mean how could anyone have thought he would actually care? It's *Leandred.* He doesn't do engagement. I can't—"

"Whoa, whoa. *What?*"

"I saw you with Leandred in the cafeteria—who didn't? It was all over records later. But we all thought it was another of his onka—"

He abruptly dropped the word before completing it, but my translator was super helpful at offering finished translations. I gave him an unimpressed look at the unkind word he hadn't finished.

"We thought it simply a friendly visit," he finished weakly.

"It was," I deadpanned.

"*It was not.* And I will never call again. I know I said that last time, but I really mean it this time." He dragged a hand through his hair, then looked up with too bright a smile. "This is just a random call. I had no intentions of using you for anything. Wow, look, you are here. I had no idea. *Random call.*"

Justice Toad beeped in warning at the repeated lies, but Bolton just kept *going.* "Tell him. Tell him it was a *random call.* Seriously, I mean it, I won't—"

I held up a hand, then quickly put it to my forehead when Bolton freaked out and plastered himself against his door, thinking I was going to blast him with magic.

My fingers were better served at my temple anyway, soothing the headache building there. "Can we just handle your call, Mr. Haynes?"

"Yes. My completely *random* call."

Chapter Seven

Beep.

I sighed, ready to leave and hunt down Constantine. "Listen, you're just digging a deeper hole by lying. You should really invoke your right to remain silent when not being questioned. Your offense has just been bumped up an entire level. I'm not going to question you. I don't care. You are going to do a penance, a service, for taking up time in the Justice System, and then you will not abuse the system again with calls to get me to show up, got it?"

"I'll do anything, *anything* to help and serve."

As Bolton tripped over himself to reassure me of his good intentions— this time truthfully—I tapped my finger against Justice Toad and thought about what Isaiah had said about campus looking to me for direction.

"Campus needs healing, Mr. Haynes," I barked in imitation of Draeger. "Do you have any ideas about how to help?"

He blinked rapidly at me—a rather disconcerting expression on the face of a guy straight out of *Frat Boys Quarterly*. Bolton Haynes had likely rarely been denied anything, living the cushy, good life.

Apparently he was not quite at Constantine's level in the hierarchy, though, if the terror that Constantine inspired was anything to go by.

"What?" Bolton asked, uncomprehending.

"How do you think students can help heal campus? Do you think you might be able to lend a hand? There are a lot of things that we can accomplish together—psychological healing, physical reconstruction, security measures, task forces—"

Words tripped from his mouth in response. "Of course, yes, I am more than willing to do my part. What a *blessing* this *random* call was."

Beep.

I gave him a pointed look.

He rallied and continued, "The fields on Fifteenth Circle, where we do intramurals, and the Seventh Circle ski runs—I'm a member of the ski club —and the greenhouses on Three. The greenies are always great at getting their plants back to rights, but they will need help with accounting, and I am excellent with system spells and my bro, Chuck, is a mad genius with motiv—"

"Great! See what you can come up with to help your fellow mage. Then share those thoughts with your friends, okay?"

"I will. I *will.*"

"Be a good citizen from now on, got it?" I said sternly, channeling my inner Isaiah.

"I *will.*"

"In the meantime, offer to help the, er, greenies, with their accounting tasks. If they say yes, let's put it at two hours. That sounds like a reasonable amount of time." Justice Toad dinged in affirmation. "Great. And if they say no, I need two hours of your concerted time revitalizing Fourth Circle."

It had seen a lot of action on Bloody Tuesday and had yet to be fully renewed, as the taunting view from Bellacia's room had continually shown me.

"Yes, *yes. Absolutely.* I will help campus in *all* the ways."

Disturbed by his increasing effusiveness, I retreated as quickly as possible, while he continued to call out reassurances and motivational quotes behind me.

More than one call followed in that vein—with people wanting to get me to their door for a peek, a picture, or a pseudo interview. I was a semi-rare, man-eating tiger on parade.

However, what was *new* was how the excitement and adrenaline rush at seeing that tiger (me) abruptly turned to outright terror upon seeing the ribbon; like a terror switch had been flipped within them from anticipatory "fright entertainment" to the fear caused by a familiar, experienced horror.

It became apparent that Constantine had done something beyond his normal mischief.

I ducked into a bathroom and tugged hard on the ribbon, trying again to remove it. For something that seemed to be made entirely of silk and deceit, it was deceptively strong.

Switching from the physical to the magical, I focused and concentrated on the magic of the ribbon and the field that had been created when it joined itself around my neck sometime during the night. I let my knowledge of warding fields come to the forefront of my consciousness and sent a trickle of magic down each thread, letting the magic within each form itself into a schematic in my mind.

At the same time, I let my fingers play over the threads. Like the stamp he had given me, the ribbon could lengthen and stretch and hold all sorts of hidden magical traps and goodies. It *already* held those things—a small carousel of artillery and destruction. Constantine was rarely without it. And though I had seen him use it in battle—whipping opponents and delivering slicing blows and even piercing one of Raphael's shields—at rest, it was more a threat than anything. Like the villainous stroking of a white cat, or placing a loaded gun on the table.

I poked at the field and watched it ripple.

I could see a dark green thread vibrate happily; an opaque, reflective one twitch irritably, and a rose thread seek each touch. The magic in the ribbon was hooked into me, but I could see the places where I could unhook it. This wasn't an unbreakable thing Constantine had done.

However there were outwardly directed hooks of a different kind. Protection and recording hooks that trailed along a thin path to

Chapter Seven

Constantine.

Ripping it from my neck would hurt him more than it would hurt me.

I sighed and fished a scarf out of my bag as the calls poured in faster, not giving me time to hunt him down. We would be having *words*.

Calls that occurred after I covered the ribbon became both easier and more suspicious. People were *excruciatingly* polite at first, but then became increasingly irritated when they failed to see over or through my scarf. Justice Toad had automatically taken care of a number of people who had tried to use vanishing or revelation spells to satisfy their curiosity, but a few of the more handsy mages had tried to hook a finger in my collar to pull the material down.

Those individuals had gotten a double dose of newthood, which was always a bad thing, as the longer a person spent as an amphibian on the floor, the more likely they were to lick it.

None of that seemed to stop others from trying, though, and I started muttering darkly as the call log tripled, then quadrupled.

"Suckers," I said, as I logged off, my hour ticking complete. The offense volume showed one hundred waiting Level One calls—the vast majority of those assuredly from gossipmongers.

Peters' canary yellow tablet was going to *wipe* most of those people. No one used the justice system and got away with it, if Peters was on the job. A few of the career-track squad members had a tablet setting that in times of extremely high call volume, could be depressed to assign all offenders of a particular level the same punishment. Since most of the false calls were Level Ones from the offenders trying to ping the system deliberately, there was going to be some *serious* wiping in about ten minutes when Peters figured out what was going on.

The good news was that campus was going to be getting a *makeover* if Peters assigned rampant cleaning duty across the board.

I headed through the Magiaduct, a little hitch to my step at the mental picture of Peters going on a Justice bender without me as the prime target.

The target on *my* back was getting through the first Layer Politics class after Bloody Tuesday's events.

Chapter Eight

CLASSY POLITICS

NEPH, BLESS HER, sent me a mental communication before I got too far.

"Doctor Greyskull showed early. I'll get our items for class, you go to Olivia. She's freaking out again about not attending class."

I sent a light stroke of thanks along our connection and headed for the medical ward underneath the dormitories.

She replied with a fond pat of her own. *"I'll meet you back in Medical in ten minutes."*

Olivia was arguing vehemently with Greyskull, who looked like someone who wished he'd chosen a different career path. Neither of them paid me any heed as I slipped inside.

"I will not allow my studies to suffer more than they already have."

"Miss Price, classes were canceled last week," Greyskull said with forced patiently. "You haven't missed any classes. All lessons are restarting today."

"Exactly."

"You can attend virtually. We do have procedures in place for this, you know. Even the combat mages—"

"Attending virtually isn't the same. You can't *feel* the magic in the same way. If I miss even *one* lesson, what do you think will happen?" she demanded.

"That you will miss one lesson and a tiny splash of classroom magic," he said in a deadpan voice.

She leaned forward and stabbed a finger emphatically into the mattress. "I've had that *man* rifling through my head for five days," she said, not softening the blow at all. "I need to figure out what I've *lost* and mitigate those losses by relearning the material."

Grey sighed. "Rafael didn't disturb any of your knowledge or memory centers—only your shields and fight/flight triggers when you encounter certain magic. I've checked. The spell hasn't changed your knowledge base, it just pings your fight response. Vigorously," he added reluctantly.

"My kill response."

"That is the one," he said.

"You are very calm about that," she said, in what was, for Olivia, a very suspicious tone.

"I have to be, Miss Price. It is part of my job."

"He talked about you, you know."

I winced.

"Did he?" Greyskull said, trying and failing to hide the direct hit.

Olivia watched his organic tattoos as they moved across his skin. "That tattoo that Ren used against him. You gave it to her." It wasn't a question. "What did it do?"

She had been asleep for that conversation.

When he didn't answer, she threatened, "I'll get it out of, Ren."

"I will neither cause you harm nor seek to keep you here past the time that you can be safely released," he said mildly, though I could see the tension in his frame.

"Ren, tell him that I'm leaving," Olivia said, suddenly acknowledging my presence.

"Er—"

"And why are you wearing that scarf?"

"Well—"

"It doesn't match your shoes. I need to go to our room, to the administration building, to the apothecary—"

"You don't need to go to the apothecary, Miss Price," Greyskull interrupted as I stared at my shoes. Were scarves supposed to match shoes?

"—to the launch site, to the Freenamel Complex—"

"You don't need to go to the Freenamel Complex, Miss Price." Greyskull was starting to sound amused, though. I tentatively changed the color of my scarf using an enchantment I'd picked up from Delia.

"—to the Shang Compound, and to the law library." Olivia ended the list with another stab at the bed.

Greyskull looked at the ceiling. "Miss Price, spell removal takes time. You know this. It needs to be purged correctly or you could end up with my feet protruding from *your* neck. Raphael puts traps into his spells and unwinding those properly takes time. Time and patience are what are needed, not harrying off into adventure and consequence."

He gave me a pointed look at the last statement.

I crossed my arms behind my back and nodded solemnly. I also tried not to picture his long feet sticking out of Olivia's long neck. Nothing good would come from that mental picture.

"I can't stay here," Olivia said, her voice sounding a little hysterical. "I must attend classes."

I cocked my head, squinting at her, trying to figure out what actually was wrong. She knew exactly what the pitfalls of her situation were; she knew she had to stay here. Why, then...?

Expression softening, I stepped toward her. "Marsgrove's not going to kick you out, Liv."

"He won't be able to stop it! Not with the emancip—" A look of terror overtook her expression and she shook her head as if unable to finish the sentence. "I must be seen to be doing regular studies. It's part of the emancipation proceedings."

Greyskull's expression was grim. "We will deal with the spell by Wednesday."

I looked at Greyskull. "The assessor comes to check on whether a person has received a correct diagnosis and treatment—can that person transfer Olivia elsewhere?"

"Yes, and the assessor *will*," Olivia said, voice pinching. "And all of it— the emancipation, everything—all of it will be for naught once I'm off campus."

Olivia would be back under her mother's control.

No.

"We have two more days, Miss Price. We will find a solution." Greyskull's reassuring tone held the slightest bit of grimness, though. He couldn't promise anything perfect.

"So, if we aren't successful fixing Olivia, we"—meaning our group of delinquents—"need to figure out how to thwart the assessor and alter his report?" I sent Patrick a mental note to get on that ASAP.

Greyskull reordered his expression into forced patience, the look of someone running low on the virtue. "This isn't a—"

"What we *need* to do is practice," Olivia said, "with the Department minions on campus."

"The Junior Department?" I considered it. "Invite a few of them into the room and see if you kill them?"

"—isn't a heist movie, and I object to your attempted murder plans," Greyskull said wryly. "Though, your bloodthirstiness is noted. This isn't the Outlands. We do have legal resources and options," he said dryly.

"You did great yesterday," I said loyally, patting him on the arm. "I have the utmost faith that without one of those devices Liv's mom had in play, you would have kept everything in line."

He rubbed his thumbs over his eyes, but I could see him smiling beneath it, a fleeting thing. "Miss Price, I need you to mentally accept that you will be unable to attend classes today. *Virtually* still counts as *present* on your record."

Olivia's lips tightened, but she nodded sharply.

"Good. Now, if Ren is amenable, we can map the spell before she goes to class"

"We don't need her," Olivia said hostilely.

"It's like I'm not the head of Medical at this university," he mused. "You are all so knowledgeable. I should just issue First-aid kits and good luck charms."

Olivia crossed her arms. "I don't want her touching the spell."

"I know, Miss Price," he said, not unkindly.

Olivia's lips tightened, then she slumped and waved an ungracious hand. "Fine."

I reached forward to give her a supportive squeeze. Greyskull smoothly intercepted my hand and tucked it into my opposite armpit.

He shook his head, muttering, "Just like Phillip. You are all as bad as each other."

Blushing furiously, I mirrored the action with my other hand, tucking it opposite so both hands were firmly clamped against my body. "Oops."

Olivia was giving Greyskull an unimpressed look that clearly said—I told you so—while vainly trying to hide her nerves.

"No touching, Ren. Just observing. Mapping. We are going to take a look at the links between the three of you and the spell itself, as it relates."

"And you? The links between the two of you?" I asked.

He didn't look away from the magical grid he was setting up to record. "I'm already quite familiar with those," he said softly.

Olivia pulled her lips tightly between her teeth and looked militantly to the side.

"Hand," Greyskull said to me. I offered it and he took a ball of swirling violet and crimson magic and wrapped my fingers around it. "Now goggles."

But unlike the pair Lifen had been wearing, the pair that Greyskull wrapped around my eyes was made entirely of cobalt magic.

The lines of magic in the room split, sharpened, and started a slow dance—a wave of color and dimension.

"Ignore the room. Let your magic ease along your roommate's. Don't poke or prod, just observe."

I followed the sound of his voice and let the magic take me. The thing I wanted most was to help Olivia, so I let magic guide me on that path. I made sure to keep my intentions concerning the spell as observation *only*.

Like Monet's *Water Lilies*, the view transitioned from soft and muted to bold and distinct with broad brush strokes and swirls of paint producing a mass of riotous color and emotion, but also hinting at smaller artistic details. Interesting techniques to explore, if one looked closely.

The spell shimmered over every dip and crevice of Olivia. The view of the spell wavered for a second, as if a second nature defense mechanism activated, then forcibly relaxed.

The magic zoomed forward and opened like a lotus flower, pushing up the valleys and ridges, with hidden notches and hairs left behind.

"He didn't hide the enchantment," Greyskull mused from somewhere to my right, voice studiously clinical, but not unaffected. "He could have concealed it in that shadow there on the left."

I looked to where the magic in his voice was pointing. There were a series of ridges, like raised paint on a canvas, where Raphael could have easily hidden something—tucked darkness into shadow and pain into crevices.

Instead, it was openly barbed and barbaric—the enchantment demanding that Olivia *destroy*.

I swallowed. There was a sheen of oil-slicked water coating the landscape. The barbs that were holding everything in place were there— worse than a tack strip on an upholstered chair. Raphael really knew how to layer a curse.

Unnatural. Man made. Raphael.

"Can the oil layer be...washed away?" Cleansed, like blowing smog from a valley?

"The layer is preventing the barbs from grinding inward. Protecting her from them. It's like a barbaric cake. Taking out one layer will deconstruct the stability of the others, possibly causing another part of the spell to kill her."

It was as if the spell was convincing Olivia's magic that she *needed* protection against the Department; that she needed to get them before they got her.

Naïve, for anyone to believe that protection magic was not a force to be reckoned with.

And Raphael had gotten the penultimate gift in Olivia Price, the abused daughter of an enemy, and someone close to me. I remembered how he had assessed her in our room after the Bone Beast debacle and our four-person ritual. He'd probably started plans for all sorts of things in those moments.

Destruction. Creation.

Related and separate disciplines. Two sides of the same coin.

"He doesn't care if the spell is detected," I said.

"No. He likely thought she'd be dead by the time anyone figured it out."

I swallowed my fury. It wasn't the time for anger.

"He told me that it was a plan for me," I said. "That he could dress me as a bomb and release me into the Department's basement." I looked away from the spell's unclean landscape. "I have unhooked some of his spells, but I'm sure he was planning to do this exact thing to me if I were ever taken. It was a contingency plan, but he used it on Olivia instead."

The entire spell structure started to shake.

"What—?"

"Ease out. Miss Price and the spell have become uneasy with our manipulations." But there was something weird in his voice, as if that wasn't the entire truth.

"We can't...do anything?"

"Patience, Ren. I would rather not use brute force to make her magic comply."

The calmed whorls of color around Olivia grew sharper, more barbed. Armed for combat.

I nodded and eased the rest of the way out.

Greyskull took the goggles from my face and gave me a pointed look, his back to Olivia, as if to say that barbed net was a taste of what we might unleash, if we continued.

"What now?" I asked, winded. I flexed my magic, feeling it hum.

"Now? Now you go to class and I create a lovely schematic. Then we begin."

I shuffled my feet. "That's it? Just the two of us?"

"A number of my colleagues would be overjoyed to work on this type of enchantment. However, that might not be in the best interests of all the parties involved."

Raphael's magic? Talking about where Olivia had been? Giving trust to an unknown?

"No." I shook my head. It was not a risk I was willing to take with the welfare of a loved one.

Greyskull was already nodding. He had his own reasons for keeping things private.

"Do I get a say?" Olivia said acerbically.

"You've had your say," he said calmly. "And you no more want anyone else gaining a peek than we do. Now, what is your choice, Miss Price?"

"Virtual classes." She held out her hand in ungracious surrender.

He floated a tablet into her palm.

"Your muse is on her way down the hall, Ren," Greyskull said.

I looked apologetically at Olivia, but she waved me off. "Bring me *Lessons from a Mage in the Wild* when you return."

~*~

Neph and I slipped into class with a minute to spare.

Every gaze turned and focused on the two of us, then zeroed in on me alone. Only the other muses in the class were staring at Neph instead, their gazes more murderous than the mixed expressions in the rest of the class who couldn't quite see Neph—their gazes vainly slipping past.

Will, Mike, Delia, and Asafa gave us tight, welcoming smiles.

"That was us under the microscope a minute ago," Mike said from the side of his mouth. "Buck up, folks."

Every seat in the thousand-seat lecture hall looked occupied, but I knew there had to be at least one empty seat, because Delia had told me days ago that one of the casualties from Bloody Tuesday had been a classmate she knew peripherally. With so many students in this class, statistically there had to be at least one casualty.

As if called by magic, my gaze traveled to an empty seat. A rose lay atop the desk. My gaze picked out another rose-laden spot almost immediately, then a third. There had been three deaths amongst our class number, then. I swallowed, but forced my eyes to look at the students on either side of the seats. They gazed solemnly back.

I swallowed again, and allowed my gaze to drift over dozens of other faces, featureless faces blending together in the haze of my vision.

Bellacia stood at the side of the room with the other four teaching assistants. Dark hair done up in her standard set of braids, loose knots, and free strands, she watched me with a smile that didn't reach her eyes.

You'd better be in our room today.

I jolted at the mental projection, but inclined my head. I was required to spend four hours with her unless I was in Medical for over sixteen hours in a twenty-four hour period.

Ren.

It was a sharper utterance. I gave a stiff nod and pushed her out. I didn't want to know how she had hooked into me.

She probably had hooks all over me and somehow, I'd probably *agreed* to them.

I'd deal with the magic, and with my roommate fiasco, later.

Magic descended across the classroom as Professor Harrow strode in front of his long desk and hitched himself upon it.

A thousand gazes focused on him.

Monday morning meant this was the first class for many. The first class, and with a subject that focused on terrorists and politics between layers.

Harrow would set a tone for the thousand students in this class—set the tone for the rest of the week, term, *year*. I didn't envy Harrow his massive job.

"I'm sure that many of you have questions, concerns, and thoughts." He held out a hand to forestall all of the questions suddenly bursting into magic around the room. "I've spoken with many of you, in and around campus, but that's not the same as seeing all of your faces in this room."

Harrow paused deliberately and looked at the three empty seats. He held out his hands, palms up, and light leaped from the centers, arcing over to each rose that sat on top. The magic swirled around then dove inside. The roses lit with brilliant color then the light settled into a soft glow.

A small blonde girl stood abruptly from the audience and held out her hands as well. Light radiated from them and shot toward the roses, adding to the glow created by Harrow.

I stared at her for a moment, brain unable to process what I was seeing. It was the girl from the battlefield. She was in this class. She stared back at me, then tilted her head and smiled solemnly.

My hands were out before I registered it, as were dozens, *hundreds* of others. Lights emanating from our palms followed the same paths. The roses burst with color and memory.

Weeping registered from the people who had placed the blooms. Harrow waved his hand to give them privacy and their faces were obscured, just a little, like a scene half-hidden by rain running down a windowpane.

Harrow glanced around the room. "The campus response to Tuesday's events has been extraordinary. Magnificent. I am honored to be part of Excelsine University."

A number of people straightened in their seats, proudly squaring their shoulders.

"We heal ourselves, we heal others. Such is the root of layer politics as well. How do we rise above our anger, our hatred, and our vengeance? How do we decide on a wise path when emotion and trauma obscure our view?"

He didn't pause to let the questions rest. "As we travel the healing road, what do we do to fix that which is beyond us? How does a politician, a citizen, decide how to go forward?"

Crossing his arms, he tapped a finger against one forearm. "How many of you want to wipe out the Third Layer?"

A good third of the room raised affirmative magic in response. I could *feel* Delia's eyeliner thicken.

He snapped his fingers and a spell took hold of the administrative magic attached to us. "How many of you have thought beyond your anger and rage?"

Some of the raised magic disappeared—people admitting their emotional states. Some of the remaining raised magic turned yellow in untruth under the administrative spell—and those people lowered their magic with tight lips.

Some magic remained—the users both truthful and still of that mindset.

Harrow let go of the truth spell. "There is no right or wrong to emotions. They simply *are*. How you choose to control them, though, is up to you. Know *why* you are making a decision and thinking a certain way. Be mindful of your emotions and how they affect your decision-making. A wise decision maker always needs to keep in mind emotions and emotional issues. Every topic raises emotions of some kind. How do you do what is right and what is needed in the face of emotional response?"

No one raised magic to respond.

"This is not a class for determining how to handle emotion, but a seminar for seeing *how* such decisions affect layer politics."

He settled back.

"The inquiry into what happened on Tuesday is in progress. And we are all in the middle of the turmoil that was left behind at the epicenter. Let's distance ourselves from campus events for today and concentrate on the effects of Tuesday's attack on the layers, as a whole. Who has a fact to share?"

Lights blinked above heads around the room—the Second Layer way of queuing for questions and responses.

Harrow nodded at a student. "Mr. Johnson?"

"There were immediate trade repercussions between the Second and Third Layer in the safe zones."

The statement was duplicated by magic on the board behind Harrow, as well as in each student's note-taking item of choice. Harrow nodded and called on another student. "Ms. Swans?"

"Salvatori Lorenzo issued a statement that the Third Layer government had nothing to do with the attack."

That, too, went on the board and in notes.

"Ms. Ng?"

"The Department moved into the neutral territory of Ventan Fields."

A murmur of magic whistled through the room.

"Unsubstantiated," Harrow said, and the statement was recorded under a special category at the right side of the board, in a goldenrod color. "But that rumor *has* been reported." Harrow didn't glance at Bellacia, but everyone knew from where that report had originated. "Let's stick to facts first and their results, then we'll investigate the consequences of what else might be occurring."

Responses were given and written in rapid-fire fashion.

"Corpus Sun was destroyed."

"The Department admitted to illegally holding Dean Marsgrove."

"The Department took hold of Excelsine, but then was subsequently forced out."

"The triumvirate reported raw Origin Magic usage."

The student who voiced that one didn't look at me while he said it, but I felt the weight of the room's gaze switch my way, as did the content of further statements.

"The Department reported that they were investigating the possibility of an Origin Mage."

"Praetorian Kaine accused Ren Crown of being an Origin Mage."

"Praetorian Kaine administered the Origin Mage box test."

"Ren Crown passed, in front of all of us, meaning she isn't an Origin Mage," followed quickly on its heels.

"Origin Magic was registered by the sensors at Sphic Observatory."

"Origin Magic spiked to higher levels than it has in thirty years."

The statements came faster and faster, and I began to slip down in my seat.

As people kept piling on damning statements, Mike said in an uneasy mental voice, *"You know...you really should lie low for a couple weeks, Ren."*

"Two Origin Magic spikes were reported in the Third Layer on Saturday," a classmate voiced.

"No more magic funsies, Crown," Saf added, using the same group connection that Mike had used—the one we had woven into our armbands.

I could feel the members of our armband group who were not in class with us mentally perking up at the shared dialogue.

I rubbed my temples as classmates continued adding damning statements to the board.

"In the memory ball, Ren Crown and the unknown man were using paint on the field. Origin Magic has been associated with paint. Kinsky, Da Vinci—"

A mental ping jarred me. I pulled my fingers away from my head, wondering who had decided to basically honk at me mentally. What were my friends expecting me to do?

"We expect you to say nothing unless called upon," Delia said as the same classmate continued listing mages who liked to paint. *"And even then—"*

Ping.

"I get it," I responded mentally, cutting her off. Statistically, at least *one* of the students in here was on the Department payroll—likely the boy who kept droning on about Origin Magic popping up wherever I was. This was the perfect opportunity to see if I would rise to the bait.

Ping.

"Stop," I mentally said, pushing the third prod away. *"I get it."*

Ping.

"I know! I won't say anything."

PING!

"Stop pinging! I'm not doing anything! You can all relax! I—"

PING, PING, PING!

I turned to the others with a scowl. What did they honestly think I was going to do—stand up and yell, *"Ta da! You got me!"*?

I opened my mouth to make a super snappy verbal remark.

PING!!.

Greyskull's voice boomed through my mind along with an even louder mental strike. *"ASSESSOR CAME EARLY."*

I froze at his words. Greyskull had been the one pinging me? But...

"But it's Monday," I blankly responded, forgetting to do so mentally. I stupidly checked my timekeeping enchantment, afraid I'd see something different. "And there was that whole thing with the tools..."

"I know," came his grim reply. *"One's heading for Medical anyway."*

"Ren?" Neph whispered, real voice taking on a thread of panic. I obliquely noticed that the rest of the class had gone silent at my off-topic, verbal interruption, but my mind was too busy with other thoughts.

The Department knew my schedule. I had Layer Politics at the same time every Monday with a decent portion of the rest of the student body. Everyone who cared about my movements knew I had this class.

It was the perfect time to ensure I was out of the way.

"Gotta go." I flew into motion, not pausing to grab my things as I scrambled up onto my seat and used one of the desks to edge-vault over the people on the end of our row. I sprinted up the center aisle stairs, leaping three steps at a time, magic giving me a boost.

"Miss Crown?" Professor Harrow said over the rise of the panicking voices in my wake.

I threw magic behind me with a half-shouted and nearly incomprehensible two word explanation of, "Doctor Greyskull!"

If the screams behind me were any indication that I had created chaos, perhaps the magic throw had been the wrong call, but I didn't falter as I slammed out of the room.

Chapter Nine

FLIP THE GRID OR FLIP OUT

SLAMMING OUT OF the building, I scattered a group of students standing on the grass and ran for the nearest arch.

Due to the already established communal network of wards, Olivia was currently in the hospital room that Constantine had been in after Bloody Tuesday, right under Dorm One. My brain spit out the fastest way to get there, through a three-arch hop.

Neph's panicked mental voice, along with Will's, Mike's, Delia's, and Asafa's, burst forth with a flurry of exclamations and information, but all I understood was that Professor Harrow had sealed the doors after my hasty exit—some sort of precautionary new security feature—and none of them could follow. I sent back a series of half-explanatory thoughts, then pushed their voices out completely and focused on my goal.

"I'm on my way," I sent to Greyskull.

There was a mirror entrance to Medical straight from the administration building that the assessor would assuredly use, but if I hurried I could beat her and reach the floor first.

Medical had been reopened to all students, so there were no credentials to scan, no checkpoints to slow me down. I skidded around the corner and started sprinting again as soon as I hit the corridor.

"Miss Crown, Miss Crown!"

I skidded to a halt, nearly sliding into the frantic woman who had emerged from a side room. She motioned to a doorway. "Through there. Shortcut!"

"Thank you!" I called out as I dove inside. Greyskull, with his bazillion concurrently running communications, must have notified his people to guide me.

I emerged twenty feet behind the heels of an upright woman who was walking briskly toward Liv's room.

* Flip the Grid or Flip Out *

Nothing was ready. Raphael's spell was still in place. We weren't *ready*.

As the woman wrapped her fingers around the handle of Olivia's door, I didn't stop my forward momentum. I plowed right into the woman, knocking her roughly against the door jamb and scattering all her papers and items to the floor. I let my body fall with the papers, then did a haphazard "snow angel" with my limbs, dispersing them further.

"Imbecile! Do you have any idea what you've done?" she hissed, leaping toward me as I continued my destruction under the guise of collecting the papers, sending magic through the fibers to make the ink bleed together. "Get away from those! I will write you up for everything from attacking an official to the ruthless disregard for personal property to setting—"

Her abrupt cessation of speech caused me to look up.

The phantom vision of another face appeared over hers, assessing me in a cold, calculating, *pleased* way. It held an expression of recognition, desire, vengeance, and *anticipation*.

I knew that parasitical face. I scuttled backward but not before a finger touched my forehead and a wave of something passed through me, making my bones ache.

"Miss Crown," it said in a voice half the woman's and half Stavros's.

"Madam Assessor," Marsgrove's winded, sharp voice said as he strode down the corridor.

I slumped in relief against the wall, letting my hands release the papers. Marsgrove always appeared, as if called by magic. I gave a slightly hysterical laugh that made him glance at me before he looked back at the woman.

"You were scheduled for a time two days hence," he said.

The leeched gaze melted from the woman's face, leaving the pinched features of the grim assessor behind as she turned to face Marsgrove. "I have no desire to prolong this inquiry, Dean Marsgrove. My time is valuable, as are my skills, and this appears to be an open and shut case. Five minutes to assess Miss Price, and I will leave you to your...duties," she said with distaste.

"You are not *scheduled*," Marsgrove emphasized. "Therefore, you will accompany me back to my office and return at the appropriate time—"

"I am Chief Assessor of the Guild of Assessors; I am the head of the Wockpat Procedural. My time is valuable and I will not be waylaid," she said, her voice like iron. "I received permission to port. I am here legally and with the backing of the entire Council of the Second Layer. That you are trying to waylay me only makes it more obvious that there is a serious issue that you are trying to hide. We have reports from an unimpeachable source that you have a volatile spell-ridden student who is barely attached to this institution due to judicial offenses. Sources of volatility and danger are issues that I would think you would be most concerned with, Dean

Marsgrove. The health and well-being of your campus should be at the forefront of your thoughts and desires. If they are not, then the Department will clearly have other problems to sort out as well."

A recording device from the floor flew into her hand and she held it out like a reporter. "Is the health and safety of your student body your top priority? We have received numerous reports that you are harboring a volatile and dangerous student. You even logged a report, as you are *required* to do. We are here to assess that risk."

Tension gripped the entire hallway. I realized that we were surrounded by staff members who had gathered while I was making a mess of the assessor's materials—and in my mental communications—everyone with one of Delia and Lifen's special armbands was listening in.

"And we are relieved to have you here, Assessor," Marsgrove said, political smile entirely false. "However, this is not your designated time slot, nor even your designated *day*, and as you say, this is an institution that relies on order and safety for all the underage mages under our protection."

"I am relieved to hear that those are your priorities, for I have time *now*. My role is to assess the magic and safety in our layer. As a result of the *circumstance* that occurred on your campus, my schedule is completely full but I *will* conduct this assessment, as required by law."

We weren't ready. We weren't *ready*. And as the assessor was completely dripping with Department magic, Olivia would 100% try to kill her.

Marsgrove smiled thinly. "I will need your tools at the end of this visit, if you continue on this course, Assessor. Or, you can come back on your assigned date and time. Your choice."

The assessor smiled. She opened her palms and three items from the floor zoomed to her hands to join the recorder, on display for the entire hall to see. "Standard tools, Dean Marsgrove, which you are welcome to examine. Your little pet has the rest of the materials I brought under her hands, probably trying to duplicate each sheet illegally while she touches what does not belong to her. I demand you search her."

I pulled my hands away and showed open palms. Duplicating her papers would have been a *great* idea and I was seriously glad I had *not* thought of it.

Marsgrove made a show of scanning *everything* in the hallway with a sarcastically sweet, "just in case."

A quick communication from the team told me that they had dropped everything in order to listen in and view the images I was sending.

"Standard replicator, reader, riveter, recorder, and ratchets. Top of the line ones, but nothing that the administration wouldn't already possess at their highest level. She knew she wouldn't need a full toolset." Loudon swore. *"They are banking on success without gimmicks."*

"And they are going to get it as soon as the assessor enters that room. It doesn't

matter how long the dean stalls. This is bad, Crown," Saf's voice said. *"Trick is ready for Protocol Twelve."*

I swallowed. Protocol Twelve was one of Trick's more insane ideas, and though implementing it would mean Olivia would be temporarily free from the Department, she would not be allowed back on campus anytime soon.

I looked through the door's window into Olivia's room. Greyskull was inside speaking to her, and Olivia's fingers were inching toward a paper that was near the bed. I could feel the magic of the paper from here—it was one of my storage papers.

Feeling a sense of inevitability settle over me, I touched my back pocket. Sure enough, the paper I had been carrying earlier was missing.

I hadn't felt her lift it from me, but more importantly, what had she placed inside of it?

Whatever it was—a magical scalpel or something worse—it didn't matter, even if I called the paper to me before she removed it. It wasn't like she needed whatever was in there in order to kill the woman.

No time.

There was no time left to figure out how to remove the spell that held Olivia in its grips. The assessor was going to enter the room, Olivia was going to kill the assessor, Greyskull was going to revive the assessor, and Olivia would be carted off to a containment cell in the Department. Any chance to remain at school and away from her mother would be destroyed.

Destruction. The thought flitted past the problem-solving centers of my brain as Marsgrove said something scathing to the assessor.

Creation. Thoughts half-slotted into a space. I looked at my palm.

I pictured a magical scalpel resting there, like the one that Olivia had used against her mother. A magical scalpel, capable of meting out healing or killing magic—related and separate disciplines. Two sides of the same coin. Actions with opposite aims. Magic that could be flipped based on one's goals.

Destruction and creation...

Before I could rethink the action, I gathered the assessor's papers in one cloud of magic and shoved them into her hands, forcing her into Marsgrove, and pushed my way into the room.

The moment the seal was breached, Olivia was in motion, striding toward the open door—the full impact of a Department employee laden with Department spells hitting her, no longer obstructed by a physical barrier or magic.

The storage paper in her hand glowed, and a silver tip protruded outward from the page where she reached to grip it—another scalpel, or something worse. I wasn't going to let the audience behind us find out.

I grabbed Olivia's arms, and before she could shake me off, I focused

Chapter Nine

my magic and *pushed*. I pushed Raphael's spell without seeking to remove it, without seeking to alter its trigger, without seeking to change its base intent even. I pushed in order to *flip* the coin.

My vision leeched of color, to a world of black and white shadows. The field of the spell glittered and wavered. Then with a "pop" like a contact lens pushed from its convex to its concave side, it inverted.

But the magic I was using continued to rush outward. Weirdly, a pool of starlight and shadow tickled my memory and I grabbed the streams of fleeing starlight, gathering them into the bough of my arms before tipping them into the nearest container that shimmered with my magic.

The magic settled and I looked at my hands. They were glowing, like I was looking at them through a film.

"Idiot," Constantine said cuttingly across the armband connection. I hadn't even known he was listening in.

"Did we just...see that happen? How—?"

The film over my vision suddenly clicked off. Oh, no. I'd visually projected all of that through mental connection.

"Hush, everyone. Not now." That was Neph.

"Lying low, though? Wasn't that the plan?" someone weakly joked, trying to raise the mood.

I swallowed.

Marsgrove was pulling me backward, face coldly furious. "Back into the hall, Miss Crown, before I—"

"Excellent." The assessor marched through the open door, but it wasn't the woman's eyes looking back at me, hungry and triumphant. "Now we are getting to the actual items of importance."

Before my terror could fully form, Olivia surged toward the assessor— the impetus, the *need*, still driving her actions—still caught by the unchanged base parameters of the spell.

The fingers of Olivia's free hand opened and closed above the storage paper, and her palm pulsed. Then Olivia's fingers were moving over the paper, slamming one corner of the page against the opposing one, forming a triangle. Then another triangle, then a curve.

"What is she doing?"

"Is she making a...weapon?"

The mental voices of the Bandits mixed together as their gazes stared through my eyes, holding my breath in their collective grasp.

Olivia's fingers moved and worked, stuttered and shaky, uncoordinated, and *angry*.

The paper was glowing with far too much magic when she thrust it toward the assessor, who pulled back in belated self-preservation—Stavros nowhere in sight when not looking my way.

In Olivia's hand was a long-toothed cadaverous dragon with a face that looked remarkably similar to that of the assessor, if created in the hands of a ten-year-old.

"For you," Olivia gritted out. "I hope you rot in hell with it."

"*What?*" the woman said, gums bared.

"I said, I hope you jot a spell on it," Olivia said, mutinously.

My jaw hung as I gaped at my roommate.

"You will rue those words, Miss Price," the assessor said, lifting her hand. "I will *not* be spoken to in that manner."

Marsgrove immediately surrounded the assessor's hand with magic of his own. And whether he was simply more powerful than the assessor or whether the administrative might of a dean of Excelsine on Excelsine's grounds trumped the ever loving hell out of a Department official, her movements were completely stilled.

"Yes, well, you can't arrest or physically discipline someone for insolence here. Impudence isn't a crime. It just shows a sensational lack of *forethought.*" That statement was *very clearly* meant for me.

However, the rest of his expression—a 180 degree turn from the stunned, disbelieving one he had displayed when Olivia started folding a piece of paper instead of killing the woman—had turned cunning. The unwavering power he displayed in his administrative persona was rapidly drawing back around him, as he realized—as we *all* realized—the changing circumstances; that there might be a *chance.*

"Since we *are* all assembled here, Madame Assessor, as much as it pains me to allow the Department to dictate any terms on a campus free from outside influence, you may do your assessment now so you can get back to your other, more important tasks," he said, wielding an extremely false mixture of casual weariness and resignation that did absolutely nothing to hide his underlying satisfaction.

The assessor stiffened, and turned to stride out of the room. "I think I will wait until the appointed time now, Dean Marsgrove." She, too, realized her disadvantage.

Three mages in the hall slid into position, blocking the door, locking the five of us—Marsgrove, Greyskull, the assessor, Olivia, and me—in place inside the room.

Marsgrove smiled in a predatory way as he smoothly stepped into the assessor's path. "I must insist. You broke the terms of agreement in coming early. I accept the new date and time for doing this assessment, without invoking the penalty clause in the contract—the one you were quite willing to invoke mere minutes ago. You have all the tools that you need, as you stated under contract magic in the hall. As you so dutifully put to record."

Magic swirled, waiting.

Chapter Nine

She was the one who had brought the recording device and used it to record her case about why she was early. And Marsgrove assuredly had a duplicate of the recording as well as of what was happening now—he played the same political games.

The Department would be shown as deliberately manipulative if the recordings were broadcast and the assessment postponed. And, at present, there was a large media battle to be won.

They held the stare down for tense moments, but with no other politically viable recourse, the assessor acquiesced and began malevolently arranging her instruments.

I felt something faint, like hope, light within me.

Helen had correctly inferred that more powerful tools would be unnecessary for the assessment—that the spell on Olivia would negate the necessity for *normal* tools. And she had also been correct in thinking that we wouldn't have been able to remove the spell yet.

No one had banked on us figuring out a way to *adapt* the spell.

"There are foreign spells all over her," the assessor said sternly. "Many of them protected within themselves, hiding the identity of the caster and the nature of the spells. Advanced protection magic. They have been perverted into something else with the magic of the other girl in the room. A complaint will be filed against Miss Crown."

"I consented to Ren's spells," Olivia said, through gritted teeth as she folded another piece of paper taken from a stack on the counter. She was on her fifth. "And I will be treated by Doctor Greyskull. I am no danger to anyone."

Olivia looked fiercely at me before she thrust a fifth misshapen animal at the woman.

"For you," Olivia gritted again, holding all five of the origami papers in her hand.

Four of those papers I didn't care about, but the one that had been a storage paper...

I anxiously watched the woman look at the creations in disgust, before dismissing them, and focusing on her arguments.

"It is illegal to use such compulsion spells." The woman marked something on her tablet. There was no need for the tablet, but as I had long observed in the magical world, people used such things to make a point.

She wanted me to know she was logging the offense.

"I'm surprised that you don't have measures in place to handle such things, Dean Marsgrove." She *tsked* and made another note, forced to fall back on her role as a government regulator. "I will log it in the Department review. When we get control of this campus that will be fixed."

"Perhaps you missed the part where your brethren were chased from campus two days past?" Marsgrove said idly.

"A mere inconvenience." She waved her hand. A small blue field popped up. "We will be back and even better prepared for the types of mages you stock here."

Like we were all tilapia in a pond awaiting the harvest.

For a second, when her gaze met mine, I could see Stavros' face flit across hers—victory, not defeat, in his menacing features.

Olivia tried to give the woman the misshapen creations again—more forcefully this time—but the woman swept her hand out, sending the papers to the floor, and strode toward the door.

"Dean Marsgrove, I will have a word with you," the assessor said grimly.

Relief nearly caused my legs to buckle. With the assessor using underpowered instruments, the actual examination had taken less than five minutes.

Greyskull followed them out, giving me a significant look before shutting the door firmly behind him.

Olivia scooped up the storage paper turned misshapen dragon, holding it tightly against her chest, then began methodically gathering the other papers crumpled on the tile. I looked through the hall window, to where the adults argued, voices silent to us, expressions clipped and cold, then knelt next to Olivia.

Olivia gathered the last crumpled creation to her with a look that was half relief and half crestfallen anguish. "What did you do, Ren?"

I tucked my hands in between my knees and scooted closer. "I...whammied you?"

She looked at the deformed papers in her hands and shook her head as a small sound of hysteria emerged from her throat.

"I flipped Raphael's spell," I hastened to add, scooting closer until our knees touched. "The inverse of destruction is construction, right? I just flipped the magic."

"You flipped the magic," she said in a deadened way, staring at the papers.

"There was a sort of slim space under the spell—I saw a place I could stick a magical fingernail and pry up the rest. His magic has some of mine laced with it, and I have some of his. And although that all sucks, it gave me a hook, an entry point, a..."

I sighed. "Look. People keep telling me that I'm going to end the world instead of remaking it into something new and awesome. And..." I fiddled nervously with the inside seams of my jeans between my knees. "That sucks. I tweaked the spell to the creation side of the balance scales instead."

"You just made a little tweak?"

"Yes?"

Chapter Nine

"You forced me to *create* things for the Department instead of destroying them."

I gave a gesture that was half shrug, half appeal. I was a creator. I didn't want to be a destroyer.

"You injected me with arts and crafts magic," Olivia said, her tone dark and disbelieving as she looked at the crumpled paper in her lap.

"Er," I looked at the misshapen forms. "That is one way of putting it."

"And it worked," she said in the same incredulous tone.

"Well, I have no idea what that one was supposed to be," I pointed at the one closest to me, trying to make it a joke.

"Ren, you can't just *flip* magic."

"Why not?" I asked. "It's just like—"

The door slammed open and the assessor strode back in. This time, though, it was with the full force of Stavros riding her face.

"Madame Assessor," Marsgrove said sharply, striding at her heels and unable to see that it was no longer the assessor in control of her body. "You completed your assessment."

Stavros—for the assessor's features were nowhere in view—ignored them and looked from Olivia to me and back again, slowly taking in everything.

And Olivia... Olivia had already called a new piece of paper to hand and was briskly folding it on the floor, anger and fear in every motion. She scooped up *all* of the creations, stood, and held them out. "Here," she said angrily.

I froze, eyes on the storage paper, which sat in its misshapen dragon form in a place of importance on top of the pile, then slowly lifted my gaze to Stavros's parasitical face.

Stavros smiled.

No.

One of the assessor's hands held out an empty cloth case and Olivia jerkily tipped the papers inside.

"Thank you, child," Stavros said, his skeletal, exultant gaze never leaving mine.

Then in a single blink of my eyes, the assessor reappeared in full view, turned on her heel, and strode from the room. "Dean Marsgrove, see me out," she demanded.

Marsgrove looked at me, wariness in his features. But he didn't know. He couldn't *know* what she had just taken. After Constantine's warnings, I had put some protections in place. Unless someone saw the paper in action, it would just look like any of my normal 2D drawings.

The adults were in the hall. They were walking away. *Away.*

We needed the assessor off campus, but I couldn't let her leave with my storage paper. I couldn't let her go. I stumbled to my feet and held out my hand to call the paper back, to blast the case from existence, to incapacitate her, but Olivia grabbed my arm.

"What are you doing?" she hissed.

"He, she, has the—"

"I *know*. Having you in prison will not aid *either of us*."

"But my—"

"I *gave* it to her, Ren," she said, agony in every word. "I transferred ownership. It is part of your *spell*. To create things *for* them. You gave me partial ownership of that paper weeks ago. I *transferred ownership* as soon as she held out her hand. You legally *can't* get that paper back unless they *give* it to you."

"It's okay," I responded immediately, automatically, to her anxiety. "It will be fine."

But panic was making my breath come fast and my vision shadowy.

I tried to calm myself, to be rational. The storage paper would paint a target on my back, but I could blame the paint. Say I got a tube of Kinsky's or something. Blame that shop in Ganymede even. Blame everything on the paint. Be fined.

It wasn't like I had put Origin magic directly inside of it only linked to me.

Communications were flying over the group connection, deconstructing what had happened in rapid-fire fashion, mainly ignoring the two of us now that the assessor was gone. With my spiral of panic muting my brain, it sounded like they were in the room with us. Dagfinn and Loudon were the two with the most to say.

"What happened to the magic she used anyway? Crown definitely used some restricted mojo. There was a "you-know-what" spike. I have the spike reader on feed now. It was timed exactly."

"That harpy didn't even blink, though, neither did Marsgrove. Why didn't the magic use show in the room?" Loudon questioned.

"I don't know. But if it had shown, the assessor would have been all over it. And Marsgrove and Greyskull, too. No. It's like it almost didn't *exist*. Serious mystery here."

"Well, it had to go *somewhere*," Saf reasoned, adding to Dagfinn and Loudon's conjecture. "Where, is the ques—?"

"Shiving imbeciles," Constantine's voice cut through. "The *paper*," he said coldly.

Pause.

I closed my eyes. But what difference did it make if they knew about the storage paper now.

"The paper. The first one? That first paper contained the event?"

Loudon said half in question, half in sudden realization. "It was in Price's hands—in the circuit of magic—when Crown did it. *She automatically used the recycler.* Holy crap, Crown."

Dread coiled in me at their words. Memory making my breath hitch. Working on instinct, I'd put the fleeing starlight into a container. A container laced with my magic.

The delinquents were still speaking as the sparked panic in my heart swirled through my limbs like a spiral of ice and I stumbled, barely catching myself on the counter, tools rattling under my grasping fingers.

"Now that you mention it, something was poking out of the paper before—did anyone else see that?" Lifen said. "Like Price was trying to retrieve something. Thought it was a trick of the light."

There was the briefest slip of a pause, then swearing issued from five different voices.

"Crown *made that paper.* The threads already had her magic in them. What if it's a—"

"It's a *storage space.*"

"And that means—"

The swearing grew more frantic.

"This is worse than the original spell on Price. *Get the paper.*"

"How?"

More urgency infused their voices, and new voices added to the sudden outpouring of panic.

"ASAP Priority," Trick said grimly. "Saf, who fits the bill?"

"Sanders, Vorlav, Ciennes."

"Vorlav's on Top Circle," Dagfinn added.

"Dag, thought you were still retired?"

"Go trance yourself!"

"Saf?"

"I'm on it."

"Tell him 'clean slate,' but get Ciennes in position too, just in case."

"Unnecessary. I got Vorlav. His motives are easy. And Moses is there, ripe for creating a distraction. I've got this. Crown, Price, *don't move.*" Saf went dark.

"Don't freak out, Ren," Will said.

A prime ranking member of the Department had one of my storage papers and was on her way with it to Stavros. A paper that, apparently, I had actively infused with Origin Magic.

"I'm freaking out, Will."

A sigh. "Yeah."

Chapter Ten

TEARS OF SUCCESS

GREYSKULL ENTERED the room, anger vibrating under his skin. "Ren? Miss Price?"

Don't say anything, Crown. We've got this handled, Patrick said emphatically, their mental voices retreating to the back of my skull as Greyskull closed the door.

"Full of entertainment, as always," Greyskull said grimly. "Now let's see what you've done."

He pulled up a scope field, along with the half-completed mapping of the spell, and carefully maneuvered both over Olivia.

"I flipped the spell," I said, shaking. "I don't know if the flip will hold, though." Like a contact lens, trying to regain its original shape.

He pulled back from his examination a few moments later, his grim expression replaced by a half-smile. "Well, you don't make life dull, Ren. How do you feel, Miss Price?"

"Like I have a killing urge to create," she said dourly.

He nodded, carefully withdrawing the fields from around her. "Along with the temporary cessation of your murder spree, the other positive is that I can see the underpinnings of the spell in a way that was invisible before."

"Can you fix it?"

He hesitated, long fingers folding the scope in his hand, then said, "Yes."

A huge blast of cheering blared across our group communications. *"Vorlav got it,"* Saf said with relish.

The paper wasn't on its way to Stavros. Why then did I feel ghostly fingers crawling slowly up my spine? As opposed to everyone else's relief, I felt only apprehension.

Greyskull tipped his head to the side, listening to something, then gave it a rueful shake. "I'm not even going to ask what just happened at Top Circle."

"It's probably for the best," I said, determined to shake off my lingering anxiety.

He shook his head again. "Fantastic. Well Miss Price, let's get you unhooked and out into the world."

Surprise painted her features. "I thought—"

"It was one of the assessor's conditions—that you are released immediately to determine your fitness. After the little skirmish on Top Circle just now, there will be even less room for negotiation of terms. Congratulations, you will be going to class tomorrow," he said with false cheer.

"But the assessor thinks the spell will fail and that Liv will kill people," I said, thinking of the ramifications. "The Department is willing to put the student body at risk?"

"The Department will do much to achieve their aims. For the good of all, of course."

I had no response to that horrifying assessment.

"You are released." He made an unnecessary show of his hands as the ward magic viscerally released Olivia, then wiped one hand down his weary face. He looked like he was one minute away from seeking out a series of stiff drinks.

"What about tonight?" I asked, as Olivia made a beeline for the hall and I tripped to get in front of her, throwing my body forward, and plastering myself like a starfish across the door. "Where do we sleep?" I asked Greyskull over Olivia's shoulder as she tried to move me.

We had planned to stay here again tonight. Being released meant my rooming madness would restart along with all the other insanity of being freed.

"He's getting away," Olivia muttered, trying to grab the door handle, head bobbing like a bird trying to see through the window. "That one, right there, I need to—"

I gave Greyskull a panicked look and he sighed, closed his eyes, and opened his palms.

Olivia slumped. "He left."

The back of my head hit the door and I closed my eyes. Flipping the spell only meant the outcome had changed—not the underlying condition. Greyskull could direct the halls of the medical ward, like whatever he had done to move the Department-laced student who had wandered by just now, but Olivia was about to be released into the *general population* and there were no overrides in place.

"I can only control the medical aspect, Ren." Greyskull's voice was filled with weary regret. "No classes for Miss Price this afternoon due to the continuing need to be in familiar spaces, and I've given her permission to attend classes virtually for the rest of the week. But the medical override for your rooming situation was canceled as soon as you flipped that spell and gave the assessor no other choice. The administrative wards connecting you to the other two rooms are in effect again. You will have to maintain the rotation schedule that is already in place until those are sorted out."

Back in control, Olivia narrowed her eyes. I had caught her up on all the rooming shenanigans, but she was going to be appalled by the reality of it in practice.

"And with the way things are going in the administration building right now, they might not get the rooming situation sorted out until tomorrow or Wednesday at the earliest," Greyskull said with a shrug. "If you feel the tug to another room, do not ignore it. Be beyond reproach for the next few days, yes?"

He looked like he didn't think that was possible and was already planning a heavy drinking session accordingly.

"Thanks. We'll figure it out," I assured Olivia. "Let's get back to our room and veg."

The faster we got to our room and settled in, the better.

Greyskull gave us a frequency that connected directly to him, and we scheduled an appointment to see him tomorrow between classes.

Stepping into the empty corridor was nerve-wracking. Greyskull had cleared the hall, but we only had one minute until it would fill again. Quickly taking the shortcut back to Dorm Twenty-five, we paused in front of the stairwell's door, then gingerly emerged into the main hall.

When nothing untoward happened, we both started to relax. But when we reached the second floor hall, Olivia stopped dead.

So did the boy walking toward us who was brimming with Department-laced spells.

The three of us froze.

With the residue of Raphael's magic enchantment still in my fingertips, I could feel the spells flowing over the other student.

Olivia's eyes squinted weirdly at him. The next moment, she was furiously *ripping* a chunk of plaster from the wall and squishing it between her palms. The boy's panic was so palpable it practically manifested in the air.

She thrust a misshapen gargoyle toward him. "Here." Her voice was heavy with vindictive irritation.

The boy scooted around us, back pressed to the opposite wall. "No thanks?"

As soon as he cleared the space, he picked up his pace, shooting frightened looks over his shoulder, before finally disappearing down a stairwell.

Olivia's gaze pinned me, her creation held between two fingers in furious appeal.

"Yay!" I said lamely, tugging the...thing...from her hand and stuffing it in my pocket.

She reached out and grabbed it before it fully disappeared from view. "I am displeased," she said viciously.

"No one's dead." I stared at the plaster she was pulverizing. "Well, that's beyond repair. But no living things were harmed."

"He didn't take my offering."

"Oh, well, that's..."

"Completely ridiculous. I didn't want him to have it anyway," she said viciously, but on the edge of tears.

"Yup. Let's go home," I said, putting my arm around her and quickly steering her to our room.

As soon as we entered, we were encompassed by the wards, each familiar protection growing thicker as both of us moved further beneath the boughs. It was like a giant, decommissioned generator kick starting itself upon feeling its inhabitants' return.

The crimp of a thousand vices loosened, and we both collapsed against the door.

I started laughing hysterically, and she started crying.

Chapter Eleven

OF VICTORY AND GRIEF

WE HAD MIGRATED from the door to my bed, curling up together, eating food from our stash and soaking up the comfort of the wards. *Our* wards. We dimmed each wards' response to hall activity and whoever might wander past.

"Was any of it real?" I finally asked. "While Raphael had you—was anything I saw in my dreams real?"

Some of it had to be. During her rescue, Olivia had referenced at least one interaction.

"What did you see?" she asked, gripping my comforter restlessly.

In a memory pocket, I captured my recollection of the dreams carefully—dulling the sense memories and my emotional responses so they wouldn't overwhelm her—and cautiously handed them to her.

She viewed them with tight lips and constricted eyes. Her gaze turned distant as she handed the pocket back and looked out the window over the grounds. "Like enough versions, yes."

She didn't offer up her own memory variations.

"And when you disappeared from campus?" I asked gently. This was ground that Marsgrove had covered with her when I'd been taking my spelled "nap."

"I ended up in a containment box at a terrorist compound somewhere in the Third Layer. I didn't have time to figure out where, though Phillip might have determined the location now with the pieces I gave him." She shook her head. "Ironically, my first emotion was relief. I...wasn't sure I was going to end up anywhere," she said with difficulty.

I squeezed her hand. I had almost obliterated part of the Second Layer thinking the same thing. Thinking her dead.

"Even better, the containment box Verisetti had prepared was to hold someone with far different magic than mine." For yours, went unsaid. "And unfortunately for Verisetti's superiors, I had taken a few precautions to guard myself against the freezing spell he placed on me at the end of last term. I escaped from the cell, and..." She smiled darkly. "And let's just say that I made their establishment unusable for a while."

"Good."

Her smile slowly dissipated. "For a few minutes, I thought I had a real chance. Wherever I was, external communication was specifically spelled against, but I was wreaking havoc with all the spells we'd been practicing. I nearly made it outside. Unfortunately Verisetti showed up—*woke* up, I guess—when I was so *close*." She set her jaw. "And he isn't like the others. I stood a chance against them. Verisetti trapped me like a mouse between lazy paws. *Easy*." She thumped her fist against the bed. "Even with all the work I put in after his spell last term."

I squeezed her. I'd been that mouse. I'd been that mouse while thinking I'd become the cat.

She shook her head mutely. "He moved our location almost immediately. The whole compound was in an uproar over what had happened on campus. He just...slipped us out while their generals argued. And the rest... The rest, you know."

"We are going to be okay," I said, steel under the reassurance. "I'm going to figure out everything."

"Yes," she said, voice going absent, mind suddenly far away. "I won't let anything happen to any of us. Ever again."

That sounded ominous. But before I could question her, voices clamored across my comm.

"Bandits, ahoy!" came Patrick's voice across the shared mental connection, as bodies collided against the outside of our door.

Olivia's face turned to the sound. She hesitated for a moment, then swept her hand out, remotely opening the door.

Patrick, Asafa, Loudon, and Dagfinn hovered in the entryway while Neph stood regally behind them, very nearly rolling her eyes. She had already been on her way over—she'd communicated her intent as soon as we made it back to the room—so they had likely swept her into their raucous midst on their way.

Olivia peered behind them cautiously, but made no movement to jump up and start folding paper objects for someone in the hall.

"We just scared the entire floor witless," Trick crowed as they barreled their way inside. "Sots all ducked into their rooms like rhubarbs. Didn't even have to use magic for it. Who wants to see a master at work?"

Neph sighed and closed the door behind her, hooking into our wards to do her normal damage control with the foursome's more manic inclinations.

I sent Neph a mental query, and she shook her head. The other "Bandits" were attending classes or other mandatory activities, but she had gotten permission to take her afternoon lessons virtually.

Babysitting all of you, she said mentally.

"Stop mother henning, Bau," Trick said, with a frenzied wave in her direction. "We can read your shouting from here and it is entirely *misplaced.* Everything is outstanding this fine day. The Queen is only half amok, Crown is only half deranged, and the Department took two to the *face.*"

"You have the paper?" I asked.

"Have the paper?" He scoffed. "No, we do not have your world destroying paper of doom."

I exchanged a look with Olivia, anxiety curling again. "Then—"

"Special gloves," Patrick said, motioning like he was putting one on. "All the Vorlavs have them. Going to be all the rage soon with you finally full on releasing the creepy." Patrick somehow made it sound favorable. He made a circular hand motion and a memory ball appeared in his palm. "Observe pure genius."

We hunched around the memory ball and Saf activated the memory of the swap that had been recorded in full detail by someone on Top Circle.

Marsgrove and the assessor were walking toward the administration building. Precisely five feet from the stairs, Magical Moses, clad in robes and holding his staff, let loose an enchantment that lifted all paper articles in a hundred yard radius like birds taking flight.

A pack of hooligans near him whooped and proceeded to skeet shoot papers from the sky to the music of the assessor's outraged screams and Marsgrove's narrowed eyes.

Marsgrove had known something was up.

I didn't spend time watching him, though. Marsgrove, more than anyone else in this situation, couldn't intervene. He could watch the carnage, but he couldn't participate. As a dean of Excelsine, he was hampered by a different type of contract magic. Especially when dealing with the authorities.

I'd researched that after his careful performance in the aftermath of Bloody Tuesday.

The scene was a flurry of booms, roars, colors and chaos, the papers bursting into confetti with each targeted shot.

Tracking the misshapen dragon paper had shown it had been hit twice, losing its shape completely.

Peters ran up, Canary yellow tablet in hand, and immobilized the perpetrators. The papers fluttered from the sky.

With gloved hands, a hulking boy who must have been the previously referenced "Vorlav" grabbed the one I had been watching and swapped it

Chapter Eleven

in a motion that was almost too clean to be seen. He handed the crumpled fake to the assessor, along with three of the assessor's other papers, and gave a respectful bow and a single, "Madame."

She nodded sharply, called the other papers to her by magic, then turned abruptly on her heel, indignantly climbed the steps, and marched into the building.

Peters was reading Moses and the hooligans their offenses, oblivious to the heist that had just occurred.

Trick and Saf had organized the entire burgled spectacle in a truly remarkable feat of time, creativity, and available resources.

As the memory dimmed around the edges, I watched the woman disappear inside the building with an unexceptional piece of paper; while Vorlav receded in the other direction with mine crumpled in his gloved hand.

"And that"—Patrick stood and dropped the memory like it was a live mike in front of an audience—"is how you—Get. Mayhem. Done."

He shimmied left, pulling his right foot along the floor in time with a dipped left shoulder, then continued the shimmy around our room. He lifted Neph's hand and she let him pull her into an impromptu victory dance.

"Yes," I heard Olivia murmur, but my attention was on Patrick and Neph, suddenly twirling in the limited space between our furniture.

Neph, the professional, had no trouble improvising and Patrick had skill of his own. Magic crackled beautifully around them.

Saf grinned and pulled both Olivia and me to our feet, engulfing us in the spell, and Loudon and Dagfinn vaulted forward to join as we all whirled together in victory.

~*~

With the spell of togetherness and victory thrumming in my veins, I headed off to a double justice shift while Patrick and Asafa entertained Olivia in our room. Loudon and Dagfinn skipped off to their last classes of the day, and after touching my forehead, Neph had murmured something about muses and duties and disappeared.

I girded myself for a repeat of the morning's calls, but the first hour of service flew by with grief calls, hilarious delinquency with the usual suspects, accidental abuses of magic, and awkwardness.

The awkward calls gained frequency, and developed a pattern, as mages —regardless of the offense they logged—stood in awe, blinked at me in a daze, and said nothing. I just pretended that each of them lacked vocal chords and was extra kind.

People still stared at my scarf, but there were no more indecent or threatening proposals.

The changes—even though positive—put me on guard. But I didn't have time to dwell on what the difference might mean.

The grief calls were still the most emotionally difficult to handle. I sat with each grief-stricken mage as they broke down, and they *all* broke down eventually, as if driven to the response upon seeing me. I always left a rose behind when the Grief Squad, as campus was calling it, showed up to relieve me and cocoon the sobbing, grief-stricken person.

The community support machine was turning into an unstoppable, amazing force.

When I'd first appeared on campus, the atmosphere had been one of every mage for herself. That self-serving attitude had shifted to a far more collegial feel, as if to say, "We are going to get *our* campus back to the way it was, get *our* people back to rights, *then* we will resume tripping you down staircases."

The community support engine, augmenting its own effectiveness by leaps and bounds, was proactively seeking out everyone on the edges. More students were admitting that they needed support and were seeking it from one of the many groups around campus that were springing up like summer wildflowers after a nutrient rich downpour.

The students who *hadn't* come to terms with their anger or pain were the ones I still saw, hence, the sobbing, furious, or dramatic breakdowns.

The Grief Squad was getting pretty good at showing up promptly and taking over, but each call of this type left me feeling a little more drained. By the time I was nearing the end of the double shift, I was only experiencing the edges of my emotions—the remaining highs of victory and the enhanced lows of loss.

I could empathize with their losses. Even after half a year, I missed Christian terribly. Some days so much that all I could do was pin my focus on something else in order to function. I intimately understood there were plenty of students who still had a far longer grief road to travel.

My emotional reserves felt scraped thin, suddenly, and I felt more removed than I had in a long time. Strange. I shook my head. It had been a long day. I needed to focus myself on what I could *do*. I didn't want to feel.

An almost foreign feeling of pleasure accompanied that thought. Weird. I rubbed my forehead and the band around my neck pulsed before I felt myself again. Time for a break. I looked at the log and chose a call that would take me outside—take me up a few levels of campus through fresh air.

Isaiah was right. We needed to plan an event. Now that the combat competition had ended, there were fewer diversions for people to focus on. More blank walls to stare at and empty headspace to inhabit. We needed to give people something positive to do, to focus upon, so that their pain could gradually and naturally work itself out, then soften with time.

I needed to hunt down the blonde to see what we could do long term to fix the emotional needs of campus.

Not so strangely, with all the upper levels reopened, groups were gathering around campus to discuss the issues still deeply affecting everyone.

As I exited the Magiaduct, I passed by one such group. A boy was standing in front of a small crowd and speaking in an unnaturally calm voice for the amount of fervor he was inspiring.

"Harmony. Concordance. Peace. The Custodians of Peace seek to ensure that all mages have equal opportunities for living well."

A slew of approving murmurs sounded.

"Ensuring peace is our highest priority. Who was responsible for Tuesday's events?"

Terse shouts proclaimed everyone from Godfrey to Verisetti to Salvatori Lorenzo in the Third Layer to Stavros, the Department, and the Excelsine administration in the Second.

"Ren Crown" was shouted at least once, as well.

That also spiked a weird feeling of pleasure—like I was absorbing it from someone else on the field.

I walked a little faster, shoulders hunched. My faster walking didn't get me away from the emotional angst and verbal accusations, though. All of the outside calls seemed to coincide with one group or another getting a little out of hand and triggering an alert, putting me in their crosshairs.

The community machine was in full swing, but everything wasn't miraculously better, of course it wasn't. There were still a lot of wounds in the psyche of campus. It felt like *weeks* had past. That I had aged a decade, when in reality, the time was so *short*.

Musicians around campus played magic-laced music that evoked sympathy, healing, pain, and the bitter struggle of reality. A string quartet full of rage on the west side of Fourth Circle juxtaposed with the lilting harmony of a flute and harp playing peaceful tones one arch away on the south side of Second Circle. A drumline produced a steady, soothing beat, while a little ways away, a bagpiper pumped angst into the air using every pipe.

And it appeared that every student with an agenda was making a pitch.

"We can no longer justify the corralling like cattle of our student population. Mistakes will be made, security might turn faulty, but we will be *free*. Vote yes on the complete reopening of campus!"

"There are no such things as safety compromises! Do not be fooled into reopening campus! Our borders are not safe!"

* Of Victory and Grief *

There were groups that wanted to root out all the evil on campus. Groups that wanted to celebrate life. Groups that wanted to pretend as if nothing had happened. Groups that wanted to take what had happened and use the experience to be better prepared in the future.

"The Bone Beast attack helped more than a lot of people realize," one girl was pointing out to a group as I walked past. "Everyone survived it, but that was due in large part to the influx of medical personnel facilitated by the Department's Emergency Response Section. There was a lot of talk in the medical circles on campus about what we could do next time if the ERS *wasn't* involved, and we *used* some of those practices on Bloody Tuesday. We saved a lot of people on Bloody Tuesday with those practices. We lost twenty-six—may magic embrace them always—but we would have lost a lot more," she said resolutely.

I swallowed, throat tight.

Every death reminded me of Christian.

A foreign feeling wiggled through me. A sensation a little too close to *revenge*. I pushed it aside.

I wanted to just...wave my wand and obliterate the need to be hunted, to end my friends' torment, to give Stavros no reason to be in power. If we were at peace, if the borders were secured and the populace was safe, there would be little need for the Department.

Step One: Get a wand.

Step Two: Live in peace.

The foreign feeling gained a small foothold of excitement. Options swirled in my mind. The entire world could be opened again... without my having to sneak around, I could implement all of the plans that I'd been unable to do.

I could go to the First Layer to hug my parents. *Comfort.*

I could go to the Fourth Layer to see its alien beauty firsthand. *Create.*

I could go to the Third Layer and fix their world. *Protect.*

I could do anything.

A feeling, greater than me—almost outside of me—fed into the notion. It felt like Christian.

I gripped the marble that contained a tiny amount of the magic that made up the Third Layer and with the trace remains of the magic of my friends. I had replaced it in my pocket when I'd changed outfits. I didn't want to be separated from it.

The edges of my vision swirled abruptly with black-and-white patterns, painting the seams and corners of the stone building nearest to me with a grungy, ripped quality.

Pleasure, assurance, and a sense of *rightness* raked through me, overlaying all of the small red flags that were popping up underneath and waving in my mind.

I could fix *everything*.

Something pressed hard against my wrist cuff, ripping the thought from me. Startled, I released the marble, letting it drop to the bottom of my pocket again, and looked up. Camille Straught was scowling at me in staggering disapproval.

"Get yourself under *control*."

Shock mixed with a crushing sense of shame as the frayed edges of my emotions became even more apparent.

It wasn't the surprise at seeing Camille—though there was a little of that. I had heard through both Axer and the Justice Squad feed earlier that all of the combat mages, barring Axer, Nicholas Dare, and Mars Ramirez, had returned to campus, and the returned combat mages were tending to campus security measures once again under the steady, capable hand of Selmarie Senthuss, the head of the Combat Squad.

The relief at having the combat mages back on campus had been *palpable*. The entire mountain had seemed to breathe a sigh of relief.

No, the shock and shame had little to do with seeing Camille Straught again.

"I'm fine. I've got it." I tried to tug my wrist free from her stone grip. With a final tug, she let me.

We stared at each other for long moments. Her steely expression matched her grip.

"I don't know what is wrong with you, but I refuse to be your minder," she said harshly.

"No one asked you to be," I said, my shame converting to a more self-protecting state.

"*No one asked...*" She drew in a sharp breath. "I should be so fortunate."

Axer, then. Axer had asked her to keep an eye on me. That same foreign feeling that had come over me was abruptly *angry*.

"Consider yourself excused," I said tightly, turning.

She grabbed my arm, spinning me back around. "And, what? Let you end my world and all the people I fight for?"

I removed her hand. "I wouldn't have done anything."

I would have listened to the red flags eventually. I pulled my hands into fists. A feeling of rightness assured me that I would have.

"Do you have any idea what happens around you?" she demanded.

At my lack of response, she opened her hand and a leaf zipped into her curved palm. She gripped it between two fingers and held it in front of my eyes.

Black-and-white swirling patterns were receding slowly on the veins of the leaf.

I stared at them, then looked back at her, a weird feeling of detachment overtaking me. It was a similar state to when Christian had first been ripped away—when I couldn't get a handle on my own emotions.

"Thank you for your assistance," I said, my *recognition* of the weirdly detached state not lessening its impact. "I will make sure to keep the feeling in mind so that I can stop it as soon as it starts."

When I could get myself back together, I'd imprint this state on my mind. Make sure it didn't happen again. Something in me laughed.

"You lack control," she said harshly.

To Camille Straught, who fancied herself the queen of control, I definitely did. I was a feral mage who was still trying to get a handle on many things in my new world.

"I'm working on it. Getting better every day." I barely held back a wince at the flippant nature of my tone. I wasn't usually quite this frivolously sarcastic in the face of my own error.

"You should be in a *collar*."

I stared at her. The weird feeling...shifted. "Why aren't you putting me in one, then?" I asked, finally. "I'm sure you know plenty of people who'd be happy to lend a hand."

"Bella thinks you *useful*."

Bellacia would. She had far too many goals for me to accomplish. But she might find amusement in throwing some of her people at me anyway—just to watch the chaos.

"You don't defer to Bellacia," I said, certain of the statement. They were friends, but unlike most people on campus, Bellacia treated Camille as an equal.

Camille's gaze was remote. "This one is for the team. You helped campus in our absence. You get a pass. A very *short* pass."

Like Bellacia and Peters, small "passes" seemed to be in effect across campus when it came to me, but the boons were running out quickly as such things did.

Camille hadn't been this angry before, though. Before leaving for the competition, even on Bloody Tuesday and during my "visit" with Axer to the Midlands, she had been full of disapproval, but it hadn't manifested itself in this white hot anger. I wondered...

"Does this have to do with Corpus Sun?"

She grabbed my upper arm. "Shut up."

"Were you there?"

"Shut *up*."

"Did you get hurt? Someone you loved?" Ramirez was currently with Axer. For whatever reason, he and Axer's cousin Nicholas had been given permission to travel on the victory tour when the rest of the combat mages had returned.

"A short pass, Crown," she hissed. "You are lucky that you didn't get anyone killed in the past few days. An *accomplishment* for you."

My stomach turned to stone, and the weird detachment shattered completely under the onslaught of fresh emotion.

"Come again?" I asked tersely.

"Death follows you. Extinction. First your loved ones, then everyone else's."

Patterns started swirling again—but this time far more fiercely.

She thrust something else under my cuff, and I nearly blasted her off the face of the mountain. The only thing that saved her was the very thing she had snugged beneath the supple, metal links.

It was drenched in Axer's magic and without my permission was calming mine. I wanted to be *angry.*

"You think I don't know your history?" she said harshly, hand still wrapped around my wrist. "You think any of your secrets safe from the four of us? The only reason you aren't in chains is because of Axer. And my support bends only so far, especially when it bends in your direction."

"Understood," I said curtly, wanting nothing more than to leave.

"Cam," a voice said, stern and gentle at the same time.

She let go abruptly and stalked toward the boy who'd appeared near us. Greene was the member of Axer's group that I knew least. He smiled kindly enough at me, but it didn't match the rest of his demeanor.

He turned on his heel as Camille reached his side, and the two of them strode off.

I watched them go and worked the fabric drenched in Axer's magic out from beneath my cuff. It was a slip of fabric, steel gray shot through with teal. I considered it and my mental state—which was starting to slip back to the loop of Raphael-Stavros-Protection-Save-Help-Olivia-Fix—then stuffed it back beneath.

A more level state of emotion blanketed me.

But it was a false state, and one I could not rely on. Camille wasn't wrong. I tapped my cuff, thinking about calming spells, protection spells, and control spells. About the nature of protection and termination. About what I needed to let go of, and what I could *change.*

I worked the fabric out then replaced it back underneath in a repeated series of movements that probably looked ludicrous to whoever was watching me—and these days, there were always eyes. Once I had about ten iterations, I felt more secure in feeling how the spell worked on me internally. I put the fabric into my back pocket—able to be recalled if needed, but left out so I could attempt to regulate myself.

I shivered and rubbed the back of my head, where I had hit it multiple times already today. Perhaps too many knocks to the head was my problem, I thought with some returned humor.

I needed to get my storage paper back. Asafa had assured me it was in "safe-ish" hands.

I sent a trickle of magic to one of the many "static" threads that connected me to my creations. A strange pulse returned, making me almost reach for Axer's calming magic fabric again. In the next moment, an offense came in for a name I had never seen on the call log.

Vitus Vorlav.

Chapter Twelve

COALITION OF NECESSITY

I APPROACHED his door warily, heart beating faster, but before I even had a hand up to knock, it opened. A large, heavily muscled guy wearing severe, expensive clothing and a dark scowl glared back. He looked like both the enforcer and the boss in a Russian mafia movie.

"Uh, Mr. Vorlav, you registered a Level Two Offense for using an illegal destruction enchantment."

He held up my storage paper in one gloved hand. "The foul thing resists."

My heart started a rapid tattoo in my chest. "Oh. Interesting. I could...dispose of that for you, if you are having problems with it."

"*Destroy* it." He threw it in my direction, then started to close the door.

"Wait!" I said, clasping the paper against my chest. Tendrils of its magic clasped me in return. "Your...offense."

He opened the door and stared coldly at me. This was not a person who typically registered offenses. This was, in all probability, his first. And with the touch-sensitive knowledge of Raphael's spell still brimming within me, I could see that Vorlav was drenched in Department magic.

Wow. How had he been persuaded to help? I looked him over. I had never seen him before, and Vorlav wasn't the type of Department stooge who regularly followed me. His magic had a specific edge that I couldn't identify.

But regardless of the reason he had registered the destructive offense—either in order to get the paper to me and fulfill whatever bargain Asafa and Patrick had made with him, or to truly destroy it—Justice Magic had to be satisfied.

"Er, how about helping out on the Third Circle?" I stammered out the additional terms.

"Fine." He tersely repeated the necessary vow and started to close the

114

door again.

"Wait!"

If looks could kill, I'd be a rotting corpse, but the door remained cracked.

I tucked Justice Toad under my arm. "Why?" I asked, trying to understand why this boy, drenched in Department magic, and who was looking at me in disdain, had helped.

"Your *muse*," he said, in a less than complimentary tone. "Revived me twice last Tuesday, along with both of my sisters, one of whom never would have made it within the death frame. You'd do well to get rid of that...*thing*. All obligations are complete, you tell Frey that, and hope that we *never* meet again." He slammed the door shut.

"Well...that was fun," I said weakly, trying to make it a joke in the empty hall, but failing miserably.

I pulled the paper from its secure position against my chest. With all the shifting magic that had been done to it, and with Vorlav trying to destroy it, figuring out what it was *now* would be an experiment all its own.

I could feel it reaching out tendrils to me, trying to reattach to its owner and I let it, pulling its magic into me. I rubbed my neck to shift the kink that was knotting the muscles there.

I logged out of Justice Toad and headed home.

Patrick and Asafa steered clear of me as I entered, gazes steadily on the paper as I moved through the room.

"I saw Vorlav."

"We see that," Patrick said, with a reserved nod to the paper, pressed against my chest once more.

"He said to tell you his obligation is complete. What did he mean?"

"Clearing out a debt, Princess, nothing more, nothing less." Patrick smiled and Saf ticked off something in a ledger that suddenly appeared in the air. "Vorlav's not our usual debtor, but he came through. The magic said that he obtained the dragon-folded paper the assessor was carrying. No worries."

A lot of people had been going to Saf since last Tuesday, wanting to clear any perceived debts. For if mercurial, fey Trick was the Godfather, then pleasant and level-headed Saf was his consigliore.

No one had approached Mike or Will or me. They'd gone to the one they thought would call them in.

"All set now, Ren?" Saf asked.

I nodded sharply.

"Excellent. Well done, everyone. Trick out!" The two of them filed from the room with jaunty waves.

Alone again, Olivia walked to me and looked at the storage paper, but didn't touch it. A frown pulled at her mouth as her hand hovered above it. "The magic is no longer the same."

"Vorlav did his darnedest to destroy it," I said wryly. "The original design should still reside underneath, though. You can change it back, if you want." I offered it to her. "Just will it so."

Olivia took a step back. "No."

"It's fine. We'll change the ownership parameters."

"Why did you give me ownership privileges in the first place?" she demanded.

"Because I trust you."

Her lips pressed together and it looked like she might start sobbing at any moment. "I gave it away." I could hear in the echo of the statement—*I gave your trust away.*

"Hey, no, it's okay." I reached for her. "It's all fine. We'll do the reset together and it will all be—"

The paper tore from my hand, Justice Toad issued an alert that I had gained an additional hour of service, and the paper dove into the grate.

We both stared dumbly at the grate for a half a heartbeat, then scrabbled forward to manually hit the reset button on its frame. Nothing.

Justice Toad beeped again and I called the tablet to hand and quickly scrolled through.

Justice acquisition. Administration locker. Twenty minute acquisition time exceeded.

"Oh, *no.*"

~*~

Isaiah couldn't help.

"Once it goes to an administration locker, it's out of our hands. You have to put in for an administrative review. You are supposed to send anything obtained during a call for review, Ren, you *know* that. That's why you took the justice hit. What exactly did you lose?"

"Just a paper for a class." I smiled overly brightly. "Thanks!"

I was pretty sure that Vorlav had been hoping for this result all along, knowing the paper would be taken. He'd been made to help us, but he hadn't needed to be *helpful.*

The Bandits were divided.

"Leave it," Olivia said, a frown pulling in her brows. "Maybe it will get recycled."

"Crown can't leave it, Price. That magic can't be *left* for someone to find," Dagfinn said, always the paranoid one.

"Administrative review?" offered Mike.

"No way. The item would have to be *cataloged* and all of its magic listed and defined. Nope, no *way*. Find it Crown," Patrick ordered, right before he started mumbling, "Should have gone with, Ciennes."

Regaining the paper meant finding someone high enough in the administration to order a bypass of the review.

I ruled out Provost Johnson, who would just up my service hours while looking disappointed. And I nixed Chancellor Barrie who was rarely on campus and under intense political scrutiny and pressure.

The rest of the deans and higher level admins would take a lot of schmoozing, and that wasn't really my forte. Maybe I could enlist one of the delinquents for it, though. I put the idea in a Plan B folder in my mind.

There was really only one person in power I could even hope to influence.

The man wasn't in his office, and it took a while to track him down. There was no administrative emergency, and if Marsgrove didn't want to be found on his own campus, he had plenty of ways to hide himself. I had to wheedle location aid from Greyskull, in the end.

I finally found Marsgrove standing on the Seventeenth Circle, at the edge of the battlefield, looking out over the valley.

My step stuttered as I passed the empty stands, not too far from where we had sprinted, then made our last stand on Bloody Tuesday—my blood and the blood of everyone who had been around me was still here, buried in the renewal enchantments on the field. I swallowed and continued my approach.

Even from a profile view, Marsgrove looked older. He was healed, Greyskull's superpowers and close connection to the dean had seen to that, but that didn't stop the heavy cast to his expression, nor the lines that seemed heavier on his face.

I stopped just short of his position.

Marsgrove was staring out over the large valley surrounding Excelsine. I had gotten used to the incredible vistas as the background behind my daily activities, but when I actually found time to focus on my surroundings, Excelsine was never short of breathtaking views.

Even if they were seen at the field edge of a massacre.

"Miss Crown," he said without turning.

"Dean Marsgrove."

I waited for the requisite sigh and a motion to approach.

We both faced the valley. The small dragons had returned to campus and were soaring through the airstreams alongside magical birds and other flying beasts. In the lake encircling the base of the mountain, large heads and sinuous bodies occasionally surfaced enough for us to see from our great height.

"It's beautiful," I murmured.

Chapter Twelve

"And far too large for one person to protect." He sounded as weary as he looked.

I rubbed at my chest.

He sighed again. "What do you want?"

Pulling my hand away from my sudden heartburn, I cleared my throat. It seemed a particularly stupid thing to have tracked him down now that I was feeling the weight of what we stood upon—of what was happening in the world at large. "So... I lost something to the Justice System and I need—"

"No."

"I haven't even gotten to the relevant part."

"What did you lose? The paper at the center of that bizarre display on Top Circle?" he asked mildly.

"Maybe," I said shiftily.

He stared at me, unimpressed. "If you are seeking a favor, do have the courtesy of not treating me like an incompetent. I put a trace on all the papers that left the assessor's hands. I saw the one that slipped into Vorlav's glove, then saw it logged in the system an hour ago."

I nodded briskly. "Great. That paper has my magic in it."

He shrugged, looking weary and jaded again as he switched his gaze out over the mountain. "So do a number of things around campus. A severe problem at first, but now irrevocably entwined with the enchantments here. I doubt we could get rid of your magic's lingering presence even if we tried."

"Oh." I gripped the ends of my shirt in my fingers and rolled the fabric over my thumbs. "That's good? What happens to the paper, though? To any of the things in the locker?"

"They are sorted by a student intern and dealt with."

Whoa. *Possibilities.* I leaned forward, straightening my fingers. "How do you get that job?"

He looked vaguely amused for a moment. "You get selected by the provost."

I drummed fingers on my arm. I didn't think my chances were good. However, Olivia's chances...

Absolutely, she answered mentally. *I'm already applying.*

Whoops. I kept forgetting to turn off my communications. I carefully dimmed the armband.

Marsgrove waved a tired hand. "Tell whichever of your friends you are contacting not to bother, I told the magic to put your paper in my locker instead."

I slumped, partially in relief, partially in unease. "Why didn't you just say that?"

"I'm feeling petty."

"Yeah, okay." I stretched out my neck and crossed my arms. "Fair enough. What are you going to do with it?"

"What is it?" he bandied back.

I looked at him suspiciously. "You don't know? You didn't investigate?"

"I know better than to touch something you created."

His bad. Axer was working up quite the immunity.

"Especially," he continued, "when you went to the lengths you did to get it returned. Attacking the assessor?"

And there was the Marsgrove I knew, tight-lipped and terrifying.

"She's not exactly making my Christmas list," I pointed out.

The weight of the world slipped free a measure with Marsgrove's naturally aggravating responses provoking normal, infuriating replies. I readied a defensive shield, though, just in case.

Marsgrove turned abruptly. "After your antics in Medical, you dare to jest? What did you think you were *doing*, Miss Crown?"

I shifted an inch away. "Saving my roommate?"

"You *do* things with no thoughts to the consequences."

"Oh, I was thinking of the consequences," I said grimly.

A rock flew to his hand, and for a moment, I thought he meant to bludgeon me with it. He angrily whipped the stone through the air, like he intended to propel it into the next county. It hit a pond at the edge of the Eighteenth and skipped three times across the water's surface. Two colorful water birds squawked and flapped, moving in case of further unexpected projectiles.

Getting a rock to skip like that when we were a level above its target position was no small feat. I was reluctantly impressed.

"There is more at stake than one person's well-being," he said, far too calmly for a man throwing stones.

"Does that mean I am to do nothing until you move me on the chessboard?"

"Yes," he said, voice unforgiving.

I touched the marble in my pocket that held a far different type of magic than one for throwing stones.

"I can feel the magic you are touching," he said evenly.

Unnerved, I stared at him.

"And I will end you, Miss Crown, if you show yourself as a threat to my home, to my layer." His voice was back to being weary, but it rang with grim truth.

I looked over the valley. "I would expect no less."

It was an oddly relieving thought—the notion that someone would put me in checkmate if the worst happened. If Raphael or Stavros got hold of me, or if I went mad from grief like I had shown myself capable... Someone capable *could* and *would* make the choice that my friends might not.

He wiped a hand across his face. "I'm tired of looking at my students and seeing victims, pawns, and dead bodies, Miss Crown."

"I won't let further harm come to this campus," I promised. Marsgrove and I were tentative allies, but I could give him that.

He laughed without humor. "That's not what I meant," he said. An aching sadness underscored his words.

I looked at him from the side of my eyes, uncertain how to interpret that. "I'll be fine, Dean Marsgrove."

"You are cursed, Miss Crown."

"That seems to be partially true," I acknowledged. "However, I also have *potential.*"

"Magic help us," he said.

I looked over the valley. "You really do have it?" I pressed. "The exact paper?"

He looked to the sky. "Is there anything you want to tell me, Crown?"

Was there?

But this was the same man who had locked me up. Who lumped me together with Raphael. Who didn't trust me—with good reason. Who would, and had already, removed me for the good of the populace.

Having him as a world-ending checkmate on me was to the good of all. Knowing that a smaller admission of power might endanger my roommate status at Excelsine was a different matter entirely.

Marsgrove was a warrior fighting for his world. He had every reason to separate me from his cousin, from his campus, from his *layer*, if he found me to be too much of an active threat.

Admitting that I was imbuing papers with Origin Magic would not help show that I was non-threatening. It wouldn't take much to blow over my increasingly thin card pyramid.

I shook my head in answer to his question. "It's nothing more than anything else I've created—all of which would make you panic. I just didn't want the paper to end up sparking a riot or anything if someone found it in the locker. It will be safe with you."

For if *anything* had been shown to be true, one thing Marsgrove wouldn't do was to fall to the dark side. He'd keep the paper in whatever secure little folder he had placed it in, just like he had done with my Awakening sketch —though he had been unknowing at the time that I had swapped the real sketch for a fake. He'd never tried to *use* the sketch, though, as evidenced by him not knowing it wasn't the true one until far too late.

And with the storage paper, permission had to be given and shared through the paper, as it had been enchanted with upon creation.

"Sparking a riot? You think you haven't already done so?" he murmured.

"No," I said softly. "Not yet."

Hopefully not ever.

"It will be soon," he said, voice distant. "The world is where Stavros wants it."

"We will fight him. I will help you fight him. I will help you save your world."

I would be his ally for Olivia. For Excelsine. For all the people and friends I had met in this world. I would work with Marsgrove. I would aid him. I would trust him with Olivia's freedom. I would trust that he would do the *right* thing for the school and for the Second Layer.

But I couldn't trust him with *me*. The frightened girl, who was terrified of losing everyone she loved.

Because I was a storybook monster. Even now, even with the pity he was feeling for me, I could see the lingering belief in his eyes. The disquiet. That I was cursed and could never overcome such a hurdle.

"I believe you will try," he said quietly. He made a little twist motion with his hand, tapping something out in the air. "Your paper is back in your room. Don't lose your things, Miss Crown." He looked over at me. "Or your way."

Chapter Thirteen

CONVERSATIONS WITH DARTS

MARSGROVE'S WORDS stayed with me. The very thought of how I could lose my way... But he hadn't been joking about the paper's return—it was at the side of the grate when I got back to my room.

As I lifted it, I poked at the magic, grimacing. It had been one of my best storage containers. Now, knots of magic and pinched conduits littered the design. Olivia had changed some of the base magic, I had thrown a whole ton of magic into it without thought, Vorlav had tried to destroy the construct completely, and who knew what had happened when it had been sucked into the justice locker then Marsgrove's magic pockets.

The results were not pretty.

There was a sick feeling to it that I didn't like—an open wound weeping. Gloom descended. That was the problem with putting too much of myself in my creations—when things happened to them, I always got the reflection.

I felt someone carefully pressing at my mind, reacting to the onslaught of emotion.

"Get rid of it," Constantine said in my head, as he quickly rifled through my visuals.

"I can fix it."

"It's toxic and dangerous."

I carefully pushed him out. But he wasn't wrong. The paper was a mess. I narrowed my eyes. I could *fix* it, though.

You can fix anything. It sounded like a reflection of my brother's voice.

I nodded and looked over to see Olivia watching me. "Liv—"

"I want nothing to do with that. Take away my permission."

"But—"

"*No.* Take away my permission from *everything.*"

I sighed, but I could understand her need. When she was free of

Raphael's spell, I might be able to convince her, but we could revisit the matter later.

I changed ownership of the paper completely back to me and tucked it under my bed. I'd fix it later. I'd fix everything.

"I'm not going to the cafeteria."

I looked up to see Olivia gripping the communication spell to Greyskull in her hand. I had obviously missed something.

"One meal, that's all you have to make it through." Greyskull's voice was calming. "And as a bonus, the roommate obligations on Ren will lessen a fraction if you go to the cafeteria together. Spending more time together in the community areas of campus means spending *less* time in *living spaces* to regenerate magic."

"Fine," she said grimly, slamming shut the connection.

"So...cafeteria?" I asked. Like Olivia, I had assumed we'd hole up with Magi Mart burritos.

I could see the problem, though, now that it had been raised. With the assessor's insane stipulation on releasing Olivia into the student population, the administrative requirement to spend a portion of the day in high-trafficked community areas would kick in.

This requirement could easily be met by being in areas like the cafeteria, main library, or Top Circle, where the community spells were the strongest. Or it could be satisfied on a normal day by traversing the regular student paths, going to classes, and being in the thick of student and academic life.

Today, well, Olivia had logged about five minutes outside our room, and that had been on our trip here.

In the best interests of everyone, it was decided that making dinner a later night affair, when most students had gone off to other pursuits, was the way to go.

This bore itself as a good plan when Olivia had six incidents on the way, and my pockets started to overflow with crushed paper. She had tried to throw the rejected papers out immediately, but had been unable to—a side effect of the magic. I was never so glad to have so many empty sketchpads and notebooks stuffed under my bed to use as fodder.

We'd agreed that, for now, I wasn't allowed to carry anything of value that Olivia might conscript, reform, and hand to someone else.

Olivia created twenty misshapen paper monsters in the first two minutes of cafeteria time. She was unable to get food without stopping to tear a piece of paper out of my notebook and create some deformed beast, so I ordered for her and juggled both of our meals with the help of a little magic.

She had initially tried to crumple pieces of paper into balls and hold them out to the recipients, but that didn't seem to satisfy the magic. The magic demanded she *try*.

My notebook was now reduced to only a piece of thin cardboard—she'd even used its cover page.

She was now using paper from one of my sketchpads. I looked longingly at the magic paper that was the equivalent of acid free archival stock and focused on the positives.

"I've been traumatized by my *adventure* in the *Midlands*," she barked out to the twelfth person who asked her what in the world she was doing.

We were wholesale blaming anything weird on Olivia's traumatizing "Midlands' adventure."

"Traumatized," I said, steering her away. The person had "accepted" the paper, so we were free to leave.

No one was at our table, thankfully, and we both took quick seats.

I inhaled half of my food—some sort of magical pasta and sauce— luckily, or purposefully, made by the Decaclops people so that it never slipped from the fork once lifted from the bowl. It was the perfect food to be eaten with one hand with no mess so that I could aid Olivia with the other. The Decaclops people always figured out what each person needed, even when the person didn't know it herself.

They had given Olivia some sort of magical smoothie with a straw. She was angrily drinking it, head half-bent, while folding sloppy paper planes on the table space where her drink would normally be. Once completed, she sent each plane flying through the air to its recipient with the aid of magic.

This actually settled the need for me to keep stuffing paper in my bag.

But within minutes, the middle of the table was piled high again with paper planes that had bounced off of shields and "returned to sender."

Far better than the few who plucked and pocketed their paper plane, an action that made me increasingly nervous.

I eyed the stack in the middle of the table and felt the papers bulging my pockets. Each sheet had a slight memory of its intent. It was time to change the game a little, just in case the few that had been pocketed were done so for nefarious purposes.

First things first though. I took the thinnest pad I had and pressed a finger against it. "Mine," I said aloud, making the pad usable only by me. I gave Olivia an apologetic glance, but she looked relieved.

Making another storage paper was off the table, but I had plenty of experience with recording enchantments now, due to Bellacia's influence. I sketched a field on the page, then activated it.

Alternating with every other bite of food, I passed each paper plane over the field and linked the magic in the fibers of each, transcribing everything that might be useful. Knowing one's opponents was always a good idea. And we might be able to discover something from the traces—

how much and what type of attachment each person had to the Department.

For every one I recorded, Olivia added another to the pile.

I could feel and mentally "hear" our usual four cafeteria companions drawing closer to our table with their own food trays.

Our eight person round table could fit ten, if we squeezed, but I wasn't expecting that tonight. In the cafeteria, the Bandits often ate separately, then met later in more private spaces.

Mike, Delia, and Will sat down in their usual spots.

But before Neph could pull out the chair to her preferred seat, someone else slid into the spot.

The plane I was holding skittered past the page field as I stared at Constantine in shock. His narrowed gaze traveled over me for a split second, before his usual casual air replaced it. He leaned back and placed his right hand on the back of my chair then began eating with his left.

Neph gave him a look of forced patience, took a seat on the other side of Olivia, and expelled the remaining chair into the floor, making us a firm table of seven for the moment.

For all of the weirdness in having Constantine sitting with us, it was a relief to be surrounded by friendly magic on all sides. I sent him a little mental squeeze along with the others and began working and eating again.

"Why are you here?" Olivia asked Constantine bluntly, her fingers quickly folding a new paper.

"Even monsters have to eat. Especially so, really."

"Why are you *here*?"

"Eating. Whatever are you doing, Price? Do you require glue and craft sticks as well?" he asked. He knew exactly what was occurring, so his statement was deliberately meant to rile.

I stabbed him in the side of the thigh with my fork. All I could feel from him was amusement, though, no pain.

"Why are you here?" Olivia repeated, thrusting the weird triangle thing she had made into the pile that was starting to reach alarming heights. There was some sort of proximity variable to the enchantment, so if someone entered the cafeteria, then turned or immediately went to the far side, the enchantment loosened enough to where Olivia could dump the half-formed paper wherever. The spell also seemed to be withering the longer it stayed flipped.

Raphael had likely expected that Olivia would be in Helen's presence quickly and without interference. I couldn't imagine if Olivia had to hunt down each person she registered as being laced with Department magic on campus.

I shuddered and jabbed my fork into my noodles, giving up on scanning planes for the moment.

Olivia grabbed another piece of paper, her eyes focusing blackly on a student who had entered the cafeteria, before she started viciously folding.

"Dear Ren and I are dating, didn't you know?" Constantine answered, tone easy, but there was an anticipatory light in his gaze. "And so are Ren and Alexander. Depends on who you ask, really. Such a juicy topic currently, and gossip in such abundance is never wrong."

I could feel Olivia's gaze swing to him, then toward me. "*Ren?*"

I let my fork drop into its cushion of noodles and gave her my best, "No clue, innocent!" jazz hand styled wave.

"It's all over the feeds. Really, Price," Constantine said casually. "I expected you to be more on top of things."

Jazz hands still in the air, I instinctively snatched the paper dart passing in front of my eyes before it could reach its non-Department target square in the face. I tapped the sharp nose of the dart with my fingertip. Olivia was getting better creasing the edges, and the dart had been thrown with enough force to do some serious damage.

"Ever my hero," Constantine drawled.

I shot him a look of disapproval and tossed the dart to the middle of the table.

Will leaned forward. "The rumors were supposed to deflect attention when we were trying to rescue you—and give Ren a reason for being around Leandred so often," Will said, in explanation, bless him. "But it didn't really do much other than kick start the gossip machine."

He really could have left that latter part out.

"It's the long game, Tasky," Constantine said.

Will nodded in acceptance, shrugged, then went back to eating. Neph, however, raised her brows at Constantine.

"What long game?" Olivia also wasn't so easily deterred.

Constantine smiled and ate a chip, saying nothing.

Well, then. I hooked a thumb at him. "It was his idea," I said, throwing him under the bus.

"I'm wounded, darling." His fingers crept from the back of my chair into my hair, and a tingle of magic wormed its way downward from his fingertips, tangling with the magic in the ribbon. I could feel a dopey smile grow.

"No. Absolutely not," Olivia said emphatically.

"Too late, Price." He let his hand drop back to the chair and the happy euphoria slowly dispersed. "Ren was having a bit of trouble with certain folks. It took a little bit to work the rounds fully, but progress has been satisfactory," he said, smile just this side of smug.

"It was pretty bad while you were gone," Will contributed, still addressing Olivia.

"I was fine," I protested. I touched the scarf at my neck, under which the ribbon was still attached.

Olivia narrowed her eyes on me.

"I had Justice Toad with me for rounds pretty much the whole time," I said reassuringly. "Speaking of which, what did you do?" I asked Constantine suspiciously. "And where were you this afternoon?"

He had only *conveniently* made contact when he wanted to give his opinion. He had been suspiciously unavailable otherwise.

He smiled. "I had a chat with a number of people. Not hard to track them down." He waved a hand. "They won't bother you anymore."

"Like a dead horse head on your pillow kind of chat?"

He tilted his head for a moment, no doubt mentally scanning something to reconcile the First Layer reference.

"Nothing quite so uncivilized," he said with a tilt to one edge of his mouth. "I just made it known that I would be displeased to hear anything untoward about my intended—"

"Constantine—"

"No," Olivia stated bluntly at the same time.

"Friend," he finished innocently.

Delia's eyes were darkly amused as she sipped her soup and switched her gaze between the three of us. She obviously found the whole thing incredibly entertaining. Mike was shaking his head resignedly while eating an enormous sandwich.

"So, will it be one bed or three this evening?" Delia asked.

"D," Mike choked, quickly swallowing the remaining food in his mouth and casting a look at Olivia's stormy face. "I don't want to end up in Medical tonight."

Delia broke her bread into chunks, a virtuous smile on her face. "Right, of course. It will be *four* when our champion gets back."

I kicked at her under the table, but Mike winced instead. Chagrined, I mouthed "Sorry!" at him.

"I've proposed to the board that Alexander might like to switch over to Bailey's room," Constantine mused.

It was my turn to choke.

Constantine patted me on the back. "He'll love it. It'll be like battling a monstrous beast every moment of the day."

Trying not to laugh, Delia pulled her lips between her teeth and kept her gaze fixed on her soup. Traitor.

Olivia looked like she wished she wasn't so busy crafting, so she could be doing a lot more stabbing.

"They told me they'd let me know by Thursday," Constantine said.

Chapter Thirteen

"You *didn't*."

He raised a brow at me. "As you say."

Delia cackled and dunked a piece of bread.

"He's going to kill you," I said.

"Perhaps. But it won't be for that particular piece of treachery," he said, swirling magic around his bowl. I automatically touched my scarf, and it was one too many times for Olivia.

"Why do you keep doing that, Ren?" She reached over and pulled the fabric away from my skin, exposing the ribbon.

She went white. "Leandred," she said, voice entirely too low. *"Explain."*

"Ren is my intended. I told you," he said, voice as irritatingly condescending as only he could manage.

I stared at him awkwardly over my shoulder, since Olivia still held the collar of my shirt. "Is that seriously what this means?"

"No," he said, with zero tells, magically or visually, as to if that statement was true.

I looked to Neph, but she shook her head. "You got yourself into this," she said.

Her faint amusement relieved me, though, as it had earlier. Neph wouldn't be relaxed about whatever Constantine had done, if it was something truly horrible.

Olivia's reactions weren't a good indicator—she'd be angry no matter what.

Mike pointed his spoon at me. "It is completely saturated in his magic and intentions. It's like carrying a giant billboard around that says, '*Approach at Your Own Risk*'."

"And '*I Am Watching You*'," Will added cheerfully and super unhelpfully. He squinted at my neck and nodded. "There's a reflection spell on top. It reflects the intentions of the viewers if they have ill designs on the person wearing the item. That makes sense, with the conflicting stories on GossipFeed earlier."

"GossipFeed?" Delia said, peering around Mike to see Will.

Will blinked, cheeks starting to go pink. "Did I say that part out loud?"

"Yes, you just admitted to listening to GossipFeed, Tasky," Delia said, amused as hell. "Might as well admit to following 'Students of Dorm Six' too."

His cheeks completed the transition to red.

"Oh, Magic, you *do*," she said, cackling.

"No, no, *no*," Olivia said, attention, fortunately, again split between folding a new piece of paper and figuring out how to kill one of us— intentionally—with the next one. One-handed folding was past her skillset, so she had to let go of my shirt. "Take it off, Leandred."

128

"No," Constantine said casually.

"Con—" I started.

"Think selfishly. It will make the wards stronger for you, as you are the roommate of my int—"

"*No*," Olivia hissed.

"Wait." Mike frowned. "Hilarity aside, isn't everyone going back to their regular rooms now? Norrissing is back with Bailey, right?"

"The wards have gotten..." I twisted my fingers in the air, then shoved them together. "All soldered and interconnected."

"Ren needs me. Price too," Constantine said, looking to *die*.

"*Never.*"

"We asked," I said quickly to Mike, trying to stave off the murder scene I was going to be in the middle of. "We sent a note to the Dean of Student Life as well as to the dorm guardians. They said everything stays in place until Axer gets back, then they'll figure it out."

"Can't damage their champion on his victory tour," Constantine said.

I looked up at the main combat table on the First Tier of the cafeteria automatically. The combat mages had a tendency to eat late, and other than Axer, Nicholas, and Ramirez, they were all back on campus, and a full shift of them were filling out the seats. More than one of their gazes flitted toward our table; no doubt talking about us.

"What *are* you going to do about him?" Delia inquired, curious gaze sharp on Constantine.

"I told you, I've requested that he be put with Bai—" Constantine started to say.

"Not about that," Delia said. "Though, if you are serious about that and it goes through, can I be there when you tell them?"

Constantine smiled. "I might consider it, depending on the compensation involved."

"Delia, don't make it worse," I said, sighing. Will and Neph had helpfully started to pass Olivia's planes over my scanning paper to record the magic, so I searched for a charcoal stick in my bag, determined to do something productive.

Delia, of course, didn't listen, and continued inciting the discussion with Constantine about Bellacia, Axer, and different scenarios of "who would win." And as if Olivia's ire was fueling a mad creative spree, paper started spewing *everywhere*. I couldn't make a storage box, but I could maybe sketch out a paper shredder.

Something with teeth. Maybe that I could set upon a few of my friends.

The edge of Constantine's mouth lifted, as if he heard my thought.

I shook my head and contemplated a design. The ideas started to flow. A folded paper with teeth that would shred anything inserted into it and scan the magic at the same time—catalog the person it had been designed for as well as their levels of attachment. And maybe attach a calming enchantment for Olivia, and a suppression field to dull the areas around us, and *where was my charcoal?*

Constantine pulled a charcoal pencil from thin air and handed it to me without looking or breaking stride in the catty discourse he and Delia seemed determined to inflict on the rest of us.

I narrowed my eyes at the implement, but reached for it.

"It's easy enough to do when you have eyes on the target," he was saying.

Something nudged at my memory. "Wait, did you hunt down *everyone* I talked to today?" I asked, frowning.

"Only the ones who needed it," he said, voice casual.

"How did..." I groaned. No wonder Bolton Haynes had looked like he might soil himself and had half-talked to the ribbon the whole time instead of me. "The reflection spell."

"It takes intentions into account. Quite a sophisticated piece of magic," he said, not at all humbly. "Worry not."

"Yeah, that's never a phrase that turns out well."

"I'm wounded, darling."

"You are not."

He smiled. "No. I must go, though. I'll see you tonight." His hand moved along the neck of my scarf and I could feel a breeze following its wake.

Mike snorted.

"There it is!" someone yelled at a table near us, and my charcoal tore a jagged black stripe down my page. My head jerked up and free fingers grabbed for my throat. The scarf had dissolved completely with whatever had laced his fingers, leaving the ribbon in unobstructed view.

Constantine was already walking away, but I could *feel* his smirk as the audible level of the cafeteria rose.

"That man is a menace," Delia said, darkly amused. But she pushed her empty bowl forward and reached into her pocket. She withdrew a scarf, throwing it toward me. It zipped through the air and wrapped around my neck.

I nodded in both agreement and thanks and reached for a new piece of paper, then realized there were only about ten pieces left in my bag. Total.

I put the kibosh on the birth of the paper monster as I realized just how much paper had accumulated and how we couldn't just start stuffing them inside a paper monster in the middle of the cafeteria. Constantine's warning about not letting others see my storage papers was more important now than ever.

"Um—" I cast another look at the pile in the middle of the table. Maybe I could design a small paper toilet instead? Normal items could be exchanged normally, like books or clothing, through temporary space, but the spell on Olivia was resisting that—we had already tried. Awakening paint might be a little *too* much, though. "We might eat in our room for the next few days, even with the community magic hit."

Olivia looked simultaneously relieved and aggravated. The lack of control was driving her mad.

"Everyone is welcome to join us."

"We'd be happy to have people over to our place too," Will said, loyally.

Mike nodded. "With enough of us, we might be able to get Greyskull or Marsgrove to hook us into the community magic system for those times. We'd do it."

"Thanks, guys," I said softly. It meant a lot, especially coming from Mike who was always measuring how much calming magic they were dosing us with.

Will waved my gratitude away, though his cheeks pinked. "I'm going to be doing a lot of work on my Shift Festival project now that we are cleared again," Will said. "Lots of pizza and pie nights. It will help all of us, the more the merrier."

I looked at Mike, who nodded once more. Mike had locked up a number of Will's projects when we were under the Department's watchful eye. How quickly times changed.

"That sounds great, Will." I carefully touched the marble that was still in my pocket. "I have a few new ideas, too."

"Fantastic. And we can get back to the lab," he said, referencing the Midlands and Okai without saying it aloud. "I'm really looking forward to getting back to normal."

I looked around at the calming spells and the remaining students—many of whom were staring back at me. Their faces looked worn and weary, but also determined. "I am too."

Normal sounded almost too good to be true. But we would *make it* so.

Chapter Fourteen

INCONGRUOUS INTENTIONS

I'd get on that normal path tomorrow, but tonight, shenanigans were still on the docket. I had a third roommate to visit. One armed with extra teeth.

Key in hand, I stared at Bellacia's door.

Olivia's return had halved again the hours that I had to spend with each person. But that still meant two hours in Bellacia's suite every day until Axer returned.

I opened the door, and sure enough, Bellacia Bailey was standing just inside, waiting. With her dark hair alternately braided and loose in sections, piercing green eyes, and carefully chosen clothing, she was a jaguar stalking her prey.

I nodded at her and closed the door. "Bellacia."

"Ren."

I subtly tried to read the newscasts and updates that were perennially circling the space.

    ♕ *Competition closes! An interview with the winners!*
    ♕ *Girl found wandering dangerous section of elite university.*
    ♕ *The Department on notice.*
    ♕ *The Bailey's Daily up 40% in views.*
    ♕ *How the events have shaken out between the layers: A Perspective*

"Looks like you've been busy," I said.

"It looks like we both have," she returned, circling a chair and coming closer.

"Olivia is back, and Axer will be back soon, so just a few more nights, then I'll be out of your hair."

"Hmmm... There's no need to rush. We're just getting started." There was something about the smirk on her face that boded ill.

"Right," I said warily. "I'm sure your roommate is looking forward to a return to normal."

"Things have become so *complicated* with the magic between our rooms. And Daddy concurs that perhaps we should leave things as they are for a *little* longer. Inessa agreed, even though her family is quite put out with mine at the moment."

I'd *bet*. General Norrissing, Inessa's uncle, was high up in the Legion. And the Legion was suffering with the Department in general for the events of the past few days.

Besides that, there was no way Inessa Norrissing wanted to be saddled with a magic share to me or to Olivia. "Your roommate doesn't want this."

"Inessa understands."

The girl in question, who was peering around the door to the bedroom, didn't seem to look like she understood at all. Lackluster hair, wan skin, and pinched expression, she had always been in Bellacia's shadow as far as looks went, and her personality was perfectly reflected by that shade—pinched and unpleasant.

If there was a prize for negative charisma, Inessa could win it.

And I had tried to turn her into a toad first term when she'd verbally assaulted Olivia, then later given her a toilet cleaning punishment when the two had fought.

To say that she didn't "like" me was probably an understatement.

Perfect.

"So, get settled and let's *talk*," Bellacia said.

"Or maybe a game of cards?" I threw out without much hope. "Studying? I have an assignment due tomorrow."

"I have it on good authority that your assignment for Professor Mbozi will be waved due to the field work you did on your little jaunt." She patted the seat next to her. "I think you have time."

Lovely. There were so many barbs in those statements that I couldn't even begin to parse which one to be most concerned about.

That I had taken Mbozi's developmental schematics for a portable chaos field could have been discovered by a number of upper level students who had been in and out of the engineering wing where Mbozi's office was located. That I had *used* those schematics to create a containment field that worked in the Third Layer during a layer shift, was something only Constantine and I should know. Unless Bellacia's recorder had been on the whole time I had possessed it, which was an entirely more frightening option.

I could never underestimate her.

Bellacia's gaze narrowed in on my throat. *Thank you, Delia, for giving me that second scarf.* Not that it would fool Bellacia. I hadn't been able to remove the whisper of the ribbon's presence underneath, and it seemed like the people who I'd rather not sense it, still could.

Her gaze met mine and she smiled, but it didn't reach her eyes. "I'd warn you, but you seem content to make the same sort of mistakes that the rest of us have."

"It's not like that." I felt like a broken record when it came to Constantine, with no one interested in listening to my scratches.

"Mmmhmm."

I shook my head. "Whatever. It doesn't matter."

"Oh, but it *does*. With how Axer...oh, but you bring me such joy, Ren."

"You and Constantine hate each other. And that's fine. But I want no part in it." I backed up the assertion with magic, pushing the intent at her.

"You don't have to *convince* me, dear. I know you don't." She smiled. "But as the pivotal piece we all play around, you don't have to be interested."

"Great. Listen, can I recommend someone else for you to play with? Bolton Haynes is in serious need of someone."

She lifted an eyebrow. "Bolton Haynes would be so privileged."

"Yeah." I sighed. "That would be too easy."

I could see Inessa, still lurking in the shadows. She looked even more sour. Maybe she liked Haynes. I wondered if I could hook her up with him. People were supposed to be happier when they were in love.

I looked back at Bellacia and frowned. "Why do you even care about playing a game with the boys? I thought you were interested in Lox now? He's a marvelous arm candy alternative."

Marvelous, if one liked the fairytale Prince who had hair that waved in the wind, and a cocky expression on his face. Wait, maybe that was the fairytale narcissist villain... Eh, still fit. He was sort of a combination of Axer and Con, without the underlying intensity they both had, but with a +3 stat increase in posturing.

I tried to stay away from him, usually, and without Axer, our paths didn't cross.

"He's back and could be a great distraction," I added. Great for *everyone.*

Bellacia's eyes narrowed and she shifted her position. "Who told you I was interested?"

Whoops. I had overheard that in a battle room, in a conversation between Camille Straught and Bellacia, when Camille had adamantly told Bellacia to drop arm candy interest in Axer.

"The room," I said. Technically, it was not a lie—it had been a *battle* room—but Bellacia's eyes subtly looked around the space of the suite, as I'd hoped they would.

"And what else did the room tell you, Ren?"

"I don't know, what did it tell you, Bella?"

Her laughter was a controlled and lovely sound. "Such fun. Come, sit." She motioned toward the chairs. "Inessa, go be somewhere else."

Inessa grit her teeth, but grabbed her bag and started for the door.

"Um, she lives here," I said awkwardly.

"And so do you, for the interim," Bellacia said, unconcerned with the other girl's ire.

The door slammed behind her.

Great. I sighed and started unloading my bag. But with Inessa gone, it *did* make things slightly easier. There were far less secrets to juggle.

I flopped into a chair. "Aren't you going to ask me what happened in Politics today?"

"Oh, I know what happened. Easy enough to piece together," she said, like a cat with a full bowl of cream in front of her. "What you must think of my investigative skills, to ask me such a thing."

"No, I'm properly appreciative, I assure you. So what happened to Keiren Oakley?" I asked. I pulled out the device Bellacia had given me after she'd hogtied the boy and handed it to her. I'd had Dagfinn look the recorder over and he had made sure that it was wiped.

She took it in one perfectly manicured hand. An expression which might have been amusement tugged at her lips as she examined it, then tucked it away. "You haven't been keeping up with the feeds, kitten."

I sighed. The constant stream of news encircling Bellacia's room had not been missed. I cast a glance up trying only to think about Keiren. Immediate search results showed everywhere I looked.

⅄ *Magicist Keiren Oakley found guilty of...*

⅄ *Oakley scion in trouble with law...*

⅄ *Broken engagement in magicist circle.*

"Psychotic episode. Not good for the bloodlines," she said in her lilting voice. "Caught with all sorts of illegal devices."

I'd seen her plant one on him, so I wasn't surprised. She was thorough enough that the devices were probably loaded with his fingerprints and magic.

It was one of the things that living with her had likely doomed me to as well—giving her a hold over me at some unspecified point in the future. My magic and essence were all over some of the things in the suite, and as a new magic user, I didn't know half of the things I should be protecting myself against. She likely had a buffet of possibilities from which to choose.

Thinking about it would just make me crazy, though, so I wasn't going to.

"Why did you do it? What did Oakley do?" I asked instead.

"Keiren was becoming attached to...an unfortunate element developing in the government."

"What unfortunate element?" It was concerning to ponder what Bellacia might consider an "unfortunate element."

"Now, Ren. That is for you to discover *for* me."

Headlines bloomed around the room.

- ⋏ *The Department in media crisis mode.*
- ⋏ *Circus of Performers: The Department puts everything into Shift Festival preparations.*
- ⋏ *Leashing Rares: A Perspective on Usage.*
- ⋏ *Who can we trust?*

I tapped my fingers on the chair. "So, how do you want to play this?"

"So blunt. That roommate of yours is hardly a good influence."

The look I gave her seemed to be enough, as she held her hands out in temporary surrender, expression faintly amused. "Fine. Off limits for now, is she? But there is so much to mine in the Prices."

"I find I don't understand magicists at all." But if Helen Price was on Bellacia's burn list, so much the better.

"That's because you are trying to fit us into one box, kitten, instead of separating the true believers from the usurpers."

"Two boxes. Got it."

She drew a finger along the arm of her chair, magically painted fingernail dragging across the fabric. I stared and four of the headlines in the room changed to magical properties of fingernail polish at my thought stream.

I determinedly changed my thoughts until only one of those headlines remained, mixed in with the other thoughts that were crowding my mind—the Third Layer, Corpus Sun, the Department, Helen Price...

Bella was watching all of it, pleased. "You need to rid your mind of some of those things. Let me take care of that for you." I could hear her voice gain a more lyrical quality, trying to manipulate me.

I tapped my scarab pointedly without looking at her.

She smiled. "Yes, let's talk about your muse."

I closed my eyes and leaned back in the chair. If nothing else, I could take mandatory naps here. Everyone would be relieved by me getting more sleep.

"What an *interesting* family of muses you hooked yourself into," she continued.

"Eh, let's talk about Lox and hooking you two up, instead." I waved a hand, eyes still closed. "I have absolutely no notion of how to do that, but I make a great sounding board."

She laughed. "Arm candy, Ren, is easy to obtain. I neither need nor desire a more serious relationship. It gets in the way of business."

I cracked an eye open and caught her smile, but her expression was brittle.

Impulsively, I whisked a rose nestled in the bottom of my bag to her lap, sending a little bit of concentrated magic with it. Marsgrove was right, my magic was everywhere on campus already.

"What is this?" she asked, the brittleness disappearing beneath amusement as she lifted the flower. A stem descended as she twirled it. "You think me one of your lambs? That I require care and healing?"

It was not, having gotten to know both of them that I thought either she or Constantine blameless in their ongoing war, but the impact to her always seemed greater. Bellacia didn't handle rejection well, at least not personal rejection. And with her spot at the top of the food chain in both birth and looks, she had perhaps never experienced it before Constantine.

She had been one more used and discarded piece to him.

Constantine was the opposite of a saint. He was exactly the type of guy girls should stay far away from. Oh, he never did anything without full, enthusiastic consent—I had been present, on the other side of his workroom door, on more than one occasion wishing I had ear bleach, and consent was *always* enthusiastic. But he was the opposite of a "call you in the morning" type of guy. Or even an "acknowledge you in the morning" type. Really, he was more an "I will never acknowledge your existence again" type.

Not exactly the thing to make a girl feel warm and fuzzy in the harshness of daylight.

His first mistake was that he had dropped Bellacia like all the rest of his girls and expected the same status quo to result.

Which *must* have motivated her vindictiveness on some level. Bellacia was no one's status quo. She had ensured his attention. She hadn't *let* him forget her.

In an ideal world, she would have chalked it up to a learning experience, dismissed him as unworthy of further attention, and moved on to someone healthier.

Yeah...

I watched her twirl the stem, examining the petals as the magic worked to connect to hers.

Bellacia relished in anything that impassioned her, and vengeance was an impassioned topic.

"It's just...for you," I said, lamely. I didn't have much experience with this sort of thing.

Christian, for all his charm, had always been a very stand-up guy. There hadn't been any need to "pick up after him." Sadie Martin, who *did* end up as Homecoming Queen according to a journal entry from my parents, would *still* be writing social media fairytale posts about their dates, should things have gone differently.

My hand tightened in reflex against my chest for a thread that wasn't there, that would never again be there.

I'd always wondered how long it had taken Sadie or her father, Christian's beloved football coach, to uninstall the invitation to Homecoming that Christian had placed in her car the night he died.

"You look like *you* might need this more at the moment, Ren," Bellacia said, catlike eyes searching for the right way to trap the mouse in me, as she twirled the stem. But she made no move to give the rose back.

I cleared my tightened throat with a swallow. "It's been a long couple weeks." I leaned forward to dig through my bag. "I have this for you, too."

I handed Bellacia a small art card that I had enchanted with three different scenarios, depending on what emotion she wished to channel. "I know you can handle yourself." Boy did I. "But I don't want you to be in any trouble on my account. If someone comes after you...play the one you want. Each has a little animated comic strip for association."

"Like *Bellacia on Report*?" she said idly, referencing the comic I had made about her to deal with my frustrations from being watched by all of her minions around campus, and to entertain Delia.

"Er..."

"I have collected all of them. You draw my nose so perfectly straight," she said, examining the card. "I love it."

"Right. Um, the card." I'd think about the weirdness that was my life later. "One animation will throw out a blast, long enough for you to slip by. Another will confuse anyone within a five foot radius for five seconds. The third will, I don't know, kind of stop time for everyone else. Make them freeze. It doesn't really stop time, just gives you a five second head start. Oh, and I put a contract enchantment on the card—as soon as you accepted it, you agreed never to discuss it or who spelled it."

I might be behind, but I was learning.

She looked at me over the edge of the card. "You made this. For me?"

"Yes. I thought you might like it? I tried to think of a journalistic thing I could make for you, but I'm sure my First Layer mind is way behind tech in that area. Maybe in a few weeks? You could tell me what you've been wanting."

Headlines spiked around the room in a rare loss of Bellacia's control, then smoothed back; Bellacia firmly back in control of the content she wanted displayed.

"Ah, Ren, you just have no idea." She pulled a finger covetously down the edge of the card. "I can't wait to see you rip out his shriveled heart."

I rolled my eyes, conversation and emotions resetting to those I could work with. "No one's ripping out any hearts. I told you, it's not like that."

She threw back her head and laughed.

~*~

Most of my toiletries and several changes of clothing were already in the boys' room, which meant that I didn't have to return to Dorm Twenty-five to collect them. And Delia had volunteered for Olivia duty—the two of them were still softly stepping around each other.

I let myself into the boys' suite—I was really racking up keys around Excelsine.

"Back from the harpy's den?"

I rolled my eyes and dropped my bag on the floor. "Seriously. You two are the worst. I don't know why you *didn't* work out."

"Boring," he said without empathy.

"I think she liked you."

True humor flit across his face. "You are adorable."

I cocked my head, thinking about her expression. "She really might have."

Something flashed through his gaze. "Do not let snakes lead you astray when you try to feed them under the boughs of forbidden fruit. They will trick and consume you."

I sighed and threw myself into the chair I always occupied. It formed into a chaise lounge the second my butt landed on the seat. I whirled my arms for a moment before regaining my balance.

"Really? You are going with this?" I asked.

"You looked like you needed one of those recliners you always picture in your mind when you think we are going to have a deep, psychological discussion."

I let my head drop back onto the cushioned back. "Fine. I'll tell you about my mother."

"Excellent. Let's start with the worst punishment you ever received." Wire-rimmed glasses appeared on the bridge of his nose and a notepad on his lap, as if he had researched exactly what the doctor/patient scenario would require.

I put on my most mournful expression. "It was soul crushing. I went without art supplies for *days*."

He hmmmed. "You murdered someone?"

"Worse. She's a chemist. I sabotaged her experiment."

Chapter Fourteen

He looked over the wire rims with extreme judgment. "What would make you do such a thing?"

I laughed, settling into the banter. "I was trying to get my brother out of trouble by shifting the source of blame. It worked. But in hindsight I think she was more scared that I nearly blew myself up." With older eyes to look back, my perspective had shifted a bit.

"Is she like you?"

"No way. She's super practical. She wants to murder me half the time—just like she did after that event. Though, the other half..." I thought about it. Thought about the ways we were alike and different. "Yeah," I said, more softly. "I guess she's like me."

Complicated feelings worked their way along the connection that had formed to Constantine, and I looked over at him.

"I'll have to meet her," he said. The complication of his emotions didn't show on his face.

I looked up at the ceiling and absently examined the wards coiled and crisscrossed in the plaster and through the air. "Someday, maybe. I can't see her now. Or my dad." Who always had my back even when he didn't understand how my brain worked. "Maybe not for a long time," I said, voice straining. "I'd lead people right to them."

"Mmmm." He tapped his fingers on his chair, and when I looked at him he had the look on his face that said his brain was actively occupied with a thought.

"What are you plotting?"

"Simple thoughts."

I closed my eyes, letting the wards extend and soak into me. The wards were always soothing here. "Your thoughts are never simple."

"Thank you."

"You would take that as a compliment."

"You are my intended," he said casually. "That makes their safety my issue as well."

I opened one eye to give him a look. "Yeah, let's talk about that first part. I know that intended has a few different meanings here, but just to be clear, we are not getting married," I said.

"Darling, I'm hurt."

"You are not." I could feel nothing but amusement from him. I pulled up my knees and crossed my arms, still leaning back. "Furthermore, what were you thinking? Neph explained to me on the way back from the cafeteria—in a very traumatizing way, thank you very much—that this is more than just a prank. That there are avowals on your part. Family ties."

"There are. It's sort of like swearing fealty."

I stared at him. With everything else going on today, I hadn't had time to research what that meant—I'd only been given the biased bits and pieces from others based on what they were most incensed by. But they'd all agreed on the fact that there was a commitment of cause that he'd made today. One that went beyond normal friendship. Like my relationship with Neph, and what her being my muse meant—a commitment that couldn't be retracted without consequence.

Helen Price's face and promise scrolled through my brain, and I could see the flicker in Constantine's expression, like he had seen her face in my mind's eye, but he looked entirely too *unconcerned*.

I pulled off Delia's scarf. "Remove it."

He waved his hand and the ribbon fell into my hand.

I squinted at it, then at him, shock turning to suspicion. "Nothing is ever that easy with you."

He smiled. "That's because I'm a lovely combination of spite and genius."

I gripped the ribbon and smoothed it out on my leg, before laying it on his knee. "You can't attach yourself to me like that," I said quietly. "Normal friendship, yes. Everyone expects you to betray me, so no one takes it seriously, and that keeps you safe. But I make too dangerous a true attachment."

"You steal the very breath from my body. I suffocate with the feelings, it's true."

"*Constantine*. This is serious."

"Of course it's serious," he said, dropping the act for a moment and leaning forward so that our faces were only inches apart. "I know what the avowals *are*, Ren. I *made* them."

"Your father—"

"Matters not," he said crisply.

"—won't approve. You publicly attached your name to mine. He's going to care. Especially when the Department succeeds in outing me, and they *will*."

"He *owes* me," he said, as darkly as he ever did.

"No. This is still salvageable." Feeling the shift in him, I grabbed his hand before he could jerk away. "Not like that, moron. I don't *need* a public declaration to call you family. And I appreciate the respite from the idiots today. But I will keep you, and the others, safe from my troubles. This avowal thing will blow over by next week, when everyone finds the next big thing to talk about. People will just say, in retrospect, that you were going after the Origin Mage for her power. And Helen will move on to the appropriate target—me. Don't put yourself *in* the crossfire."

He stared at me, unreadable for a moment. "I've had women try to save me before," he said idly.

Chapter Fourteen

"Then that means I'll be yesterday's trash soon on that part of the equation, but *we* will still be friends."

He smiled with a far truer lift of his cheeks. "Don't be foolish. I told you before, I'd never let you go." He touched my chin, tilting it up toward him. "I could remove the danger, you know. Lock you in a room—a tower—"

"My hair isn't long enough," I said automatically.

"But you *would* spin me gold. So many things better than gold. Truer." His gaze dropped to my lips. "I would keep you in the finest of materials, handcrafted with only you in mind. The finest paints, in a tower so high that you would have no cares."

"A gilded cage?"

"Yes." He whispered, and an ache grew as he smiled crookedly, all wrong. "A gilded bird in a gilded cage. Bright and charming and beautiful. Always admired."

His voice, full of memories, made me ache. I touched his skin.

He shuddered and laughed roughly, withdrawing his hand. "They say you turn into your parents—that everyone does eventually."

"I think you can turn into anything, should you want it enough," I said softly.

"Do you?" He looked at the ribbon, gave it a flick, lengthening it into a six foot lash. He had used it against Raphael and against Kaine. "I thought to become a murderer."

"I know."

"So what shall be the goal of a man who no longer sees the path beneath his feet?"

"Choosing bricks or pavers to make a new one?"

"Better than a shovel, at any rate," he said easily, though the complicated feelings coursing through him were anything but casual. "I'd rather twist the road to my purposes, rather than start anew."

"Then do that. I will help."

He smiled. "I know. If only I could keep you. That you need to be free is the cruelest beauty."

"So do you," I pointed out.

His eyelids slid halfway closed. "I would give up my freedom for the right cage."

"Well, you did, like, temporarily adopt me today. We could make the world our cage."

"I've never had a sibling." He tilted his face to the ceiling. "I think I would spoil one rotten. Do beware."

I did exactly what I would do to Christian. I batted him with magic. After a very brief moment of shock, he batted me back, and we traded magically barbed spells for half a minute.

"Not that I don't enjoy all this foreplay, but I was—"

"ARGH!"

"—trying to tell you how much I plan to spoil you with all sorts of courting gifts."

"No. No you were not." I pointed at him. "You said *siblings*."

He started laughing. Actual laughs, not one of his affectations. "Well, the aristocracy is always a little unstable."

"Argh. Forget it!" I threw up my hands.

"You did say you wanted to give them something else to talk about." All of his darkness had vanished, like it never existed.

"No, no, I said I didn't want you to burn for me."

"I always bur—" He fended off two more attacks, laughing again. "Think this whole thing through, darling. What are people talking about?"

"Your insanity?"

"And Alexander's. Instead of yours."

I sighed and dragged a hand through my hair. "Helen Price—the *Department*—is going to *use* you. When they out me as the anti-Christ you can bet they will drag you down with me." I rubbed my hand over my face. "They will drag everyone down with me."

"Now you are just being a braggart."

"Constantine—"

"The problem is you can't *control* what happens to any of us. So, unless you want to turn dictator and suppress the masses—which I fully support, by the way—then you have to let people make their own choices." He tapped the ribbon draped across his leg.

I stared at him. "Who are you?"

"I'm your inten—"

"For the love of all—"

An aggressive knock on the door interrupted the circling argument.

Constantine waved his hand and the door opened.

Olivia and Delia were standing in the hall. Delia gave a jaunty wave and disappeared, leaving Olivia alone with a satchel of her personal items and a mulish look on her face. She stomped inside. "I can't believe there are more sleeping wards *here*. Better to get this over with."

"You are welcome, step right in," came Constantine's falsely polite response. A snap of his wrist and the door shut behind her.

She gave Constantine a dark look. "I don't want to *be* here, Leandred."

"Should we be readmitted to Medical?" I asked, looking between them.

"No," came the response from both of them.

"Right." I looked between them again, then shrugged. "Homework?"

A large table immediately appeared in the middle of the living space where a coffee table sometimes sat. It looked exactly like what I had pictured in my mind. I blinked at the table, then looked down at my cuff.

Olivia narrowed her eyes at the table, then looked at me. "How much time *have* you been spending here?"

"Yup. Homework!" I said quickly changing the subject.

~*~

The potential nightmare of the evening dissipated as we *did* get to work. Olivia had a weeks' worth of personal catch-up to do, as well as assignments from today's classes, so she quickly got on task. I started on all of the work I needed to do on my individual study and Mbozi's assignment.

Olivia fiercely worked through her classwork—immersing herself in the virtual feeds again—while Constantine ensconced himself in his workroom for half the time, and sprawled in a chair next to me, negligently flipping through the pages of a book the other half.

Olivia and Constantine mostly ignored each other, though Constantine made a few disparaging quips when the spell to create would seize Olivia. The fading spell was further neutered under the plethora of wards Dorm One suites afforded, but there were also a lot of Department-laced students walking Dorm One's corridors, making Olivia twitch.

Overall, I counted it as a win.

Until it was time to sleep.

I didn't have class until ten tomorrow, but Olivia started early every day, and Constantine had an eight o'clock meeting with Stevens. I had planned to stay up late, but there was no way those two would retire while I was still up, so I sighed and consigned myself to staring at the ceiling until they fell asleep. I could sneak back into the living room as long as neither put alarms on me.

I stopped short in the entryway of the bedroom. The room had converted itself to accommodate a third person.

A giggle escaped. It was a little hilarious.

"What are you laughing at?" Olivia demanded. Constantine ignored us both, moving around me to fiddle with the magic on his side of the room, which had gone from a half to a third portion.

"It's just... I never expected to do co-ed summer camp. At a magical university. On a mountain that could someday, possibly, eat me."

Olivia's brows pulled sharply together. "The mountain isn't going to eat us."

"Pssh. This place will totally eat us at some point. No one will convince me otherwise." I patted the wall. "It's okay," I assured the building, and the mountain through it. "I'm sure it will be quite the adventure."

Olivia's shoulders tightened and she looked at Constantine like she was readying herself to defend my craziness, but he just lifted an eyebrow, not the least surprised, and continued what he was doing to the wards over his slimmer bed.

Olivia's muscles didn't relax—as if she wasn't sure whether to be relieved with this development or incensed. But I had spent entirely too much time with Constantine for him to be anything but aware of my antics. Sometimes Olivia selectively forgot this.

And sometimes I forgot that the others had no idea how much time Constantine and I actually spent together. Other than Will, no one ever *saw* it. We were usually on our own.

Whatever. "This is totally summer camp. I never went to an overnight camp." I'd done very little outside of building my world around my art and my brother—neither of which had required me to do much away from home.

"I like this," I said, looking around the room with more enthusiasm. The wards were humming, satisfied, almost as if they were amused.

Olivia deliberately stalked past me and staked out the middle of the three twin beds, glaring at Constantine as she dropped her things on top.

Constantine barely looked up. "Price, you realize Ren's been staying here without you, right, and has no concept of personal space?"

"I just bet. And that stops now."

"Really? I think you have no ide—"

I tuned out their bickering and jumped into the slightly smaller version of Axer's bed that I'd been sleeping in. It put me between the door and the two of them, the perfect defensive position.

The wards hummed happily.

"I think this will work out just fine," I said, interrupting them, and feeding a little more magic into the ward set.

"Of course you do," Olivia sounded resigned. "You'll have all of us living in a happy commune at some point."

Neighborhood maybe. I liked *some* space.

And Olivia couldn't fool me. She was embracing the community vibe that was growing ever stronger in our group. Of course, I was pretty sure she would pick just about *anyone* other than Constantine—except for maybe Inessa and Bellacia—as a camp mate, but she was embracing the community aspect tentatively with both arms and all magical tentacles.

I frowned. Did—?

"No," Constantine warned without turning. "Stop thinking."

I deliberately thought of a ton of magical tentacles hugging him and sent all of it—mental pictures and fluffy emotions—toward him.

He fumbled the thing he was trying to put on his nightstand and looked at me, revolted. I just laughed, happiness filling me.

I pulled out the marble filled with Third Layer dynamics and stared at it, letting the lamplight filter through.

"You are still carrying it around?" Constantine's voice was unreadable, and suddenly, so too were his emotions.

Olivia looked at the marble with a narrowed gaze. "What is it?"

"It is a window into what might be," I whispered, turning it and letting the magic catch the light. "It is *possibility*."

The possibility of freedom. Of peace.

A little thrill of excitement bounced somewhere in the back of my mind. *Do it*, it seemed to say.

Constantine's eyes narrowed and he looked at my bed, then at the ward lines.

"I won't do anything in here with it," I said reassuringly.

"That's not—" Constantine cut himself off, finger stroking his ribbon, gaze losing focus as he tried to work something out in his mind.

It loosened something in me, seeing the ribbon back with him in its natural habitat. A weird bit of satisfaction filled the space where the mental voice had urged me on.

Olivia's eyes caught Constantine's play of motion, too. "You aren't reattaching that, right Leandred?"

The briefest flit of emotion crossed Constantine's face before he wiped it clean. "As you say."

"It would be bad for Ren," Olivia said darkly.

"You should be concerned with removing your own attachments then," he said, voice barely showing interest in the jab, his brain still working on whatever puzzle he was mulling. "All those leashes you've been handling say otherwise, though."

She stiffened. "You'd know, as you *designed* them."

"As you say."

Olivia's eyes narrowed. "You aren't reattaching it."

"I don't have to reattach anything, *Price*. She's like a bait shop that lets anyone grab anything they want off the shelves. *Think*."

"And a new shipment just arrived!" I said, trying to forestall bloodshed. Olivia growled as I pushed her into the bathroom to brush our teeth. But a few hip-checks and toothpaste spells made her relax and smile.

Soon enough, the lights were out and we were all tucking in.

"Good night, Liv! Good night, Con!" I quipped.

Constantine gave an aggravated sigh, but I felt his light brush across my mind, a mental caress for good dreams.

"Good night, Ren," Olivia intoned, as seriously as ever.

I had thought myself consigned to staring at the ceiling until they fell asleep. But surrounded by the feeling of the companionable wards and lifelines of two of my closest friends, I quickly fell to sleep with Axer's dragon clutched against my chest.

But in my cocoon, I had forgotten the dream wards with three of us hooked in wouldn't be the *same*.

Chapter Fifteen

DREAMING IN ORIGAMI WAVES

WAVES OF WATER lapping at my face gave way to a brilliant midnight sky as I lifted toward it, clothes shifting into something shorter and dryer.

Knights on horseback galloped across the stars, bright constellations against darkness, as the dreamglass formed in a far more usual way. A phoenix and a dragon soared gracefully together above the horizon, flames of blue fire lighting the scene. Bands of ultramarine and white flowed and mixed together, an amalgamation of protection, chivalry, and power.

Papers, both antique and crisply fresh, cluttered up one corner of one area, and portraits containing shifting faces littered the walls. Familiar faces, mostly, were surrounded by symbols, diagrams, equations and illustrations that I associated with each person—crowns and swords, plants and rings, patterns and components.

Along the edges of the glass, shadows lurked, creeping and searching for holes. Those too, unfortunately, were normal.

And in the center, Axer stood—an invincible sentinel waiting. He looked me over with eyes almost too blue in the reflections of the dreamglass.

Something flitted through memory, a recollection that was too quickly lost in the ether of the dream with his gaze connected to mine.

He looked at my throat. A number of expressions too quick to parse traveled over his face and through the shifting walls of the dreamglass.

"I see the rumors are true," he said, lifting a finger.

I reached up, automatically, to touch the ribbon encircling my throat. "I can explain—"

"About your roommate becoming a trash artist."

I realized a moment too late that there was nothing around my throat and that he was indicating the papers cluttering up the corner of the dream behind me—papers that were forming into shapes and patterns while my subconscious worked around the details, trying to figure out how to solve the problem.

"Oh. *Oh.*"

He didn't precisely smile, but a devilish, amused gleam lit his eyes.

"It's not funny," I said.

His gaze was wiped clean when it met mine. "No."

"Constantine—"

"I know what he did."

I let my hand drop. "He's making himself a target. You all are."

"We were targets already." He cocked his head, looking at the flow of my thoughts across the landscape. "I have never been anything other than a target."

I watched my symbolized Top Circle memory of Kaine, Stavros, and Axer dance across the glass. It was hard to argue against Axer being a target. We had, perhaps, tentatively drawn even at this point on the target scope. He was an older, established fear. I was uncertain terror.

"Price and Leandred, even your muse, know the stakes—knew them well before you did."

"Olivia has been drafting emancipation papers for weeks."

He nodded, unsurprised. "She's always been an untapped potential, but stunted. Her devotion to you will gain her much. She could be a force."

I let my fingers scoop a puff from a dream cloud and form it into a pen. Even in my dreams, I wanted to chew on something.

Olivia...no, I knew her path was going to be a better one. It had to be. But the others...

I watched a Valkyrie thrust her sword into a monster in the illustrated swirls of the dreamglass. Camille Straught hadn't been wrong.

"Ah," Axer said, pulling his fingers through the images. "She shouldn't have done that. I'll have a talk with her."

"No." I sighed, trying to control my thoughts so he couldn't read *every* one of them. My subconscious wasn't exactly cryptic, and I really didn't want to share my more embarrassing thoughts. "It was my fault. I lost control for a moment. She wasn't wrong about anything she said. And she shouldn't be forced to be nice to me." Or to like me.

"It's not you," he said distantly. "Or at least not totally you. She takes a lot on herself; feels she has a lot to live up to." He shook his head. "Her time will come to decide, and when it does, her decisions will be her own."

"*You* trust her."

"Of course. But with my life and four others, not yours. Not yet. There is work to be done to gain you a spot in her list. You need to gain her trust. She guards her charges well."

Chapter Fifteen

I stared. "Are you trying to...? You are. You're nuts."

"A consequence of having the forces of the world at my fingertips," he said with an unrepentant smile.

A strange pond suddenly appeared, but he waved it away, changing my dream as easily as he changed whatever else he wanted.

"Sometimes I wonder if I shouldn't be wearing more wool," I said. Sheep vaulted across the sky in emblematic reflection.

"You are too unruly a beast for the flock." A weirdo purple sheep was suddenly doing barrel rolls and ramming into the sheep in front of it, pushing it off course and causing a wooly pileup twelve deep.

I sighed. "I'm okay with Straught not liking me. I stand against a lot of her aims." I looked him over. He looked good. Healthy. "No worse for the wear now that you are starting your victory tour?"

"Nothing a week of press events, tight smiles, and careful nodding won't cure."

I shook my head—it felt like far more time had passed since we'd watched the closing ceremony. "Congrats, by the way. I watched the Freespar highlights." Axer had killed—well, *murdered* or *slaughtered with excessive force* was more the way to put it—everyone. *Literally* killed everyone, though they'd all been successfully revived. "You didn't leave anyone in doubt of your scariness. You are right. You are a target all your own. Maybe I need to stay away from *you*," I joked.

He looked past me, at something shimmering at the edges of my dream vision. Conflict tightened his too-blue eyes. "Possibly more true than you know." Darkness pulsed outside the dreamglass, rolling over it in waves.

"Okay, scary. Tone it down." I patted his shoulder.

He looked to the glass dome above our heads, as if asking for patience. The purple sheep did another barrel roll across the glass, bleated in triumph, then hit a tree.

A dragon, black as night, unfolded itself from the massive boughs, lifted the sheep by its scruff, and set it on its feet. The sheep bleated, then launched itself into the air, morphing into a hummingbird as it flew.

I scratched my chest, perplexed by what that meant.

"Well, I'm happy you triumphed as scariest mage, but I think it's neat that there are three winners and that the competition committee allowed it."

"Were pleasantly persuaded is perhaps a better descriptor."

"Ah. They only wanted you?" A sole Second Layer champion, a *repeat* champion.

I was quite familiar with how that worked, with Christian and his two time state championship football team. Repeat champions weren't just twice as prestigious. There was an exponential quality placed on a second win.

Melancholy colors muted some of the dreamglass swirls. There'd been no chance of a three-peat for Christian.

"Nice and tidy," Axer agreed. "It might have been best if I'd not participated in Freespar." He looked to the corner where a knight was fighting monsters with one hand tied behind his back. "I'm terrible at losing, though, and if I had lost, the officials—Second Layer lackeys, all—would have tried harder to figure out who poisoned me. They'd eventually have blamed Biato, who did actually do it."

I recognized the name as the Third Layer competitor who was one of the co-champions.

Little lights flickered angrily around me and the paint in the moving illustrations streamed toward me, pulling on all of them like a knitted knot being straightened. They smoothed into feeding lines flowing directly into me. "Someone poisoned you?" I inhaled and my tone tightened. "I thought —"

He lifted the light closest to him and smoothed down the magic with a soft motion. The rest of the lights relaxed, and began happily frolicking again. The paint released and the illustrations reformed.

I stared at the dancing lights. Connected to me as they were, my mood shifted with them, relaxed and almost ebullient.

"You are dangerous," I said, finally.

He let the little light fall, so that it, too, could dance. "Biato sent his brother with us to Corpus Sun, so don't think too hard about maiming him. I should have let him win the whole thing."

"Should have? You fixed the competition?"

"With a thousand events?" He looked amused. "No. I just took advantage of the opportunity presented in the last events to even things out. Freespar gives the most points of any event, and I had a choice of who to target first and last. I simply whittled them in a desired order. Having three champions is too rife with possibility."

I stared at him, not even able to comprehend how he had successfully targeted and eliminated competitors in the midst of the carnage I knew Freespar to be.

"What possibilities?"

"The chance to *chat* as we tour. Things are moving quickly. Allies are essential."

Energy infused me. "You can tell them that I think I can fix the Third Layer. I captured a sample of the last event. And I used the recycler to hide my magic. I have a few ideas. Like *pockets* and *domes*. I just need to—"

He lifted one of the lights and gently stroked it again.

I grimaced at the forced calm shifting through me. "Too much?"

"Don't do anything until I get back."

"Yeah, phrases like 'keeping a low profile' and 'being normal' are getting a lot of use around here, too."

He looked amused.

I looked at the papered area in the corner where my mind hadn't stopped working on the problem of Olivia's spell.

"I'd have thought you'd find this creative explosion fascinating." He walked over and crouched in front of the papers, observing the patterns, then moved a few with his fingers, examining the ones beneath. His eyes moved rapidly, reading the spells and my thoughts on each.

Don't trust him, a voice whispered, startling me. I looked around the dreamglass, but nothing looked out of order and the shadows were all safely outside.

I rubbed my chest, then my throat, a little unnerved, but there was only silence where the voice had been.

"Ren?"

"Sorry." I physically circled my subconscious thoughts into a swirl, then sent them winging off into the ether. "When are you coming back?"

He was still studying the magic that I had done. "I don't know. They are talking about extending the tour. The other layers are pushing for it with their champions."

Little spikes of worry pulsed around the dream. "It's nearly the end of the term, though. You'll miss classes." It made me uneasy to have him off campus for that long.

He eased my worried thoughts with a calm hand along the edge of the glass. "We are catching them through virtual feed. And the other combat mages are back."

I nodded.

He smiled. "It won't be much longer and the extra time allows me to put things into place. Many things."

Don't trust him.

I swallowed. "Okay. Great."

He touched my chin, tipping it up. "Something is wrong."

I deliberately muted the recollection of the oddness. I trusted Axer pretty completely. I had no idea where that thought kept coming from. "No, it's just been a long week."

I could see his mind working, and his gaze tracked something across the dream before returning to me. "Get some sleep. Dawn is cracking here, and I need to have a chat with someone else in your room."

"Don't hurt him," I said immediately.

He looked amused. "Constantine Leandred doesn't need anyone to protect him in a dreamspace."

"I just watched you *obliterate* people who are considered the best fighters in five...two...however many layers. *Worlds.*"

"Strangers," he said offhandedly. "No one knows how to kill you like family. Don't do anything drastic tomorrow, small purple hummingbird-sheep."

I flipped him off.

Axer gave one last swipe across the glass of the dream, a half-smile on his face, then he was gone. There one moment, gone the next.

And like it had been *waiting*, the dreamglass shifted and my gaze went to the shadows poking at the holes.

I knew what they were. And I shouldn't approach them. I knew this. But something in the shifting dream urged me forward.

Find out.

Whether my subconscious was telling me to face my fears or gain answers, I didn't know.

I clasped the metal dragon figurine, which had become a physical entity in the dreamspace once Axer left. I reassured myself that if I got in trouble, it would pull me back to the guys' room. I could leave at any time.

Christian's face appeared in one of the portraits and he smiled in encouragement.

Encouragement from the twin of my subconscious or not, I knew better than to invite the shadows inside my space where all my secrets could be laid bare. I stepped out to meet the darkness.

My step into the starfield of dreams was brief. The shadows wrapped around my ankle and another dreamglass whirled toward me, then pulled me inside.

Unsurprisingly, Raphael smiled at me from the middle of a sterile, white room—an uncomfortably empty slate. Nothing upon the walls let me read anything from him. Kaine was nowhere in sight.

Something in me was irritated by that, but the feeling fled quickly.

It didn't matter. I checked my body, which morphed in and out of the consciousness of the dream, and clasped the dragon—my safety totem—to my chest.

"Hello, Butterfly."

"I beat your spell."

"Did you?" He pulled his hand through the air, twinkling starlight like dust in the path of the motion. "Tinkered with it maybe, but I feel the tendrils still in place. A brilliant little piece of tumbled magic, but I think with a little effort I could flip it back. Grey's fondness for me will always be his downfall. He doesn't have the balls to call in those who could truly strip the spell bare without my aid."

"You've done enough."

"Sufficiency is a useless descriptor in master plans," he said lightly.

Chapter Fifteen

"There is always so much *more* that can be accomplished."

"What happened to Kaine?" I asked, looking around again.

Raphael smiled, but instead of the fond golden gaze I was used to, dark shadows swirled within his eyes. "I ate him."

Nausea curdled my insides and I moved my clenched hand from my chest to my midsection. "What do you mean ate him?"

I could see the shadowed slivers slipping from the shade of his pupils into the gold of his irises.

The dreamglass cracked as my mind forcefully decided to wake up.

Raphael put out a hand to the glass, and the cracks halted. His eyes were darkly amused. "It was the quickest and safest thing to do here. I don't want you being eaten. Not yet."

The thought of Kaine—anyone—being eaten, was enough to make my mind revolt and flee.

Raphael tilted his head watching the cracks widen beneath his spread fingers. "It bothers you that much? Well, I don't think you will like the alternative."

He waved a hand to smooth over the new cracks, then reached into his mouth and pinched something shadowed there. Pulling it out in one continuously long string, the shadows were pulled from his eyes—the inside end of the string. As soon as the end of the long shadow emerged, he threw it to the corner where it bloomed into the life-size body of Kaine.

Kaine was completely still, but for his eyes, which immediately darted to Raphael and filled with a horrible promise of death, then focused on me, filling further with dark purpose.

"Behave," Raphael said in a voice that was equally amused and terrifying. He waved his forefinger in a little figure eight pattern, a threat, and I could see Greyskull's tattoo embellished on his fingertip like a thimble of ink pulled over the digit.

Kaine shied back. The movement was almost infinitesimal, but his previous stillness brought it to view.

Raphael smiled fondly at the inked finger. "Such a lovely gift. Do thank Grey for me."

I was pretty sure Greyskull had not meant for Raphael to be using his gift in this way.

I licked dry lips. "Nothing more adverse was done to you in the fall?" A more insane Raphael was something no one wanted.

"From Kaine? Oh, he did some damage." He tilted his head and I could see the echoes of shadowed lesions. "But he was quite battered from the attacks he sustained from you and your pets. Fantastic job, Butterfly."

Kaine's eyes focused on me, filled with even more hate.

An answering hatred rushed through me, an emotion I was unused to feeling.

Raphael jerked his arm suddenly, then flicked something away, his eyes widening in faux surprise. "Butterfly, is that you spreading your wings, trying to hook into me?" He paused to examine his arm. "I'm so proud."

I frowned. "I'm not doing anything. I don't want to be attached to you at all."

He watched me for a moment, then shrugged as if he believed me. "It could be so many things. That spell you flipped—naughty girl—and the things you are letting that boy do to you, calming and influencing you. I thought you didn't like the games we were playing."

"They aren't games and Axer is nothing like you."

His head tilted back and he laughed. "Is that what you think?" His gaze met mine and it was both amused and malevolent. "That he is doing these things out of a sense of honor?"

"No. Yes. Both. He obviously has some plan that I'm part of. I'm not stupid."

"No, just naïve. And trusting. I've always liked that about you. Now where exactly are you?"

He didn't step closer, but I could see him rifling through images in my mind, the pages of a picture book flipping across his eyes.

I stepped back and clutched the dragon to my chest again.

"Mmmm..." He hummed. "So close to the correct triangle, but not quite there. Still, it's not inconsequential, the magic that you have assembled in that room. Soon. Soon it will be the time to strike. Without Kaine, the shadows the Department tries to keep hidden will slip away. The time will be—"

I felt it this time. The magic that hit Raphael emanated from me, but wasn't *from* me.

He grabbed me by the front of my shirt and dragged me toward him. He was staring at something—maybe my clavicle, maybe my throat, then a terrible series of expressions moved across his face. Anger bloomed, then a terrible knowledge, and finally, dark intent.

A wash of his magic encased me, and for a moment, I felt freer than I had before. Unleashed.

He released my shirt and started pacing, gaze never leaving mine. "How did you manage that, Butterfly?" he asked, far too mildly for the sinister expression on his face.

"What?"

"Your terrible lack of foresight and the loss of your freedom."

Crap. I touched my neck, but the ribbon wasn't there in this dreamspace. Still, a trace of it must have shown.

His pacing grew more restless. "It has always been to my advantage, your dangerous levels of trust, both in yourself and others. That you do not learn quickly enough to guard yourself is both a blessing and curse." His steps became furious. "For all of my plans..."

"What is going on?" Raphael was mad—a mind sickness that was likely permanent—but he was almost always in *control.*

"Death's sweet embrace. She comes sooner for me than I had planned," he muttered.

"Raphael—"

"But she will be no less welcome." He was suddenly in front of me and his smile was sharp and a little sad. He pulled a hand down my cheek. "When the time comes, I will not let you linger in chains either. Your death will be a bittersweet event, but I will make it *true.* I will not allow you to suffer long."

Shadows flitted through his eyes again, and Kaine's image flickered in the corner, as if he couldn't be two places at once.

"What do you mean? What are you talking about?"

I was officially terrified. Raphael, for all of his insanity, I understood...well, understood wasn't the right word, but his actions followed a pattern. A pattern that had been twisted from love and protection to pain and destruction. Kaine, on the other hand... All I knew of Kaine was evil.

"I can make this work. Traps placed in want of another are always the best way to trap in turn. For greedy hunters stay near the traps they most want sprung. Tell your new friend that I look forward to his destruction."

He smiled. It was not a comfort.

A wave of his hand and the previous feeling settled over me, heavier than before. I found myself flat against the smooth expanse of the dreamglass, delicate spikes pinning my limbs in place.

"Your death comes swiftly, and I mourn it already, Butterfly. Pinned to a board, wings fluttering and stuttering. I will make certain they *all* suffer, though." He walked closer, shadows overcoming the whites of his eyes. "I offer you a last gift. Two last gifts. Your friend can do so much damage in other ways. For you, well, the power of a last plea. My poor little butterfly."

A pencil thin snake was winding down his arm. He rotated the limb in 180 degree turns so that the snake remained in view as it slithered around in its descent. Each rotation, another head grew on the snake until there were four of them.

As it reached his wrist, its four sets of eyes met mine. He sliced the end head off with his fingernail. The three remaining heads grew agitated, all staring at me with feral eyes. Before I could react, the middle head reared forward and sunk its fangs into me. The dreamglass shattered with my scream.

Chapter Sixteen

ESCAPED ENCHANTMENTS

OLIVIA AND CONSTANTINE were long gone by the time I dragged myself out of bed. I had tossed and turned under strong silencing wards most of the night after my nightmarish encounter with Raphael, trying not to wake them. At some point I had felt Constantine spell me, though, with murmured words.

Whatever he had done had muted my nightmares.

I was going to be having a lot of them. I shuddered, and made myself think of other things—like whether Olivia and Constantine had fought over time in the bathroom, and if I could figure out how to view the memory of that battle.

One thing was for sure—no more stepping outside of my dreams.

I wanted to starfish face first back in bed and coil the remnants of Constantine's sleep spell back around me, but my morning class was *Engineering Concepts in Warding* with Mbozi and I knew he'd want to talk about the ward that I had successfully activated in the Third Layer. For once, he might actually be looking forward to seeing me. The thought was enough to get me outside.

"Ren!" I turned to see Olivia racing toward me.

I perked up a little as she neared. She looked better. "Hey, Liv."

She frowned as she turned me at the shoulder and started walking us back to the Magiaduct. "You look terrible."

"Yes, it's a four coffee morning, I think."

She nodded distractedly, her gaze darting from one group to another as we moved.

A little shot of adrenaline roused me from full stupor and I tuned more fully into her, sensing the quiet panic underlying her more vibrant state. Raphael's final monologue bloomed in my brain, and with it, suspicion and panic. "What's wrong?"

Chapter Sixteen

"I haven't created a single thing this morning," she whispered.

"Er...that's good?" Please, let that be good. I looked around us. Students with armbands and memorial gear were walking to and returning from classes. None of them had 'DEPARTMENT' stamped on their foreheads, but... "Maybe people are revoking their Department ties. Or maybe once you make something, you don't have to do it again—like you are successfully killing them with the gift?"

I'd take either of those options. As much as the origami fest had been amusing at first, I was glad she was walking alongside me normally now—well, as normally as possible, with her nearly frog-marching me.

"No. I've felt no less than twenty Department connections, some of them new. But they didn't cause me to *do* anything."

I frowned and examined her face as if I was going to capture it on canvas. "You look good, like way better." Flushes and spots of color were in the correct places, no more pasty zombie tones. "Maybe the spell was only good for a smaller period of time than Grey thought? Maybe it wore off during the night?"

She looked at me seriously. "Do you *really* think so?"

"No." I rubbed my forehead, and internally swore. "It...maybe...I had a dream last night about..." I waved my hand and finished the thought mentally since we were outside our wards. *Verisetti.*

"About or *with?*" Her expression changed from nervousness to fury.

"I won't do it again," I said quickly.

"*Ren,*" she growled, gaze focused ahead.

I sighed. "Yeah, I didn't think you'd be amused. But seriously, it's—"

"*You* are going to Medical."

"Yeah," I nodded. "I'll drop you off there."

"Not for *me*, for *you.*"

"It will make me feel better to get you there safely, yes."

"No, you idiot, *you* need to go to Medical."

"That's where we're going. Then I need to go to class."

"No."

"But—"

"*No.*"

Greyskull took one look at the way Olivia strong-armed me into his office and registered my morning class as "virtual" via medical exemption.

I sighed and flicked my finger in the air to signal Greyskull's coffee pot. "That was my one chance to see excitement in Professor Mbozi's eyes."

"I'm sure there will be others," he said, pulling two stone chairs from the floor.

"Lies," I muttered and sat, cup whizzing into my hand.

"The spell is as good as gone because Ren has been having *conversations* at night," Olivia said, crossing her arms next to me.

I winced.

Greyskull pulled an examination spell over me. A jumble of unclear images shot by too quickly for me to catch. "You do have something. A bite of some kind."

I hid my face in my cup.

"He *bit* you?" Olivia said in horror.

I spewed the liquid from my mouth. "No. A *serpent*, a serpent bit me. Oh my god." I wiped my chin with the back of my hand and cast a cleaning enchantment everywhere else. I eyed the floor critically. Passably clean—which meant no more magic brooms unless I enchanted them. *Yes.*

"A serpent bit you. Nothing to worry about then," Greyskull said drolly. "They are all quite harmless. It's not as if I see firesnake bites and burns twice a week and have to reattach necrotized limbs."

I called over a new cup of coffee. "It had four heads," I muttered into the steam, pretending it could hide my face. "He beheaded the first one."

Greyskull stilled. Then he pulled a spell net over Olivia so quickly that she startled. He didn't pay attention to our surprised noises, just worked steadily, ignoring everything else.

He finally sat back in his chair, eyes pinched. "Where?" he addressed the question to me.

I braced myself at the look in his eyes. "In a dream."

"The spell is gone," he said. For some reason, he didn't sound happy about it.

"Completely?"

Greyskull shook his head, lips tight. "The damaging parts, yes. They were cut. The remnants are withering as we speak. Gone completely by midday, I'd estimate."

"You are certain?"

"Yes. A four-headed serpent? Taunting." Greyskull looked far older than his true age for a moment. "Rationally, if Miss Price didn't kill someone right away, the gambit was a loss anyway. But, why not leave it in place to cause havoc and occupy resources?"

"Because he has something much worse planned," I said softly, finishing his thought.

He nodded, then shook his head as if he was just *done* with it all. "Let me take a few more readings, Miss Price, just to make certain. But it looks like a perfectly clean cut. Banishing the remnants will take minutes."

"No," Olivia said.

We both looked at her.

"I want this part of the spell. The part that lets me identify who is connected to the Department," she said darkly.

159

Chapter Sixteen

"It's Rafi's spell," Greyskull said gently.

"And now it's mine," she said grimly.

"It is withering, Miss Price, even as we speak."

"All magic can be duplicated and recreated if you have the right tools," she said.

He said nothing for long moments, then tipped his head. "Very well." He pulled out a replicator.

"What are you doing?" I asked, unnerved by their conversation.

"Duplicating the spell, examining it, then turning the other cheek," Greyskull said.

"Liv—"

"No," she said grimly. "I *want* that spell."

"Liv—"

"I know what I'm doing, Ren."

I watched Greyskull carefully capture a copy of the spell, already moving on the assumption that I'd be convinced.

"I'll help," I said.

"I know," she said, almost resigned.

We worked in silence as Greyskull cleaned the spell trails on Olivia and Olivia stared at the captured duplicate in her hand. I helped with any devices or magic that either needed, moving from one to the other in an economical and spell-enhanced dance I had learned from Neph to ease the flows of magic in the room.

"It's done," Greyskull finally said.

"*Thank* you. I'll be back this afternoon," Olivia promised. She clasped his arm, then mine, then made her way out of the room, determination in every step. I watched her go with the duplicate tucked into her pocket. Unease filled me. I started to rise, planning to follow her.

"Not you. Sit." Greyskull pointed.

"I should—"

"Ren." He looked weary as he began cleaning his tools. "Tell me about your dream."

I sank back into my seat. "You can't tell Marsgrove," I said.

"Ren—"

"I know. Believe me, I know. Raphael is putting something bigger in play. But Marsgrove doesn't think rationally when Raphael is involved. If he knows that I followed the shadows... He might remove Olivia from our room. And she needs me. I swear I won't leave my dreams again."

He sighed, eyes slipping closed. "Shadows. Of course. Phillip should know. His strategic mind is a match for—"

"Please," I pleaded. "My dream wards are good. I just...stepped out of them." I didn't even know *why* I had. It had seemed a far better idea at the time, the memory of Christian urging me on. "I won't go out there again."

Greyskull said nothing for a moment, then, "How is he?"

"Scarier," I said immediately, shuddering. But it was a *relief* to be able to talk to someone about it. I didn't want to tell Olivia or Constantine or Axer, a voice within me rebelling at the very thought. My words tripped over themselves trying to get out. "There's something weird going on between Raphael and Kaine. Like they are together, but still hating each other. I don't like it. Kaine terrifies me."

"It's a terrible thing to have those two joined together in any way." Greyskull's voice was grim.

"Raphael ate him," I whispered.

Greyskull narrowed his eyes and leaned forward. "You saw him do it?"

"I saw him pull Kaine *out*." Just the memory made me want to gag. "He was saner after...saner for Raphael, at any rate. Then at the end, they were kind of flickering together again."

Greyskull tapped his lips, brows furrowed. "I wonder—" He shook his head, fingers moving to his temples.

"Yes?" I prompted, when he didn't say anything more.

"No. I have no unbiased position on this matter. You should tell Phillip." He held up a hand to forestall my automatic negation. "I won't tell him, but you should. You should tell him the entirety of your dreams. He has always been the strategic thinker, and he does so with a far clearer mind. He has been able to completely divorce himself from his emotions." Greyskull smiled without mirth. "It's a blessed skill."

I understood not wanting to be able to feel anymore. I swallowed around the grit in my throat. "Raphael said to thank you."

"As ironic as it is, that's not a relief to hear, Ren."

"Yeah."

I didn't tell Greyskull that Raphael was using his tattoo to torture Kaine. There was a dark side to Greyskull that might be pleased by it, but the knowledge would cut him, too.

I pulled a rose out of my pocket—there was a small enchantment in this one that paused grief for a few hours—and set it on his knee. "I'm sorry."

A small smile slipped across his mouth as he lifted the rose and tucked it into his shirt pocket. The sorrow receded slowly, though, as deep sadness was wont to do—consuming small moments before they could stick. "Me too, Ren."

His hands adjusted magic in the other rooms he was remotely tending. Even when Greyskull went scarily *still*, like he had with Helen, he was always in some sort of motion—as if stopping would cause him to drown. "Tell Phillip."

"No." I looked at my connection thread to Olivia, strong and pulsing with life. I couldn't risk it.

"You aren't going to be able to beat Rafi at the game he is playing," Greyskull said, gaze serious, harder emotions once more buried beneath his normal tranquility.

I shook my head. Greyskull's words had proved true so far, though— Raphael was always a step ahead.

Greyskull took my hand, startling me, and a silver infinite trinity symbol on his forearm lengthened, pulling into a looped line, then slipped along his skin, bleeding down into mine.

"He has nearly two decades of experience over you. If winning is the goal, you need to change the game."

As the tattoo hit my skin, the line blurred for a moment, then morphed into a hummingbird. It flew along the whorls and lines of my fingers and palm, mapping them.

Greyskull tipped his head, as if disquieted at what the tattoo had become as the bird slowly turned purple and gold, then inspected its new home.

"The hummingbird. Purification, balance, life. The goal or the game, Ren."

I watched the tattoo he had given me shift around my palm, fly up my arm, then bleed into my skin.

~*~

After the events of the morning and my need to understand what might have happened, I sought out Constantine and told him I was bringing food.

"Not Magi Mart?" he asked, a little relieved, as he took the container from me.

"Takeout from the cafeteria."

"A picnic? Darling, you shouldn't have." A checkerboard table cloth appeared on the surface of the table.

I pressed my finger against the cloth and little two-dimensional ants started crawling around.

"If they eat my food, I'm spelling you double tonight," he said, opening his container.

I peered at him over the top of the lid as I opened mine. "Thanks for that, by the way."

He shrugged. "You were all over the place, and I didn't think Price would recover if I pulled you into bed with me to calm you down."

"Her reaction would have been...exciting," I agreed as we both started to eat. "In the bad way. But thank you, I actually slept a little after you spelled me."

A hummingbird wing peeked out from under my shirt cuff. I rubbed my forehead.

"Bad dreams?" Constantine asked, his tone a little too indifferent to be true.

I tucked an escaped lock of hair behind my ear. "Something like that. Did you, uh, did you have any visitors last night?"

He watched me for a moment, fork suspended. "Perhaps," he said placidly. "Don't worry, there was little bloodshed."

"Con, did you...what was in the ribbon?"

His eyes narrowed and his fork dropped. "What did he say?"

"He didn't say anything. I just need to know."

He pushed his food container forward. "What are you asking for specifically?"

"Did you put something on me that would try and incapacitate Raphael?"

"No." He sat back, abandoning his meal fully, and pulled his ribbon through his fingers. I watched it move—it looked no different. "That type of sorcery was for plans now exterminated."

I leaned forward and sent a soft stroke of magic to him. He pulled his fingers from his wrist to elbow and lifted the magic up to examine it before letting it fall back into place to flow through him.

"I will never understand your levels of trust." He leaned his head back against the wall, tipping his chair back, and watched me with sharp eyes. "Tell me why you are asking about Verisetti and about my plans."

"I met him in a dream last night."

The chair's legs immediately hit the floor and Constantine sent out mass beams of magic. The magic zipping around the walls and ceiling pulsed in answer. "Our wards should not have allowed that," he said tightly.

"I...might have stepped out of my dream."

His eyes slid shut. I heard the echo of his mental swearing. "Ren."

"Right."

He leaned across the table and I leaned forward to meet him as he touched my temple. "Show me."

I let the memory play.

He pulled back minutes later, his fury barely restrained. "It is I who have been pulled down the wrong path. I *will* kill him."

"No." I swore, grabbing his sleeve. "It's nothing I'm not used to."

"You shouldn't be *used to* anything like this."

I stared at him.

He pulled a hand down his face. "I see the irony, yes."

His anger returned quickly though. "But how *dare* he say that I leashed you. I've done everything *but* that these last weeks."

"Raphael deliberately seeks discord. Especially in friendships. He said from the beginning that I shouldn't have them." I shook my head. "Don't

163

listen. I don't. I just needed to know if there was something in the ribbon spell." I touched my throat. "Everyone is reacting so wildly to it."

Constantine didn't say anything for a moment, then, "It will protect you when you need it. Don't step out of a dream again."

"I know."

"You say that too easily." He leaned forward on his forearms. "Ren, Verisetti is dangerous, but with Kaine involved..." He ghosted a hand across his stomach. "You can at least trust Verisetti to wait for whatever mad moment he has planned to use you for. Kaine wants to destroy you."

I shuddered and unconsciously sent a wave of magic to his midsection. "Kaine wants to destroy everything." There was no *life* to Kaine. He had been raised a shell, and that shell had never been filled.

"I can kill Verisetti, but I don't know how to kill a shadow. Do not leave your dreams." He watched me silently. "Promise me."

"I promise."

I rubbed the back of my neck.

Why was it that the more I promised that—to myself and others—the less it felt like I'd keep it?

Chapter Seventeen

TEAM BONDING

Stevens rescheduled our regular afternoon session to a double on Saturday. I tried not to feel too much relief at not getting the third degree from someone else today.

I headed back to Dorm Twenty-five and read a few unsatisfying dissertations on dreamglass encounters. Grimacing, I shoved the research to the side and stared at my ceiling. Something about the encounters felt inevitable.

I looked over to where my personal photos were displayed—the duplicated ones I'd left here. I looked at my brother waving at the camera. With the spell on Olivia gone and my mission to safely retrieve her now complete, I felt strangely adrift.

Needing something else to do, I lifted my corrupted storage paper from under the bed and stared at it. The broken and intertwined magic snaked around the page.

Maybe not. I shoved it back under.

I rubbed my temples and tried to ease the weird ache that was growing worse.

Justice Toad croaked with an incoming message from Isaiah.

Intersquad meeting. Meet on the hour. Mandatory.

An intersquad meeting meant the combat mages would be there, ready for a complete transition back to the norm. Transferring the security of campus back to the combat mages was what *everyone* desired. I could almost feel the combined relief of the entire Justice Squad.

The wards and powers of execution had already been transferred upon their return from the competition, but there were plenty of smaller magics that had been entrusted between the squads that needed to be yielded.

I was eager to give back the campus magics Axer had given me.

Chapter Seventeen

Someone on his team could transfer them back to him upon his return. Olivia was free, campus was healing, and all I wanted to do was veg with our expanding group and be *normal*.

I checked in with Olivia before I left. She responded mentally with, *"At Patrick and Asafa's, see you at dinner."*

Well, that was good, at least.

Arriving promptly at the meeting time, I was taken aback by the number of people gathered, and I wasn't the only one visibly surprised that it wasn't just the Justice and Combat squads at the meeting point on the Eighth Circle field.

I wandered over to Peters. He tossed me a half-frown, still as uncharmed with me as ever. Now, *that* was normal. Still the upright servant of the law, Peters would rain fury upon me if I stepped out of line.

I looked at him with a mixture of new eyes and old. Empathy, the great equalizer.

I nodded my head at him, toward the new additions, then back at him, tacking a grimace to the motion. He blinked, taken aback by my fraternal communication, then frowned, looking for the trap.

Peters hadn't changed a bit, but my *view* of him had. I could empathize with him, even if our ways of doing things might forever be at odds.

We had both lost brothers. And while he had channeled his grief into justice, I had channeled mine into protection.

He shifted, uneasy with whatever he saw on my face, then said gruffly, "The Neutralizer Squad was called here too. None of us knows why."

Surprised, I looked around us again. Now that he said it, I could see semi-familiar faces that roughly fell under the same label in my mind.

I hadn't had a lot of interaction with the group. There had never been a reason to stick around after putting in a request for a neutralization. There was a setting on Justice Toad that called in a neutralizer when a student needed help removing an enchantment and didn't want to go to Medical.

The Justice Squad didn't deal with removal, only justice in punishing the perpetrators of magical crimes. And the grief punishments, the calls I actually stuck around for, didn't require neutralization, they needed something far more personal.

Therefore, having had little interaction with them, I was unnerved by their dissecting gazes as they looked me over like a piece of freshly cut meat.

I edged closer to Peters, a movement I never would have thought possible a week ago.

"Maybe they are going to neutralize any remaining spells?" I offered.

"They've already been doing that. But, it's as good a guess as any other," he said gruffly.

* Team Bonding *

The Neutralizer Squad hadn't been called in to help with the security circus involving the Peacekeepers' Troop. Their primary function was fixing problems *after* they took place. They'd been quite busy over the last week, however, helping Medical where needed, then rushing out to aid campus when we'd been released from the Magiaduct.

Isaiah discharged a nonthreatening, calming magic used to quiet large groups and gain their attention. Selmarie was alongside him, as well as an older girl I didn't know.

"Campus will reopen completely on the Saturday before finals week." Isaiah used both hands to calm the murmurs that rose at his statement. "I know there are valid arguments both for and against this occurrence. But Shift Season demands it happen, and the politicians and board have deemed that campus reopen, so it *will* happen, and we need to make sure it happens *correctly*, no matter what our personal views on whether it *should* be done."

I had mixed feelings on the subject, and based on the uneasiness wafting from the trisected crowd, so did many people around me.

Isaiah looked around the crowd, split into three as it was.

"That means we need to scour every inch of campus proper. Make sure anything foreign that was left behind is found and disposed of. The levels below Eighteen will have to be scrubbed as well. We've be given dispensation to go through those levels ahead of the rest of campus, in order to clear them out."

Magic shot into the air, indicating questions.

"Peters."

Peters nodded at the acknowledgment of his turn to speak. "I support this endeavor; however I do not know why the Justice Squad is involved?"

"It's a good question. The combat mages routinely sweep away threats and the spell neutralizers take care of magic left behind. Those of us in the justice aspect—who do we serve justice to when our enemies have fled? The answer to why we are being involved is two-fold. First we have been trained in the last months to support the Combat Squad above and beyond our support in years prior, and because of the breadth of the job ahead, we are needed in that capacity.

"Secondly, the thriving spirit of the last few weeks has strengthened *all* squad communication and work," Isaiah said. "Campus needs cooperation more than ever. The student body needs to see a united front. And it was suggested that working together in teams to help campus might benefit us all."

Oh no. I tried to shrink in on myself as Isaiah nodded in my direction.

I heard Peters sigh audibly as he followed Isaiah's nod. What he was thinking about me at the moment was beyond my ability to parse.

"Warrior, judge, healer," Selmarie added in her capable, businesslike manner. "Trinity magic will strengthen all sides of the service triangle."

Selmarie and the female head of the Neutralizer Squad were both obviously respected by their squads, just as Isaiah was with ours, if the lack of questions after Selmarie's pronouncement was anything to go by.

"Stand by for assignments," Selmarie said.

Some combat mages and justice members looked resigned, others invigorated. The neutralizers looked especially excited and shifty. The whispers I could hear from the pocket of neutralizers nearest to me were not a good sign.

"—to take her apart."

"—need to know how to neutralize her."

"—how she dismantled that dome."

I squared my shoulders. Being dissected was not new. I'd put up with whatever came my way.

A familiar face and sardonic expression pushed through the pocket.

I sagged with relief as Lifen strode toward me. "Thank God."

She laughed. "You should see your face."

I grabbed her shoulder. "Say you are on the Neutralizer Squad and will be my partner. *Promise me this.*"

Since Axer was still at the post celebratory events, I couldn't be paired with him. Being paired with Lifen was lifesaving, no matter who our third was from the Combat Squad. Even if we were stuck with Camille Straught.

A ghost of a smile worked its way over Lifen's lips as she looked at me. "I had some extra hours to give to campus. Mistress Sidonai was happy to make room on the team for the next few weeks."

I didn't question how Lifen—or whoever had informed her—had known about the intersquad plans. I never questioned how the club network got their information.

"Chen," growled one of the boys from the Neutralizer Squad standing nearby. "What are you doing?"

"Teaming up, Todd," Lifen said, tone approaching boredom. *Halren Todd*, she indicated mentally to me. *A real winner.*

"We haven't been assigned," he barked.

"Time for assignments, then," she said, as if she couldn't care any less about the topic. "Ren's good with it, and so am I."

He scowled at her. "That's not how it works, especially for someone like you."

I bristled at the slur to Lifen, no matter that we *were* actually on the squads due to delinquency—or at least we usually were, since Lifen had volunteered this time.

My bristling pulled his gaze to me and it was all I could do not to recoil at the scientifically hungry look that bloomed.

168

* Team Bonding *

He turned back to Lifen, scowl darkening. "There's a hierarchy, and we all want a piece of—"

"Ah good. One of you from each squad?" a new, but familiar voice interrupted.

We turned as one to see Greene from Axer's team throwing a small ball of magic into the center of our inhomogeneous group in the way that the most respectable of mages introduced themselves through their magic.

"Elias Greene," he said, the introduction magic reflecting his name, winking in greeting. He flipped the front section of his light brown hair back. His equally light brown eyes were looking directly at Lifen, making it heavily obvious that, even if his magic wasn't screaming with it, that she was the one he was addressing from the Neutralizer Squad.

"Waiting for assignment seems a beastly endeavor. I'll join as your third, if you'll have me," he said casually, standing with one hand loosely tucked into the pocket of his tailored trousers. "Selmarie is just as happy when we find acceptable matches ourselves."

Lifen looked him over slowly and deliberately, then threw her own ball of magic at his in a graceful toss. The little balls collided, then fused, seeking knowledge, before dissipating with a tranquil air.

"Chen Lifen," she said, introducing herself last name first, as was her custom. "Pleasure."

"Is all mine," he said, rather smoothly, with a disarming smile. "I've seen your designs with the garrylic metals. And the casing for the Latsky device? That was you, wasn't it?"

She regarded him through unreadable eyes. "It was."

"Excellent. Crown," he said, turning to me. He was the oldest of Axer's group, at twenty-one, and always projected a gentlemanly demeanor. But there was something simmering beneath Greene's amiable expression that spoke of an endless patience—that he could wait years for the perfect time to strike.

"Greene," I returned, somewhat warily.

"Do you consent to the three of us working together?"

An expert in combat devices, Elias Greene was by far the most sociable and outwardly approachable of the five members of Axer's group, but he was also the one who never quite answered the questions he was asked. Ramirez rarely spoke in groups, but Greene was the greater enigma.

I had always felt that whatever came from Ramirez, though spoken in few words, was truth, whereas Greene had a refined way of never giving straight answers.

Patrick rarely gave straight answers to outsiders either, but his dissembling was more jocular in nature. Greene's disarming pleasantries were more dangerous to my mind, because Greene typified trustworthiness in a way sharp-eyed Patrick never would.

In my peripheral vision, Halren Todd jabbed a finger toward me, mentally communicating with someone.

"Yes, I consent," I said quickly, going for the devil I knew, and nodded at the magic in Greene's question. The magic happily conjoined the three of us.

Halren Todd's complexion turned a mottled red. He was clearly incensed, but very few people challenged anyone in Axer's group, and Todd was no different. He turned and stalked away.

Peters looked at the sky, as if seeking divine intervention, but didn't say a word as he headed after Todd toward the squad heads.

"Excellent," Greene said, with a clap of his hands and an aristocratically friendly smile. I felt a little ripple of magic. "Selmarie just sealed it."

I looked over his shoulder. Todd and his cohorts had just reached the squad heads, all vehement voices and dramatic arm gestures. Isaiah pinched the bridge of his nose and gave me a very pointed look.

A sheepish shrug was my only available response.

Isaiah visibly sighed, then waved us away, as he got pulled into the fray.

Selmarie looked like she wanted to enact Todd's murder herself, and I had a feeling that regardless of Greene's words, Selmarie would rather have done random assignments than deal with the Neutralizer Squad's griping. But no magic snapped out to break our group tie.

Camille Straught stood to the side of them, poised and strong like the Valkyrie she was, avenging gaze on me.

"I thought for sure I'd end up with her," I murmured.

Greene followed my gaze. "Yes, well, there's been enough bloodshed these past few weeks, don't you think? How about we take a look at campus."

He snapped his fingers and an enchanted slip of paper appeared an inch above them. Greene plucked it from the air. "Eighteenth Circle, battlefields, Midland's edge," he read. He held out the paper to Lifen, who was a "don't believe it, check it yourself" kind of girl. "Good assignments. Always pays to be first."

That is the assignment, Lifen's mental voice confirmed through our communication loop, before she tucked the slip of paper into her pocket.

Greene smiled, apropos of nothing.

I narrowed my eyes as we began the trek down campus, eager to get away from the arguing neutralizers who had started to throw tantrum magic.

"You get your way a lot, don't you?" I said to Greene.

"You're mistaking me for Axer, Crown."

"Not even remotely."

"So suspicious." He smiled, as if pleased. "Now, Chen, may I call you Lifen? Let's speak about that lovely piece of metallurgy that I've heard about with—"

And so it went.

Other than my serious distrust, tagging along with Greene was pleasant. The entire Combat Squad was beyond competent, but because Greene relied so heavily on devices, most of our encounters with rogue elements entailed herding and cleverness more than actual fighting. In the absence of regular foot traffic on the lower levels, unruly beasties had taken over, like spiderwebs forming over untrod paths. Greene was always prepared with some gadget or gizmo or plan, and his tailored clothing never suffered a crease.

The great thing was that after each encounter, Greene handed over the device he had used and allowed us to examine it. It wasn't until after we examined the third of those devices that I realized that his openness and disarming questions were a calculated attempt to learn how we would deal with each device so he could improve upon his designs and overcome our defenses.

While slotting us into an appropriate villain level status.

Worth it, Lifen said mentally, as she checked the inner workings of the stationary net that he had used to capture a spawn of filnibbles. *Besides, I told him the wrong answer deliberately two devices ago. I'd totally have used an incitement spell.*

Greene flicked the stationary net back into a metal band around his wrist, arrayed under his tailored shirtsleeve. "Lovely, isn't it?" he said to Lifen as she leaned over interestedly to examine the design of the bracelet container.

Greene was the gentleman equivalent of an academic assassin.

I sent that thought to Lifen.

Tasky and Loudon are going to be so pissed, Lifen said mentally, touching the metal.

That you are getting to feel him up? The master device-inator?

That he's letting us examine everything he uses. Definitely doesn't hurt that he's also hot, she responded.

That sent me into a coughing fit. A second spawn of filnibbles popped up from the ground. Greene whacked me on the back, and an honest to god cane appeared in his other hand with a silver fox head handle.

"They should only spawn once a week. Try this." He handed the cane to Lifen, who would take care of the needed neutralization.

All in all, it was a pleasant outing, monster-wise.

It would never do to forget that underneath his tailoring, Greene was just as lethal as the rest of Axer's team. But he didn't seek outrageous beasts to fight—*cough*, Axer, *cough*—so we weren't in much danger of being mortally wounded. And Greene was attentive, interested, and encouraging —the perfect scientifically minded aristocrat and gentleman. When it came to brainstorming what to do about whatever situation we found ourselves in, he was a captive audience.

Should have been a huge win.

Especially in contrast to Axer, who was flat out *demanding* as a partner and who always led me all over the worst areas of campus, demanding I *do better*. And while I always *did,* since his brand of disappointed encouragement *made* me give him my best, it had been both emotionally and physically draining at first. Only when I'd become used to working with him had our relationship led into the ideal output between emotional effort and result.

Watching Greene handle problems with his devices was academically interesting.

And...boring. Unchallenging. Those devices were already made. I wasn't interested in problems that already had solutions.

I missed Axer.

I rubbed my chest and rolled my shoulders, then activated Justice Toad to record the remnant of a spell adjacent to where the battlefield dome had been raised. Someone would need to reexamine it in a few days to make sure it was truly gone.

"Good show, Ren, Lifen." Greene smiled disarmingly. "Going for the hook between the two spells. There was a spell on Top Circle with a similar detonation pattern."

There had been. Loudon had placed it.

And that was the worrisome thing, really. Greene was continually seeking and receiving information in small ways about our group dynamics and what we were working on.

Dangerous.

I said as much to Lifen mentally, who hummed in agreement.

He turned to me. "And you would ask your friend Delia to make the fabric for the fitting? And your friend Asafa to imbue it with the right amount of intensity?"

I stared at Greene's disarming smile for a long moment. It was as if he'd read my mind and was calling me out on the shared thoughts.

Very dangerous.

Lifen seemed to find him amusing, though, which was even more disturbing.

A morbid bystander, I watched Greene take it upon himself to completely charm her, which was about as Herculean a task as it sounded. It was absorbing and terrifying to watch. I kept as silent as I could—

answering questions with nods or head shakes, not wanting to reveal anything more than I had to.

Lifen had been as surprised as I had been at the information we had revealed in a few simple responses to him at the beginning. But she had caught on quickly and blithely played the game. Near the end she caught my gaze and winked.

Greene was going on about how wonderful he'd found a specific project that he very obviously assumed had been spell activated by Lifen.

"And you have to be trusted to hold the spell," he said, voice admiring, trying to gain her acknowledgment to the fishing hook.

"Yes, it's a delicate balance, but then you know all about that with the cloaks," she responded lightly.

"Yes, it's a simple matter of..." He trailed off, then gave a rueful shake of his head. "Good show."

It was something that the combat mage teams never spoke of, even to each other—of who held the magic for the group cloaks—for that person would be targeted specifically for it during combat. It was always tacitly assumed that Axer was the holder for their team, since he had the horsepower for it while simultaneously doing the dozen other things he had to keep track of in a battle.

"It was but a paltry victory against the silver tongue you wield," Lifen said with a smirk.

"Always a dangerous gambit, when you play at social engineering," he acknowledged ruefully, swinging his cane. "Give just enough without giving too much. Trust is a hard weapon to manipulate without giving some in return."

"You wield it well," she said.

He winked. "Thank you. Perhaps I could continue to wield it against you?"

Lifen blushed.

The world is ending, I mentally sent to Neph and Delia. *Pack my bag.*

"In fact, what do you say to—?"

I had let the two of them handle most of the problems, but the demon that appeared suddenly in our path made every bit of lethargy flip into adrenaline-fueled magic.

The demon howled as I ejected him into a holding tank on the Fourteenth Circle, using one of the expulsion paths Axer and I had set up together to handle rogue monsters. The small cloth tucked in my back pocket, drenched with Axer's magic, tingled.

A calculating look appeared on Greene's face, for a moment so brief that I could have imagined it. "My word," he murmured. "Good shot, Crown. Lucky."

Chapter Seventeen

Finally, *finally*, as we headed back to the Magiaduct as the sun sank into the bumpy horizon, Greene got down to business.

Without breaking stride, he turned and walked backward, looking between the two of us, a small device resting in his open palm, extended toward us.

Lifen eyed the device, making no move to take it. "Interesting bauble you have there, Greene."

"Isn't it? And here I am sharing it with you."

"Does that mean we have passed your little test?" Lifen replied.

"With flying colors," he said, far too easily.

"Right," Lifen said, gaze moving from the device to his face. "Binders are illegal. You can earn a twenty month magic limiter for having a facilitator in your possession."

"Which is why having a shielded one is such a coup."

Her expression didn't change. "Pass."

"It would only be used for an afternoon. We would give as much as we would take to work out some terms. To give you something *better.*"

"No."

He smiled. "We want to protect our interests, and you want to protect yours. They are intersecting at a particular point, don't you agree? This would just ensure we are all...friendly around that intersection. No catch."

What is he talking about?

He wants to bind us all together, Crown. For a limited amount of time. For something specific, but yet unspecified. Lifen's mental voice was tight and filled with conflicting feelings.

I looked at Greene, who continued to smile. *Like bonds of servitude? No way.*

The bonds work in reverse as well.

"You know that my intentions are true." He tilted his chin toward Lifen's metallic right earring. Lifen's expression didn't change, but something about her posture shifted.

It was poor form to ever think that the items that mages wore and carried were magic free. Every object had a purpose. I had never guessed at the function of Lifen's earrings, though.

"As you say," she said, tilting her head and letting the setting light glint off the metal. "However, you are beyond capable of twisting your words."

"I will make a more concerted effort at this bargain, then." He twirled the device around his palm. "We gain only what you willingly give, and vice versa."

"Mmhmm," she said.

"Take some time to think it over. In the meantime, it would be lovely to gain an introduction to a few of your friends," he said, voice easy and uncomplicated. "I have a set of mages that I routinely buy from, but a few of you are far too creative to let slip by."

This isn't Regency England. He can approach any of them on his own, I sent to her.

I knew Will, at a minimum, had done business with Greene before. Greene was the most approachable member of an elite group on campus, so lots of people approached him, and he was rumored to always be on the lookout for interesting baubles.

It's the game, Crown. It's all in what he isn't saying, Lifen said.

What, like, "Fair Maiden, me swooneth if you don't doth take my handkerchief to your bosom!"

More like, this is my playground, take note, shivits.

Oh, like you wouldn't take his handkerchief, I needled.

Greene smiled. Lifen's eyes narrowed and she abruptly switched off my mental connection to her. I cautiously switched off all of mine, too, just in case. I eyed the device in his hand.

Lifen, though, kept her gaze on his and fished a paper from her pocket —the one he had handed to her with the campus assignments—and lit it on fire in the palm of her hand, then ground the ashes to dust between her palms.

"Pity," he said. "I was rather hoping to hear your response."

"I'll grind your balls to dust next."

"Now that is cause for a swoon." He held out his hand with the device in it. "A trade for a guile. Look it over to your heart's content. Tamper free, by my magic I so do vow."

She narrowed her eyes, but took a handkerchief from her pocket and scooped the device inside.

I activated my comms after I felt Lifen reactivate hers. Her reactivation meant that whatever Greene had done to listen to us this whole time had been destroyed with the paper.

If you put that to your bosom, I swear I'm going to—

Shut up, Crown.

"Think over what I said; discuss it with your group. You all did a fine job Bloody Tuesday," Greene said. "Better than fine. And there is something absolutely fascinating about the ouroboros you each wear around your necks. We'd like to leverage all of that and more. But we want to minimize the other parts." His gaze switched to me. "The parts that are a little too close to the events at the end of last term, Crown, and the ones with you haring off to places you shouldn't go. Got me?"

"Perfectly," I said, voice clipped.

"Excellent. So, let's speak about you keeping a lower profile and what we can do to help."

Chapter Seventeen

I twitched. "I'm already on it, thanks. Ask Axer."

"See, when it comes down to it, *that* is truly the part that concerns us," he said in a contrite way that I didn't buy for a second. "Most of the time he stays iron-faced and above reproach, but Axer can be flashed silver when he wants—bright and reckless—and when he is, he is always unapologetic for it. He doesn't expect for a second that you are going to maintain a low profile. All of his plans take into account that you will go as barmy as Cam expects you to."

I stared mutely at him.

"And Axer has plans upon plans for that insanity. However, Cam, Lox, and I don't want to go down that path, if we can help it. You seem like a fine sort, and all, but I don't want to die for your mistakes."

"I don't want that either," I said tightly.

"Well, Axer has already marked you, so now we all must scramble to make sure when the bomb does go off, it is as contained as we can make it. He'll do everything in his power to maneuver around your control problems. Probably give you all sorts of things he shouldn't," he said, far too casually. "We'd like you to gain control over all of it on your own."

"Working on it."

"But not really enough, no?" He twirled something into existence. It was one of my newer roses. It was leaking magic, almost visibly. "Putting a little extra oomph into things, aren't you?"

Lifen looked bored again, but I knew she wasn't. She was recording all of this for later use. And probably trying to figure out how to get even with Greene for listening in on us the whole time.

"What do you really want?" I asked him. "What is all of this dancing about?"

"Simply to talk," he said easily. "We figured it was time to do a little scoping of our own, without Axer around to stop it."

"What, you want to get to know me?" I asked dubiously.

"Well, of course. And Axer is such a protective bastard," he said with a trace of fondness. "But you can surely understand our cautions. What with how people see and treat him."

Like a god and demon. I knew the feeling.

"Deducing your intent is necessary," he said. "As well as taking action from what we discover."

I blinked, and Lifen's expressionless mien couldn't fully smother the sudden amusement I could feel from her, though she stepped just the smallest bit closer to me at his hint of threat.

"Wait. Are you...are you giving me a shovel talk?" I asked, confused.

Greene's expression brightened. "Ah, what a delightful saying! Very descriptive. Why, you could use the shovel as a burial tool, or as the bludgeoning object. A very apt First Layer solution. So creative without the aid of magic. And a rather messy cleanup without that aid, which rather adds to the imagery." A shovel magically appeared in his hand in place of his cane and he gave it a considering glance. "And, yes."

Lifen's laughter rang in my head, and I could feel her relaying thoughts among the other streams in our loop, but I noticed she also shifted closer to me, just in case.

As much as I was stupefied by Greene's words, my flight response wasn't buying that I would get bludgeoned in full view of campus, so what must have been a bewildered expression made me frown dubiously.

"What about Ramirez? You only mentioned the three of you. How does he fit into all of this?"

He waved the hand holding the shovel. "We'd all follow Axer to hell, but Ram would stay with the devil—take Ax's place—if Axer got caught. He won't interfere with anything Axer wants to do. And the shovel talk, as you call it—well, he wouldn't bother. He'd just slit your throat in the night," he said pleasantly.

Lifen gave a sharklike smile. "It's a good thing that Ren isn't alone in the dark then, isn't it?"

"Mmmm," he agreed. "That is a good thing. A point in her favor. Do look over the bauble. I will see you both Thursday. It has been a *pleasure.*" He gave a charming smile and bow, then split from us with a parting gesture of gentlemanly magic.

Camille and Lox were standing at a nearby arch, waiting for him. Camille's stare, focused on me, was no less chilly than it had been the day before. A group of other combat mages stood a little apart from them.

The others didn't hide their stares either. But that same watchfulness and wariness that had been there before Bloody Tuesday—the "why did Axer pick her" type—had magnified into something far more complex.

It was no longer a question of why he had picked me to act as his campus scout. Actions and events that had slipped by the public at large had not slipped by the combat mages. They knew exactly what I was capable of. What they were going to do about it was the question they seemed to be wrestling with.

Camille, Lox, and Greene seemed to have their own plans for that.

Lifen steered me toward another arch.

"That was the weirdest thing in a week full of them," I reflected.

"It was definitely an unexpected start to the evening," Lifen agreed dryly, rolling the device Greene had given her out of the handkerchief and between her fingers, no doubt wondering if it was adequate compensation for Greene listening to our private conversation the whole time. Lifen could be just as vindictive as the other Bandits in meting out revenge.

Chapter Seventeen

"I can't believe Greene gave me the start of an 'if you hurt him' speech." I shook my head. "So weird. I thought friends only did that when people started dating?"

Lifen's face pinched as she looked at me, gaze searching. Then she chortled—laughing in a way that I hadn't thought taciturn Lifen Chen capable. She wiped at one eye and patted me on the shoulder. "Thanks, Crown."

I sighed. "Whatever. So what are we going to do about this bonding proposition thing?" I waved at the device. "They can't really want to bond themselves with us, even for an afternoon. I don't buy it."

"Oh, there are tricks here, for sure." She smiled. "But tricks are our domain."

"Great." I sighed again. The last thing I wanted to do was hook myself to Camille Straught.

She eyed me. "You need to figure out what Alexander Dare has done to get them running scared."

"Be friends with me?"

"That is a bad thing," she conceded.

"Hey!"

"But it does give perks, like seeing what it takes to terrify a combat mage."

Chapter Eighteen

SHIFTING

I WAS FLIPPING through mental connections—trying to gain better control, prove that I was not completely incompetent, and determine how to keep the future "Greene's" of the world from eavesdropping, when my hindbrain latched onto "eavesdropping" and I whooshed into a connection without express consent.

The voices turned crisp and clear.

"I'm not using the debts for that," Trick said, but in a far different mental voice than I was used to with him. This one was conciliatory in tone —but not like the feigned one he affected for Liv and Saf, where he was playing at the role—this was a true yielding to a higher position of power. "I will use them, but for campus gains. It would do us little good to be seen as the purveyors of the disaster. For people to think that *we* were the ones who set up the attack."

Trick, who had a well-deserved reputation for capriciousness, was all business here.

"Patrick—" came the threatening response.

"You know the public will do so, Father. Simon has agreed with me."

"Your brother has a soft spot for you."

"But not a blind spot."

There was silence, then, "Fine, handle them your way, but you will give ten percent of the results, as expected."

"Of course. Good evening, Father."

Patrick disconnected the call to his father and twisted the connection to me in pain. "Crown."

"Sorry...I don't know how this happened," I said, standing on my tippy toes, alone in my room, but as if someone had twisted my ear in their hand, then pulled upward.

Chapter Eighteen

"You eavesdropped on my secure line," he said, far too placidly.

"Seems to be the case," I said, trying to vainly control my magic into not attacking him remotely. I could feel my shields reaching out mental tentacles to grab him in his room.

He dropped the magic. "You are going to make Dagfinn go bald."

"Sorry. Seriously. I don't know—"

"I know, Crown," he said, sounding tired. "Come by later."

I took Olivia with me. Just in case.

"My father wants me to use the debts we've been collecting across campus for...other things," he said, once we were all inside the wards.

Uneasy about what that might mean, I took solace in the fact that it had sounded like Patrick wasn't going to do that. "But you won't." It wasn't a question.

Olivia looked at me. "How do you know?"

"Because of what he was saying."

He laughed, but it only held half its usual humor. "You are breaking us, Crown. Trying to make us into good people."

I stared at him. "I'm a delinquent."

"A delinquent who *cares*." He looked tired. "It's a contagious disease, it seems."

Back in our room, and after viewing a full memory retrieval of the events, Olivia explained that the conversation I overheard was Patrick defying his father and saying that the debts he had been collecting on behalf of the Bloody Tuesday aftermath would *not* go to Dominic O'Leary.

Many of the students at Excelsine had powerful parents—parents who could be influenced by their children's debts to a mobster who *wanted* laws passed or events buried.

Invaluable debts, really—like Vitus Vorlav's—that could be cashed in terribly at some point.

Olivia smiled, obviously of a different perspective. "Patrick is brilliant, if he uses the debts for campus. Every person here who has their debt going back to the community will trust Patrick, at least a little bit. If they need to deal with an O'Leary in the future, they'll deal with him. It will benefit him in untold ways."

I nodded along, rubbing my neck absently, used to Olivia's more Machiavellian way of looking at things. I had noticed the new respect Trick and Saf were getting—not just the fearful respect they used to, but a deeper kind. Win-win, as far as I was concerned.

Olivia sighed. "You are hopeless," she said, reading my unspoken response and my lack of interest in any political plotting.

I nodded again. "I think I'm okay with that. Can you imagine if I got scarier? Campus wouldn't survive."

* Shifting *
~*~

By the time night fell, everyone connected to us knew the spell on Olivia had been removed. The knowledge brought with it a strange comfort of safety—of being cocooned on campus until exams. What could go wrong with the Department banned from campus and the students secured inside?

"Layer shifts, layer shifts, layer shifts!!" Will said eagerly, laying out all of his vast materials.

Delia rolled her eyes and spelled a pillow behind her on my bed, takeout box in hand. "Here we go."

Will, Mike, Olivia, and Neph lounged across the other spaces in our room as we all ate and chatted over cafeteria takeout boxes, taking advantage of some well-earned lethargy.

There was something weird about being in our room, though. I looked out the window, frowned, and scooted from my bed, switching with Mike to claim the floor spot next to it. That didn't seem to help, though. I felt a little worse even. Maybe I was just getting too used to being elsewhere?

"This is the last full moon before they start." Will bobbed a bit in his chair as he stabbed something in his container that looked like chicken—if chicken meat came in green.

Delia looked at him critically. "I confess that I thought you'd be crazed before this point. You surpassed my expectations."

"Crazed? Crazed? This is the *best time of year.*"

Will had been talking about entering the Layer Shift Festival since I'd met him. I hadn't had the first clue what a shift was back then.

Having gotten up close and personal with magic backlashes since, I was a little more clued in. Exhilarating and terrifying, in a land of surreal existence like the Third Layer backlashes *fit.* I wondered how it would work here in the Second when the Department loosened the controls and let the layer work itself out on its own. It was a scheduled period between the fourth and fifth full moons of each year, so I was expecting something pretty anti-climactic.

"If you use your project to skim the mageball team's clothes, I need you to give me advanced warning so I can be there," Delia said, stirring her food, and looking at Mike from beneath her long lashes.

Mike, who played the intramural sport, leered.

Olivia pretended to gag as she flipped a page in her spell book, discarded container already on her desk.

"No, just a few last tweaks on the skimmer. It's time to start on some *new* ideas." Will rubbed his hands together. "Ren, notebook."

I promptly flipped one out, pen in hand.

"Right," Delia said, looking between us. "Crown cornered the market on crazed for the past few weeks, so you had to take a backseat. My estimate was obstructed. Welcome home, Tasky."

"We'll get early data, test some hypotheses, secure a path...never waste shift season," Will said seriously, pointing at me and ignoring Delia completely. "It's the most important season for scientists."

I nodded in agreement—trying not to hear what Delia muttered to Mike —and Will chugged full steam ahead. "First, we want to think about *facets*. Then *duplicates*."

I sketched notes with one hand while I ate with my other. Neph, sitting between us, occasionally pulled the magic from one of my notes to another, in case I missed anything while Will was talking too fast. The recording enchantment took care of most of the dictation, but the real key when taking notes for a person who went off tangent so frequently was in the *organization* of those notes.

"And that one makes me think about air. No, *steam*. You know, we could use steam for the other thing, too, Ren. And, hey, what about graphene for that. No, the *pads*. We could graphene the—"

I pulled his second-to-last sentence into the little word whirlpool I'd drawn in the lower right, and his last sentence into the wordpool I'd drawn mid-left of the page. The wordpools could be enlarged so just their own contents showed, or they could all be spiderwebbed to show the overlap between concepts, as the paper had a timestamp feature on it to track mental brainstorming progression.

"We can try three of those on the ant farm mobile circuit," he said enthusiastically.

I tapped my lips with the pencil. I didn't have a wordpool for ant farms. I started sketching one.

"Seriously?" Delia demanded, arms crossed and no longer lounging. "That's the tenth idea you've spouted for testing. How many motherloving projects do you have lined up, Tasky?"

"All ten are viable," he said defensively.

"Yeah. I have like three *hundred* viable project ideas," Delia said in a deadpan voice. "That doesn't mean I have enough hours in the day to do anything about them."

"Well, I'm most excited about the first three," he conceded. "So we'll spend two hours a day on each of those next term, and six hours on testing the pad."

Delia's eyes narrowed, then her expression went entirely too relaxed. "Are you and Ren taking classes too?" she asked innocently.

Olivia gave a little twitch in the corner.

"Three. But they all credit with Shift projects, so that should only add a few hours a day."

"Plus sleeping," Delia said, winding magic around her finger as if she wasn't winding up someone else in the room. Olivia's head had lifted and she was now glaring at Will.

"Sleep is for *after* the fifth moon," Will said to me.

I nodded, but then caught Olivia's scowl and immediately started to slowly shake my head, palms out.

"What does that mean?" Will asked, brows furrowed, as he tried to sort my action into something concrete. "Ten hours of sleep a week?"

Neph sighed and nudged him. He looked around and immediately straightened.

"Oh! Sleep. Yeah. We'll sleep." He shot a furtive look in my direction. I furtively returned it.

Mike rolled his eyes. "Convincing. I'm not letting you skim people's clothes off after this term," he warned as he crumpled up his wrapper and threw it into the chute. "Not that I don't love your results, but I still haven't found half of my clothes from last term. Let's make sure your next few ideas are nudity-free ones, yes?"

Delia smirked and opened her mouth.

Olivia held up a finger, never breaking the glare she had concentrated on Will. "Peoples, no."

"Just because you don't want to see Bessfort in the altogether—"

"I really do not."

"—doesn't mean that all of us won't appreciate the sight."

Mike fluttered his eyelashes at Delia. "I'm shocked and flustered. Me? You want to see my—"

"*No,*" Olivia stressed, still glaring.

"—manly calves?"

"So manly," Delia agreed.

"William," Olivia said warningly.

"Lots of sleep!"

"Right," Delia snorted. "But speaking of manly, I heard you had quite the afternoon, Ren," Delia said, turning her riling in another direction.

"Very manly," I agreed.

Delia leaned in. "Was Lifen really flirting with Elias Greene?"

"Lifen Chen?" Will looked so disturbed that he missed his food container, stabbing his knee with his fork. "Ow, ow, ow. Flirting?"

Mike rolled his eyes. "You'd flirt with Greene too, if you thought he'd give you his tech."

Will looked thoughtful. "I don't think anyone would be surprised by that, though."

"They flirted for like two thirds of the time we were out there. It was a nightmare. Greene was listening in on us the whole time, too—he hooked some spell into her. Then he got all weird about Axer and said they want to do some sort of binding with all of us."

"No," Olivia said firmly and immediately, making a note of something in her book.

The rest of them, though, sat in gobsmacked silence. Neph's entire body had stiffened.

"That's what Li meant then," Delia murmured in some recollection, shaking her head.

Will opened his mouth, but nothing emerged. He closed it, opened it, and then tried again. "Who?"

"Axer's team," I said, gaze drifting back to Neph in question. But she was once more handling the streams of calm and comfort in the room. She smiled at me as if nothing was amiss. Brow furrowed, I looked back at the others.

Will was still staring, and Mike looked as if he was tiredly reconsidering his place in the universe. I could see Delia look at Mike in the way that meant the two of them were carrying on a conversation apart from the rest of us.

"Axer Dare's team wants to do a binding...with us?" Will asked.

A quick long distance chat with Axer had gotten me nowhere. He had displayed no surprise at the item Greene had given Lifen, and had showed only the smallest change in expression when I hinted that his friends thought I might harm him.

In response to all of it, he had maneuvered me around his workroom and opened a view on one wall that allowed me to see all of the breathtaking sights he was experiencing on their victory tour across the layers. His deep, soothing voice made me forget all about his weird friends.

He'd deliberately distracted me.

Drawing myself back to the here and now I said, "Greene gave Lifen some illegal device for doing it. Lifen is setting up a meeting over at Trick and Saf's this weekend to look it over and discuss options."

"No," Olivia said, flipping a page.

Will nodded slowly. "I'll be there."

"You will not, because there will be no meeting," Olivia said without looking up.

Will never looked away from me. "You do know what a binding could mean, right?"

"Not a clue."

"Good, because you *aren't doing it*," Olivia stressed.

"Lots of horsepower," Will said. "*Lots*. And during *shift season*, we could totally use that on some of our projects." His voice picked up his excitement. "We can talk about it when we meet to complete the notes on

Project #2."

I shrugged. "Okay. I'll draft at Bellacia's. I can meet you at the normal time. I'll start on project #3 while you spec #4, then we can go over #5 while—"

"There will be no binding and Ren is not helping with all of your projects like some glorified assistant," Olivia said, glaring at Will.

"Er, she—"

"I want to help with his projects," I assured Olivia.

"You are too helpful, and I hate when Leandred is right," she muttered. "No binding, and you can help William with *two* projects."

"But—"

"Listen to Price, Ren," Delia said, ignoring the way Olivia blinked at her. Olivia was still getting used to Delia agreeing with her on *anything*. "We need to go over the exchange parameters, at the very least. Agree to nothing with the combat mages. And don't think I didn't see you sketch out a design for the headwear I told you about earlier or the paper snow cone for Mike. All of us will take up your hours for the next three months, if you let us."

"*William?*" Olivia intoned deliberately.

"Of course, of course. Two projects." He gave me a furtive look, which I returned with a slow nod.

Neph batted both of us across the tops of our heads.

~*~

At Bellacia's, I rubbed my chest and drew out a series of diagrams, trying to figure out the exact nature of how the magic could be collected on Will's Project #3, while mulling how to get Olivia to let me help her with the Department spell. She'd run into an issue with it and had been angrily flipping pages when I left, muttering about Patrick wanting to add a reverse enchantment and how it was killing her.

I was happy the boys were helping, but I felt like *I* should be doing something too.

As always, news feeds were continuously streaming around the walls of Bellacia's living room, reporting all the best "Bailey Bits." While the victory tour was still big news, media attention had started to switch to the next big thing, and there were a number of reports on pre-Festival events— wondering what wild or wonderful new bits of tech might be unleashed this year.

The normal murmurs of unrest littered the edges of the feeds as well— terrorist plots, strange magical blips, and general feelings of unease.

"Shelle Fanning reported that tech and security innovation will be key this year," a reporter said. The background switched to a large media event.

Feet kicked up over the arm of a chair I'd conjured, sketchbook in my lap, I ignored the murderous looks I could feel from Inessa. Hey, if I was going to be forced to be here a few hours each day until Axer returned and we all went back to normal, then I was going to make myself at home.

I felt worse, though, the more time I spent with Inessa in the room—as if her murderous glares were physically affecting me.

Shelle Fanning, the mage in charge of media and publicity at the Department was speaking in an upbeat tone on the main feed. "We are looking forward to all the wonderful things the scientific communities in our layer have developed. We are expecting a great season. And every country is working together to make sure we have the best festival yet."

The Department proxy was on her A-game, deliberately ignoring any questions about anything other than those things that were for the good of the layer. Her communications all came across as optimistic and forward-thinking.

"Your freedom is fleeting," a silky voice said from a report on the side. "Enjoy it while you can, Ren Crown."

I gripped my sketchbook and pulled my legs down, looking around the room. Inessa sneered at me, but immediately went back to her book. There was nothing that indicated she'd heard the voice.

"That's right," the voice cooed. "It's only you. Better that you come to me. I won't have to hurt your friends that way."

Inessa kept reading, the magic around her unchanging.

I took deep breaths. There was no way Stavros was in the room. I carefully searched the feeds on the walls, isolating and dismissing each before moving to the next.

"We are promoting the 3 P's this year," Shelle Fanning said on the main feed, smiling at a question from the media audience that was tiled around the screen like a virtual auditorium. "Progress. Protection. Process. They are intrinsic to our stability and advancement. We don't want to progress too quickly. We don't want to process too much. We must be careful with our rights. Care and thought should go into each step."

Lovely talking points. Taken alone, the Department sounded like a great institution of protection and progress.

"And that is why you can't and won't destroy us, Origin Mage," the voice said, and a flash of Stavros' face led me to a sliver of a feed on the eastern wall. "There are hundreds of thousands working here that believe every word she speaks."

Shelle Fanning continued talking in the other feed—an optimistic force to be reckoned with. She portrayed the "can do everything" sort of woman who seemed to define everything that women were supposed to strive for: career, family, country, home. She successfully juggled multiple roles singlehandedly, while plastering a smile on her face.

* Shifting *

The only thing she seemed to be trying to hide behind that smile was *exhaustion*. I could buy that this woman believed everything she said.

"You don't believe it," I murmured to the voice.

Inessa looked up and sneered at me, as if she thought I was speaking to her. "You *would* think we should be stripped of our given rights and stability."

I shook my head and rubbed my chest.

How someone could justify thinking well of the Department when surrounded by people like Stavros and Helen and the praetorians, I didn't know. But, then, if you didn't know Helen Price was an evil woman, she came across as a coolly competent one. She was the epitome of the cold, intelligent decision-maker on the outside. Her coldness just spawned from her heart.

But the Stavros-like voice wasn't wrong, not everyone in the Department could be evil. The working Joe's, the everyday citizens who thought they were doing right, the people who believed in the 3 P's would never accept that the organization they were working for or believed in would ever work against their aims.

I had just been unfortunate enough to experience some of the Department's loveliest charms up close and personally.

"Get *closer*," the voice said.

There. That one. I threw a slice of magic at it, and the feed snapped. I breathed deeply, feeling like my airways had reactivated, and let my head drop back.

"That was my open link to my father." Inessa grabbed for the ends of the magic and tied them back together, restarting it. There was a noticeable absence in the line this time, though, like a redialed number that hadn't yet recaptured a virus.

"Are you going to destroy each magic in our rooms, one by one?" Inessa demanded. "Start small and work your way up to everything we've built?"

The Department's loveliest charms...shared by Inessa Norrissing.

"I plan to destroy nothing." I shakily pulled my sketchbook back into place and tried to figure out where to restart my drawing, thoughts muddled by adrenaline. "I'll take that one out again, though, if it threatens me further."

"You are disturbed. There was nothing even on it. The thing that *will* be on it is the evidence against you that Daddy's troops are currently searching for in Corpus Sun. You should be in prison," she said bitterly.

I stared at the notes I had started for the Department spell. They blurred in my view.

"Bella thinks you useful," Inessa said, when I didn't respond. "But you are rotten."

I cocked my head toward the ceiling and let my head drop back, feeling weary. "A rotten fruit with a worm at its core?" I tapped my pencil against my lips. "What if it's a magical worm? What if it's eating the rot and replacing it with something fresh and tasty."

"This is not a joke."

"No," I conceded, but sketched the idea anyway. "I don't know what you want me to say, though. I definitely do not fancy prison or being leashed by a psychopath."

"You have no idea of what you speak."

"Perhaps not. Do you?" I examined her. "What do you think Enton Stavros plans to do with all the power he is consolidating?"

"Something that won't end this world like *you* are going to do."

I poked my pencil in her direction and watched her flinch. "Newsflash, Magicist. We are all capable of destruction or peace."

"You—"

"Have less ability than you do, probably, on how to strike the government where it hurts. Sure, rare powers allow for rare events, but the terrorists and Department are doing a mighty fine job of taking out plenty of settlements and towns with normal everyday means."

I wondered where the magic went. What did they do with it? Knowing the Department—just thinking on what they had done at Top Circle on Bloody Tuesday—they probably sucked the magic out with each blow.

I wondered if anyone had ever cataloged how much magic had been in place immediately after the destruction of the Third Layer, then referenced it against present levels. Would the amounts be the same?

Surely the terrorists had that data. I looked at the room's ticker tape for the answer. Data and figures scrolled.

The Third Layer categorically maintained that they had less—and that their levels were steadily decreasing every year. The Second Layer denied this in every publication, only putting in a caveat that *if* their levels were decreasing, it was because the Third Layer hadn't put in proper safeguards and safety nets against leakage. The Fourth Layer couldn't be arsed to respond with anything other than various politically worded forms of, "Touch our magic and die, Second and Third Layer Scum."

"Trying to figure out how to crush our society, you feral *shasta*?"

"Nice. Resorting to slurs. I think that means you lose the argument." I watched the ticker turn into debate rules and nodded. "Aren't you on the debate team?"

Inessa threw a sickly bolt of yellow at me.

With academic curiosity, I watched it absorb into my outer shield, then regather into a ball and propel itself back at her.

Inessa flew heels over head into the wall. Bellacia swanned into the room as her enraged roommate was trying to de-pretzel herself in order to launch another attack. Peters appeared in the hall through the still open door.

"Miss Norrissing?"

"It's her," Inessa raged, spitting, and pointing at me. "She's to blame."

"Miss Norrissing," Peters said severely. "You are being charged with a Level Two, on account of a Level Five attack on another student. This lists Miss Crown as the one attacked."

"She's not a student. She's a *monster*."

"You aren't helping yourself, Miss Norrissing."

"You are on her side. She's bewitched you. All of you."

"I assure you, that isn't the case," Peters said, somewhat drily.

I was starting to kind of like him.

"She's a monster, an Origin Mage. Why can't anyone just *say it*? She's going to kill us all."

"Miss Norriss—"

All at once, magic weirdly skittered over my skin. I wiped a hand along my arm, trying to get rid of the phantom feeling, then headlines pulsed around the room with a screeching sound.

Bellacia skidded to the wall and pulled out no less than twelve streams, actively searching through them. Twelve more, than twelve again, the streams built upon each other, creating a geometric monstrosity of spelled news.

Headlines began to poor out of the combined streams, headlines screaming to be read.

Feral Awakening! Major Landmark Destroyed.
Destruction Recorded Across Three Layers
Is This the Magical Apocalypse?
Origin Magic Will Destroy Us All
Five Things You Can Do NOW to Save Yourself

Bellacia's headlines changed every moment with each new piece of data added, updating each news item to make it more relevant, more compelling.

And then the visuals began to appear: A recording spell of a woman smiling and waving in front of the landmark Faruza Bridge just before it exploded behind her; a family hunching over as rubble and shrieking, tentacled monsters—blown from the water—rained upon them; and old footage of a "National Treasure" sign being erected in front of the bridge years ago.

Inessa wailed, loud and distressed. I jerked at the sound. People were shouting in the open hallway where Peters still stood, eyes wide on the broadcast.

Behind him, I saw Constantine leaning against the opposite wall. He looked bored, but his eyes were tracking what was happening through the open doorway.

Inessa pointed wildly at me, speaking to the others. "There will be more of this. Feral Awakenings are a *sign*. They are one of the *signs*. She's going to kill us all." Ferocity lit in Inessa's eyes and Peters' tablet shrilly beeped as if it read something on her, some intention, and was already listing a punishment if she went through with it.

Her wild gaze narrowed in on me, like lightning pinpointing a target in a savage storm. "Unless I kill her first." She lunged for me.

She didn't get a whole step before Peters neutralized her, freezing her mid-lunge in a physically impossible position without the aid of magic. But it was if he'd frozen the whole tableau. All of us stood in shocked silence. Constantine broke it as he relaxed back against the wall in the corridor—which meant he'd been in previous motion.

Everyone stared at Inessa, who suddenly started screaming.

I clapped my sketchbook shut. "And that's my cue."

I hurried from the room, and Constantine easily kept pace with me until we reached his suite.

Olivia, Neph, and Will skidded inside, eyes wide, five minutes later.

So much for some well-earned lethargy.

Chapter Nineteen

FERAL DREAMS

MY DREAMSPACE unfolded into a pearl dome under the stars.

Axer was already there. He rose as I appeared. "Are you okay?"

"No. Can't say today ended in the way I thought it would."

Image upon memory image scrolled in the paintings that were displayed on the walls. One held my memories of Constantine plotting revenge against Inessa—easily deduced as his representation by the assassins dispatching her in various creative ways and wearing insignias in the same violet shade of one of the connection threads I shared with him. There was another image, of Con trying to reassure me in his normal, superior way—talking about disregarding what the insects thought, and behind him those symbolic insects were crushed and wiped into swirls of red.

Another painting depicted Olivia trying to make me practice things that would take my mind off the news, while alternately plotting Inessa's downfall as well, something she easily dredged up the motivation for.

In a different painting Neph and Will were reassuring me. Other images were of things and people that had grabbed my attention.

Like the newscasts... the animated paintings were shifting as my mind tried to work out different puzzles.

"The...feral disaster made it hard to fall asleep," I said with difficulty.

The news had quickly made the circuit and induced a wave of uncertainty that the media and Department had capitalized on. I had *felt* it in the community magic at school—the ripple of unease.

The feral Awakening in the First Layer had happened in the same earth spot as the Faruza Bridge in the Second Layer and a barren area of Outlaw Territory in the Third, triggering the destruction across the layers.

Will had said it happened sometimes. His painting spoke the same apologetic words that he had told me earlier, "Feral Awakenings can act like bombs. Pinpointed all in one spot, you know? The destruction ripples out."

Chapter Nineteen

Even in memory he looked anxious, until finally, Neph stepped into his dream frame to reassure us both.

Raphael had made more than one "blown up" reference during my Awakening, so it wasn't a complete surprise. But it filled me with sadness. Someone like me, like Christian—with no idea what was going on—had suddenly been filled with way too much power, and no idea how to use it.

Axer pulled his thumb slowly along my forehead. It lessened the tension I hadn't realized I had been holding. "Bad memories?" he asked softly.

"Yes." Of anyone, he was the one who would understand my memories of Christian's Awakening.

A feral mage had died today. But at least...at least the mage hadn't been hunted.

"Those three men who attacked my brother...they are in jail, right?" I asked, somewhat desperately.

He rubbed his thumb along my cheek, cradling the side of my face. "We processed them immediately. Awakening thieves are the worst of scum. There is no judicial lag for that type of crime."

I closed my eyes. The feral mage still might have been terrified when his power sparked, but hopefully... Hopefully, there had been a little awe mixed in. I remembered looking at Christian's fingers sparking like lightning. It had been an amazing moment.

I sent out a small entreaty into the dreamworld for that to have been what the feral experienced—that the awe of Awakening had engulfed any sense of fear.

Axer looked around the rapidly shifting art of the dreamscape. "Come. We'll go somewhere else."

I automatically looked to the shadows stretching across the dreamglass —their tendrils winding around it, always looking for cracks to enter.

"They will follow," I said.

Axer barely spared the shadows a glance as he smiled at me. "They can't follow where we are going."

Axer could hold his own against anyone, but I didn't want to initiate a fight between the four of us, even in dreams. Raphael, Kaine, Axer, and me? We might as well be The Four Horsemen of the Apocalypse.

Axer pinched one edge of the dream and drew it inward toward the other edge, then set it whirling. It twisted the dream like an hourglass made of paper with us inside.

"I promised I wouldn't leave my dreams," I said, watching the dream twist with ill-concealed curiosity. I really wanted to know what he was doing, but I'd made a promise not to leave to everyone who knew about Raphael.

"Don't think of it as *leaving*." Axer winked at me and stepped from one twist to the other, as if it was a normal thing to do, his body twisting with the motion into a space that wasn't two-dimensional, or three.

And me? Of course I followed.

He twisted the dreamscape again and we stepped, once, then twice, then a dozen twists, until one winding triangle was the one he wanted. "Here."

The dream untwisted, and it felt like the same dream at its base, but everything looked different—and the cares and fears I had been carrying melted away, one at a time with each twist.

"How did you do that?" I asked, automatically stepping onto the path the dream had stretched before me, going over what I had just seen in my mind and trying to figure out how I could do it in the future.

"I have a cousin who is naturally talented in dream walking and dream taming, and also in making talismans. That"—he pointed to the dragon that had appeared on me as it was in the real world—gripped in my hand against my chest—"is one of them, and I have one connected to it."

"Do you need the talisman?" I couldn't see one on him, but that didn't mean much. Axer was adept at hiding whatever he wanted. "Can you do it without?"

"Yes. Like any skill, dream manipulation becomes easier with repetition, especially if another dreamer gives you such unfettered access. Are you trying to figure out how to do it without me?"

"Yes," I admitted.

He smiled. "The worlds you will break and create... Come."

He parted a curtain of ivy and I followed him into a magical grove. The ivy rustled as it fluttered back into place, screening us from any outside eyes. A small waterfall of silver and gold cascaded over colorful rock into a pond, kicking up foam. Fish soared over the foam in small arcs.

Starlight fireflies flew through the air, lighting upon my fingertips and shoulders. Iridescent flashes of light and texture reflected from the dark sky above and off the curious, incandescent airborne creatures into the pond. It was like watching a reflected meteor shower in crystal clear waters.

I could feel lingering worries captured in the paintings of my mind numbing with each traced light. Not disappearing, but creating distance.

"Do you like it?" he asked, smiling as I knelt at the edge of the water and trailed my fingers along the surface, blurring the lines and pulsing waves of light outward. Iridescent fish darted under the surface, following each motion of my hand as if they were the ones mesmerized.

"Yes." Axer fit the whole tableaux so well, too—magical, beautiful, and with an edge of danger that I nevertheless knew would never hurt me. "I wish it existed outside of your mind."

Like so many things, if *only*. If only I had time to create everything that I wanted to make, or to fix everything that needed to be fixed.

Chapter Nineteen

"It does exist," he said, far too easily, prodding one of the pods in the ivy. A large brilliant flower in blues and greens bloomed outward. "This is an exact replica of one of the waterfall groves on our island."

I shook my head, but smiled as I watched him coax open another flower. The fish darted around my fingertips, brushing ever so gently against my skin. "Only you would have more than one waterfall. How do you choose which to visit when you have so many choices?"

His gaze met and held mine. "There is only one for me."

Emotions rippled through me, and even in a dream, I could feel magic tingling in my fingers, clutching the dragon in his room, in his bed.

A flower opened behind him, and I switched my focus to it, unable to maintain his electric gaze. The flower was different from the others. Protruding from its center were thin vials instead of stamens.

"That's a strange looking bloom."

Complicated emotions flickered across his face as he followed my line of sight—his sigh caught in a non-existent breeze. He withdrew one of the vials and held it in his fingers, staring at it for too long without saying anything.

"Are you okay? What is it?"

"It's a chance." His fingers tightened. "A gamble. A risk."

He pulled a stirring rod from the mass of vines.

They didn't look like the man-eating vine, but I had to ask. "Are those —"

He looked amused. "No. Maybe someday, though, if they had a tender living there." His words were easy but something in his tone was not.

I looked around, like he always did in my dreams, trying to figure out what he meant, but nothing seemed to translate. The ivy was tickling my feet, reaching soft petaled fingers outward, and the fireflies were hovering, as if trying to grow closer.

"You need a gardener?"

He smiled, clearly amused and radiating *fondness*. One of the fireflies flew around his head, then lit onto my shoulder, looking at me expectantly.

"I don't know what you eat," I told it.

Axer dipped the rod into the water, and the liquid swirled clear and opalescent at the turns of the stick to form a yin-yang of mixed, creamy light.

"Beautiful," he said.

He lifted the rod and deftly let the liquid slide from the tip into the vial. As the liquid filled the vessel, the vial bulged like blown glass. It filled, then dropped into the pond, sealing its own end like a self-sealing balloon to form a sphere, a bright orb bobbing along its surface. The orb drifted over to a reed-protected spot on the opposite bank, gently encapsulated in its own brilliance, where it joined two more.

Odd, I hadn't seen them there before.

"What are they?"

"Merely a provision."

"In case of what?"

"Need." The edges of his eyes were tight.

I stared at the globes then at the pond sparkling with life. "We should fill more, then."

He rose and steered me away. "No, one draw is easily overlooked and replaced. Come, I have another place to show you. It has the best dream food."

It did. It also had dragons you could fly spirals on, and underwater caves with Atlantean-like treasures that one could take a lifetime to explore.

There were dreams of puzzles and puzzle boxes that were diabolical to unlock. Axer coaxed me into solving what must have been two dozen of them.

But we didn't chase a single monster—sometimes we didn't do much of anything at all, sitting in companionable silence—and I didn't feel a second of boredom.

When Axer returned me back to my dreamscape, though, I couldn't help but look at the ever present shadows squirming along the base of the glass. They were smiling.

Chapter Twenty

TAKING CONTROL

THE NEXT MORNING, I woke with Constantine and Olivia. We bickered about plans for the day as we brushed our teeth.

"Murder and mayhem."

"Forgiveness and order," I countered.

"You can't even say that last one with a straight face," Constantine said to me, unimpressed, buttoning up his coat as he headed for his eight o'clock. "The day I see you dictating *order,* is the day the world ends."

"I'll show you the end of the world," I shouted after him.

Two people shrieked in terror down the hall. I hurriedly shut the door, then pressed my back against the wood as if that would somehow hide me further.

"Nice job," Olivia said sourly, lifting a book. Constantine's amusement overflowed our connection, even as he walked away.

"It's going to be a great day," I said brightly. Then I looked at the headlines—still full of the "feral disaster" and my smile slipped.

Axer's confirmation about the Awakening thieves being in jail hadn't settled me the way I'd been hoping. He had done a great job in distracting me again, though—I had meant to ask about what his group wanted, as well. The dream escape had been lovely, but in the light of day, there was a lot I needed to do.

What usually happened to the magic in an Awakening? Raphael had taken mine, but even mages who Awakened before sixteen—non-feral mages—had Awakenings. Had all the feral's magic gone to the destruction itself?

To Olivia's consternation, I set up a board with everything I could find about Awakenings, the Faruza destruction, and the feral that had died.

Eighteen. Brown hair, brown eyes. Glasses in some pictures, contacts in others. Liked track and soccer, and books about magic. The latter was especially gut wrenching. Two siblings. Seemed to have a pretty normal existence—nothing too strange, no obvious warning signs.

The Department alarm had gone off five seconds before the explosion —the grid that monitored the First Layer for magic use had issued an alert, but it hadn't been in enough time to mount any sort of response that could have saved him.

The explosive nature of an Awakening after age sixteen had rippled through the layers.

I touched his graduation photo—the one I had scraped from newscasts —the one he or his parents had likely submitted, or were planning to submit, to the yearbook. Christian and I had gotten ours taken the previous summer. My parents must have received them by now.

I cringed. Sadness and pain rolled through me at the thought of my parents opening the albums showcasing our smiles, hopes, and dreams— half of which would never be realized.

This boy's parents and siblings were just starting that hideous journey. Just like the relatives of the Excelsine students who would never again walk the campus paths.

Something rumbled in the distance.

Why didn't you save me?

My fingers pinched the graduation photo, and suddenly my brother's face superimposed itself over the top, then a moving picture of my parents opening a photo album full of his images appeared on top of that.

I dropped the picture and ran from the room. Even Olivia calling after me didn't make me pause.

A faceless person I passed in the hall chuckled in a voice that sounded far too much like the one from Inessa's wall.

I barely waited for Greyskull to acknowledge me before barreling inside. Olivia, following at my heels, spilled into his office behind me.

"Flowers?" I asked a little desperately.

He studied me for a moment, then tipped his head, dark eyes going soft. "Of course, Ren." He closed the large paper book he was reading, pressing it back into flat, electronic form.

"You're busy," I said, cringing a bit, and actually taking a moment to sort through my panic.

"No. Never for this." He pulled up the little table where we had worked before. The look on his face said he knew. He understood.

"What is going on?" Olivia's arms were crossed the way they always were when she didn't know what was happening and didn't like the fact.

"We are going to make some of Ren's flowers. You are welcome to help," he said, with no expectation or judgment.

We had made thousands of roses at this point, so getting started was easy. The amount of magic I wanted to stick inside them was not.

"It's okay, Ren," Grey said softly. "You are working too hard. We can take as long as they need."

They. Yes. I couldn't take the time for me, not yet. But *they*, I could do they.

Olivia frowned as she watched me fumble again, then elbowed me and snatched the magic into her palms. "You are putting too much in, Godzilla."

An unwitting laugh burst from me. We had watched three different Godzilla movies when she'd stayed with me over winter break. She had found them humorous for all the wrong reasons— *"They could use a spell, Ren. Right there. What is wrong with these people?"*

"I'm helping," she said grimly, as if I would say no.

"Okay."

Her expression eased and she nodded firmly, then held out her hand to help me ease the spell into the folds of a rose.

"Does it help?" she asked softly, after we'd been working for a while.

"Yes. Even when sometimes it feels like nothing will."

"Okay," she said quietly. "Okay, Ren." Something firmed in her expression.

We made three hundred roses.

~*~

I felt far better, but on the way to politics class, magic shifted over my skin, like ghostly fingers playing a tune across keys beneath my flesh.

Neph stopped next to me, looking at me curiously.

I felt the blast when it happened. Alerts started issuing all around us seconds later.

"Another feral!" someone said.

"The origin is in First Layer Asia," shouted another.

"Tsunamis wreaking havoc all the way into the Fourth," said a third.

I rubbed my skin, the ghostly fingers playing their tune again, placing blame on me for not being able to do anything. Neph gripped my arms, sending calm through me.

The Bandits were yelling across the armband link and asking whose terrifying mental images had just blasted our communication circuit. Constantine and Olivia had gone straight to the source—me—and were demanding to know what was happening.

I sent reassurance down their threads.

Will took care of the others after a shared look with Neph when we took our seats.

To say that chatter about ferals was at an all-time high in *Layer Politics*

* Taking Control *

101 was an understatement as Professor Harrow fielded questions, even from students who had previously had little to say.

"How can we find ferals faster?"

"What is the current system that is in place?"

"Should we restrict other layers from trying to find them?"

"Professor, sir, are we going to be discussing Origin Mages and Magic?"

Even as one student in a class of a thousand, at that question Harrow looked at me, tapped his chin, then looked back at the student who had asked. "The second to last week of class has always been dedicated to those topics. What has happened in the past and how we use the next Origin Mage. What would it mean to have an Origin Mage in the mix in current events?"

My breath was coming in shorter, more frequent exhalations that I could tell even Neph was having trouble regulating with her calming spells, because Harrow wasn't *answering* anything. He wanted us to *discuss* and *formulate*.

It felt like I was plummeting toward something without knowing how to work my parachute.

I called a little magic light to appear above my head in question, and every gaze turned to me, including those of my wide-eyed friends.

Harrow nodded at me, expression caught between interest and reticence. "Miss Crown?"

"How does the Department find a feral *before* the new mage explodes?"

He considered his answer for a long moment before responding. "They use Origin Magic."

"How? *How* do you use Origin Magic to do it?"

A ripple of communication waved through the room. I didn't care. Everyone had been talking about me for weeks already. The question of *if* I would be discovered was moot; the real question was *when*.

With knowledge of how to use Origin Magic, I could do *much* given time —like find and encapsulate the ferals of the world before they exploded. I could *protect* them. Magic itched against my skin, wanting to unleash and feed the notion.

"It isn't discussed, Miss Crown," Harrow said simply. "The use and manipulation of Origin Magic is state guarded information. As to 'why' that is, that *is* actually on topic for this class." He moved into a more permanently seated position on the desk. "Powerful mages are not trusted in the system of the Second Layer."

Another ripple of communication passed through the lecture hall.

Harrow half-smiled. "At a school of bright, talented mages, this view is always particularly problematic."

He tapped a finger against the desk. "As discussed, partial regulation is

199

sought by some factions. Flat out control by others. A good question to ask is what is the definition of power? Where is the power line drawn?"

He pointed to a boy in the front. "Are you a mage that should be watched?" The boy startled at the attention, knocking a device on his desk to the ground.

"What about you?" He pointed to a girl on the other side of the room, who shrunk down in her seat.

Harrow calmly surveyed his audience. "What about Miss Bailey?"

Bellacia kept one eyebrow arched as she gazed around the room, completely at ease with the regard as she watched the reaction of the crowd.

"Look around you." Harrow indicated the room at large. "Some of the most powerful mages you will ever meet are attending this school with you *right now*. Where do you draw the line on who gets a say, who freely uses magic, and who is a danger to society?"

Bellacia raised a perfectly manicured hand, palm facing away from the audience, her control cuff displayed on her wrist. "Thus our societal agreement."

Harrow nodded and hopped off the desk. He pulled his fingers through the air, calling up diagrams and class bullet points and quotes that hung in the air like marquee signs and set them floating around the room.

"We've talked about this in general terms, especially as it affects the layers and how societal agreements differ between layers and even between and among countries and towns within layers. Social agreements are at the very core of communities, and navigating those contracts are what layer politics is all about."

He hopped back on the desk, holograms floating in the air around him. "But what does it mean for Origin Magic? This magic is the very *essence* of what makes up the fabric of our system, our *existence*. The layers are a magical construct. They can be changed; they can be *destroyed* by the magic that constructed them."

Another ripple of communication ran through the room, this time with an unease that was more familiar.

"Is this something that should be openly allowed to be studied? Origin Magic *can* be learned." He held out a hand to forestall the louder ripple of conversation. "Again, state guarded information on the *how*. But like *any* magic, there are those naturally talented at it—those with the innate ability to manipulate it—and others that, through intense study, can learn it."

Question lights blinked around the room.

"There are five people in the Department who share the duties of seeing to the Origin Magic of the Second Layer, and three at any time who control it. The Triumvirate." He tapped down on a piece of magic, which made all of the question lights above our heads extinguish. "We will get to that. And no, this isn't privileged information; it is just not often shared." He sent a pointedly amused look Bellacia's way.

"We have shared this knowledge," Bellacia said with a smile. "It is not my fault if people aren't listening."

But I knew how she could bury one thing and raise another. I'd seen her do it. The items that she wanted seen were promoted far above, while she carefully buried tidbits that she didn't want to gain attention. Sure, the reports were still *there*, and she could point to them later—"Look, we tried to tell you, look at the date of the article"—but it was a carefully crafted game.

Harrow continued the lecture, aggravatingly touching on *parts* of the information I needed while telling us the rest was either restricted or outside the scope of the class. But I didn't need parts, I needed *wholes*.

After a quick search through the class databases and information grids in a streaming room after the lecture ended, I could see that I wasn't going to find what I needed the sanctioned way, though.

Harrow had confirmed what I had felt during both explosions, however —that Origin Magic *could* be used to identify people who were on the verge of Awakening.

The tricky thing, as Will had said to me once, was the all-or-nothing burst of magic from people over sixteen-years-old when they Awakened—all that pent up energy surging forth.

No one had figured out how to adequately find Awakenings that happened that quickly.

But then, Origin Mages were rare. And when found, they were often not in charge of their own projects or destiny.

I firmed my lips.

Restricted information? Well, if there was no class that could teach me what I needed to know, there were other ways.

It was beyond time I found them.

Chapter Twenty-one

ON ORIGIN

I WENT TO DRAEGER, and since I had to retrieve his cartridge from Dorm One, I accessed him in Axer's workroom.

Draeger bloomed to life, looked around, then frowned.

"I know," I said quickly, flinching. "There are some really outrageous new things in my memories. It's been... Well, the craziness continues unabated."

"I'm reading that, Cadet," he said, a bit grumpily. Draeger was far too controlled to tap his foot, but it sure looked like he wanted to.

I had been kind of hoping for a hug, not ire.

"I'm going to learn how to wield Origin Magic," I blurted.

He looked at the ceiling of the room and blew out a breath. "Finally. The mole knows it's been sticking in your craw for months." He abruptly frowned at something in the corner of the ceiling, squinting his eyes, thick neck jutting toward whatever he was trying to examine.

I didn't care what was in the corner. I could do nothing but stare at him, floored by his words. "You are programmed to be a separate entity. A mentor. I...I thought you would tell me not to. I...I thought you might leave me, if I refused," I said softly.

Draeger switched his gaze to me, examining me, just like a real person might. "Thought I'd try and talk you out of it, did you? I told you before, Cadet. I was created to be what you needed, imbued with a sense of *you* upon creation. And, also, I am a facsimile of Lieutenant Marcus Draeger, who had, what one might call, a loose moral compass when it came to seizing that which opportunity presents."

"But...Origin Magic," I said lamely.

"It is a powerful weapon. No different from other magics, except for the fact that the structure of the magical worlds run on it. The five layers are like a massive five-floored brick building that exclusively houses wood carpenters. Except for you, who are a *mason.*"

My life would have been infinitely easier if I'd been surrounded by oak in this analogy.

Draeger read my expression and shook his head. "The creators wanted to have a system that could not be easily hijacked. They needed stability. The history books say the choice of magic was easy. Origin Mages are creators and tend not to be controllers. They usually don't give two hoots about anything outside of their creations." He tapped his head. "All goes together—the outlook, the interests, and the magic that gets called and transformed. Wielding Origin Magic is really just understanding the set of streams that compose it, and inherently knowing how to manipulate them."

"Can anyone do it then?" Like Harrow had said?

"Bits of it, sure. It's like learning any code. But magic has properties that are still unexplainable. Most mages like to just say they are 'gifted' or skilled in some way. Others try to break magic down and explain why each person might get a different gift. The most common theory is that a person's entire life force combines to create affinities. Some mages skilled in one thing suddenly change later in life to being skilled in something else, due to trauma or circumstance. Some mages just naturally wield certain types of magics. And Origin Magic promotes the least amount of natural users."

"Wielding it is seen as such a bad thing." I could picture the revulsion on Marsgrove and Camille Straught's faces and the gloating in Bellacia's.

"The system is built on it. Many a dark age—and there have been *many* across the layers—happened because of an Origin Mage's tinkering."

That was great.

"Periods of enlightenment, too. Fear not, Cadet! You are made of good, strong fiber."

"Sure," I said without cheer. "That's why I have permanent community service."

"Hijinks! Raccoon feces! The danger lies in getting led astray in your judgment—thinking you are helping the world in some way while listening to insidious voices. And terrible things can be done with powerful mages under a leash. You will almost assuredly never think to take over the world —I'd bet on a turtle-monkey's great-uncle before you—but if you get led or leashed by someone with less than stellar morals..." He shook his head. "End of the world scenarios, Cadet. But if you wanted a philosopher for a mentor, you should have chosen that Zen guy! Gopher pucky! Weak moral fiber. Get your head on straight! You never capitulate!"

He raised a fist as if threatening something in the room.

"Okay." I straightened my shoulders. With Draeger's explicit permission, my last vestiges of doubt fled, and my skin tingled in excitement. "I'm ready. Let's do this."

Chapter Twenty-one

I would learn how to be an Origin Mage and everything that meant.

I stared at Draeger. He stared back at me.

"What, you think I'm going to teach you, Cadet?"

"Yes?"

"What am I going to do—pull it out of my squirrel?" Draeger crossed his arms, and frowned.

"Yes?"

He stared at me.

"No?"

He huffed in agreement.

"Er, then...?"

He pointed at me. "You already know where to start, Cadet. It's right there in your rodent brain."

An image appeared, projected onto the wall. The black-and-white book in the library sat imperiously on the cupola's railing, watching me, even in my vision.

I took a step back and grimaced. I could already imagine everyone yelling at me—their shouts becoming muted as the book ate me, chewing up everything that was Ren.

"But you are my mentor," I tried again. "You are made to read my magic."

"If you wish to proceed as you have been, but with just more awareness of what you are doing, then we'll meditate our squirrel brains out," he grumbled. "But if you want to explore that specific type of magic usage— you need to gain knowledge that neither the original Draeger, the mentor program, nor *you* possess. That irritating Verisetti fellow who spelled you has some knowledge—I can see his magic and how it layers through yours —but he, too, possesses magic outside of my parameters, and reading those defenses gives no more knowledge of what you *can* do, just what it seeks to make sure you *can't*."

Wow, that was *extra* grumpy. Too grumpy for the situation really, since he had fully endorsed my learning plan.

I frowned at him. "What's wrong? You sounded like you wanted me to do this."

He pursed his lips and tilted his bald head away from me.

"Nothing's wrong," he said dismissively.

Grumpy.

I tilted my head as well, to examine him. The magic that made up Draeger's existence, that activated upon me calling him, and formed with the memories—both mine and those contained in the cartridge—was connected to the room in streams of green. He looked broader and bolder in the battle rooms, he was thinner here.

"You don't like it here," I concluded with some surprise.

"Course I don't. Not my homestead," he said gruffly.

"But we work in different rooms in the battle building." I frowned. "I mean I often get a room in the first corridor, but we've moved around a lot."

"Blank slates, Cadet," he boomed.

I looked around, then came to with shocked understanding. "This room is filled with Axer's magic. You don't like his magic."

Draeger had always thought it hilarious when Axer stomped me in the battle rooms.

"Traps and stickiness," he said, lifting his foot as if the floor was covered in tacky glue. "Unnatural ties everywhere on you. And there's some other weird and new magic inside of you that I can't get a read on. I don't like it and since you have access to campus again..." His look was full of dark expectation.

"The battle rooms next time. Promise."

And finally, I got my gruff hug.

If I sniffled a bit, no one had to know.

~*~

Helmet in place, I headed into the chaos of the fourth floor of the main library.

Books were flying around even more wildly than usual. They circled me immediately, chattering noisily. I smiled, unable to stop the small lift in mood that the books always brought.

"Not too much to eat lately, eh, boys?"

The usual suspects circled me, as well as a few hopeful newcomers—*Hiding From the Authorities, An Epidemic of Delinquency, DIY Magic, Fix Yourself and the World Around You, We Are Watching You, Leeches and Leashes, Seed Magic,* and *Patterns of Thought.*

"Not today, my papered friends."

I was interested in only one book. I stared up into the cupola at the regal book that always surveyed the floor imperiously from overhead. Cover tilted toward me, it waited. But it was a mistake to ever think it a passive tome. When it had helped me with the enhanced sense book at the beginning of the term, I had known then that it would demand things from me if I leveraged its knowledge.

I already had a debt to it that I hadn't repaid. A long green line of obligation.

"Can we speak?" I asked, my gaze fixed on its cover.

It stilled completely, then hopped from its perch, great black-and-white covers outstretched as it turned slow circles in descent.

Chapter Twenty-one

Tension gripped me. I knew the Fourth Floor books well at this point, but there had always been an imbalance when it came to this book and to me.

As it grew closer, it caught itself on a turn and soared off to the edges of the room—toward the pedestals that housed the dangerous and classified books.

It landed on a black stand, empty of any adornment, beautiful in its simplicity. Small crystal brackets rose to encase the bottom edges of its hard cover. The book neatly stepped sideways to avoid being clamped down. The brackets again tried to grab hold of the book, but it stepped the other way. The solemn dance continued as the clamps repeatedly tried to engage.

Down the row was the love spell book the girl had wanted to use on Constantine months ago, along with *The Twelve Black Steps* and *Death Magic*. I had been expressly cautioned against checking out any pedestal book, so I had used other resources to find the resurrection information I'd needed.

I looked back to the black-and-white book. There were no words on the heavy cover, only a thick, swirling Mobius strip that was winding its way around the cover threads.

There was no sign in front of the pedestal, but a quick spell showed the entire pedestal was wrapped with wards. Seemingly, millions of wards—some of them new, some very, very old.

I glanced around quickly. We were still weirdly alone. "This is your pedestal?"

It dipped the top of its spine and sidestepped another bracketed grab.

"Can I read you apart from the pedestal?"

It snapped shut, thumping the air like a sonic boom. The wards around it pulsed outward, thick and unfriendly—it's version of a negative answer.

The book rose in the air and flew to a semi-circular table, landing imperiously. I sank into the chair across from it as its inked pages flipped open. I could see words and diagrams, but everything was blurry. There was some sort of spell blocking it from being read outside its pedestal.

The books that had previously been circling me were now perched on the bannister with many others, tipped forward, watching. I looked at the rare book in front of me, focusing my gaze on the top of its spine, where the signature pages were magically bound together. This close to each other, the connection thrummed between us.

I hadn't wanted to acknowledge it before, because I *knew*.

"You are a book about Origin Magic or Origin Mages, aren't you?"

The book snapped shut and its front cover pulled upward in a puffed-chest gesture.

Resignation welled within me. "Yeah."

The book regally wobbled toward me, covers parting with obvious intent.

A weird, foreign sense of excitement gripped my chest, but heretofore unknown impulse control seized harder. "Wait."

I had a sudden image of every Junior Department stooge running in here to grab me. Of my temporary safety and freedom being stripped away completely.

The book stopped and snapped its pages together, displeased. It took another threatening step forward, one step away from knocking off my helmet and grabbing my head.

I thrust out my hand. "Okay, okay, just wait, let me think."

It stood like Draeger had, irritated, barely patient, but willing to let me have a moment. I *wanted* to read the book, and the book could construe that intent.

But I needed to be cautious. Jumping into things feet first had caused past problems.

I looked back at the wards circling its pedestal. If I squinted enough, I could see nearly invisible tendrils extending through the air encasing the book. "You've been here a long time, haven't you? Seventy years, I'd bet. Maybe I can...unravel the wards tethering you? Free you?"

The threatening posture shifted, and the Mobius strip on the book's cover pulsated. A different sort of tension stole over the book. It still wanted to grab me, but it wanted its freedom even more.

A quick glance around showed I was still humanly alone. I walked back to the pedestal. Sensing my intent, the book landed atop it again and began its dance of avoidance with the clamps. With the book on top, the wards glowed brighter.

I had spent weeks of sleepless nights studying wards, and I had died entangled in the clutches of extremely strong ones that had attached to the shield set that still surrounded me. That practice, and that mistake, had allowed me to fix the wards on my parents' home. I would fix this, too.

As incentive, now that I had acknowledged the content of the book, I had a feeling I'd get an unsolicited face-hug if I didn't work quickly. It was the Godfather of the cupola—it wouldn't accept a "no" for long.

I examined the ward patterns closest to the surface of the knotted mess. There were at least fifty of them. The first seven were clearest. I committed them to memory in sequence, forming a paint palette in my mind and burning a black "1" into the corner. Lilac, blonde, eggplant, mint, carnelian, azul, forest. The first block to unravel. I'd need to decode the possibilities for each color then come back to determine the exact warding intentions of each.

The real conundrum was the ward glowing under all of them—a dark grey, shadowy swirl someone had slipped inside. I was academically familiar with the type from working with Will. It was a port spell—old and powerful...and pointed. It probably wouldn't port *everyone* who touched the book, but a dollar to a donut, if *I* touched it and was recognized as an Origin Mage, we were going on a trip.

I had a feeling part of the destination name would start with a "base" and end with a "ment."

The book watched me intently as I stared in turn. I could no longer deny this part of me, though. I *wanted* to find out about Origin Mages and Magic. I needed to find out what I was and what it meant to be an Origin Mage.

If I wanted to beat Raphael, to beat Stavros, to figure out how to save the next feral, I needed to embrace it. Even if it meant that I would be outed to the world.

The book tipped its left corner suddenly, taut with concentration. I followed its gaze.

A lanky boy I'd seen before was peering around the corner of the stacks. He was one of Bellacia's informants. And he was recording me interacting with a book on Origin Magic.

"Perfect." I sighed. My "outing" was going to happen a lot sooner than I'd anticipated.

The Origin book ruffled its pages in a tsunamic wave of paper, then threw one corner into a sharp, militaristic point.

A book from the cupola dove. The boy looked up in time to see the book's trajectory, but not to do anything about it as the book opened its giant maws and clapped them around his face.

Worst Nightmares flowed in an eerie script across its cover.

The boy's recording spell shattered like crystal dropped on concrete and the boy gave an ear-piercing shriek as he scrambled backward, trying to shove *Nightmares* from his face.

I was in motion before I knew it, lifting a giant eraser and throwing it at the book's spine. Already running, I followed the action with a second one that I pressed up against the bottom portion of the book, where the signatures were bound together by glue. It immediately released its hold, gave its own squawk, and flew in circles in the magic updraft that extended around the cupola.

The boy stared at me, white-faced. Heck, I felt like I was mirroring his horrified expression.

I dug out a crumpled rose from my pocket and pressed it against his chest.

Impossibly, his eyes went wider.

I could hear the books ruffling in the air. Something was coming in for another pass, and this idiot hadn't worn a helmet. The only mages who didn't wear them were the combat mages and the students who were willing to be plastered all over the pages of the books.

"*Run,*" I shouted.

Whether the book had shown him his worst nightmares, detailing them in ghastly strokes upon its pages, or shared the nightmares of others, it would still have been horrifying.

He ran.

I whipped back to the Origin book, heart stuttering fitfully in my chest. "You can't do that."

It splayed its pages out in a "we have to eat, too" kind of gesture.

I put a hand to my forehead. "Not...not as a punishment for me. If people come in here without helmets, then they know what they are getting into, but don't go after them because of me."

It rippled its pages in a shrug.

"In less exciting news..." I sighed. "It's going to take me some time to unwrap you."

There was no sign of surprise, but tension thrummed through its binding. Disappointment strummed through me as well. I rubbed my chest.

"But I'll do it." The promise strengthened the debt thread to the book, making it pulse a brighter green. "In exchange, in the interim, maybe you can help me cobble together some knowledge from other books?"

It bristled, spine straightening imperiously.

"No, I know," I said quickly, soothingly. "Nothing would be as good as accessing your information. Definitely. But if I check you out with that ward in place, the Department goons are going to nab me and I'll never be able to free you or help anyone else. I need a little time and some additional skills. Ones I know how to use."

It contemplated me, and for a moment, I thought it might just blast my helmet away and be done with it, but it flicked its spine and three books zoomed down.

Rare Mage Skills in The Wild, *When Art Magic Blurs the Lines*, and *Understanding Creation* all bobbed in front of me, eager little sparrows ready to serve.

I tentatively extended my wrist for the first one.

The black-and-white book blasted into the air, circling back up to the cupola. It landed on the rail, but its gaze never strayed from me.

~*~

I headed back to Dorm One filled with knowledge and a bit of euphoria from the three books, plus a bonus fourth.

Even walking in on Olivia and Constantine arguing did little to diminish my joy.

Chapter Twenty-one

"It's not that simple, Price," Constantine was saying with a sneer.

"Nothing ever is for *most* of us," she said, a little vindictively.

"Good talk?" I asked brightly, dropping my bag.

They immediately focused on me.

"Where have you—?" Olivia frowned. "You're glowing. Why are you glowing?"

Constantine crossed his arms. "Seriously? She probably hugged a radioactive seal because it was adorable and looked like it needed it."

I scratched my neck. My skin was prickling strangely. "Sorry for worrying you."

"Why would anyone worry?" Constantine said with a bit of a sneer. "You send a flurry of terror, then determination, then nothing. No one *worries* about these things."

"I forgot to turn my communications back on, didn't I?" I checked my armband. Everything had been strangely silent, but the books had been *fascinating*. I hadn't even thought—

"Exactly," he said grimly.

I cringed. "Sorry."

"What did you do?" Olivia demanded. Even Constantine was looking at me darkly, united in this one thing with her.

"Nothing?" I tentatively reached for both of their threads to get a read on them, realizing too late that it hadn't just been my frequency communications; all of my connection threads were *muted*. I blinked at the threads—how had that happened? I concentrated on my connections and they all came blooming back into life like a surge of wildflowers suddenly blooming across a meadow.

Constantine grabbed his elbow and never had I seen such physical relief cross his features before. Olivia rubbed her chest, and she looked like she might cry.

"I had no idea. I'm so sorry." I tripped over the words.

"Ren, what did you do?" Olivia asked, softer this time.

"I made a deal."

They both froze, small movements pausing, caution and consternation mirroring their expressions in a strange way.

"What deal? With whom?" Constantine asked tensely.

I rubbed my wrist. The three books that had been clamped there had imparted some interesting knowledge on ward structure, rare mages, rare beings, and magical artifacts that a fourth book *Memory Enhancement* had glued, at least temporarily, into my brain.

As a side benefit, my brain had clamped down on the section on the life force hooks and how they related to, and differed from, warding.

"I think I might be able to help remove your life hooks, Liv."

"No." Constantine's voice was oddly implacable.

"What? Why?" I said, stopping abruptly in my tracks.

"I forbid it."

"You can't forbid her anything, Leandred," Olivia said, then turned to me. "You aren't doing it."

"Because *you* telling her what she can and can't do is any better," he said spitefully.

Olivia lifted her chin.

I looked between them. "You want the life hook gone, Liv. And I know the removal of the other spell went sort of—" I wobbled my hand back and forth "—but this one won't have the same traps."

"The nature of the hook, and it being in place for so long, means you can't *remove* it," Olivia said, chin high. "My mother has to release it."

Dark feelings were emanating from Constantine. How could I not have noticed that all the currents that usually flowed in and out of me were missing?

"There must be a way to destroy it," I repeated. There was always a way.

"No. You aren't getting *caught* for a shiving spell that can be routinely switched," Constantine said, angrily swiping a hand through the air.

"Routine? Putting Liv's life in someone else's hands—"

"Once transferred, the spell starts to fade. Price will be released after a period of time." He swiped his hand the other way. "The hook will be removed by someone who has taken extensive vows—tortured death vows —never to use it. Now, back to you, *darling*. What deal did you make?" Constantine's voice was implacable as he tapped a finger on a bicep.

Maybe I shouldn't say. A voice deep inside me cautioned that I should say nothing. *Keep it to yourself.* The voice sounded oddly like Christian.

But it felt like secrets kept would be secrets that could come back to haunt us. I powered through the caution.

"It was a knowledge trade. I'm going to release the Origin Book in the library from its servitude."

Something inside of me, maybe the euphoria from the books, leaped in excitement again, making it hard to remember, later, which one started yelling at me first.

Chapter Twenty-two

IN ROOT

IT HAD TAKEN a lot to get Olivia and Constantine to stop yelling so that I could explain. Neither cared about faceless people I wanted to put myself on the line to help.

"One of those faceless people was my brother," I said quietly.

One of those faceless people had been me, and who knows what might have happened if Raphael hadn't siphoned most of my magic? He had created the volatile situation around my own Awakening, so I wasn't inclined to be *thankful*, but it remained a fact that he hadn't killed me—something the thieves hadn't done for Christian.

The authorities hadn't gotten to Christian before the thieves did, and they hadn't beaten Raphael to me.

Olivia and Constantine's connection threads softened, though each of their faces still looked implacable.

"I need to know how to use my own magic," I added softly. "It's time."

"Fine. Figure out how to free the book," Olivia said. "But don't free it *yet*. Promise me."

"Promise," I said quickly. I wasn't freeing it *today*.

Olivia seemed to realize her mistake. She pointed at me. "I ban you from further life hook research."

"But—"

"I will help Price guard the hook," Constantine interrupted before I could argue. His expression showed his distaste at the words. "You will do something magnificent but stupid otherwise."

"Yes," Olivia said, with an equally repulsed grimace.

I sent a mental note to Neph full of overriding delight—s*eriously, pack our bags.*

Constantine—who could be securely trusted when it came to his promises—was going to help *Olivia*. And she was going to *let* him.

Olivia was getting better at relying on other people—her network slowly spreading wider—but Constantine was still a "rely on Constantine or Ren, and no one else" kind of guy.

Relief swept through me.

Both had relied solely on themselves for far too long. And Constantine was in a far better position to help with the hooks than anyone, having been through it himself.

A sudden, beaming smile threatened to burst from me—I didn't have to do everything, and I had missed that feeling so much since Christian's death.

I struggled to conjure a woebegone expression and a sigh. "Okay. I'll let you two handle it."

From their identical frowns, I was only half successful at the ruse.

I escaped before either of them could back out.

I sent a mass of *thanks, love, trust* through Constantine's threads, as I escaped. Resigned acceptance, irritation, and grudging fondness returned along the path.

And I could still *help* in my own way.

I headed down to speak to Greyskull.

He wasn't alone in his office. I rubbed my chest as something quickly fluttered then fled. Stevens looked me over with sharp, critical eyes. Something flitted through her gaze as she stared at my torso and her brows drew together, but then she shook her head, as if mistaken about something, and her gaze went back to my crown.

"You were right," she acknowledged to Greyskull. "But this is all I will do."

He watched me strangely for a long moment, as if I'd appeared through sorcery. "Sometimes, fate is a strange creature. Come in, Ren. You are here, so you can help. Four is better than three for this anyway."

I entered a bit warily. Professor Stevens had rescheduled our lab, so it was the first time I had seen her since she had thrown the Department off campus and helped get us to Medical.

Our last conversation flitted through my mind. She met my gaze, stony and aloof, but fire burned in her eyes.

Stavros' daughter.

His taunts from the previous night flickered through my thoughts.

I stepped closer to her, and she didn't shy away—the badass woman that Stevens was would *never* back away—but her negative body language was easily read. "You don't want to do whatever this is," I murmured. "You don't want to be here."

"No. As I told you, it is better for everyone if I remain on the sidelines." She looked intently at the magic around me—as she had months ago when she had first detected Raphael's spell on me. "But on certain topics, Grey is always right."

"I'm speechless," Greyskull said wryly.

But I ignored him, needing to clarify something that had become more important over the last few days. "I heard you talking to Helen Price, before Bloody Tuesday. She has something on you."

A crisp smile slashed across her face, but didn't reach her eyes. "Everyone has something on everyone here, Crown."

"Can she get to Olivia through you?" I prodded quietly. My priority to protect her hadn't changed.

Something in Stevens softened. "I'm not the piece on campus she will try to move for that. We will do everything to support your roommate's emancipation. You can believe me on that."

I nodded, another piece of relief slotting into place.

Greyskull motioned behind me. "You're late."

Dean Marsgrove walked in and closed the door.

For all of my thoughts on Marsgrove as an ally, my fingers automatically flew toward my bag and my lock picks before I forced my hands into my pockets. Other students weren't the only ones these days suffering from trapped claustrophobia.

"Phillip," Stevens said.

"Lucy," he replied just as sharply. He looked exhausted again—not magically this time, but weary, like the leader of a country who had far too many concerns to deal with.

Greyskull didn't bat an eyelash. "Behave."

"Er, what's going on?" I asked, fidgeting.

"I would think it obvious," Stevens said brusquely, pulling sharp implements out of her pockets. But, I was pretty certain her ire wasn't for me.

"A risk assessment and spell manipulation," Marsgrove said, staring darkly at both Stevens and Greyskull. "Why is she here?" He pointed at me.

"She showed up," Greyskull said calmly.

"As she frequently does," Stevens muttered.

Marsgrove squinted at me. "She's glowing."

"Also frequent," Stevens muttered a bit more caustically.

"What did you do?" Marsgrove asked me suspiciously.

"Just spent a little time in the library," I said quickly—and truthfully.

"Phillip, leave her alone. Ren, over here," Greyskull called, motioning.

"So...?" I queried, shucking my bag and doing as directed.

"Your roommate wants to use part of the spell that was placed upon her. And while she has been diligently—more than diligently—breaking it down, there are a few...personal parts that we might be better able to

214

identify and remove. And Lucy wanted to see it," he said offhandedly.

Stevens shot Greyskull a sharp look. Marsgrove looked peeved.

Had Greyskull told Marsgrove about the dream and the spell getting cut? I looked at Greyskull. He slowly shook his head.

Relief swept me.

My gaze caught on Stevens, though, and I winced at her raised brows and knowledge-filled eyes. I had never said he couldn't tell Stevens.

Well, I was always being warned about my bargains.

"Tricky," I muttered.

"I thought you might approve such a tactic," Greyskull said unrepentantly.

Marsgrove looked between the two of us suspiciously. "What are you two whispering about?"

Greyskull waved a tattooed hand. "You won't be actively touching the spell, Ren." He looked at me, gaze adamant. "Do you understand? You are an inactive participant I'm going to pull into a magic share."

I didn't even know what we were doing, so I just nodded.

Marsgrove muttered about my "sticky fingers" but took his position around the examination table, looking both mulish and resigned. He was always at his grouchiest when Raphael was the subject of a conversation or event.

Greyskull pulled magic up with a soft swish of his hand, and a full hologram of Olivia popped into place—Raphael's spell all over her. "Let's see what we have."

Color and geometric patterns bloomed everywhere—graphs and charts and symbols, little pumping icons that morphed into other shapes. I touched one and it vibrated as if it had been tickled, then bloomed, showing at its core a colorful golden stamen in the middle.

Greyskull's magic very lightly tugged mine. With all the magic we'd performed together over the last week, it was ridiculously simple to give permission. I understood the basics. I had done a four person magic share with Olivia, Will, and Neph, so I knew what was involved. And Raphael's magic seamlessly connected to theirs, making mine slip right into position like a greased fish.

"His magic is all over hers again," Marsgrove said grimly.

"Yes, but that's not why we are here," Greyskull said calmly.

Greyskull's hand gently clasped the air around me and looped it together with the strands from the adults.

I could feel their magic binding together and pulling on mine. It wasn't an unpleasant sensation, but it was a little weird. I rubbed my chest.

Marsgrove's emotional fatigue was almost sentient. I shook off the immediate desire to make it better—Marsgrove wouldn't be pleased by the

Chapter Twenty-two

attempt.

Since I was only a conduit, and they didn't need me for active participation, I poked and opened the little constructs that danced like live beings in the air.

The three adults hovered over the image of Olivia's prone form, scopes and constructs fluttering around them. A grid of spell points overlaid her image in blue and green dots.

"Ren flipped it here." Greyskull pointed to a particular set of spell attachment points.

"The girl is stupidly brilliant," Stevens said, frowning.

"Hey!" I objected, in the middle of opening a small purple globe. I was ignored.

"A dangerous combination. The whole thing could have been catastrophic," Marsgrove said. "We need to do something about her before something happens that we can't undo."

I waved a hand in front of my torso to indicate that I was right there, listening.

"So far everything she has done has been quite delightful," Grey said. "Look at F8."

"You would think that," Marsgrove said darkly to the first statement, but looked at the designated point. "F8 is a focal point, agreed. D12. But you didn't see her with the Dare scion," he continued the double conversation. "Or attend the family's latest 'meeting' in Itlantes."

"I have seen them together, actually," Grey said just as unconcernedly. "Y37."

"Then you should be more frightened. That there will be war isn't a question. It's how big it will be. M89."

"I'm standing right here," I said.

"The wards around them certainly provide fodder for gossip. M88 not 89."

Stevens' gaze flitted upward. "Two pact? And I agree on 88."

"Oddly, it's three."

I gave up on getting riled and concentrated fully on what they were doing, identifying each place where the spell was anchored with miniature hooks.

A little residue on the spell's edge grabbed my attention. I reached out to touch it and Greyskull mildly zapped me without looking my way. Whoops. I shook my hand to remove the sting and tucked both hands in my armpits in an attempt to keep them still.

Greyskull had told me initially, before the spell was removed, that attempting to remove one of the hooks without removing the whole set could backfire extraordinarily, leaving Olivia with no knowledge of friend or foe.

But there was a smudge. Right there. I just wanted to remove it.

The shared spell focused on my desire to tinker, and heat started blistering my skin.

"Stop thinking," Greyskull said to me, not unkindly.

"She's going to end us all," Marsgrove muttered. "In some misguided attempt to *help*. There was that Origin Mage back in the six hundreds who tried to end hunger, remember that story? Make sure you read that one, Crown."

"Shut up, Phillip."

They worked in tense tandem for a few minutes, identifying hook points and spell intentions with clipped tones.

"I...I do just want to help," I said.

Marsgrove looked at me, expression softening the smallest bit. "I know, Crown. It's not so much you as all the rest of it. The Dares don't do *subtle*. They court disaster."

"They always do," Stevens said perfunctorily.

"This time it's worse. We stand upon a precipice. If they choose the wrong moment—"

"Maximilian will never make that mistake."

Marsgrove's lips tightened. "You haven't seen the boy with her then. You have no idea what horror is coming our way if he jumps."

"I listen to the winds, same as you," Greyskull said mildly, though I could see the tension in his fingers as he carefully separated spell threads.

Stevens's silence was oppressive all on its own.

"Julian is going to be a problem, too. *Plans* need to be in place. To deal with all of them," Marsgrove said, a little magic pulsing from him as he too-forcefully pushed at one of the threads, emotions overcoming his care. "I wish I hadn't attended that damn summit. I could be in denial like the rest of you. Happily frolicking with the Origin Mage and her magic around campus."

"I'm listening to all of this, you know," I said.

"Do you think I'm trying to hide my thoughts?" Marsgrove asked without looking up, and deliberately took more care separating the next thread under his fingers.

"Well, it's doing you a fat lot of good being vague and creepy. I don't do subtle either."

He looked offended by the creepy part. "Fine. Don't speak to Axer anymore. Or Olivia. Or the Leandred boy. Or the O'Leary boy. Or the Bau muse. Or anyone else with Third Layer ties, which includes the Peoples' troublemaker. Anyone with ties to O'Leary is also out, because they all spiral back to him. The communication and demolition mages are destined for government pickup within months of graduation."

"What about the Bailey girl?" I asked testily. "I haven't seen you moving to sever that tie."

"There are certain things on campus I can't influence once they are in play. I was off campus when that pact with the devil went into motion. Take the Baileys down with you, if you want. A pleasure for us all."

"I suppose Mike and Will are off limits as well, since we are making a list."

"William Tasky and Mike Givens make fine, steady friends, but they will be irreparably tainted by ties to you."

I swallowed, lifting my chin. "So for my benefit, I shouldn't speak with all those on your first list, and for their benefit, none of those on the second."

Marsgrove looked up at me, finally, gaze steady. "And that is why it is pointless for me to give you warning."

I crossed my arms. "Knowledge is power. You can say, 'Ren, a tornado is coming, don't use weather magic for the next two days,' or, 'Ren, there's a taskforce after Neph. Make sure she stays low.' I can take direction, you know."

"Ren, don't use any magic. Ever again."

I firmed my jaw.

"No?" A fleeting smile ran across his mouth before it took a downward turn. "The plain truth of it is that it doesn't matter what warning you are given, the path may change, but the end will be the same. Sometimes a flame just burns too brightly. Such is how it has always been with particular mage types."

"Give up, eh?"

"No. Be *prepared*. And I mean that for all of us."

"Quiet," Stevens barked harshly. "Both of you."

Marsgrove looked at her, then bent back to his work.

Twitchy, I wanted to continue the argument, but Stevens wielded the power of disappointment over me too well. I swallowed my comments and concentrated on the magic as they worked together.

Inside their trinity, their magic was incredibly familiar and collegial, flawlessly parting, ebbing, and flowing together. And they were working with my magic just fine, but that fourth organic part of their set was missing.

Raphael. The protector of their group.

"Lassiter sends his regards," Stevens said, apropos of nothing, and yet, I recognized the name as their fifth friend, and wondered if my thoughts were flowing through the others due to our current connection. "He also said, and I quote, 'Not on your life.'"

"He's siding with Rafi," Marsgrove said, no surprise in his expression.

"He's siding with no one," Greyskull's voice sounded weary.

"Neutrality is a fairytale construct," Marsgrove said sharply. "A myth served to those who are protected by others. For those who don't have to do the dirty work themselves."

Grey flexed his fingers, tattoos dancing upon his knuckles. "You are such a funt sometimes, Phillip."

That word translated very negatively in my translator.

"And you are—"

Their voices grew in volume and the spell...wiggled. I stared at the wiggled spot, as their tones grew far more heated.

The residue had been carefully wiped over the last five minutes' work, but there was a little ribbon of something wiggling around, hiding beneath the other spells. I twitched, watching it. Four smaller ribbons fanned out from the end of the central one, then pulled back together. It looked an awful lot like...

One smaller ribbon poked out and a little tongue of magic hissed, then three other heads answered.

My hand darted forward, and my body ignored the electric zap sent from Greyskull as I grabbed the writhing creature between my thumb and forefinger just as I would any snake in the grass, right behind its biting heads.

There was an upheaval in the room's magic, but I ignored it as I stared at the serpent, bringing it closer to my face. It smiled at me, four times.

"I like snakes," I said to it. "But not when they are toying with my friends."

It gave four hissing laughs.

Marsgrove grabbed my wrist. "How?" he demanded, grip firm, gaze rigid.

I automatically tried to work my way free of his grip. I had to force myself to stop. "It was wiggling, vibrating under the spell."

It was the truth. A sliver of the truth, at least. Something in his gaze said that he knew there was more.

Everything in me screamed that I say nothing about the dream, though. What if Marsgrove tried to take me away from Olivia? He could. Olivia was completely under his control as a ward of Excelsine. When Axer got back and our rooming situation went up for review, Marsgrove could separate us. He had the authority and there were alternatives for housing now.

And Marsgrove might think separating us the best alternative. He had as plainly said so, telling me to stay away from her.

No. Marsgrove was an ally in keeping Olivia from Helen, but he wasn't an ally in keeping me *with* Olivia. I couldn't trust his response to Raphael

Chapter Twenty-two

invading my dreams.

Greyskull, bless the man, was already in motion. His expression was caught between still being ticked with Marsgrove, the amusement that so frequently blanketed him whenever I did anything stupid, and a deep pain as he looked at the snake. "Good job, Ren. Hold him so that I can..." He opened small magical pliers and secured them around the wiggling serpent. "Excellent."

Bringing it closer to his face, he shook his head slowly, watching the writhing heads that were watching him in return. "Rafi." He sighed, then collapsed the spell net that was connecting the four of us to Olivia.

"The rest is what Miss Price requested."

"Right, since the poisoned hook accidentally showed itself to Crown. So *serendipitous*." Marsgrove's voice was all hues of sarcastic.

Fear and panic took me. "It was when you started arguing. It wiggled."

That shut up Marsgrove so abruptly, that the temperature and mood of the room dropped like a heavy stone pushed from a table.

None of their gazes met, and without another word, the session was over.

Greyskull was putting their equipment away. Marsgrove was staring furiously at the wall, and Stevens was gathering personal items and striding from the room.

Marsgrove released a ball of explosive magic at the grate, then followed Stevens' path, slamming the door behind him.

Completely unnerved, I looked toward Greyskull seeking an explanation. "What did the argument wiggling mean?"

Greyskull shook his head, lips tight. "Old wounds." He looked at the bag, eyes pained.

His expression was steely when he looked back at me. "Now, why are you really glowing?"

"No...reason."

He sighed.

It was worth it, though, when I delivered the spell remnants to Olivia and she fiercely got to work on whatever she had planned.

~*~

After a quick Justice Squad hour and another session with the books, I was glowing even more brightly, and I was overflowing with insane ideas.

I happily ran to meet Constantine at the vault. I could feel he was in a much better mood, too. The muting of the threads had really upset him. But I was going to make it up to him with a few of these ideas—there were *so many things* we could work on.

"For the love of everything, darling, stop *sharing*," Constantine said as I neared. "I can't take any more of your elation. It's giving me stomach cramps."

I tried to cap my emotional bleed through, but couldn't. "Sorry. Unlike that book that muted connections, this one enhanced them and I stuffed them all your way. Just wait until you see what I have for you."

"Better be *fantastic*." But through his long-suffering look, I could sense his anticipation as he opened the vault.

We both stuttered to a halt. There was already someone inside.

"As I thought," Stevens said, looking between us, arms crossed. "You should have scheduled your sessions under a shell name, Leandred. Too bad for you both. These hours are now mine. Both of you get in here."

"But—"

One look from Stevens had me shutting up.

Constantine examined her, tapping his forearms. "And if we don't?"

"You will, if you want that assignment you've been nagging me for."

He narrowed his eyes, then looked at me, as if asking what I wanted to do. I blinked at him—of course we were going to do it. I didn't know what his assignment was, but Constantine rarely asked for anything. That meant whatever Stevens was threatening him with was important to him.

He narrowed his eyes at me, then turned.

Oh. *Oh.*

I grabbed his arm and pushed him inside. "You're the idiot. It's not a sacrifice. Stop being a martyr—it's terrifying."

Stevens' expression was fiercely elated as she looked between us. It was a strange expression coming from her.

"Even the best planners forget the outliers in this game," she murmured, then set us to a grueling set of creations.

My glow was gone by the time we were done, but I felt weirdly freer.

The shadows stayed out of my dreams that night and Stavros didn't whisper in my ear at all.

Chapter Twenty-three

BIRDS, BANDITS, AND BOOKS

But two lovely dream jaunts with Axer full of puzzles and enchanted groves, and a series of positive reports concerning projects wasn't enough to quell the edginess I started to see creeping through campus.

Excursions with Greene and Lifen—and sometimes with Camille Straught's or Lox's groups angrily and silently tagging along—were maddening and uneasy. Especially since Olivia had put the kibosh on a binding, not trusting the motives of the combat mages.

I certainly received my fair share of glares from Camille and Lox—as if I was somehow making everyone's lives more difficult just by existing.

Complicating the weird dynamic with Axer's group were the shady Neutralizer Squad members on Camille and Lox's teams. I felt like I was tagging along with Emrys again—regularly being set up to show some extraordinary, banned power—but this time so a group could figure out how to take me down.

"Ow!" I shook my hand from where it had gotten shocked by one of the neutralizers. Again.

"Oh, I'm sorry." The girl, Faun, stared at me intently. "Are you angry?"

I gritted my teeth and focused on *calm*. "I'm great. Moving *on*."

Five minutes later, I felt a prick of blood drawn from my arm. I slapped a hand against the cut. "What the hell?"

Faun quickly scooped my blood into a vial.

"Okay, no. Give that back." I held out my other hand.

She tucked it into her vest. "No." The other neutralizer hovered behind her, staring creepily over Faun's shoulder at me.

Magic rose in me. I looked at Camille, who gazed narrowly back.

I focused on the feeling of Axer's cloth, even though it wasn't under my cuff anymore, and turned back to Faun. "I must ask you to return that to me."

The girl peered at me. "You feel angry, don't you? What are you going to do? That's the third time that I've—"

"It is," Peters said. "And if you don't give her the blood back, I'm going to issue you four citations myself."

Peters, who was the Justice Squad member on Lox's team, and an athletic girl named Yarza, who was a good fit for Camille's brand of long expeditions, were seriously frowning at the neutralizers. Lifen just twirled a stick between her fingers looking bored.

But I'd seen the limp Faun had sported earlier. I hadn't given it to her.

Greene, Lox, and Camille, while they never provoked, also never interfered with what the neutralizers were trying to do.

It was a certainty that I was being tested. I didn't enjoy the feeling or the reality of it.

"Should have just done the binding, Crown," Greene said, twirling his cane. "We could have gotten a nice feel for your intentions, and the true natures and power levels in your group."

Lifen raised a brow. "You aren't afraid you wouldn't measure up?"

He smiled slowly at her. "Of that? Not in the least."

"You two are horrifying. I want to switch teams." I drew a mental cartoon of the two of them and sent it to Axer.

I was very, *very* careful to keep the rest of the conversation to myself, though, because Greene was never shy when it was just the three of us on rounds. Therefore, when he wasn't flirting with Lifen, most of his conversation revolved around Axer and how I negatively influenced him.

He was blunt and informative about it, too.

"He's more reckless because of you. One week into winter term, he changed a plan he had been carefully building for years. A plan he had already laid the groundwork for. Three weeks in, his new plans revolved completely around you instead. Interesting, don't you think?"

"Riveting." I sighed.

I did a lot of sighing during campus rounds, and very carefully kept my thoughts hidden from Axer during my dreams. I was getting the tiniest bit better at concealment.

Which was good, since I'd been having embarrassing thoughts about wanting him back on campus.

I locked those thoughts down tight and increasingly requested destinations outside of my dreams to hide my jumbled mindscape where all my secrets could be found.

He always made sure we stopped by the relaxing grove every night without fail—a place where all the worries in my life could be set aside.

"As soon as Axer gets back, these little jaunts will be cut short completely," Greene said.

Chapter Twenty-three

"What?" I asked, startled out of the memory. "We won't go there anymore?"

Greene frowned slowly. "Did you want to return to the Eighth Circle sloughs?"

"Oh! *These* jaunts."

So used to people reading my mind—either through the armbands or Axer's and Constantine's abilities—I blanked my thoughts immediately.

The energy around Greene quickly changed, narrowing in on trying to read me. Greene couldn't read my thoughts, but he could put a lot together with very little—my responses, my sudden blankness. Putting pieces together was his superpower.

He tapped his fingers on the cane he held. "I see," he said in aristocratic consideration, gaze skirting over me as if he could find the dragon figurine just by looking for it. "Why I am surprised, is the question. Yes, best to needle in as much as we can now. You will be hidden completely soon."

Greene was weirdly free with his dubiously verbalized thoughts.

"Best entertainment available on campus, Crown," Lifen said, darkly entertained by every second.

Entertainment had taken an especially weird bend in the weeks post Bloody Tuesday and Recovery Saturday (as Patrick had deemed Olivia's rescue).

I found Olivia pouring over an origami text one evening. She held up a hand before I could form the question. "Don't ask. I can't stand to be terrible at anything."

Her paper creations—now freely formed—got a lot better after that. She continued helping me make roses in Medical with Greyskull. It seemed to soothe something in her too, something left over from Raphael. And she was able to imbue some of her own soothed terror at being trapped into the roses—something that I hadn't thought to do.

I sometimes found her crafting the bases with Greyskull before I arrived. It seemed to be helping both of them.

And I was making sure to very *carefully* regulate the amount of magic I added to the roses. Greene and Camille weren't wrong about being more careful for everyone's sake.

On the other end of her projects, Olivia was getting close to gaining official recognition of her emancipation—striking while the poker was hot with her mother's unconscionable use of the life hook.

I did my utmost to be the best sounding board I could possibly be while she crafted her arguments.

Popularity-wise, the Department was rebounding from their political hit double-time as a result of their quick response to addressing the "feral" situations, increasing their "good works," and burying anything that smacked of an "undeserved" police state. Their perceived sadness over the deaths of the ferals in the First Layer was also entwined with greater promises of safety.

Shelle Fanning had done a marvelous job of combining empathy with security concerns.

"A national landmark was destroyed, and three countries were harmed by floods, but we are already rebuilding," she said one night on the main newsfeed. "No one was permanently killed. We will be taking a closer look at monitoring future Awakenings, as it had been brought to our attention that more might occur soon with the uptick in Origin Magic that has been occurring—a concerning event that we are working to get to the bottom of quickly."

And there it was, simmering just beneath the surface. That I would cause further destruction if not dealt with.

Bellacia, or her father, had cashed in on the game—letting the Marsgrove story stone sink, pulling back from reporting on the Department's ills—and had gotten increasing media access spots elsewhere in the Second Layer because of it.

"That's how the game is played, Ren," Bellacia said one night. "But don't think I've forgotten. I haven't. Due time comes to all. Enton Stavros is up to something and I will be the one to reveal it."

I didn't understand such games. To me, it was far more black and white. Government evils? Rip them out. Government goodworks? Pump in money and magic.

Bellacia thought my ideals "cute." Her smile grew more strained, though, as like Greene, she realized that whatever "access" she had to me was coming to a swift end. Because the fallout from the Inessa situation had cemented that I *would* be getting out of the dreadful roommate dilemma. Olivia had righteously submitted eighteen different complaints, and Marsgrove had finally written her a note saying, *"It's in the works. Please stop sending requests about student safety—you are giving the Dean of Students an aneurysm."*

Even with the odd attempt to hunt and catch me around campus, though, people were being very *nice* to our group. Some mages were sincere, sure, but others...the ones who immediately expressed interest in the instruments we were using, like Greene, or in knowing more about all of us —especially me—were suspect at best.

Trick, manically, was most concerned about the ones who seemed genuine, and he had put a moratorium on allowing knowledge to go beyond anyone in the inner circle.

"Oldest trick in the book. Throw out a few duds, easy marks, maybe a few intermediate ones, make us think we've routed them, then wham, right in the face with the affable, *helpful* worm we let in."

"Do you think maybe you are being a bit paranoid?" one of the guys on the edge of the inner circle asked.

"You don't achieve power by being blind, Jameson."

So everyone who approached me had to be filtered through them first. I was told I could be nice, helpful even, but never to give out information and, "Dammit, Crown, no magic!"

It was hard not to help when someone was in need, though, so I continued to give things when the Bandits weren't looking.

"Run each one through Price first," Trick said the seventh time I was caught. "Symbiosis, Crown. You love everyone, we are suspicious of everyone. You make all of us feel warm and fuzzy; we make sure you aren't taken advantage of. Win-win all around."

Sometimes I wondered about our group.

When I wasn't wondering about our group, free moments were spent diving into books on wards, ferals, and suppositional Awakening procedures, helping Greyskull with roses and healing enchantments, Justice Squad, classes, and assisting friends. "Assisting friends" ran the gamut between creating characters for advanced gaming projects, stitching enchantments, metal alloys and dyes, material creation, legal wrangling, weather and dance spells, identity charms, explosives, recycling magic, and trying to keep people's clothes on when Will "skimmed" things.

In between those tasks were other, smaller aids; like assisting mages wherever I found someone in need on campus (without getting caught by Patrick)—because it was as if giving out that first rose, and the hundreds of subsequent ones, had connected me to something more.

The growing community vibe on campus was on the brink of something, no matter what Patrick mumbled suspiciously about. What that brink was, I wasn't sure. But I put in extra effort to nudge it positively whenever I could.

Still, with the end of term barreling toward us and the anticipation of campus reopening on the Saturday before finals, the weird got weirder.

Headed to the library to do some studying with the books, I was saying a quick goodbye to Olivia when a knock came. Already bundled up with bag in hand, I opened the door—never a good idea when the presence on the other side registered as "unknown."

Three mages in black hooded robes stood very solemnly on the other side.

"It is the seventh month of the Hummingbird," the middle one intoned gravely.

It was still the third month of the year last I checked, but no matter. Maybe hummingbirds had their own calendars. I edged my lower half behind the door and nodded, like you were supposed to when confronted with people on a high.

My nod seemed to both relieve and add tension to their robed frames. "We seek your blessing for the Vernal Equinox, where balance rests on a knifepoint each year."

"Er. Sure."

Olivia started swearing behind me, then the door slammed between my face and the group of three.

She pointed at me. "No answering those questions or the door!"

"But—"

"Ever!"

She was looking even more frazzled, trying to reword—for the hundredth time—one of the arguments that she planned to use in her upcoming court battle. We'd helped her draft most of it the night before, but she was stuck on the opening sentence, saying that it had to be *perfect*.

"Yup," I said, nodding to her in much the same fashion as I had to the hummingbird dudes.

She narrowed her eyes and I nodded far more quickly and edged back to the door.

The figures were still in the hall. I pulled the door shut behind me, gave them a sheepish shrug with my mouth pulled out and down, then pointed at them, at me, at the general direction of Olivia.

I made an additional set of muddled hand signals for, "wow, look at the time" and "can't talk right now—but, hey, nice robes!" and "you need to talk to my lawyer," then, I grabbed the new set of pamphlets attached to the outside of our door and busted out of there.

It wasn't the first group that had come to the door. And at least this one hadn't tried to abduct me. That had been embarrassing for everyone.

I flipped through the pamphlets as I walked. Better that than watching people react as I passed.

The Moral Obligations of Origin Mages, Volume 1. The paper looked as if someone had stayed up all night scribbling their thoughts out—I'd give it a read so that they wouldn't feel too bad.

How to Use Power for Purpose looked like it held some pretty good info on a quick flip through, so I stuffed it in my bag as well.

And vying for my new personal favorite title—*Give Up!* which also had the cute subtitle: *Make the Ultimate Gift of <u>You</u> to a Government or Scientific Study.*

I dumped that one into a trash toad that was hopping along the path, mouth wide open, tongue flicking to catch stray magic and rubble. The greenies had been spawning them left and right. I gave it a sidelong glance as it hopped its enormous belly down a lane that wound between a knot of

Chapter Twenty-three

slightly damaged buildings on the Fourth Circle.

Will? How many toads does it take to—?

His answering mental groan made me grin. *No toad jokes, Ren! I almost got eaten by one on my way to engineering. My latest portal pad is not trash!*

Two people coming toward me gasped at my smile, and I quickly picked up my pace.

Midlands tonight? We'd already been a few times to visit the rocks, who were awesomely holding down the fort, but I had picked up a few stab-worthy tools earlier in the day that Guard Rock would get a kick out of, and I could use a break from campus proper.

Yes, please, came Will's desperate response.

"It's her," one student whispered to the other as I passed.

With all the frequency and mental talk, students weren't all that subtle about letting me hear them. Perhaps pointedly. With a populace so hooked into each other's thoughts, they didn't bother to try and keep open discussions private.

One of them brushed past me and I felt two spells collect and siphon into the gem that the Bandits had given me to handle such things. I sighed. I had more tracking spells in that thing than a crabshark on a sardine hunt.

"The Origin test didn't—"

"I don't care what that test concluded. It's supremely obvious. Look at all the data points. Data point A, she—"

Someone plowed into me from behind. I pivoted into strike position before I recognized the culprit.

"Going to take my face off, Scary?"

"I wouldn't know where to begin," I said, as Delia hip-checked me, wearing a smirking grin on her face as we started walking again.

"That's because my cosmetic application is an art in and of itself. I heard that you were going to end the world today."

"No autographs."

"Like I want your scrawl tattooed."

I pointed to the Third Circle arch to indicate my direction. She nodded and we went through.

As we curved around the arch point on the other side, away from view of the group who'd been gossiping, Delia subtly looked around—cautiously, like she was very capable of when she wanted to be—then tucked a heavy object into my pocket.

"For you. From the people with the thing."

I nodded. From the Ophidians, then. "I wasn't expecting anything back. I said so in my note."

"They are bargain oriented people. And you obviously made an impression."

Constantine had probably made far more of an impression. The thought made me grin.

Frost Viper, the call sign of the Ophidian girl I'd ridden with through the Third Layer had been easy to accompany. Constantine's ride with a trio of the other snakes had been a far different experience.

I still had to look up what exactly a Frost Viper *was*. Each member of the gang had a snake call sign to protect their identity, many of the names from taxonomies I'd never heard of.

"Well, I didn't do anything." I had tucked a rose into Frost Viper's satchel after the ride, then sent her the kit I'd taken on our trip to the Third Layer, but that wasn't much. "But I'll thank her for whatever she sent and think up another gift to give."

"You sent them something that is basically life support. And you did it for free." She looked at me like I was an idiot.

"It didn't cost me anything," I said uncomfortably, looking around at the wealth of magic around us while thinking about the dearth in the Third Layer. "I'm hardly a philanthropist."

She shook her head. "That rose wasn't free. You needed all your tricks on that trip. But you parted with one. You do that a lot."

I stared at her, uncomprehending. "We didn't need it."

"You didn't know that at the ti—no, you know what?" She patted me on the back. "Where are we headed?"

"To the library?"

"Why do you make statements sound like questions?"

"Ugh. What's a Hummingbird?"

"A small bird that—"

"No, great, this is going to be one of those days." I rubbed at my temples. "Some weird dudes. Or, maybe not dudes. They had a dudeish vibe." I waved a quick hand, then snatched it back when people crossing our path ducked. "Anyway, three dudes in black robes were outside my room talking about hummingbirds and the equinox and periods of time. Any ideas?"

"Send me a picture."

I pulled the memory up, then paired my connection to Delia along with her frequency and sent it down the metaphorical tube.

"You are getting much better at that," she said. Her head cocked to the side. "Looks like the Layer Equilibrium Society. Shift season is a big deal for them."

"Shift season seems to be a big deal for everyone," I pointed out. "Even the ones who just want to predict doom and gloom."

"Keeps us on our toes," she agreed. "I am going to rock the shift changing fashion line I have almost finished—thanks for the dye additive, by the way, I don't know what you did to the agent, but it resisted the shift simulator by a multiplier of point six."

"Great! I'll make some more. Constantine and I will be in lab tomorrow. I bet we can increase the results by a factor of two after the first week of test results."

"I'll have to thank Leandred? How uncomfortable."

But she seemed more amused than anything.

With the weeks dwindling before the shifts started, students had been ramping up the use of the shift simulators on campus in order to get their last—or first—tests in before the real thing began. The resulting small tremors that ran through the mountain were almost pleasant.

As if I had conjured one by the thought, a tremor vibrated the ground and I smiled.

A group passing us screeched, hands pressed to their cheeks.

"That's not her, you morons," Delia bellowed over her shoulder. "How long have you gone to school here?"

I scratched at my neck, cringing. That was one of the side effects of any resemblance of a shift. Everyone looked at the Origin Mage. Or, perhaps more accurately, the "we are pretty positive she's an Origin Mage, we are just working on proving it."

"Tell me that Shift Season—with its constant shifts—will stop those reactions," I said.

"Shift Season brings out the weirdos, the fanatics, and the panicky," she said, eyeliner drawing itself into little swirly whirls at the corners of her eyes in a simulation of her own brand of eccentricity. "But for the more philosophical disciplines or sects, it's more social experiment than anything else. Watching how people deal with the issues that the layer shifts always bring. Seeing how resilient we are. The aim of groups like the Equilibrium Society is to watch what happens during the season, then to remove items, creatures, or mages that put the layer out of balance."

I stared. "Oh, wow, that's not foreboding at all."

"Well, they can't just go around willy-nilly removing things or killing off people. We do still have laws and justice around here."

The Department just seemed to get a pass.

"Why would they want my blessing, then?"

She shrugged. "There are lots of disparate groups in that particular sect. They might think that you will aid in the season, rather than making it apocalyptic like the rest of us are betting on."

"Delia!"

"Truth," she said, unapologetic.

The main library came into view, towering with its beautiful glass and magical steel trappings.

"I'm Fourth Flooring," I told her in dubious tones. Hardly anyone ever ventured up there with me other than Axer, who already ruled it.

"Cool." She removed a knit cap from the temporary pocket space that was connected to the wardrobe in her room. "You want one?"

She produced another without waiting for an answer, and put it in my hands.

I examined the complicated knot work and magicked threads. The subtlety between functional and stylish was a line Delia loved to walk. And like most everything Delia wore, the hat was on trend. "Do you wear it under the helmet?"

She stared at me in revulsion. "Do I look like I wear a safety helmet?" she demanded.

"No?"

"The answer is N-O with a thick exclamation point, not a question mark, Ren."

"Got it."

I tugged the offered hat over my hair. "This will be the same as having a helmet?"

"Of course not," she scoffed. "That's why they are called *safety* helmets. Seriously, Ren, sometimes I wonder about you."

"Yeah, what was I thinking?"

She ignored the dry tone. "I've seen, like, a hundred pictures of you on the feeds in a shiving helmet. Unacceptable. That's why I'm going with you and you are going to wear what I made for you."

I rubbed my chest. I'd probably be fine with just the knit hat. Probably be fine without it, to be frank. The Origin Book, lord of the cupola, had given me a sort of immunity, now that it wanted something I was trying to provide.

Delia, however...

"I don't want you to be eaten—"

"Pssh. Let's go, Crown."

I readied a spell, anyway, as the first book swiped down for a pass at her. Before I let the spell fly, the book recoiled as it opened its pages near her head. It shot back through the air, squid style.

My hand fell, unused magic still moving along my palm. "What—"

Delia tapped the purple threads of her hat. "Eraser gum woven in. Won't last forever, and the more that approach, the more the magic dwindles. We've got about an hour. But it's the stylish mage's alternative to helmet head."

She thumped a palm against my knit hat, enchanting the sound to mimic the clunk of hitting a helmet.

"If I get my soul sucked out, you are totally to blame," I said.

Chapter Twenty-three

"Responsibility accepted."

I waved to the Origin Book, who stared hard at Delia, then seemed to reject her as a threat, imperiously flexing its cover in a lordly "proceed" command.

I set up at a table under the cupola and three books immediately flew down, dancing on their little cornered feet as they waited to be acknowledged. I looked them over as I took a seat, unable to see their spines yet, and wondered what titles the Origin Book had sent today.

One of them hopped forward and I held out my hand. Information about field wards ran through me, absorbing into my mind. The full knowledge never completely remained, but it was all about the connections. And I could use the tail of the magic to a significant degree. I still retained some of the abilities from the enhanced senses book—the first book I'd been gifted here.

Delia watched the clamped book for a second, head tilted. "I can't believe no one has been able to capture that on recorded memory. The books don't do that normally."

I did an encompassing gesture with my free hand to indicate magic, bargains, and probably death were involved.

Delia shook her head. "It's just a matter of time, Crown. I knew there was something fishy you were getting yourself into. You are lucky you have us." She froze for a moment, in the act of pulling something from her pocket. "Me, I mean. You are lucky you have me," she said with a sniff.

She pulled a blanket out of her pocket half a foot at a time—like a magician with a never ending handkerchief—then threw it on the floor. She stretched out on her back, feet on the seat of the chair next to me, staring up into the cupola.

I watched her, to make sure she was okay, while also trying not to go cross eyed at the visual buffet the clamped book was serving up on wards.

One eye closed, Delia made a little gun sign with her fingers and shot a zap at one of the books diving toward her. She blew the end of her finger and little wisps of purple swirled around the edge.

"Like the First Layer, yeah?" she asked, wanting confirmation of her weapon.

"Without the purple smoke, magic, and flying book, close enough."

She proceeded to shoot each book that came close. Within a few minutes, the books took it as a challenge, and there was a great buzzard tornado of bound paper above us.

Nothing like calling a little more attention our way.

I sighed and gave her a little spell that tickled the books. The tornado grew in size, books flying and scampering around her shots of magic.

Worst Nightmares gave a little shake of delight as it evaded three of Delia's zaps and spiraled up into the air—a biplane evading ground fire.

I couldn't imagine what this might look like outside the stacks that surrounded the cupola's interior. With a quarter of the books on the Fourth Floor participating in the spectacle, swooping in the magical updraft and taking turns diving at the smirking girl on the floor, it must look like the apocalypse was starting.

No, nothing like calling a little more attention our way.

The great thing about Delia hanging out on the Fourth Floor, though, was that she zapped encroaching books *and* encroaching students.

Few students other than the combat mages or the ones specially trained or training in library arts ever entered the cupola's area. The few students who *did* risk it were all, to a one, trying to get footage of me.

"Oops," Delia said unapologetically, as she zapped the feet of her sixth mage with a spell that made him swear and dance around like his shoes were full of fire. "Didn't see you there."

A few minutes later, I caught her frowning. "How do you *usually* keep people from recording?" she asked.

I cringed. "*Fleeting Memories* has a leaking problem and copiously drips ink on people hanging around the cupola."

"That is horrible," she said, voice filled with delight.

Delia had amassed fourteen Level Ones by the time we left.

"I'm not letting you go back," I said, wincing at her tally, even though it had been a huge relief not to be an inadvertent accessory to people losing their memories today.

"What? Just you and Lifen get to do all the fun stuff? I can totally turn these offenses into community service." She couldn't even keep her tone serious.

"Besides, the Justice Squad has been hilarious," she continued. "Did you see Peters? All six of the times he had to charge me in the last hour? He wants to maim me so hard, just on principle, but I saved his best friend on Bloody Tuesday," she said in a tone that was far too casual. "He gave me stitching duty the other day, and keeps adding to it."

I had wondered what "adding on an hour to your previous punishment, Miss Peoples. *Please* cease spelling everyone," had meant.

It was also kind of interesting that after the sixth time Peters had shown up, people had stopped approaching the cupola. I was pretty sure he had stayed on the other side of the stacks for a while. I could imagine him stopping people from entering with an endless stream of resigned sighs.

"What does stitching duty involve?" I asked.

"Bunch of fiber arts do-gooders putting together memorial pieces and helping the indigent. It's all very upstanding citizen-y." She waved a hand.

"Are you racking up hours so that you can work with them while pretending you aren't there willingly?"

"I don't know what you are talking about, Crown. I can't stand those do-gooders."

"Right," I said as seriously as I could manage.

But each time Delia was available, she accompanied me to the Fourth Floor, racking up double digit offenses every time, and smiling all the while.

Chapter Twenty-four

SHIFTING PRIORITIES

WITH THE FULL MOON sliding back into darkness, shift season excitement ramped up big time in the scientific community while shift terror ramped up for everyone else. The shifts would start on the next full moon.

I was hoping that it would provide the distraction so desperately needed as people shifted from shock and anger to longer term despair over lost friends, and that it wouldn't be what Bellacia's feeds anticipated—panic.

The shifts themselves were too valuable a testing point for me to ignore, and after researching Kinsky, who had stayed out of the Department's hands for a few years, I saw *opportunities*. Kinsky had done a number of projects at the Zantini Institute under the direction of a Professor Mussolgranz that the public—even those awful art store people back in Ganymede—thought perfectly acceptable works.

I could slip a number of things under the radar if I did it as *school* work.

However, with the amount of scrutiny I was under, I couldn't just go start fixing *layers*. That was a one-way kennel ticket I couldn't yet fight.

I wanted to fix the Third Layer. I wanted to identify every person in the First Layer who held the potential to Awaken. I wanted to support and help rare mages. I wanted to protect my family and friends, I wanted to fight to keep people out of the Department's basement, I wanted to be a great Origin Mage.

Do it all, said an insidious internal voice.

I rubbed my chest. I wanted to do it all, but I had learned a little bit of caution.

I could bite off a few pieces of the world-saving pie that *didn't* scream Origin Mage, because anything I tried that smacked of Origin Magic was going to be highly scrutinized.

Chapter Twenty-four

My other less *acceptable* projects would need to be done under the cover of darkness.

If I could *pace* myself, I would be on campus for four more years—plenty of time to save the world.

Right now...right now I could try to save those like *Christian*.

When Professor Mbozi saw me heading toward him, he sighed and muttered something that sounded like, "She'd cheerfully drag a guillotine in her wake."

I laughed nervously and smoothed both hands down the sides of my jeans. I had practiced this speech.

"Hey, Professor! So, I noticed you had an opening for independent projects next term. And I'd like to refine the portable chaos field design—utilizing it as both a viable containment field and shield—a switchable spell. I think that it will be a useful addition to the scientific community. I'd like to attempt this under your supervision."

I worshiped Mbozi, his classes, and his knowledge. The man knew everything about his chosen field. And if I could pull off the project, I could make something that could be used in the event of an Awakening—protecting the layers by putting the mage under the field and protecting the mage from *others* by using it as a shield. Even better, under supervision, no one could claim it some wacko Origin work. It could be used in real time by real people. People who weren't me.

Getting the field *to* the Awakening mage would be part of step two, and would require Will's input. He had wanted to play with portal pads that could traverse layers since the day we met. It was *how* we had met. It felt prophetic, almost, coming full circle to the moment when I'd realized the magical world was real.

Step two, Ren, step *two*.

Mbozi tapped one of his books. "You want to take a revolutionary design that few can even conceptualize, and not just realize it fully with all the charms and triggers, but also have a way to subvert it to its opposite track?"

I thought it over for a moment. "Yes." I deliberately avoided making it sound like a question.

We had talked about the success of the singly-tested field finally—and Mbozi was one of the very few who knew about my Third Layer trip, though he had deliberately stated that he didn't want details outside of the field test results—so he knew I had gotten the field to work. Making it *reliable,* however, was a step far harder to achieve. And being able to flip it added a level of complexity that far exceeded the original aim.

"What are your plans for conclusion-testing?"

"The layer shifts. It's shift season soon," I said as earnestly as I could manage.

"You plan to only test here?" He looked down his nose at me, and crossed his arms, as if interpreting that to mean I was lying and planned to trip off to the Third Layer when no one was looking, with a pink parasol and butterflies trailing from my hem.

Pink wasn't really my color, though. And there were some things that I clearly could not take upon myself at the moment without risking those around me.

"I also have a group that can test in the Third Layer," I admitted reluctantly. "I was planning on sending advanced beta tests to them."

I'd exchanged another recycling kit with Frost Viper, who had gifted me with a strange copper branch in return. It, too, held magic that I had yet to identify. The Ophidians seemed game to try my items, though.

"Dare I ask whom?"

"A biker gang in the Outlands?"

Mbozi stared at me for a moment, then shook his dark head. "We'll just list them as 'friendly parties' on the sheet."

My heartbeat jumped. "I can do it? You'll take me on?"

"Miss Crown, wild pegasi couldn't keep me from your project."

~*~

I entered Constantine's workroom, grinning like a loon.

He didn't look up from the delicate gears he was securing to a wreath of black. "You got him to agree."

"Yes."

"I don't know why you were afraid he'd say no. Mbozi's not an idiot."

"He looks at me like I'm going to announce my intention to turn the sky green every time I approach."

"You could do it," Constantine said, carefully nudging a gear into place with his artist's fingers. "I know just the shade."

"Would you—"

"Yes."

"You don't know what I was going to ask."

"Don't I?" A ghost of a smile worked his lips, and he turned his head just a fraction toward me, looking at me through a lock of hair. "The answer is yes anyway."

"I should make you do part of my community service," I mused, kicking back in the chair across the table from him. "That would serve you right."

"Go ahead. I can't say no to you either, darling."

"What do you mean, either?"

He smiled—though it was more of a smirk this time. "Either, one or the other, all of the above."

Chapter Twenty-four

I let my head drop back so I was staring at the ceiling, but could keep him in my peripheral view with a shift of my eyes. "Will you work on the project with me?"

He looked over, gaze somewhere near my chin, then went back to his meticulous work. "I told you we would work on it when we got back from hell. We are in hell no longer."

"But you have your own projects—"

"Of which you did six last week," he said, closely eying an internal mechanism. "And the fibril canopy you want to create for your field— twelve naked nymphs bathed in whipped cream sea foam couldn't tear me away."

"Mbozi cited wild pegasi."

"The man is a gifted engineer, but I question his imagination."

"Will you have enough time with your classes and Olivia's thing?"

"Do you think you are the only one who can multitask dozens of things?" he murmured. "I'm offended."

I sat up and drummed the fingers of one hand on the table, while chewing my thumb knuckle on the other.

"I thought up the canopy for you. Based on the discussion we had about those fibers you wanted to try."

His gaze shifted and held mine. "I know."

"Okay." I nodded, as if that would extinguish my lingering guilt. I could ask for help. I could. I could keep asking. Like I was trying to tell the Ophidians, who kept returning items to me, as if one deed required repayment.

I had almost always been the one to insinuate myself into other people's projects, though. Even with Christian. Only when I'd gotten myself into deep trouble on campus had I rolled over—usually a little too late—to ask for help.

"Your emotions pain me," Constantine said bluntly, once more concentrating on his task. "I can't imagine what use guilt serves if it makes a person feel like that."

I sent a jumbled packet of emotions his way.

He sighed. "Ren, I could give a cransee's arse about most of the things I was planning to do this spring. The only thing that mattered was the project that I put on indefinite hold, for which you *should* feel guilt," he said, his light tone. "My schedule is quite free, and entirely yours next term."

I slumped. I was glad he was focused on projects other than revenge on Raphael. Still—"I'll make it up to you."

He stopped working for a moment, fiddling with the tool in his hand, then looked at me and said, "You already have."

He said it simply, and I felt an enormous feeling of kinship, all of a sudden, centering on my neck then pushing downward toward my chest. Constantine's eyes followed whatever magic he could see traveling.

"I'm happy to take advantage of you. Guilt is stupid." He rubbed his chest. "Hold this gear in place."

~*~

Stevens said yes to the project as well. When we gathered to discuss preliminaries, the professors exchanged glances heavy with meaning. Constantine and I were given all access passes to the vault for spring term, which was huge—and also something of an apology from Stevens, who was allergic to apologies. She was adamant about joint work hours between the three of us now, so it was her way of allowing us our own secret projects.

I had copied the vault's wards as best as I could upon first heading out to work in the Midlands. But the chaos wards of the vault were still predominantly Mbozi's, and they were a work of art in their details.

They were details that I could use to improve my own, and that would aid me in unhooking the book. I was definitely going to use my all access pass to do both.

And as a bonus, I could lower the door while smiling sweetly at the mages who always trailed me trying to get recordings of me doing shifty things.

No more sneaking around, unless required.

Chapter Twenty-five

ATTACKS OF EXCITEMENT

AS THE WEEK before finals wound down, the small ground tremors became increasingly more common.

Not all shift projects *used* shift magic. Many of them, like Will's, were for prevention of the magic buildup. Or in Loudon's discipline—detangling knotted magic or trying to actively recycle it—like our Third Layer travel kit had.

The company that Trick and the others had formed—Trick now calling all of us Bandits United as a joke—was working on monetizing those kits and putting them in the Hawker's Festival next year.

They were going to make a lot of money at some point.

Olivia rolled her eyes one day and said, "The idiots want you to know you'll get your agreed upon percent and so will I." Olivia had argued that I could ask for more—my type of magic was unique, so I had a competitive advantage, but as far as I was concerned, it was all a win-win. I was never going to be that interested in business. I could help out when needed and pursue other shiny things.

Trick, Saf, Kita, and their expanded crew had their own spring project planned—running the shift magic through a series of relays that powered and caused fluctuations in the game fields themselves. Designed to keep gamers on their toes with a series of world and frame changes—ones that mimicked what might actually happen during an unanticipated shift—their project was a bit diabolical.

I sketched out a series of designs for them one evening while Constantine rolled his eyes in the background. With my hours and the speed at which Olivia, Constantine and I regenerated magic together, his living room was becoming the most common meeting ground. Even Olivia had grudgingly moved most of her active projects into a corner of the room.

* Attacks of Excitement *

Mike, Will, and I were splayed out on couches there on the Thursday before finals.

"The Fifth Layer is not a broken wasteland like the Third. It's like...electricity, alive all the time. Hoary and mysterious is the Fifth Layer." Will's fingers did a mystical dance. "We should totally go there for break, Ren," he said enthusiastically.

"Right, because that makes sense," Mike said, waving a half-hearted hand through the air. "Let's go on a field trip to *hell*."

Olivia had left us to "do actual work" on a legal brief cum final term paper, while Neph was studying a complicated series of detailed postures for one of her exams and needed the space in her room to dance.

I could understand why they had abandoned us.

Mike, Will, and I had been lethargically trying to study for our politics exam together, but had gotten sidetracked consistently, materials forgotten at our sides. Even Delia had bailed on us.

The exam was Monday, but Monday was still *forever* away, and there were so many other shiny things to do rather than prepare what to answer when given: yes, no, a, b, c, d, e, give your argument, write an essay, make lightning, shoot a fireball, or none of the above as choices.

"There are layer jolts in the Fifth, though. *Jolts.* And we could stop by the Third, cause a few shifts. I could get some great data before we even begin the season," Will argued.

"You don't have a *permit*, Will," Mike said, as if he'd repeated this argument far too many times and was *done*. "For *either* layer."

"I bet I could get Dean Mar... Or Proctor Vel... Okay, maybe next year." His voice picked up enthusiastically again. "Next year, Ren, we are *going* to the Fifth Layer."

I looked at my fingertips and rubbed my thumbs across them. I had learned some *very* interesting things today from a Fourth Floor book entitled *Between Layers*. Campus was being released from its bonds on Saturday, and Will and I were both free after Wednesday. I could get us to the Fifth L—

"Don't even think it."

I looked at Constantine, who was on the end of my couch, and who I thought had been ignoring us. I raised a brow at his statement, but he didn't look away from the book he was reading. It was a real book, too, the covers bending gently, like palm fronds over his fingers.

"I didn't say anything," I said.

A page of the book flipped without any motion from him. "You practically shouted it." His eyes tracked words on the new page.

I looked at my fingertips. I *could* do it, though—get Will where he wanted to go. The idea of it—making him happy—outwitting restrictions—

sent my heart racing.

Do it.

"Absolutely not." Constantine's voice brooked no argument.

"But—"

"Because no one would *hunt* you the moment you stepped foot from campus?"

"I'm learning—"

"Verisetti or Stavros or even Price's forsaken mother? What about the terrorists in the wind? Or the magicists who slaver over the Bailey's reports and think anyone with a modicum of talent should be cuffed and leashed? Or the Equilibrium Society that thinks you will end the world?"

"The Layer Equilibrium Society asked for my blessing, actually."

"They did?" Will asked.

Constantine looked down his nose. "I'm starting to understand why Price is so obstinate and dour all the time."

"I'm not saying that—"

"Do you want Tasky to get arrested?" he asked, switching tactics along with the timber of his voice.

"Of course not," I said automatically.

"Because William Tasky is on the list of idiot students who will show up on a layer scan."

"Hey!" Will sputtered though it wasn't without some sheepishness.

"And the Fifth does layer scans all the time. They have to." Constantine looked at me pointedly. "Oh, have you not *researched* this yet, Ren? Do you know what a layer scan is? Were you just thinking of going off half-cocked to give your friend a moment that he wanted? How embarrassing," he said, turning his gaze back to the page.

"Ugh. Fine. *Understood.* You don't have to be unpleasant about it." The feeling of possibility retreated under forced sense. I rubbed my chest and whatever strange sense of disappointment registered there at being unable to go.

"I am exceedingly adept at the skill," he said, with only a small glance upward—quickly returned to the page. "One must play to one's strengths."

I put my chin on my hand and leaned my elbow against the back of the couch. Weird feelings were coming from him. "You're worried."

He made a sound that on someone else might be called a snort, but was too refined on Constantine. "It seems to be an integral state of being your friend."

My jaw dropped. "What do you mean?"

Will's gaze was unabashedly darting between us, as if watching a match, while Mike was trying to be a bit more circumspect.

Constantine pointed a long finger at Mike without looking at him.

"Givens, tell her," he commanded.

"First, let's get something straight, Leandred. I'm not your minion," Mike said to him. "Second, yes, you make everyone worry, Ren," he said to me, carrying out Constantine's directive.

A freezing wave swept through me, from head to toe, but sat most heavily in my stomach, leaving me numb.

Constantine looked up, eyes narrowing, obviously able to sense the change.

I smiled. It felt all kinds of wrong on my face. "Oh. Well, that... I didn't... Okay."

Mike seemed to read my numb panic as well, and hastened for reassurance. "It's a normal part of being a friend, Ren. I worry about Will every damn day."

But that was different. And I was happy Will had someone to look after him like Mike did. I didn't want to be anyone's burden. I was supposed to be the one holding everyone else's burdens. It was *my* job. I was the protector.

It was my job. What if...

The flipping patterns on the table didn't reveal any secrets, and I only realized I was staring at them when long fingers turned over my left hand. Constantine moved his fingers along the metallic cuff that was always in place. Mostly in place. Sometimes in place. It was my fourth, after all. And I didn't—

"Shhh. It's okay," he said, interrupting my spiraling train of thought.

The fingers of his other hand drew a half circle around my neck, and magic zipped along to complete the path.

A feeling of family, calm, love, and support surrounded me.

"You never removed it," I said, referencing whatever magic had been placed by his ribbon.

"Of course I didn't," Constantine murmured.

I could hear Mike's aggravated sigh in the background.

"How many books did you speak to today?" Constantine asked me, ignoring everyone else in the room, as usual.

"Nine."

"You are taking too much," he said.

I opened my mouth to argue, then shut it. "Yeah, okay."

There was another surging sense of family—like a reward given for not being stupid.

"Magic," Mike whispered, and he was looking at Constantine like he was a masked alien who would reveal himself at any moment.

Mike looked at Constantine's hands—his long fingers—then at my neck. "It's a leash," Mike whispered. His expression was of thunderstruck revelation.

Constantine froze.

I frowned. Constantine had used them on me before—I knew what one felt like when wielded by him. "No it's not; nothing has been taken from me."

"That's not what I m—" Mike cut off abruptly, gaze switching to Constantine. Some fight played out between them in minute facial tics. "Fine."

"It's a community magic, nothing more," Constantine said dismissively. "When campus opens, we need to be prepared."

I frowned at him. "Prepared for what?"

Magic screeched and shook, like a TV signal on the fritz.

As if our conversation had conjured them, a group of Third Layer terrorists appeared on an emergency news broadcast.

A small woman in all black gear stood in front of a military group.

"For nearly forty years have I watched the gears of the world grind over us," the woman said. "No longer. You think yourselves safe? Then this will be your new beginning."

"Frela Vey. Fourth on the top ten list," Will murmured.

"She's a fighter?"

"They all are, to an extent."

"She's small."

"So are you," Mike said with amusement.

"I'm not a fighter."

"No? Aren't we all?"

The woman—Vey—on the feed continued.

"Look at all of you. So content in your vast homes with your comfortable household magics."

With Godfrey destroyed, Raphael on walkabout, and Leonach Lorenzo still pretending to be a politician, a new person had stepped in to fill the Third Layer terrorist leadership void, and a quick search with Will and Bellacia's gifts said this one had quite the history.

Frela Vey was as petite as she was hard. Poised as she was ruthless. Gone was Godfrey's pseudo-aristocratic tone wrapped around working class rage, and in his place was a small storm of darkness.

She was wearing a dark suit that was both flattering on her form and armament all its own—a battle cloak that had been magically drawn into a suit around her. Her hair had a forties-like curl and weight.

"We've been reliably informed that it's only a matter of time now. That pieces are in place. Enjoy our magic while you still have it, because we will be taking it back."

She waved her black baton, I felt something weird tug at my chest, a shadow crossed my vision, and destruction descended upon the land.

~*~

Even Axer wasn't able to calm me completely at first. Everyone had given it a try.

I felt it was partially my fault, though. The tug. Raphael. The box, somehow made whole. My magic was out there, taken from me, and doing things that I didn't want it to do.

"Verisetti couldn't have fixed the leash through a dream," Axer said, sitting in front of me, the grove vividly alive around us tonight. "Not without your permission."

"He put something on me. He's always putting things on me." I scraped at my arms. "Spells everywhere." Even Draeger had said the traps and stickiness hadn't been a sole product of Axer's workroom, after we'd moved back to the battle rooms to practice. That meant they were on *me*.

Axer stopped my hands. "Before, when he was using the leash, you were rendered immobile. You said this wasn't like that. Maybe it is just the feel of similar magic. When...when my mother uses her magic, I can feel it, like a tug that connects us."

"You think there's another Origin Mage?"

"No, but there are other people who can manipulate Origin Magic, especially when working together. You take too many burdens on yourself."

He rubbed my arms, then let me go. "We'll be back Saturday morning for the opening of campus." He shot a look at me through the hair that had fallen across his eyes. "I've been away too long."

I nodded and trailed my fingers through the water. Abruptly, my tension drained—like it had slipped into the waters and rippled away. The pond always reminded me of something on the edge of memory.

"Better?" Axer's voice was both questioning and tense.

I cupped some of the water in my hand and let it escape between lazy fingers. "I miss you." Flowers suddenly bloomed around the grove in reaction and I quickly got my mouth to behave. "I mean, I haven't fought a monster in weeks. Greene is not a sport hunter. I'm getting rusty."

I concentrated *very hard* on the abruptly still water and let the silence stretch.

"How goes it with the books?" Axer finally said.

I relaxed again, pulling my fingers along the surface. "I'm learning all sorts of things. They make me tired, though. My roommates badger me about it."

Even Constantine was giving me the stink eye when I tried to stay up late. "I am getting more sleep now than I've had for months combined," I said wryly, looking up. "And I removed a second set of wards from the book today."

"Did you?" There was an intensity to the statement that was greater than usual.

"Yes. Do you disapprove?" I frowned at him. "You never said you disapproved."

"I don't." He produced a puzzle box and handed it to me.

I stared at it, but took it from him, turning it in all directions to examine it. "Another? I'm beginning to think that you're training me to break into whatever passes for an international bank in the Second Layer."

He nudged me in the side. "Solve it."

Chapter Twenty-six

COMMUNITY

THE TERRORIST ATTACK—taking out a travel hub somewhere in Second Layer Africa—spiked many of the traumatic fears on campus that had been slowly healing.

As spooked as part of the population was, though the reopening of campus *was* going to happen.

The three squads had done a thorough job canvassing the levels all the way down to the twenty-second. But the arguments concerning the reopening still occurred in the nooks and crannies where students liked to hang out.

"I don't want campus reopened at large. It will be worse."

"It *must* be open spring term for shift season."

"I don't want campus *closed*. At least this way, we can *escape*."

The uncertainty and subsequent panic prior to finals week was messing with the minds of many students. It was messing with them in a way that wasn't productive for anyone. And I felt a responsibility—a responsibility to campus, to my stolen magic, to all the things Raphael had done since I'd Awakened.

I thought about Bellacia and how she played the media and news. I thought about Olivia and how she made her arguments. I thought about how I had always liked to be in the background, letting things happen instead of forcing change—in myself and in the world.

The community groups had existed before my arrival on campus, however, my first impressions of wickedness and mayhem on campus had confirmed early on that "helpful" groups weren't the dominant ones.

Now, though... Everywhere on campus, I could see small pockets of mages actively helping each other. A horrible impetus had spurred the change, but a sense of community—maybe one that had always been waiting, waiting for a moment to unleash itself—had bloomed in the wake of the attack. A tentative bloom, but there all the same.

Helping others deal with their grief had vastly improved my own ability to handle my sorrow. Even with the old dreams coming back, more and more—the old thoughts, Christian's voice whispering to me at odd times— I felt stronger. Better able to deal with the backward slides that always threatened. I was at a mental health point, finally, where I could at least recognize the backward slides. Where I could find ways to cope that weren't as destructive.

I thought about the underlying good will that was strumming through campus. I could let it continue as it was, hoping that it would continue to be nurtured and grow, or I could *use* it.

There was an opportunity here, and—clutching yet another pamphlet shoved into my hands proclaiming my duty to the world, Isaiah's words about rallying people, and my own desperate desires to have my magic do *good*—I forced myself to take a step toward it.

My first call was to the blonde from the battlefield, who still walked the grounds with my magic illuminating her from the inside—who had spearheaded much of the rehabilitation of spirit around campus.

Finding her was easy. A sketch drawn during politics weeks ago had yielded her name from the first person I asked.

The weird thing was her complete lack of surprise upon seeing me at her door.

A large smile bloomed across her rosy cheeks and her aqua eyes twinkled. "It's so good to see you, Ren." Her smile fairly brightened the room. "Sari Tarkovar," she said, introducing herself. "Come in, come in."

Her roommate, a bushy-haired brunette with a kind face, squeaked upon seeing me, but recovered quickly and busied herself setting up a little tea table.

Somewhat bewildered, I sat and automatically lifted the delicate rose-wrapped teacup that was placed in front of me. Deliciously magical-smelling scones were placed on the table with a little pot of jam. The scones tasted as good as they smelled.

Both girls, introduced as Sari and Bess, sat with their own cups of tea and smiled happily as they lifted them to their lips.

I wondered if I had somehow found the good fairy mound.

I rubbed a hand over my eyes. I really shouldn't have let the book on *Non-Mythological Beings Through the Layers* have its way with me yesterday.

"We have everything ready," Sari said, hands crossed graciously in front of her. Bess nodded brightly.

I paused, teacup halfway back to its small, decorative saucer. "You do?"

"Of course. We've just been waiting."

"For?"

"For you."

I nodded. Sure. Fairies knew things.

"We aren't fairies," Sari said, grinning, eyes bright.

I pointed at her, forgetting for a moment that some people saw that as threatening motion from me. "You just read my thoughts, Fairy."

She laughed, seemingly not in the least worried about the gesture. "You are in our room and I have a life link to you."

Oh, crap. Olivia was always warning me about these things, but did I listen?

My teacup hit its saucer. "A life link, like a hook?"

"No, saints, none of that." Sari put a hand out to pat mine. "Just a link, a connection. An added awareness from where you shot me full of magic. And do not worry, you have wonderfully protective shields. I can just get the thoughts that are meant for me to hear."

Yeah, that wasn't quite a relief.

She laughed, cheeks dimpling. "I would never abuse such a link. Have no fear. There are easy ways to limit the input. And links go both ways."

Constantine had said that long, long ago, but unlike Constantine, who had made that statement then taken full and immediate control of the connection and what leaked through, Sari did the opposite.

She opened the link—the connection—wide.

I could feel the happiness streaming through her, the understated power flowing beneath. She felt undiluted hope and appreciation for everything around her. She was a coiled buffet of promise and love. I stared at her as positive thoughts of *we will help you* and *we will do this with you* continued to strum through the link.

"Do you know why I've come?" I asked numbly, under such an onslaught of affirmation and euphoria.

"To change the world," she said.

And the desire and the fear coiled in me. Many history books the Origin Book had picked for me lately had transferred stories of Origin Mages over the ages and their grand plans and destructive ends.

"Campus first," I said.

She nodded, light shining around her—some of it visibly my magic. "Campus first."

"I have an idea for Saturday. And with the right timing"—I touched my memorial armband; most of the students still wore them—"we can involve all of campus. Quiet the fear. Give back the power."

Giving campus back to *itself*, to its denizens. That seemed important.

"You wish to do a unity band," she said.

I looked at her, at the thought softly plucked from the surface of my mind. "Is it a bad idea?"

Chapter Twenty-six
A smile bloomed, this one quietly gentle. "No, Ren."

~*~

My next stop was to Bellacia's.

"Your last hours here, Ren, before your *guardian* is back—I suppose a little gloating on your part is allowed," Bellacia said, lounging in the command chair in her workroom, watching me closely as I entered and dropped my bag onto her guest chair. "I'm sure Leandred suggested parting words. Hurry up, then. I deserve all of them for my machinations and intrigues, and now you are free of me, blah, blah—"

"Yeah, about that..."

Her eyes sharpened and her chair went upright as she leaned forward, uncrossing her legs. "What do you have, Ren?"

"I have a proposal for you."

~*~

My third stop was to Trick and Saf's room, where all the Bandits were gathered.

"Unity band," I said, as I bounded in, out of breath. "On the Eighteenth Circle. Tomorrow."

Sharp glances were traded throughout the room and even sharper nods.

I furrowed my brows. "Why does it look like you're planning something?"

"We are now planning a unity band, of course," Patrick said smoothly. "Now, give us the details."

~*~

The idea spread like wildfire. The Bandits and Sari and Bess had a *lot* of connections. And with the goodwillies ready for the rush, Bellacia's network released the idea in a viral tidal wave. It took about three minutes for nearly the entire campus to be locked in.

Chapter Twenty-seven

UNITED

IT HAD TAKEN all night for Professor Wellingham and two other professors, along with ten students to determine the ideal spots for everyone to stand. There were complex algorithms of magic and sympathy to account for and not much time to do it. Keeping friends and sympathetic groups together strengthened the magic in an area, but there was also a desire to spread the magic throughout. To interconnect our magic like an interwoven, unbroken Celtic knot work, a design that could never be undone.

Isaiah and Selmarie, along with the other club and student group leaders around campus, had readily endorsed the plan. The detractors and cynics on campus had been taken care of with a swift reminder that they could opt out, but that any influence they wanted to have would be lost in the event —the community magic would not contain theirs.

Not even the fieriest detractor wanted to be left out of the ability to influence.

Patrick and Asafa had done a little "debt assistance" work on their own, as well—taking a slice of each debt—"A little bit from the top, Crown"— for anyone who participated.

The line of mages stretched long miles around the perimeter of the Eighteenth Circle. Fifteen thousand students, two hundred faculty members, three hundred staff and administrative members, and five hundred adjunct employees lined the invisible barrier that would reopen campus to the world.

Nearly every student had turned out, even many of those less excited about campus reopening. The prevailing sentiment among them seemed to be that if campus was going to reopen, we were going to make it *ours*.

I'd shoehorned Constantine out of his kingly throne to participate, dragging him through three arches before he'd taken my wrist and said I'd made my point and he'd help. He looked blackly amused as he gazed at the Eighteenth Circle barrier—the one that he had helped destroy on two occasions.

With the combined weight of our community magic, we would dissolve the barrier, then cross it, pulling the community magic downward, to reconnect to the cities and towns on the lowest quarter of the mountain. We would take back our own defenses. This was *our* mountain.

And we would heal it, and each other, with each small step.

Frequencies powered down one by one as everyone got ready to wield the magic that we'd need.

A small commotion caused me to look left, then right. Even though I couldn't see them, I could hear the whispers as Axer, Nicholas, and Ramirez arrived back on campus and stepped into their designated spots miles away from our position and each other's. Everyone had a defined spot—only Constantine, and the others who had joined at the last minute, had needed to be worked in.

And of those, Constantine was, perhaps not surprisingly, the biggest thorn in everyone's side.

"I'm either next to Ren or not here at all," Constantine had said, tone bored, but words and gaze resolute.

Wellingham had looked like he wanted to commit murder, but he had made it happen, shifting ten other mages to cardinal points opposite us.

"You are such a jerk," I whispered to Constantine.

"Unrepentantly."

"I should never have brought you."

"Decidedly."

"How do you even get away with this kind of thing?"

He shrugged. "Power."

"This event is supposed to be about *community*."

I felt him smile. "I'm adding my power to the community."

"Con—"

"Don't worry, darling." He fished a vial out of his pocket and started unscrewing the cap. "I'm already making it up to you."

"*No.* What are you doing?" I hissed as he tipped the lip of the vial toward the ground, the action hidden as his body turned toward mine and I instinctively imitated the physical gesture. The liquid fell between us, then immediately seeped into the ground and began to spread in a clear glaze that caught the edge of the light—just enough light to know it was there since I knew where to look.

The only thing that stopped me from nervously glancing around was the rule drilled into me by Christian long ago—never make it seem like you are doing something shady, *especially* when you are doing something shady.

"I'm helping," Constantine said, answering my question, his mouth pulling into a smirk as he screwed the cap on the empty vial and slipped it into his pocket.

I looked down at the spreading, clear magic with a mixture of resignation and regret. "Are you taking hold of the wards?" Maybe putting a hook in them so that he could easily do as he wanted at a future point?

"Tempting. You'd be angry, though."

The only emotions coming from him were light, playful—maybe with a little resignation wrapped in there, but positive feelings flowed across our bond.

"You are amused," I said. "What was in the vial? Why are you suddenly so amused?"

He tipped his head. "It's...freeing, this shift in perspective. It's all rather insignificant in the grand scheme of things, but you want this—for campus, your new home, to be happy and free. Easy enough to assist with, so here I am."

"I had to drag you here."

"It wouldn't be a *game* otherwise. You would have been far more skeptical had I come willingly. You'd never have bought it and I'd have been made to stand elsewhere, relegated to being *good*."

I looked at him, then slipped my hand around his arm and squeezed. "I'd buy it."

Bonds wrapped around me—family, fondness, and something slightly darker and more fatalistic. He squeezed my hand beneath his, then pulled away before I could identify the last feeling.

"It's a good thing your hero is back," he said, pushing the hair from his face. He didn't look in the direction where I could feel Axer's presence like a beacon, but Constantine's connection to his roommate was likely stronger than mine—I could feel the exact spot on which Olivia stood, directly on the other side of the mountain, opposite us—and Axer and Constantine had been roommates and in each other's lives for far longer.

I had my guesses about how long—I'd bet a storage paper that their relationship pre-dated the death of Constantine's mother.

"You are glad Axer's back?" I asked skeptically.

"Your tower," he said lightly. "Temptation triggers even the darkest of creatures without good reminder. Alas, that I am quite aware you'd never survive the fall."

"You're a weirdo."

Another wave of amusement and fondness traveled the bond. "Would you rather I drag you to hell? I could be convinced. I'm a fickle creature. And a selfish one. Self-sacrifice is really not my color. Look at me right now, so drab."

"Yeah, drab—that's what that girl who *literally* threw herself in your path on our way here was thinking."

He sighed. "Alas, drab isn't nearly enough to hide my overt physical attractiveness to lesser mortals."

"Right. Well, maybe next time try a nice 'No thank y—'" Motion on my other side made me glance over to see Greene stepping into place next to me. I blinked at him. "What are you doing?"

He had been placed close to Lifen and Delia about a quarter turn away from me. I'd heard the girls' lewd commentary over the joint communications before everyone had muted them.

"Balancing the two of you," Greene said. "Wellingham is going to birth a canary otherwise. Cam and Bellacia are on the other side now, flanking your roommate with the others already set up there, to level the three of us in the spell."

Yikes. I sent waves of calm and embracing feelings to Olivia. She did not feel pleased with her situation, but she accepted my reinforcement.

Constantine shrugged at the look of reproach I sent him. "Alexander, Ramirez, Lox, Senthuss, your muse, and all of your little friends are spaced at points between. It's a better distribution. Besides, the community mages are the ones handling the brunt of this experiment, and they are still cardinal to each other all over this twee little grid."

"But not the power," Greene pointed out, trying for casual, but not quite attaining it. "No one who has been listed should be next to each other. Having the four of you at compassed points would have been the best distribution. But someone didn't bother to say he was showing up, then threw a tantrum when he did."

I peered at Greene's aristocratic posture. It was strange seeing him so tense.

"The four of us?" I asked.

Greene's gaze switched to me and eased a fraction, before returning to Constantine. "The four of you involved in the room switch. The five, really, with Bailey and Price close to each other. The absolute easiest configuration."

"If only it were a switch," Constantine said, ignoring everything else, tone dismissive.

Greene's lips pulled tight. "Intentional sabotage will invoke retaliation."

Constantine looked at him for the first time. "Sabotage? I heard about your little chat with Ren. Chats, really. Do you think poor Alexander doesn't know how to handle himself? I could see how. Automatons do have a hard time with emotion. Perfection doesn't like *messy*."

Greene, who I had rarely seen in conversation as anything other than gentlemanly, affable, and easygoing, was suddenly anything but. *This* was the warrior on the field who destroyed.

Constantine's gaze chilled. "You will find your threats don't go as well with me as when you say them to a girl without a clue of what you are warning."

"No." Greene pulled himself together, re-erecting each gentlemanly affectation as he laid his hands on the handle of his cane. "I don't need to threaten you for you to know the consequences should you interfere solely out of spite."

I could see Wellingham and a female professor on small wisps of magic, circling closer to our location. The Eighteenth Circle barrier pulsed, its last minute counting down as the administration started to unhook the magic.

Constantine looked at Greene like he was an insect trying to gain access to his watermelon. "Surely you don't think saying such a thing will work in the way that you want it to. I hadn't thought you as stupid as the others, but perhaps I will have to modify my respects accordingly."

"If you really want to touch the web you've spun, Leandred, and see what will happen should you pull a thread, so be it."

Constantine's caramel eyes reflected a void for a moment—a darkness I hadn't seen in him in weeks. "You have no idea what web I've spun."

The more wound up Constantine became, the more Greene seemed to relax. *Testing.* Whatever test Greene was running was giving him the desired result. "Not all of it, no. Only two people truly know you, one of those cursed with it, and the other supremely naïve. But unlike Lox, I don't underestimate people starved of affection."

Darkness spiked in twelve directions at once.

"*Community,*" I said, grabbing hold of Constantine's hand and *squeezing.* "Yay, *community.*" I sent everything I could through the grip Constantine was fighting to be free of, while I pinned Greene with the least impressed look of which I was capable.

Constantine fought for a moment more, before abruptly relaxing, dark tendrils dissipating in the wind. One dark brow rose at me, and I sent him an equally flat expression in return.

I stepped back so that I could stab both men with finger gestures without having to move my body too much.

"The ceremony is starting and you will both do this," I said fiercely. "We are doing this *together.*" I stabbed both fingers at the ground.

"Of course, darling. I'm here, aren't I?" Constantine looked bored again, all further thoughts stuffed into the dark chasm he kept swirling at his center for just such a use—his own purple and black vortex made to store anything unwanted. I hadn't known how he could bury emotion so quickly until I'd accidentally stripped away that privacy with my paint.

Chapter Twenty-seven

"As you say, Crown." Greene tipped his head, utterly composed once more.

Wellingham and the other professor flew by on their wisps, sprinkling dust over us as they flew.

As soon as the dust hit my skin, the community magic pulsed. I could immediately feel the edginess from the boys on both sides of me and I let some of my magic flow to Constantine.

Constantine acquiesced—just a small defiance still present—but one that he shed the moment my magic sought his.

Greene, on the other hand, accepted the community magic as it hit him, without needing any prodding. But then, Greene had pledged himself to the defense of Excelsine, like all the combat mages. And while this was not a combat maneuver, it was in defense of campus, all the same.

With our acceptance, the community magic linked each of us together—like it had done during the Lightning Festival—spreading from one mage to the next in a golden net.

Golden lights blinked between us, tendrils of gold bridging between one mage and the next.

One of Bellacia's magical recording bubbles that were orbiting the mountain circle, recording the event for one of their outlets, sped past us overhead.

Within a minute, the barrier between the Eighteenth Circle and the lower levels of the mountain dropped. It was just a shimmering of the air visually—there one moment, gone the next—but the weight of the spell dropping reverberated through the ground and community.

I had wondered how the coordination of so many people would be handled, but that was the beauty of the spell dust—and of the common desire in each of us for what we were trying to do.

Campus cleansing, possession, and freedom.

The magic urged us forward, and, in tandem, we took one step forward, then another.

The gold of the spell seeped into the ground, into the dirt and magic that made up Excelsine, connecting us to campus, and campus back to all of us.

It was a heady moment. And with it, I could feel another magic reaching up, asking permission. Recognizing the maker, I immediately acquiesced, and I felt the magic move along the roots of my connections, filling me with the same gold light.

I heard a gasp, then another. I followed the surprise blossoming through the community magic to the ground in front of me. Little zips of gold were diving in and out of the ground in front of us, as our magic kept spreading. Like little gold dolphins swimming and diving at the prow of our growing ship.

They grew in length, breadth, and luminescence, shooting forward further with every step forward. They hadn't been in the briefing materials about the spell, and the echoed surprise around the mountain affirmed that I hadn't missed anything on my own. I examined them, as we continued to walk and spread the magic. Of all the things that I could compare them to —like dolphins and nucleic light—the thing that they most reminded me of was the man-eating vine.

I looked at Constantine, who was now a dozen feet away as we walked down the mountainside on our vectors. We couldn't use spelled communications, but I didn't need one to read his smug expression and the questioning tilt of his head as he looked at me.

I grinned, knowing that he would read my response as a yes, I definitely liked them.

And the community magic did too. There was a feeling of wonder through the community circle—a feeling that was often lost in a world of wondrous things. But the gold lights were a manifestation of the magic. Constantine had created something to show the spirit of the magic, and in turn, that manifestation was *accelerating* the magic, increasing it as mages actively promoted it, forming an unbroken circle that spread further, that was *more*.

I shook my head. The things that man could do if he were working for the light.

Though, it was very likely he had conceived the base of the spell out of a desire to do evil, so, there was always that Catch-22.

On my other side, now nearly twenty feet away, Greene was studying the golden lights that were spreading farther and farther in front of us, the little zips growing into long jets of gold, pushing down the mountain, making the ground glitter in front of us. But everything was happening so quickly, and in such a euphoric haze, that I couldn't parse his expression.

Each step took all of us further apart, physically, but the community magic made it seem like we were bundled together, in a net of comfort, euphoria, and possibility.

The feeling of community spread throughout, linking all of us together. We would not be undone.

And just when we reached the stairs between the nineteenth circle and twentieth, the golden light burst in a tsunamic wave that rolled over the lower levels, linking up to the townspeople and city folk below, who were watching and supporting us.

The magic dimmed to a light, warm weight—one that lingered. Everyone was searching faces, farther away now, and internal communications were restarting sporadically as people questioned whether we needed to walk further.

"*Spell secured,*" came a voice from the ether.

A number of people immediately headed down the mountain and disappeared through one of the off-campus arches. I noticed a number of them pull fingers along the arch, though, as if telling through the community magic that they would be back.

I smiled, a little goofily, and looked to see Constantine sauntering toward me. Greene strode in from the other side.

"That was incredible!" I told Constantine. The euphoria was going to be slow to dissipate, I could tell. I could even feel Olivia reluctantly agreeing, way over on the other side of the mountain.

Greene smiled at me, gaze moving to Constantine—calculation in the depths of his eyes—then he tipped his head. "Indeed. Later, Crown."

He walked a few steps, then became a streak of light, moving in the extended travel magic that had suddenly opened back up. He was likely going to rejoin his colleagues.

I turned to Constantine and bounced from my toes to my heels. "I want to do that again."

Constantine sighed, wearing his jaded default expression. "Price is correct. We would all frolic in the meadow, if it were up to you, then snuggle in our bunks, humming each other to sleep."

I poked him in the side. "You'd love it. You helped this frolic. That liquid—it was an amplifier?"

"It allowed me not to have to walk down the whole blasted mountain."

I nodded, since that *had* been the plan. "How did you get it to spread so quickly?"

He looked at me and I could feel a slight ruffling of my thoughts as he plucked a theatrical mental image from my brain, making quick jazz hands to match the image. "Magic."

I elbowed him. "Did it just need a hook?"

"An easy conduit."

"Just one?"

"Just one, when that conduit is you."

I tipped my head, considering how that could be done. "My magic trusts you, so it accepted the hook and spread it, causing it to catch the community trail, from my group to each mage that trusts each of them, and so forth, until everyone had tapped in?" I could see from his expression that I was on the right track. "You are lucky that my magic automatically accepts yours."

There was something in his eyes. "Forever."

Gaze connected to his, I thought about the void, and Greene's cutting words. I touched my neck, then his arm. "Sorry about the whole, 'hand squeeze, don't obliterate the mountain' thing."

"Sorry?" A shadow of a smile curved his lips. "It was like watching a beautiful dark master rise. Next thing you know, you'll be puppeteering me around the Third Layer."

"I will *not*," I said, voice full of horror.

He laughed, eyes sparkling. "Pity."

"Seriously, I'm sorry." It felt like an imposition somehow, like I had forced him to be someone else for a moment—even if that was preventing him from accruing a Level Five and splattering combat mage guts everywhere. I didn't want to take his choice away.

He tapped his leg, grin fading. "I could have overpowered you—you give far too much of yourself, even when you pad your side with the power of creation itself. You may have stayed my hand for a moment, but you didn't force me to stop. No, your eternal disappointment was what kept me from plucking out Elias Greene's internal organs and splaying them in a circle of sacrifice, and I have full control over my reaction to disappointment."

"That's great," I said, relief underlying my grimace. "And thanks for the mental picture. My nightmares were just starting to fade."

"Any time you need an actual memory, do let me know, I'll be happy to create it."

I peered at him. "Greene's not harmless."

"Neither am I."

That was true. "Do you dislike Greene and the others because of Axer?"

"They exist—I dislike them on general principle."

I poked him again. "You aren't as much of a misanthrope as you pretend."

"I'm every bit of one."

Will and Olivia caught up to us one level up, converging from their points around the mountain.

"Price, tell Crown that I hate humanity," Constantine said, almost lethargically.

Olivia scowled. "Were those your halcyon lights?"

"No."

"They were great," Will affirmed.

"You are mistaken."

Will frowned. "But they were spelled to Ren."

"It could have been from any of you underlings," Constantine said dismissively.

"Nah. It was either her spell, or yours. The rest of us would have gone through our own networks simultaneously. Only you would go through a single point." Will, always good-natured, seemed to find this completely

Chapter Twenty-seven

acceptable.

Constantine's eyes narrowed.

I patted him on the arm. "Don't worry, everyone still thinks you're evil."

"Then they aren't blind."

Neph joined us, and her magic full of warmth and happiness mingled with mine. The muses had been happy to be part of the campus magic, not subservient to it or controlling.

At the arch that would take us to a north field in front of the Magiaduct, Constantine tilted his head, then with a brush of his fingers against my ponytail, he turned and took an arch in the opposite direction.

Used to him doing such things, I continued on with Will, Olivia, and Neph.

"It was really incredible," Will said. "The community magic alone was great, but what Leandred did—"

"I question his motives." Olivia frowned.

"Yeah, but that's your job, not mine. I think it was brilliant." Will bounced a little.

Neph smiled affectionately at him.

"He didn't want to walk all the way down campus," I said as we neared the Magiaduct's arches.

"I can actually believe that," Neph said dryly at my side.

Tingles started in the connection thread attaching to my chest. I started walking faster in the direction they pulled me toward—one of the outdoor tunnels that led through the superstructure had a crowd in front of it.

I began walking faster than Olivia and Will, who were in front of us, so I placed a hand on both of their backs and pushed them into a faster pace.

Irritation spiked from one; surprise from the other.

"Ren, what are you—"

But I wasn't listening anymore.

The crowd parted and I saw the person my heart had been pulling me toward—the last of my set, back where I could protect him too. He was lounging against the western wall at the edge of the tunnel, looking straight at us.

People were congratulating him—not quite touching, but making affirmative gestures near his space.

He stepped out of the crowd, neatly parting it—a magnet that attracted and repelled, leaving him untouchable.

I threw myself toward him. He caught me in a hug.

"You're back!" I said.

His arms were firm around me. He smelled *real.*

We had been communicating for weeks now by dream, but seeing him in person and touching him provoked a feeling of anticipation that was

260

both exhilarating and new.

"Congrats," I said, pulling back, big grin stretching my face. "How was politicking?"

He smiled. "Political."

A cleared throat from the side made me look over to see Olivia tapping her foot and pointing unobtrusively at the crowd, some of whom looked gobsmacked, while magic moved over the calculating eyes of others.

"Oh." I scratched my neck. "I'll see you later?"

"After I waited here for you?"

I smiled, and I could hear Olivia sigh in some sort of pained release of air.

The crowd parted as we fell into easy step, moving through it to enter the Magiaduct. "How was your trip? Are you here for good?" Feeling euphoric, I bounced a bit as I walked. "Where are we going?"

"To our room," he said. "And yes. I told you I wasn't leaving again." He looked amused as he watched me.

His gaze moved over my group, which was following. Will was dismissed quickly—Will was an open book and Axer had assuredly mapped him out long ago. He tapped a finger against his thigh while looking at Neph, then moved on to Olivia.

"Price."

"Dare."

"You look recovered from your adventure."

"I am. Thank you." Grudging as it was, there was sincere gratitude in Olivia's words.

He tipped his head. "Interesting tales in the layers right now. You are going to emancipate?"

"I have already, I just need it officially stamped and the hook removed. It will be done during the break."

There was something strange in Axer's gaze for a second at the mention of the life hook, then he nodded and turned back to me. "Good idea on the unity band."

Flushed, I was too full of goodwill not to give a dopey smile. "I barely did anything, but I think it worked really well."

"It did. And you did more than you think. Only a third of those participants would have turned out last spring."

"The numbers grew because of the fallout after Bloody Tuesday, more than anything," I said softly, looking around at the battle scars that were slowly disappearing.

"No."

I looked at him and felt a curl of amusement at his implacable tone. "Well, if you say it isn't so, then that must be true."

Chapter Twenty-seven

His smile was accompanied by crinkling at the sides of his eyes. It set off a furious beat in my chest.

I cleared my throat. "Are you, uh, studying for exams?"

"Not anymore."

I frowned.

He looked equally amused by my confused expression. "I've already taken them."

I blinked. "Really?"

He looked at me from the sides of his eyes. "Why are you surprised?"

"I shouldn't be. All those papers in your mind," I mused, then shook my head. I could hear Olivia suddenly swear behind me. "I guess I just figured you'd take the campus-wide offer to get out of the exams, since you had to deal with the chaos of the last few weeks."

Exams had been made "optional" in a wide number of classes—decreed by the administration in the wake of Bloody Tuesday. But many students were powering through, happy to have something else on their minds. The ones who were opting out—no one faulted them.

The students who had slipped away after the barrier was released—stepping right out of the unity line and through an off-campus arch—had likely taken the offer.

Fingers pulling along the arches...

I had high hopes they would all be back.

During dream sessions, I had never asked Axer about classes or exams. He'd kept the topics of our nightly conversations away from school and world events. Strange, I guess, now that I thought on it.

Occasionally, he asked specifically how I was progressing on something, and there was always, *always* a puzzle he challenged me to solve, but most of the time he took me to interesting and imaginative places to see and explore, talking about legends, myths, history, and art in the layers.

I poked him. "You seduced me with all those visits."

He looked sideways at me. "Did I? I thought I'd been failing quite miserably. It's been a humbling experience."

"You, humble?"

"We all know how terrible I am at it."

"I'm happy you are back."

He looked at me. "Me too."

I felt fingers brush along my back and turned.

"We will see you at dinner," Neph said, indicating Will next to her in the gesture.

I stopped and gave them both hugs. "Okay. Thanks again."

Neph hugged me tight, and I felt her fingers brush over the scarab in my pocket, as if to reassure herself it was there.

* United *

Olivia, Axer, and I continued the trek down the hall to his room.

Upon entering, Axer looked around surveying the changes.

Stuff was littered everywhere—some of it not even Olivia's or mine. And there was no evidence of Axer's expensive club chairs or Constantine's mismatched antiques. Instead there was a conglomeration of couches and bean bags. The Bandits had been using the living room as a headquarters since the guys had so much space and spending time here satisfied nearly all of my roommate requirements.

Still. Looking through fresh eyes, I wondered why Constantine hadn't *said* anything. All he'd said to the Bandits in the past few weeks was not to enter his workroom or the bedroom. He'd been implacable about those two things, eyes dark.

He *had* offered a small, smirking reward for trying to gain access to Axer's workroom, though.

No one had taken the bait.

"It's a bit of a mess. I hadn't realized..." I rubbed the back of my neck. "You had to have seen this already, though, right?"

Olivia looked between us, eyes narrowing. She knew we talked, but now that I thought on it, she didn't know about the dreamsharing. I guess I hadn't told anyone about that, which seemed weird, now that I thought about it.

I opened my mouth to rectify that forgetfulness and Axer slipped into position beside me, lifting my hand. I blinked, staring at him instead.

"It is your room, too," he said. "You can do with it as you wish."

Olivia narrowed her eyes. "Why did you *and* Leandred agree to this rooming debacle?"

"Would you rather have had Ren stay with Bailey permanently?" he said mildly.

"No. And that's not what I'm asking, is it? You and Leandred hate each other and yet you left her under a roof with him."

"Constantine is like a dragon. He guards with fire the very few things he considers his."

Her brow wrinkled painfully. She looked between us, then shook her head. "Leandred is vile, but I've made my peace with him. You are the one I'm watching now," she said, eyes focused on Axer.

"As you should," he said indifferently.

She looked at me. "Ren, don't be stupid." Then walked to the bedroom.

I looked at Axer. "So, now that you are back, where are we off to first?"

He smiled.

~*~

We traipsed all over the mountain. And even Guard Rock was happy to see Axer again.

Constantine barely acknowledged us, when we returned. He did roll his eyes at me, though, when I poked him into finishing one of the projects that I'd been helping with.

I pushed him into his workroom.

"We were all hoping you'd finally abandon us," he muttered, sweeping the non-project papers into a bin.

"Ha. You're stuck with me."

It took me thirty minutes from that point to realize he had somehow managed to glue my ponytail together.

That night, upon entering the bedroom, I started to giggle.

There were four beds in the room.

Olivia held up a finger at me. "No."

"*Camp.*"

"*No.*"

"Oh, come on, Liv," I wheedled. "We'll be back in our own room tomorrow. *Camp tonight.*"

"I'm not making those sa-more things," she said.

"S'mores. And just a little—"

"*No.*"

~*~

Arranged in the middle with Olivia, with the boys on either side, I slept really well.

Nothing could go wrong.

Chapter Twenty-eight

DEALS WITH DEVILS

THE NEXT MORNING, the roommate magic broke, and Olivia collapsed onto her bed in Dorm Twenty-five, starfishing on it, like she was reclaiming the sheets. "I have never been so happy to be back in my own room."

"You were in here 24/7 before."

"*Exactly.*"

I smiled a bit at that, setting my things up around my bed and putting toiletries in the bathroom. "It wasn't so bad, was it?"

"It was wretched."

"Constantine helped you."

"He's wretched."

"Their rooms are really nice."

"Wretched."

"This sounds familiar. Are you going to take him under your wing like you did Trick and Saf?"

"You take that back."

I tried to hold in my laugh. Constantine was nothing like Trick and Saf, and the fun relationship Olivia had with the two boys was nothing like the cold detente between Liv and Con.

She pointed from where she was wriggling into the covers. "You would have squirreled us in there for the next four years, making "secret" mooneyes at Axer Dare while not noticing them in return."

"Hey!" My face started to heat.

She waved a hand in my direction. "I know. It's disgusting. At least we can agree on one thing—Bellacia Bailey is gone. Wiped. No longer in your life."

I rubbed my hand along my neck. "Yeah... About that..."

She sat up sharply, everything about her on high alert again. "What did you do?" she asked, voice low.

"No, it's fine! I canceled my debts to her. All of them." I spread my hands. "It's a really good bargain."

I'd also gotten the Unity Band out of her. Her support of it had enabled the viral spread. It had brought everyone together. Worth it, all on its own.

"Bargain? *Ren.*" There was a sharp note of censure in Olivia's voice.

"I spend a free hour with her three times a week, that's all," I said quickly. "Easy!"

"Three *hours* a week? For how long?"

"...ever?" At the look of death, I rallied. "I mean, while we are both at school. I added that part in there. Yay, me!"

"Norrissing tried to *kill* you, and she *lives* there."

"I don't have to deal with her. That's explicit. I included that in our agreement, thinking of you," I said earnestly. "Bellacia and I can meet anywhere on campus for those hours—they can all be done in one chunk even—or we can hole up in her workroom."

"Hole up in her *workroom?*"

"You should see it, it's pretty magnificent," I admitted.

"You gave her continued access to you."

"Yes, but I have continued access to *her*, too."

Olivia crossed her arms.

"It's like...I'm a reverse spy!"

Her fingers started tapping.

"I can determine loads of information just from her room's feeds." While giving her only three times the data from me.

"*Ren.*"

"Yeah, okay." I tucked my hair behind both ears, gaze flitting away. "I knew you weren't going to like it. But she's not all bad." At her disbelieving look, I rallied harder. "It will be fine. It's been fine!"

Bellacia was actually a resource that I couldn't access in other ways. A Second Layer magicist born with a silver spoon and a plethora of powerful magic. Both Dare and Constantine had impeccable pedigree, wealth, and immense power, but they spun things their own way. Bellacia spun what the *world* saw. Because she was in *charge* of what the world saw.

"She would make a great ally," I said.

"I've heard those words before."

I winced, because Raphael had said them.

"Far better than an enemy, anyway. And, as I said, she's not all bad. She's...kind of funny?"

The kind of sharp humor that came with a blade, but...still funny!

"And smart," I said. There was no denying that.

"And self-serving and manipulative and evil," Olivia finished with disgust.

"...we can work on that."

Unsurprisingly, the others didn't take it much better, especially Neph.

"She has an agenda," Neph said at lunch. For once, Neph was the one stabbing her food.

"Of course. Everyone does," I agreed.

"That's not what I meant, Ren."

"Yeah."

Constantine...well, Constantine took it the worst. He ranted for a little over twenty minutes about stupid decisions and trusting untrustworthy people, then stalked into his workroom to "make something."

The one who had the least to say about it, surprisingly, was Axer, who sported a small smile as we stretched out on the floor of his workroom, like we had done on the banks of rivers and on cliffs made purely of imagination in dreams. It was doing strange things to my insides, though, to be near him in person.

"I'm sure you'll be fine," he said, dismissing the topic as we alternately worked on abstract spells and continued little games from the dreams.

"You win for weirdest response yet."

His smile lengthened half an inch and he bounced magic to me which I bounced back. He was more relaxed than I had ever seen him. His long, athletic frame was splayed out as he absently played with magic for sport rather than using it for a competitive need or to save the world. He turned his head to me. "You could do worse than having Bellacia Bailey think of you as a resource to be protected."

Head on my arm like I was going to perform side stroke on the floor, I popped a little mushroom cloud of magic from the floor. "Until I end the world."

He pulled the magic to him, the little cloud inverting in his palm. "Not even then. You just have to do it in a way she'll agree with." He twirled the ball of magic, then threw it back at me. "Solve this."

The magic spread out and I looked at the seemingly random shapes and squiggly lines of the puzzle—number seventy-two in the ones he'd been giving me—and watched as the shapes shifted and moved under my gaze. No, not that way. I nudged one, then moved the others around, shifting them into a position that *seemed* right.

I rolled the magic back to him twenty minutes later.

He smiled and ran a finger along its edge, then tucked it into a small, carved box before producing another ball.

I eyed it without taking it. "I'm never going to pass politics at this rate."

"No one cares." He nudged the magic over, and the swirls became more pronounced and interesting.

Chapter Twenty-eight

My fingers inched toward it. Axer's puzzles were complex and intriguing, much more interesting than studying for politics. My other classes were set. *Individualized Architecture and Design* had been an independent study class, and the final had been a project that Will and I had worked on and completed together, with permission. *Engineering Concepts in Warding* was going to be a walk in the park. I had gone far beyond the class parameters already. Individualized study with Stevens was the same. I'd done everything I'd been asked to do and then some.

Politics, though...well, it wasn't my field and I really needed to study. I didn't want to *fail*, but my fingers inched closer to the puzzle. Surely just another thirty minutes—

The magic was scooped out of my reach and Axer sighed.

"What are you doing?" I asked, looking over. I had been about to take it.

He looked at the magic, then rolled it into a corner. "Terminating the world. Come here."

I eyed him, but pushed myself upward. "I told Ori that I didn't want any booster whammies," I said, guessing at his intent. "It's cheating."

I had been informed of that when I'd been denied access to the Fourth Floor earlier. No students were allowed on the Fourth Floor during finals week when they still had active finals to take. Apparently it had been a problem in the past—students selling their souls to the books for a quick bit of knowledge.

Ori, as I'd taken to calling the black-and-white book, had offered it to me anyway—shocking the magic out of me by appearing visually in my mind. It had gone on to inform me that there was a secret way of passing knowledge through the floor of the Fourth and into the Third Floor via a streaming room.

I'd kindly passed on the book's offer, but had shown it through the connection that I had gathered enough information to remove five more of the interconnected wards around the book as soon as I could access the Fourth Floor once more. Ori had been happy enough with that not to push me to take its offering.

It was a little bit of "an offer you can't refuse" type of book.

While I had been dawdling in reveries, I hadn't realized how close Dare had gotten.

He cradled my cheeks, fingers touching my temples, the skin behind my ears, and the sides of my neck.

"Erm." Everything burned where he touched—a prickling warmth that didn't hurt, but felt overwhelming.

A smile spread slowly across his lips as his gaze touched on my parting mouth. My eyes were suddenly taking in too much light and a flush was working its way over my skin.

He murmured, "Are you saying I could have saved my humbling simply by helping you study sooner?"

"What?" I wondered if something was wrong with my translator, because I was far too warm and none of that made any sense, even with him speaking *English*.

He shook his head, but the smile stayed, as did the look in his eyes—a fondness mixed up with all sorts of other things.

"Show me what you've learned in class," he murmured.

I closed my eyes, because I couldn't look into his anymore without thinking mad thoughts. There were all sorts of idiotic ideas fluttering through my mind. But I was getting better at meditation and control too, and I cleared my thoughts, tucking the sillier ones back where he couldn't find them.

I concentrated on politics class, letting him riffle through class lessons, assignments, lectures, and the out-of-class studying I had done.

The pads of his fingers lingered on my skin for a moment, then pulled away.

I opened my eyes as he touched his hands to the ground. Images and assignments appeared around us, all at once. His gaze flitted between the images, text, and amorphous bits of thoughts and magic, fingers connected to the room's magic.

The muscles in his arms clenched, rippling tension all the way down into the back of his hands. A thin book appeared above his lap, then dropped. He caught it before it fell completely.

The room's decor morphed from information central to the tranquil scene of the grove.

I smiled at our surroundings, reaching out to touch one of the fish that was virtually swimming across the floor.

He gently pushed my hand away. "I see this setting was the wrong choice." The setting changed to a garden—lovely, but unremarkable.

"Wrong choice for what?"

He opened the book and ran his eyes along the first page. "Paying attention. What is the title of the person who leads the Triumvirate?"

I blinked. "I don't know."

"Who is the current president of the United Republic?"

"Er."

"What is the only way to enter a plea concerning a criminal act across layers?"

"I...have no idea."

He stared at me, then pointed to the side wall. "Learn it."

Visually sticking to different symbols, in the way I always learned best, were the answers to each question, "pinioned" in the garden—small signs of information in the three vegetable beds, scribbles across the bubbles in the water trough, answers attached to each bug and animal that hopped through in a specific formation—forming a visual path for my mind to travel and collect.

I stared at him, wide-eyed, as he began to lead me through the garden, asking questions and allowing me to memorize the information and tweak any object or path. I continued to stare at him after each piece of information was cemented into place in my mind.

He had cross-referenced everything I *knew* with everything that had been part of the class that I had either zoned out on or missed, and he had specifically set up the garden to quiz me on what I didn't know.

He reached over and tucked a loose strand of hair behind my ear, touch lingering as he smiled. "It's like you forget about magic."

"How did you know?"

"It's also like you forget that I've been in your dreams."

"But—"

"Ren." He produced the same ball that he had had before our too-intense study session and relaxed back onto the floor, staring up at something on the ceiling that only he could see. "Seriously bad for the ego."

He threw the puzzle ball to me. "Solve that."

I stared at the puzzle and did.

~*~

With Axer back and being seen with me all over campus, it was like people suddenly remembered I was different again.

"You're a feral mage," one girl said eagerly as she jumped into my path.

"Er—"

"What's it like, being feral?"

"Um—"

"Is it like being a time traveling caveman?"

"...what?"

"Do you just become, like, suddenly smarter?"

I squinted at her. "No."

"Do you feel like you are going to explode all the time?"

"I try not to eat too much junk food before bed."

"Do you feel the deaths of the other ferals?" asked a mage in a bright orange shirt. A large crowd was beginning to form. "What about this one?"

A picture of devastation was in his palm, and for a moment, his face held the smirk of another.

Any humor I had started to feel turned cold.

"How do you feel about the Department's proposed initiative?" another asked. "And why does this keep happening?" An image was shoved beneath my nose.

I stared at the picture of devastation in his palm. There was something strange about it. A man stood at the side of the image, too blurry in the curve of the memory to make out his features, but there was something familiar.

"What initiative?" I asked, unsettled.

"How did you do it? How did you handle the Awakening magic?" someone else asked.

"Everyone has an Awakening. You had an Awakening." I pointed, scooting back. "Ferals just have them later, it's the *only* difference."

"But it means you have a non-magic mindset for so *long*."

The orange-shirted mage pushed that one aside. "So, *do* you feel their deaths?"

"I need to get to class."

Except I didn't have class. No one had class. It was finals week. But I pushed through the crowd.

For some reason, I headed to Bellacia's.

"What is the new initiative?" I asked Bellacia as soon as I entered, then pulled up the newscast of the image the boy had held in his palm, zooming around the edges for the picture of the man.

"Not even a morning has gone by. I knew you couldn't stay away." She stretched, turning to me, lethargy entirely feigned, her gaze far too sharp. "Ferals are a scourge. The Department is simply proposing a way to minimize Awakenings."

She tossed magic to me that was rife with headlines, and I dropped my search in order to catch it.

A recording of Shelle Fanning handling her regular duties sifted through the air. "We seek the permission and the *empathy* of our fellow mages, to grant asylum to teenagers in the First Layer who show signs that they are beginning to manifest magic."

"They want to lock them up," I said grimly.

She didn't deny it. "Better for them. Better for all of us."

"They are mages, just like you."

"They are not mages like me, don't be absurd. They have no loyalty. No formation to the system. They are easily seduced. It is best for them to be inculcated straight away to our views; else they think they can change things. They make a mess."

"Aren't *you* seeking to change things?"

"I seek truth, not change."

"So you just want to know what is going on, but not do anything about it?"

"Exposing the truth creates small change. Most people get outraged, then go back to their daily lives. I give them that outrage, sell news, and see not the slightest bit of change on an overriding scale." She fanned out her fingers.

"But Stavros," I said. "You want his truth."

She narrowed her eyes. "There is something rotten there. Something that needs to be dug out."

"But not to collapse the whole system?"

"Decidedly not."

"And ferals seek to collapse the system?"

"They go on and on about *redoing*, as if it is easy to build a world. A society. As if we are a bunch of children's blocks that can simply be re-formed."

I looked around the room, at all of the information careening around the walls. "Why do you tolerate me? Why do you still want this connection?"

"Tolerate you—as opposed to, what? Extinguishing you? We aren't in the business of extermination in the Second Layer. We leave that to the Fourth. Once a feral has Awakened, all we can do is to deal with them and the havoc they will wreak. But you? You have been pinioned to the Second Layer, and Excelsine, specifically. I worry not that you will betray your home. You aren't the type."

Neither had been Raphael Verisetti.

I shook my head. "How do you feel about life force hooks?"

She leaned in, little recorder whirling, as always. "Who are we talking about?"

"Does it matter? Do you have an opinion on them?"

"Don't be rude, Ren," Bellacia said idly, leaning back, tapping her finger on the three rings she wore on her right hand. "They are a touchy subject."

I knew Bellacia well enough now to know when all I had to do was patiently wait and she would continue.

"Most people don't misuse them. Should that ruin it for everyone?"

"There are other ways to ensure primogeniture protection." I had looked it up. "Inheritance terms can be done in multiple contractual ways that don't include giving someone a way to kill an heir that doesn't meet your standards."

"They are a tradition."

"Just because something is a tradition doesn't make it good."

"What would you know of it," she said, almost absently, the way she did when she didn't have a ready argument or response.

"Are you actually serious?" I demanded. "Do you have them on you?"

She smiled at me like I was a small child. "Of course I do. And, no,

Daddy would never use that. But what need has he to?"

"What if he goes crazy? What if someone is taking advantage or controlling a person?"

She waved a hand. "That's part of the magic. You have to *mean* it."

I paused. I had thought, maybe, that whatever had been done to Constantine had been a psychotic break—that maybe Stuart Leandred had had one and been trying to atone for it ever since.

"So, if someone is furious, they won't engage?"

"A certain level of furious, sure." She shrugged.

She shrugged like this was all of little note. It boggled the mind that she could have such disparate views on traditional society, her place in the world, Stavros, the Department, and her fellow mages. It's like she made up her own set of norms to follow, and those norms became absolute.

"I don't get you," I finally concluded.

"Ren, I'm simple. A simple girl looking for truth in the world."

"But you aren't looking for truth," I said bluntly, watching her eyes narrow dangerously. "You are looking for what you want truth to be, then building a picture of what you want to see around it."

"I think you should be caref—"

I leaned forward. "You could be doing it, looking for truth—you are a brilliant reporter. But you don't seek *new* knowledge. You will never find truth if you only look for confirmation."

"Is that what you think *you* do? Search for truth?"

"No," I said, just as bluntly. "But then I've never said that's my goal, whereas you maintain it to be yours."

"Poor Ren, looking to spend the rest of her life in a lab, hooked up to a machine," she said with a doctored smile.

"Probably. If there is a way I can fix that, I should, shouldn't I?"

"There is no path that won't lead there for you."

"Then there is no path for you that will lead to truth."

She smiled. It was a brittle thing full of the challenge that she wanted to present, as well as the rejection of that same challenge.

"I'm bored of you now. Get out."

I gathered my things and headed for the door. I paused with my hand on the knob. "The thing is... You've already decided on your truth. So what is there left for you to search?"

The spike from the connection thread—the very, very unfortunate one that I had to her—was painful in its furious intensity.

"Goodnight, Bellacia." I shut the door behind me and headed to the Origin Book.

The faster I got it unhooked, the faster I could fix this world.

Chapter Twenty-nine

FINALS AND FREEDOM

RELEASED FROM roommate entanglements, I was back to spending my time however I wished. I hadn't realized how keeping track of all my hours had been so stressful until I was liberated from it. My activities didn't alter much, but the relief from *having* to do them in a certain order or for a certain amount of time was highly freeing.

The latest set of book wards were dastardly—it had been five days since I had undone the last bunch and I was stuck on one of the oldest ones in the current set. There was a balance and a dance to it—release too quickly, and the Department gets a new ape; release too slowly, and that could mean another feral gone.

Freed from campus requirements, people were coming and going from the mountain at rapid rates. Only registered students or people occupationally attached to campus could do so, but underneath the golden light of the unity band there was still a discordant thread and students watched the off-campus arches—monitoring anyone who came through while running surreptitious (or not so surreptitious) scans.

It became a running joke that bringing volatile substances onto campus meant you got a free strip search. The Justice Squad had to get involved a few times before it started getting better.

My Monday final in politics went off with only a minor hitch. Axer's personalized mental study guide had made the quick answer portion of my politics final easy—all I had to do was follow the different connection points of the mental garden to answer the questions that had definitive answers.

The harder questions were the philosophical ones, the essay questions. What did I think should be done about the Third Layer? How would I use an Origin Mage? What did I feel was my duty as a Second Layer citizen?

My answers had left me with an itching notion, a need to *do* something.

* Finals and Freedom *

My Tuesday final with Mbozi was challenging. He added extra questions and credit opportunities that went beyond the regular final and into concepts I didn't know the answers to—and that was always exciting.

Mbozi resignedly stared at my stuffed answer book as I handed it in—my spelled words wiggling around on the edges of the enchantments overflowing the magical binder. "Have a restful break, Miss Crown. Please."

"I will! I can't wait for spring. See you soon!"

He gave me a rare smile. I headed to the vault and Professor Stevens with a spring to my step because of it.

Stevens had been on point and all business since Medical. We had returned to our regular working relationship where she was the master and I was the harried apprentice. But at least now I knew she was on my side. Or, at least, not *against* me.

After commandeering all the hours Constantine and I had scheduled to work together, we had made huge amounts of progress on creating superior paint. I sent a smug thought into the ether. Raphael could suck it.

Today being the "final" was really more of a formality, than anything. I took the opportunity to broach what had been long on my mind—even more so since my politics final.

"You told me I had to save the world."

Stevens scrutinized me over the beaker she was holding, as if wondering what I was doing, breaking our detente on the subject. "You do."

"Will you help me?"

She didn't say anything for a moment, then, "No."

I tapped one of the beakers. "It's...an enormous task that I'm currently incapable of, and you won't help? That's a bit unfair, don't you think?"

"It is extremely unfair." Abruptly, she sighed, smoothing a hand over her tight bun. "You can't risk having me help you, as I've said."

"Because of your father?"

"You can't trust anything he touches." Her gaze narrowed on me. "Anything."

"I trust you."

"Which is why I will not help in your plans," she said simply. "However, this—" She pointed around us "—this I can do."

Outfitting me with a knowledge of materials, readying me for a war that was not yet upon me. Like Greyskull, who slipped knowledge into conversation, or schematics into creations, Stevens was helping me without giving direct aid.

Though Greyskull had slipped up a bit on that. I touched the hummingbird tattoo fluttering under the skin of my wrist. Stevens looked at me sharply for a moment, then returned to what she was doing.

It reminded me of the interconnectedness of their group, and of how that dynamic could be affected by their choices concerning me.

"Professor, do you want me to ask Professor Mbozi to be my mentor going forward?" I asked softly.

I hadn't declared a focus yet, but I'd been aiming at architecture or engineering in the First Layer. And though that seemed like ages ago, I was still interested in everything engineering related, as harried Professor Mbozi, who was likely correcting my test right now, could affirm.

Something loosened in her shoulders. "We plan to share you, depending on how the joint shift project goes. I am willing to assist in all of your *academic* ventures. And I...you are a good kid. Keep doing what you are doing and collecting your allies, and when the time comes, you will stupidly figure out what you need to. Now, stir this twice," she said briskly, "and make sure you get the infinity knot *right* this time."

I gave her a quick hug. She was appalled.

~*~

Will and I had already completed our architecture project, but we needed to sign off on the paperwork and turn in our creation during the designated time block. As soon as we did that, I could get back onto the Fourth Floor and unravel some more wards. The contract magic would register me as "complete" for exams.

I headed to Will's room, where he was elbows deep in the guts of a portal pad.

"I thought you were done with testing?" I asked as I closed the door.

His eyes were a little wild, his hair sticking out in all directions. "I have to enter it into the competition Sunday, Ren, *Sunday*."

Neph, priority one, Will's room, I sent to her with a humorous mental picture of his Einsteined hair.

There was a weird absence in the connection to Neph, though. I shivered at the feeling and poked at the connection in concern. *Neph? I was just kidding. Will's fine. Are you okay?*

Like a connection slowly reforming, her connection grew warmer. *I'll be back in two hours. Don't worry about anything you feel in your connection threads. I have to go,* she sent mentally, then "switched off" again.

I frowned at Will. "Do you know where Neph is?"

Will twisted his enchanted screwdriver. "In Granobia. All muse meeting. Layer-wide. She said she would be back by dinner." But something was off in his expression.

"Is she okay?" Unease flowed through me.

"Sure, sure. She'll be fine."

I frowned at him. "Do you know what the meeting is about?"

"Yeah, Neph was tight-lipped, but I saw it on the feed earlier. The

Legion is trying to figure out how to use the muses against the terrorists." He rubbed the back of his neck. "No good is going to come from that."

My frown deepened, but abruptly, my thoughts went muzzy. I scratched my arm, blinking. I refocused on what Will was doing.

"What are you stuck on?" I shook the lingering bad feeling away. "You just got the ability to transport two people—cramped and squished—worked out."

Which I totally blamed on Will viewing the memory of Raphael and Kaine's inglorious exit from Corpus Sun.

I narrowed my eyes at Will. "You are trying to add something else to the pad at the last minute, aren't you?"

He sheepishly pushed his design journal toward me. "Yes?"

Leaning forward, I followed Will's bubbled portal pad sketch with my fingertip. He had drawn with one of the pencils I had made for him. Will and I weren't naturally sympathetic in magic—our magic was neutral—but we had easily come up with ways to make devices sympathetic to both of us, which circumvented any need to rely on what we'd been born with in order to work together.

I pushed magic along the thin lines of charcoal, and they readily jumped to my command as I cleaned and expanded the sketch. "An emergency system?"

He grinned. "You are always so concerned about getting caught in a pad. I thought we could work a kit into the outer ring."

He tapped one of the lines I had just traced. My finger lifted and returned to the start of the ring. He leaned forward over the pad too; always interested in the art magic that came naturally to me.

The outer ring would still need to be thin. Or have the ability to expand its own lip. Zipping and unzipping itself magically...yes, that had possibility. I put my finger down and a zipper formed beneath the trailing line. The zipped tines worked together as I pulled. It had to be flexible. I went over it again, imbuing a feel of flexibility. The sketched zipper took on a more malleable look, but it would make sense to consult with someone in garment construction and stitching magic to see what options already existed and could be used.

Delia was on my list of people to see. I'd run it by her.

I looked at Will, my finger tapping the drawing. "We are going to be working until Saturday night on this. It will take some serious research."

"I know!"

We exchanged smiles.

A sudden ping made Will frown and his fingers pressed beneath his ear. I fumbled for the connection to Neph.

Four hours, now. Sorry.

Chapter Twenty-nine

I rubbed at my chest.

"They wouldn't hurt her there."

At that alarming statement, I blinked at Will, shifting my gaze away from my lap. "What do you mean *there*? Where?"

He frowned at me. "At the muse meeting. Their magic is nullified in a gathering that large, especially with Second Layer officials present, no magic allowed."

"Why would... Are there other places where they *would* hurt her? Why would not having magic *help* her?" Panic was swiftly overtaking me.

Will must have felt it, because for once, he fumbled for a room calming spell. "Whoa, whoa. My pad isn't set for double transport if my room explodes."

I grabbed the edges of panic and emotion and funneled them into a stream that I exhaled with a ten-second breath. At the end of my exhale, I felt more in control again, as I'd been practicing separately with Draeger and Axer. The latter, ironically, because he thought I relied too heavily on Neph's influence.

"Ren, you didn't look up what I told you about muses." Will's response was more statement than question.

"No." Will had said something at my parents' house. It felt so long ago now. I had forgotten about the incident with Olivia and Neph completely, in the wake of the terrorist attacks. "Tell me now?"

He looked conflicted, like he did when he hoped a topic could be resolved by reading a fact-driven, philosophical text instead. "I thought Delia gave you all those books?"

"I didn't want to look at propaganda."

He rubbed a hand over the back of his head. "You can't hold family against someone," he said in warning.

"Of course not." Warm feelings suddenly suffused me and my worries slipped away. "You know what, don't worry about it, I'll ask Neph."

Will looked at me strangely. "No, I have a few minutes, and you should know. I can't believe Delia hasn't brained you with it yet."

I rubbed my head, feeling weird all of a sudden. "Yeah." It was like some distant memory was trying to creep in.

"Neph's uncle was branded a terrorist and taken into Department custody last summer. Caused a big split in the muse community. His whole commune was punished."

"That's why Neph had to leave Sakkara," I murmured.

I pushed past the feelings trying to make me look away and focused on the ceiling, letting Will's encyclopedia and Bellacia's internal news feed tell me about Ahmed Bau. His speeches on the Second Layer included the titles:

✡ How Mages Thrive Through Domination
✡ How the Magicists' Views Will Be Their Own Downfall
✡ Revolution of a Calmed World
✡ On the Necessity of the Soul Plague

A few featured delightful subtitles as well, such as:

✡ When you are all burned to a crisp, the muses will dance upon your bones.

"Charming." It made a lot more sense why everyone kept reacting negatively to the man's name, though it was like thinking about him gave me a weird headache. "Why hasn't Stavros, you know, terminated him already?" It seemed like something he would do. "Put someone else in charge of the Alexandria commune?"

"What better way to keep the muse communities in line than by pinning one of their own as evil? We touched on it a little in class after you left that day to get to Olivia. Harrow talked about past political policies for the Fourth Layer and magical beings. The other communes hate him—they hate Neph's whole commune—because all muse freedom has been curtailed to an extent in the wake of his sentencing."

"Can't the other muses get rid of him?"

"The muses are allowed only a few secrets, but how their connections work is one of them." Will frowned at something in the feed, tapping his pencil. "Ahmed Bau's views aren't all wrong, is the problem. Terrorist sympathizer is too simplistic a term. He's an opportunist trying to use the unrest to forward his own aims. He wants muses to be free, which is the main concern."

I stared at him. "Ummm...don't we want muses to be free too?"

Will grimaced. "It's complicated." He took in my expression and tripped over himself. "Of course we want them to be free, but there's all sorts of —" He waved his hand "—and—" He waved his hand again, punctuating it with a little downward stab like it was a complete sentence.

"You can't wave your hand as word explanation inserts if you actually want me to know what you are saying."

"Ugh." Will looked agonized. "It's complicated."

"So is transdimensional travel. I don't see you shying away."

He grimaced. "We want Neph to be free. Free for all things. But we don't want Ahmed Bau or people like him to be free."

"Because he sucks."

"Yes. Specifically, because—"

Chapter Twenty-nine

A soothing calm spread over my mind. Will's voice became a low hum in the back. I looked at where chocolate and sand connection threads attached to my heart.

Neph. I should go to her. Help her.

The soothing calm spread through the threads, and my brain followed, unwinding from its tense state, the past few minutes slipping through my fingers.

"Sometimes loyalties are twisted and not easily unknotted," Will said grimly, finishing a conversation I had long lost track of.

I frowned and touched my threads, vibrant with life. There was something tugging on the edges of my consciousness. "But sometimes, if a rope has been abused long enough, you just need a tug," I murmured, even as it too tried to slip away.

Before the thought fully disappeared, I threw it in a bunny-eared loop around the bright green debt thread to the Origin book.

Chapter Thirty

A USE FOR A MUSE

AFTER WILL AND I worked on his pad upgrades and turned in our project, I spent two hours in the library unraveling some of Ori's wards—finally, *finally* getting the one I'd been stuck on—and getting chomped by fluttering pages. Delia, done early with finals, had already gone home for break, but she must have enlisted aid before she left because Axer showed up as I entered the library's atrium.

The books were endlessly interested in Axer, so he made a wonderful diversion, and he made certain no one else breached the cupola while I did my thing. Ori watched him from the cupola, oddly intent. Axer's gaze frequently strayed to the black-and-white book in return.

An hour into the unraveling, I stared in bafflement at a bunny-eared attachment to the green debt thread, wondering how it got there. I slowly unraveled it.

"Ren?"

I looked over to where Axer was staring at me in concern, fending off books without taking his gaze from me. I could only guess how long I had been staring at what had been revealed to me.

"I'm okay." I sent him a wave of comfort, then gripping the loop in shaking fingers, I looked up at Ori and asked for very specific books, ones outside of Origin Magic. Ori, freed from ten more wards, and happy with my progress, complied.

What I found wrapped around my mind was both maddening and heartbreaking.

A thousand lost memories returned with a vengeance. I didn't know what showed on my face or in my threads, but warm hands suddenly clasped mine.

"Ren." Axer peeled my fingers from the book, and there was a strange combination of empathy and resolve to his expression—like he had expected an outcome and been unable to prevent it. "I've never been supportive of that bond, but even I can see the strength of it. She'd do anything for you and vice versa. Sometimes people do things out of fear of losing that which they love." His expression clenched with some inner turmoil.

He threw the book into the air and the pages caught on a breeze, then curved on an upward spiral draft. "Come on. I'll let you try to beat me in the battle rooms."

Sparring with him—using my creativity and art against his force and military strategy—helped my brain to sort through what Neph had done and why.

I felt the moment Neph stepped onto campus, and immediately stopped my attack and picked up my things. Axer leaned against the wall, not trying to deter me.

I paused before him, then instinctively reached out and gave him a quick hug. "Thank you."

Complicated emotions were quickly shuttered, but strangely, the one that stood out the most in him was *hope*. Axer had never been a proponent of my muse bond, as he'd said, but it seemed for a moment almost as if he were desperate for me to forgive her.

He seemed almost reluctant to release me.

I looked up at him in question, but he just smiled. "I'll see you tonight."

I nodded and fortified my thoughts as I exited the battle building.

I could feel Neph's magic, along with her connections to the other muses, flow across Top Circle as all of them emerged from their usual port.

Where, usually, I would only feel her entrance and the calm, happy feelings across our bond, with the switch that had been flipped by the books, I could feel all the other things she'd been hiding from me as well—anxiety, desperation to make sure her flock was safe during her absence, unhappiness from whatever had been revealed at the meeting.

All things she had been shielding me from.

I heard the murmurs from people I passed—their discussions of the muses returning and the rumors—and I felt the twitch in my connection to Neph as the first hit landed.

I saw the second hit with my eyes—ribbons of air leaping out like tentacles to squeeze—as I ran toward her. I threw a ward spell that would take the brunt of the attack, and sprinted toward the small crowd, activating the enhanced senses the identically titled book had temporarily given me again.

"What are you going to do, Bau?" the other girl was saying. She looked like she, too, had been hit. "You shadduch shast. I don't care what you had to do to get Colm Adrabi to put that spell into place—I'll take a thousand lashes until you *surrender*."

Neph said nothing, gaze cool.

"Do you see what they are going to do to us? You either use the magic, give her to one of *us*, or you turn her in. You are doing *nothing* for us."

"You say that like I have any reason to help you, Aira," Neph said. "You made up your mind about me before I ever arrived on this campus. And where once I would have given you my complete devotion, I found a more than acceptable alternative. I'll never give her to you."

The girl, Aira, vibrated with anger, and the ribbons of air squeezing Neph tightened. "You are a *disgrace* to the community. Selfish, prideful, *stupid*."

I skittered to Neph's side and slashed a hand through the ribbons of air, completely releasing the magical grip she had on Neph.

Neph stared at me in horror and I felt the mental net upon me tighten in an almost painful grip. I stuck up a mental hand and met the grip with one of my own, holding the net above my mind. Neph's horror magnified into terror. I tried to send my own feelings of calm to her, but everything was muddling with the anger I felt toward the girl who attacked her. I tried to calm my breathing.

"Are you listing your own traits?" I asked the other muse, Aira. "Do I get to add on to the list?"

"This is none of your concern, Origin Mage," Aira spat. But she didn't reengage her grip on Neph. "You are probably the reason for Adrabi's spell, too. You are a troublesome infant in all of this."

"Flattering." I turned to Neph, trying to ignore the cocktail of emotion spinning within her and the tears I could see welling in her eyes. I tried for a businesslike tone to keep her from spilling them. "Why isn't this pinging the Justice Squad?"

"They have no authority over individuals in our community," Aira answered before Neph could. There was something about her posture that said she was used to speaking for others. "We get punished as a whole and have an internal justice system to spread it out, no matter what Colm Adrabi thinks."

Adrabi was one of ours, a Bandit, and I remembered him saying that he was putting something in place to help Neph after Bloody Tuesday.

"Right. So before Adrabi's spell, you got away with everything and Neph got blamed?"

Aira's smile grew meaner. "His spell won't last forever, and you aren't helping her, Origin Mage."

I took a breath and let it exhale slowly. "Neph, you have my permission to use my magic in any situation you find yourself in where another muse threatens you," I said calmly, letting my magic back the statement, sealing it visibly in the air.

Both Aira and Neph stumbled back, and I could hear gasps from the other muses who were around us. One of them—Elyn, I think I'd heard her called—blanched, her face draining of color.

"How... You..." Aira whipped toward Neph and the seething hatred in her gaze held an edge of deep jealousy. "Go ahead then," she said to Neph. "Wipe us out, *slagga*. Take everything we've worked for and—"

Her sentence cut off as sound suddenly ceased to emerge from her throat. She clutched at it furiously, mouth trying to issue words.

There was no physical component to the spell, no choking, just the absence of sound. I calmly held the focus of my mental pyramid entirely on setting the curse against her so she couldn't use that word again without the Neutralizer Squad stepping in—a curse for a curse.

I leaned toward her. "I'll take this one," I said, almost gently, as Justice Toad pinged an alert against me.

Her chest was heaving with anger when I released her. "Do you think that is the only descriptor I can use?"

I answered quietly, in promise, "I think that I will barely notice the punishment should I need to spell you for each one."

"She's not even the most powerful muse on campus," Aira hissed. "If you put your lot with the rest of us, you will be served far better."

I said nothing, just tilted my head to the side. I didn't care if Neph was the least powerful, though I had my doubts that this girl spoke the truth. Something of my thoughts must have shown in my face, because Aira's expression grew uglier.

"End our community then. Our *lives*. A Bau with an Origin Mage—the world will fall to *despair*. Then we will *all* be taken."

I tucked my arm through Neph's—whose mental state felt similar to someone going into shock—and started to walk away, tugging her with me.

"Enjoy it while your little pet lasts, Origin Mage," Aira called behind us. "She *loves* you, but she'll never be able to keep you, and once a tie gets cut between a muse and her charge, or her *community*, it can never be reattached. *Never.* Just ask her about Sakkara. *Ask her.* And the tie *will* get cut. Have fun while it lasts, Nephthys. You bring *ruin* to us all."

She disappeared in a swirl of skirts.

Only with her absence did I feel the tightness of my shoulders, and that Neph was shaking, and that I was shaking. I got us through an arch that came out near a little grove on Third Circle and steered us toward a bench.

"She sucks," I said.

Neph tucked my head into the crook of her neck. "She's not wrong," she murmured shakily. "She's not wrong."

"She is."

"You shouldn't know. How do you...? Why are...?"

I let the calming magic she always exuded sink into me, like standing in front of an open oven after my bones had gone cold, but I didn't let the other parts—the far more manipulative ones—sink in.

"It doesn't matter. I'm here," I said.

"I know it is temporary. I know. I know," she whispered.

"It's not temporary. It's what we make it."

"If only that were how it worked." I could hear the tears in her voice.

"We will make our own rules," I said implacably.

I touched the marble in my pocket—always in my pocket. I could fix this world.

"Come on, back to your room," I said, keeping the marble tucked inside.

~*~

Neph danced, gentle light flaring and arcing from her body as she went through the movements of the form. She always danced, especially after meetings with the other muses, and I could understand why now. It was both for the emotional release of the dance and for securing hundreds of her spells.

Waves of sympathy and calm fluttered over me—things I had taken for granted as being *Neph*.

I let the magic of the dance work some of its enchantment, and I thought about what the books had shown me, while a bubbling cauldron of emotion welled within me.

Neph looked at me, concern on her face, obviously feeling some of it through my fortifications. I could feel the enchantment she was trying to place.

"It's not going to work again, not completely," I told her gently. "I got schooled by an immunity book earlier. Somewhat literally and painfully."

Her eyes slowly closed and she came to rest, silks swaying around her in a gesture of fear and defeat.

I touched the magic of the net I had let her place—I could feel it against my skin. "Every time someone mentioned your uncle or the muses or you, I started to say or think something on the subject, then abruptly forgot."

Pained resignation flitted across her face. "Yes."

"Why?" I asked softly.

She sank to her knees in front of me and offered her wrists. "I've wronged you."

"Er." I turned them over and took them in my palms. "Let's just, like, actually have a conversation about this. With no whammies involved."

"Our abilities—the way our magic works—seek ties. We aren't solitary beings. And mages, for good reason, don't trust us. We have powerful abilities that you have never seen, and hopefully *will* never see." She skittered her fingers along the edge of her skirt. "Instead of the one-to-one ties that we used to have with mages—a symbiotic existence—in the past few hundred years, there has been a banding together with each other instead."

"Is that...good?"

I'd seen enough from the books that I understood, a little bit now, why Delia, Constantine, and Axer were never quite supportive of the bond. Giving a muse power put a mage at a disadvantage, should the muse decide to take control of the bond. Except for Will and Mike, the one thing I felt like the mages around me were failing to take into account, though, was how deeply Neph guarded that trust.

The two guys had been the only ones completely accepting. I wondered if it was because of how they'd met her—caught up in the first bursts—they had likely felt the magic and intentions on both sides of the nascent bond.

"It is fine. It works and we are able to attend schools and live in the Second Layer. We would be restricted to the Fourth, otherwise, with the other magical beings that require sustenance that is not entirely food related."

She looked at me as if I might freak out.

"Mages are pretty reliant on magic, too." I'd seen a student last week who'd stared at the shoelaces on a conjured pair of "hip First Layer shoes" like he had no idea how they worked. "That you might suck a little off the top and convert it into happiness and calm doesn't seem all that horrible."

I felt her amusement and relief softly vibrating our bond.

"You couldn't have thought I would care about something like that, though." I tilted my head, sifting through possibilities. "You are protecting me from your community."

Freed from the enchantments, and *knowing* Neph, it wasn't hard to put together a rough reason why she had been spelling me.

Her face crumpled. "The less you know about them, the less they can influence you. If you know *nothing* of my uncle, he can do very little to you directly."

"But he's in prison."

"He's always there—a specter, far away, with little direct magical influence right now, but still *there*," she whispered. "I knew you were powerful from the start, but I had just hoped it was a...normal kind of power. And you were...perfect. You needed me just like I needed you—and I've never felt like my abilities were more useful. Everything clicked, like I had found exactly what I wanted to do with my life, what I was destined for. It quickly became obvious what you were, though, and I..." She shook her head. "I'm selfish. I don't want to let this go."

"Well, good." I frowned. "You are *my* muse, but more importantly, you are my friend. We'll figure it out."

"No." Her expression was pained. "I...I need to figure out how to let you go. But I have you all tied up with me, and until I untangle everything, you must let me place the veil again—the spells. The more you know, the more at risk you are should he be freed."

"No."

"Ren—"

"You know," I said, propping my chin on my hand. "I gotta say this is all a bit of a relief, I've always felt like the only one benefiting in this relationship."

"*Never.*"

I smiled and sent a wave of *friendship, love, and calm* to her. "But that's what friendship is, right? Give and take. I want you to concentrate on your own things without worrying about me."

That made me think uncomfortably of Mike and Will and Constantine —saying that everyone worried about me.

She nodded. "You will always come first."

"*Give and take*, Neph," I said softly. "Let's just make sure this bond is even. Even in all ways."

"Okay." Neph nodded, with absolutely no intention of follow through visible on her face or in her threads. This was going to be an uphill battle.

I frowned. "You've been struggling, and I didn't know." This was the most deeply unsettling thought—that I had been ignoring her troubles. "I don't want that."

"I hid it from you. Deliberately. I didn't want you to know."

I drew her up next to me. "Did you think I would leave you?"

She didn't respond, and it was easy to see the effects of past trauma— whatever had happened to her at Sakkara, whatever the problems were in her own commune.

"I won't." I backed my words with magic. "I never will."

~*~

My hour with Bellacia revolved around the same muse theme.

"There's a tidbit of gossip going around that Aira Melphine had a fit earlier today," she said. I could tell Bellacia was still irritated with me, but there was something new and determined to her expression.

"Is there?"

"Quite unpleasant and unattractive," she said, her smirk saying that she was pleased about it.

"How would you even know, Bella, you can't see her," I said, concentrating on the magic I was trying to conjure.

"I can see Aira quite fine. She's head of the guild."

I looked up, curious at that. "Really?"

Bellacia pinned me with a look. "I see that Delia wasn't lying about this before. You have to be educated on this matter."

"I'm good, thanks. Learning up." I raised a fist in the air.

"Not quickly enough. And your learning is lazy due to your *fondness*. Do you know why muses are regulated?"

"Because you people hate freedom?" I said, offhandedly, trying to will a little ball of flame into existence. Axer and Constantine played with their diversions so often that I thought I'd give it a try. A small burst of flame lit, but then erupted every which way, and I spent more time trying to corral it than making it a power statement.

"Without that little bauble of a beetle you wear, I could make you do anything. Tell me—how do you feel about that, Ren?"

The scarab warmed against my chest. It was a reminder, both good and bad, of what Neph had been doing for me with her community. She had paid for the scarab in some way.

"Unfavorably. I doubt that anyone likes the idea of being out of control."

She leaned forward intently. "Exactly. And that's why we regulate. That's why *I'm* on a list. I'm a powerful mage, Ren."

I made the flame dance and gave her a look that I hoped conveyed that if she gave a villain speech, I was conjuring ear plugs.

She smiled. "All rare mages should be on one. It is the only way to keep society stable."

"So you say. And yet that didn't stop you from using *your* powers against me."

"Exactly. Exactly. And what happened?" She tapped a finger to her temple. "The correct processes were in place to stop me. The Justice Squad was called, Professor Harrow was alerted."

"But you could still have gotten the information out of me— information about a muse, ironically for this conversation—before anyone intervened in your Level Two Offense," I pointed out. "Just like you took a hit for Oakley's attack, yet were clearly able to plant all sorts of things on him first. Justice Magic is good, but it isn't a cure all. We aren't a police state."

"I received a Level Three Offense."

"That's because you didn't stop the attack when you were warned. Don't mince Justice System words with me. That is one area in which I feel qualified to argue."

She hummed. "You've earned worse than a Level Three."

"Yeah, and you don't see me arguing about chaining everyone up," I said, rolling the magic around.

"I don't want to chain *everyone* up."

"No, just us weird and dangerous folk. Funny thing about Neph, *she* has never gotten a Level Three. Not even during the battle. She maintained correct behavior the entire time. Above reproach."

Bellacia drew a long-tipped finger along the arm of her chair. "So passionate in defense of her. So true to her."

"You'll never convince me otherwise." I drew a small thread of fire into existence, pulling it from the elements that Excelsine so abundantly had—shared resources for all students to use and play with. In approaching the Third Layer problem, the trick was going to be in how to leverage such a thing without bringing the whole system down.

"So passionate in defense of someone whose abilities you don't even know."

"I know Neph's heart."

I let the fire trail and snake through my fingertips, then pulled a thin stream of water droplets into my other hand. I waved my hand faster to watch the droplets separate, then dragged them more slowly to form a little watersnake. He snapped at the droplet in front of his mouth.

"Did you know that muses don't just inspire inspiration, they also inspire despair? Pain?"

The watersnake launched itself in shock at the nugget of fire and steam blasted from my palm. Bellacia caught the steam cloud between her fingertips in the air and pulled it downward, rotating it so that it sat suspended above her palm in a vibrating mass of energy.

She rotated my vapor cloud around, separating it back into its elements, then scattered them. They extinguished and vaporized in the air while I stared.

"Dear, dear, Ren. And here I was told that you were learning all about the duality of abilities. Why would you be surprised at the flipside of a muse's?"

I firmed my lips and didn't respond. In my frenzied research earlier, I had concentrated more on the net of spells—the veil Neph had placed.

"On a mass scale, they can cause entire nations to fall," Bellacia said. "Imagine it, despair streaking through the population instead of innovation and inspiration? It would be Gaminga all over again."

A quick look upward at her tickertape magic, told me that Gaminga was a devastating extinction event in the Second Layer thousands of years ago. I hoped Bellacia was catching my less kind side thoughts in the ticker's corner that had her name all over them.

But the ticker did the job it was spelled to do and headline after headline on muses scrolled by.

"Everyone wants to say that Origin Mages are the cause of all the dark ages and periods of enlightenment, but everyone forgets about some of the other fascinating and dangerous beings who bring down empires."

I thought of the flags on Top Circle. And of the magic that called us all to the field. Of the magic that the muse community wielded that influenced many things on campus. Neph had given me a pass more than once when the muse magic was controlling everyone else.

I wondered again what that had cost her. The guilt of it weighed upon me.

"Regular mages can band together and do terrible things as well," I said.

The Third Layer terrorists were proof of that. Not all of them were powerful like Raphael or Godfrey or Vey.

"But muses aren't regular mages. And they have a base control that can't be affected by a mage unless...proper rules and contracts are put into place."

"But there is a contract," I said woodenly, looking at my tablet and watching the information scroll by. "The only reason they are here instead of in the Fourth Layer is because of the contractual obligations they swore to mages."

"Yes." She leaned forward. "And *that* is what your friend's dear uncle seeks to change—even now from his prison spell he speaks of revolution. Of flipping everything in favor of the muse community. He threatens untethering them from the community bonds of the Second Layer and unleashing despair upon the lands. He wants them to be free."

"That..." I swallowed dryly. "Freedom isn't a bad aim."

Her gaze was intent. "It is hard to trust people, Ren. Everyone must be regulated for the safety of all."

I stared at her, trying to add it all up—to add *her* all up. "Why are you seeking to expose Stavros, Bellacia? You have the same aims."

She leaned forward even more, laser-eyed, her gaze almost zealous. "That is just the thing. I don't think we do. He speaks, but it only emerges as the truth when played from the mouths of puppets. Stavros is doing something for his own ends. And mages like Keiren are in on it."

"Doing what?"

She frowned, some of the crazy receding from her gaze, and leaned back. "They say they are implementing plans for the good of everyone, but it's not adding up. I can hear the tones in their voices. They aren't *ringing*."

Audition and voice control were Bellacia's skills, not mine, so while I could conceptually understand what she meant, I had no way of verifying it.

"Politicians lie," I said.

I had hoped it was different in the Second Layer than in the First, but some truths seemed universal. It was just much, much harder to get away with here.

We had covered some of the major case studies in politics. With truth stones in play, people had to get pretty creative, but it could be, and had been, done—to devastating results across layers.

"So many mages in the Second Layer *forget*. So many willfully ignore our history, our past battles, what the current signs point to. The astrologic forces and seers are up in arms, and though I'm ever a skeptic, there aren't nearly enough opposing predictions to mean that they are all wrong," she muttered. The tickertape lurched with her thoughts, and I tried to catch the headlines, but she gained control quickly.

"Something very bad is being put into play," she said with difficulty.

I thought about Omega Genesis, and whatever it was the Department had planned—a horror that unsettled even Marsgrove.

"The truth, Ren." She watched me, expression unwavering. "You will help me find it."

Chapter Thirty-one

REMINDERS OF NORMALITY

THOUGH THE CONTINUING rumors and unsettling portents were persistent, the last day of term approached like a blinding light barreling down on campus through a tunnel. Mages finished with exams lazed about, while others ran around, trying to get their last ones done.

Dragons flew in the breezes, silliness resumed along the paths, multi-player sports and games spilled across Top Circle and onto the regular upper level fields. Mages were changing their clothes and faces again, regaining a sense of normality for some.

It gave me hope.

I spent the last afternoon before everyone left for break lounging around Top Circle and soaking it all in—watching the festivities, reveling in the natural magic that was running through the mountain, feeling the increased sense of harmony, and waiting for a shoe to drop.

"Did you sign up for classes," Olivia demanded, sinking down next to me.

Axer was stretched out on the lawn on my other side, Greene, Ramirez, and Straught similarly sprawled next to him. They had finished playing a magic, blood-gushing version of rugby that Christian would have loved.

I had missed being a spectator. I had always loved sports, especially those that involved my family members. Watching the pick-up rugby game and cheering had been nostalgically reminiscent of days long past.

Axer had been strangely relaxed ever since the Neph incident and he'd taken me on two—*two*—impromptu outings to the Midlands that involved food and sightseeing instead of fighting monsters and taking tests. I had been discreetly checking him for foreign spells ever since, but hadn't detected anything untoward yet.

"Yes," I answered. "*Volatile Engineering* with Mbozi, special projects with both Mbozi and Stevens, *Explorations in Art*, since Marsgrove is being lenient—I think Stevens chewed him out about my campus permissions, since I have unrestricted vault access now and it seems pretty silly to restrict me from art classes—and *Death and Resurrection.*"

Olivia looked sharply at me at the last one. "Who encouraged you to add that one to the list?"

Axer, lying on his back with his eyes closed, raised a hand.

I thumbed a finger at him. "It didn't take much convincing, though. I need the history credit, and it is an apt choice."

"What about Nephthys? Did you talk to that professor together?"

I looked at the flagpoles and the magic streaming in, out, and around them—concentrating on one in particular that always pulled my eye. "Yeah. She runs a course on bonded pairs and groups in the fall—with a specialty in muse bonds. The professor said we could visit an hour each week to talk things through. Neph is reluctant."

I trusted Neph with my life, but I wanted to make sure she had her *own.* That she had options, if hanging around me for the rest of her life turned out to be, you know, not in the game plan.

"It's a good plan." Olivia nodded decisively.

I leaned back on my hands. "What about you? Get everything you wanted?"

Olivia's list of classes was always exhaustive.

"Yes. I also got the intern position taking care of all the items in the justice locker."

I gave an evil laugh. "Excellent."

"I'm not allowing you to have your wicked way with whatever I find," she said disapprovingly, though I felt her own dark satisfaction slipping through.

"No, no, of course not." I was quite happy to let her have her own wicked way with whatever she found.

"How did you get that position?" Camille asked, from her sitting position next to Ramirez. She'd only glared my way three times in the past hour. I felt we were making progress.

"I'm a ward of the school." Olivia lifted her chin. "I need to pay my dues, like any good citizen. I simply asked the provost."

The provost was a weird guy—he'd assigned me community service to the *Justice Squad,* after all—but even he would think stringent, *usually* rule-following Olivia a good fit for the position.

"You should join the Combat Squad with Crown," Greene said.

"I'm not joining the Combat Squad," I said pointedly. "I'm not even staying on the Justice Squad after my hours are up."

Axer smiled without opening his eyes. "And when will that be again?"

"...someday."

Chapter Thirty-one

Bellacia folded herself gracefully into position next to Camille, though she had a stylish travel bag at her side indicating she would not be staying. "Well, don't you all look like campus' best protection detail. I'm certain everyone is feeling like you are just the mages for the job. I can't tell whose blood is whose."

Greene, always immaculate outside of combat mage activities, flicked some of the dried blood on his forearm close to her expensive bag.

"Charming. I'm off to cover the festival activities. Wish me well, Ren."

Olivia looked at her in distaste, then deliberately focused her attention elsewhere.

"No one needs to wish you well," I said bluntly, but not without some humor. "I feel like I need to wish everyone else there well. I am sure you will crush everyone who needs crushing."

Strangely, Camille looked at me with the slightest of smiles.

"You say the sweetest things," Bellacia said, with a tip of her beautifully styled head. "Don't get into trouble without me here to record it. In fact, use this at every opportunity." She tossed over a device that I automatically grabbed from the air.

Olivia held out a hand without looking and I put it into her palm.

"I'm not using that," I said. "I'm certain you already have fifteen people scheduled to follow me around."

"Ten, actually. Do you think I need to increase it?"

"Goodbye, Bella. Have fun terrorizing the citizenry. See you when you return."

She would be doing an internship for the first month of spring, recording everything about shift season. I had promised to do all I could to hunt down information on Stavros in the meantime.

"Ta, Ren. I'll write an extra terrifying Origin Mage story during break, just for you." She gave me a salute, Camille's arm a small squeeze, ignored everyone else completely, then sauntered off toward the administration building, and likely the port to the Second Layer Depot.

"I don't know what Lox is thinking," Greene muttered.

"Thinking? I don't recall anyone diagnosing him with that particular ailment," Axer said, eyes still closed.

"It's everything below the brain he excels in," Camille said. "She's going to eat him alive. I can't wait. Do you think he'll blubber? I think he'll blubber."

Ramirez held up a ten munit bill. Camille plucked it from his fingers with a satisfied smile.

Greene held out his own. "Put me on the square for scorched reproductive parts."

Olivia looked over at them, blinking, but I was used to this kind of ribbing with Christian and his friends, and I'd seen the combat mages *literally* chop arms from each other in "play."

"Article about his family's incontinence and monetary woes." Axer held out a bill, otherwise looking for the world like he was sleeping. I'd bet every bit of gambled money, though, that he knew where each person on the field stood, like an overpowered magical bat.

"There is literally no way a scathing article wouldn't be involved," I agreed.

Axer held up another bill and Camille snatched it, too.

Camille looked at Olivia, and something interesting was happening behind her eyes. "What about you, Price?"

Olivia examined her, and there was a collective silence for a long moment. "Is there a square for all of the above?"

Camille's smile was slashing. "There is. You want it?"

"Definitely."

~*~

I helped Will pack his shift project. He had invited us home with him for the break week and festival, but the unanimous decision was that I not step foot from campus.

"Remember to eat," I said. "And make sure you charge the extra magic before you do the demo."

Will's hair was going every which way, as if he'd already accidentally released the charge twice—straight into his skull. "I made a note. Mike promised he would spell-marquee it across his forehead in the audience during the presentation, just in case."

I laughed a little at the picture of that. "I wish I could go."

"Me too, but we'll record everything. Next year, Ren," he promised. "Next year we'll be praying to the gods of science and leftover pizza for as long as we need. No one will even remember to check on us."

"Imagine the stench," I said dryly and he snickered.

A content silence descended as we packed the last of his project into the magical storage case.

"I'm glad you worked things out with Neph," he said, as we finished.

"You've always been supportive of the bond." I thought of what Axer had said about how he hadn't been. "Why?"

"When you introduced her to me, it was like the sun was shining everywhere all at once around you both." He smiled, gaze going distant in memory. "Bondings are rare between mages and muses due to centuries of distrust—it takes trust on both sides. Anyone could see you were good for each other."

"Only you and Mike, and very reluctantly, Olivia, were supportive before Bloody Tuesday."

The amount of life debts Neph had earned on Bloody Tuesday had completely turned the Bandits around. I hadn't heard a peep from any of them since, even Delia, who had once been the most vocal.

Will frowned. "Maybe it was because Mike and I were the first ones you introduced her to? I'll never forget that day. Maybe some of the bond was revealed to us in ways that it wasn't to others."

I nodded, that thought backing up my previous one. It had been hard to get Will and Mike to see Neph, but after they had, it had become much easier for me to unveil her with a simple introduction.

Now that I thought on it, subsequent introductions hadn't even revealed Neph to be a muse. The ones who had stuck around, or already had suspicions, had figured it out quickly enough, but it hadn't been a point of conversation in quick introductions.

"It probably doesn't hurt that neither Mike nor I have families who care about that type of thing," Will added. "Ingrained family notions are hard to shake."

I thought on Bellacia's words. And about Neph's state of mind after the encounter with Aira. About any encounters she might be having when she was out of my sight.

"I'm worried about Neph. She's...fragile right now. Apprehensive."

"Yes, but she'll be okay," Will said with a small smile. "Because she has you. She has all of us."

I smiled at him. "We can build our own commune?"

"You've already built a community, Ren," Will said softly. "We'll beat everything together."

Chapter Thirty-two

BREAKING TIES

MOST STUDENTS abandoned campus immediately following their last exams. Even the squad mages were on loose rotation, coming back to campus only for the most egregious of monsters or trouble. The nice thing about the Second Layer—and the shifts resetting all the twisted travel magic every year—was that mages could pop in and out wherever visas and contract magic allowed.

Olivia and Neph joined me for easy squad duty around campus, halving my remaining hours as we basically wandered around talking and enjoying the views. Olivia was taking to our mandatory stay on campus with zeal.

"This is the first time I haven't had to attend the Department's Spring Ball," Olivia said with relish. "I always hated that thing."

Olivia's emancipation and hook appointment were scheduled for Wednesday. The Department had demanded my presence alongside hers, but Marsgrove had invoked some clause to stop me from attending. Evidently, my parents had assigned guardianship rights to him while I was on campus.

Of course they had—he'd been filling their heads with how great school was going to be in helping me control my new powers...right before he had locked me away. I couldn't believe I hadn't guessed that he was my temporary guardian before—no wonder he had had so much control over me when I'd first arrived, and before I'd learned magic. Currently, though, it was a big win that Marsgrove had control. My parents' contact information would be in Department hands otherwise.

"The Department wants you to step off the mountain," Olivia said grimly. "No way is Marsgrove going to allow it."

"I won't step foot from campus, don't worry," I assured her. "You think he'd let us poke around downtown, though? Axer's birthday is coming up, as are Mike's and Loudon's."

Chapter Thirty-two

Marsgrove looked like he would be happy if we all disappeared into a hole in the ground, but he waved at us to go ahead.

"Don't go farther than where campus bleeds into the business district and staff neighborhoods," he warned. "The lower levels still have travel restrictions in place—visa permissions are required to port in—but it is slightly less secure than the twenty-second and up."

Safety adamant in her mind, Olivia turned me into a slightly doughy teen boy, then Neph into a reedy one, then she morphed into her own version of disguise.

I poked at my new skin, watching how the enchantment worked. "Is this really necessary?"

"Only if you want to go."

"Looking great." I gave her two thumbs up.

We spent quality hours searching through stores and taking tea in a charming little shop. The tea shop was a pretty hilarious experience in our teen male disguises. It was only on our way back to campus with our birthday purchases in hand that things spiraled out of control.

"I'm going to check the muse poles on lower campus now so I don't have to do it later," Neph said. She had made a deal with the school to be the on-campus muse for the week—which had the dual benefit of keeping her on campus and the other muses away.

"Oooh, we'll come," I said. Each "check" produced a nice pulse of magic that felt like a soothing bath, a foot massage, and a blanket cocoon all in one concentrated blast.

Olivia sent our packages to the dorm and we accompanied Neph to the poles on the Twentieth Circle.

She placed her hand upon one and it lit briefly with white light before going dormant. I gave her a hopeful smile and she nodded. I stuck my hand to the next pole in the rotation and smiled as I felt the ends of the magic roll over my skin. A beautiful melody echoed in the air.

I disengaged my fingers, happily wiggling them and feeling the dwindling zings. "I'm all for these checks."

Olivia rolled her eyes, but she always sneaked in a few touches too.

Neph placed her hand in the same spot where mine had been. She had assured me from the first time I'd touched one that she could reset anything my magic accidentally did. "We each have one that is ours specifically to power and guard—to spread our magic across campus. This one belongs to a muse who makes the loveliest music."

I'd learned very quickly that Neph's pole was the one on Top Circle that always drew my eye. I'd seen her pull her fingers over it many time since the veil over my thoughts had been removed.

I wistfully listened to the dying notes of the beautiful music. "It must

298

have been upsetting for the muses in charge of these poles when campus was on lockdown."

Neph's expression was grim. "They have been our least luminous members these past weeks."

"Whose is this one?" I asked, touching the next one on Circle Twenty.

Light flashed, then shot through the ground like a lightning bolt across the grass. A dark tendril followed the path, disappearing in the distance.

I backed away. "Was...that supposed to happen?" It hadn't happened with any of the others, and I'd been touching a lot of them.

"No." Neph stepped toward the pole, brows furrowed.

A flash of darkness and light zipped back up the path. An eerie ring of shadow encircled us and I felt my frequency gem go cold.

Olivia immediately had four shields up and her hands outstretched.

A man appeared on the edge of the circle, straightening up from a crouched position, as if he'd been transported that way.

But...we were on campus. I stared down at the circle and the thin cord that snaked down the mountain.

"Nephthys," the man said, lifting his head. Sunken eyes and a look of hunger did nothing to diminish his presence. "You've made it worth the wait."

Neph went absolutely still, like a deer wanting to bolt but frozen by headlights surging toward her. The unfamiliar man's oddly magnetic gaze darted between us, tracking lines and magic.

"What terrible forms you have taken," he said as he examined us. "You let the mage—the spawn of that hag—put magic on you? Let me wipe you clean."

Olivia stepped forward threateningly.

"What are you doing here?" Neph's voice cracked.

The man smiled. "My favorite niece, of course I would visit."

Oh, *oh*, that was not good. A random weirdo, no problem. Neph's crazy uncle who was supposed to be incarcerated? No, not good.

I inserted myself into the space in front of her, eying the ring of darkness and sending tendrils of magic to determine its composition.

"How are you blocking the proximity of my frequency?" Olivia was surveying Ahmed Bau as if he were week old gum stuck to her shoe.

"The bonds, little spawn," he said, looking at Olivia. "They extend quite a far distance, too, when I'm so close. You've all given my niece quite the boost." Greedy eyes took in the threads streaming from Neph. "A bonus. But the real prize..."

His gaze went hungrily to me. "He said it would be soon. The Day of Reckoning."

"Who?" Neph's voice cracked.

"What does it matter? Another mage trying to rule us who will fail. Your mother is trying to displace me. She even instituted a veil after yours was lifted from your mage, but it was too late, far too late. I will punish her, of course. I can feel all of them again." He closed his eyes and flexed his fingers. "But I'm feeling lenient at the moment with the lovely gift you have given me," Ahmed Bau said. His voice—everything about him, really—was strangely compelling. "Given all of us. The one we will *use*."

"Never," Olivia said succinctly.

Go, I sent her mentally. I couldn't mentally flag anyone else, and Neph was unresponsive, but I could still reach Olivia in the circle. The magic of the circle was connected mostly to Neph and to me. Olivia might be able to fight through it.

He'll take you by the time I get help. Even her mental voice was grim. *Our best weapon is time. Someone will notice the vacuum of our absence.*

Neph's connection thread jerked the tiniest fraction, as if she'd heard us. "How are you here?" Her voice cracked, but she kept speaking. "How did Elyn give you access? You should be in prison, and the campus guild would deny you entrance even were you free."

Elyn was a muse, and one hundred munits said that had been her pole.

"You didn't think I was the only one ready to start this revolution? She had the same motivation I did—and the same assistance from new friends."

A shadow swirled through his eyes.

I blindly grabbed Neph and violently started pushing her back, keeping myself between her and her uncle. We were on campus. Ahmed Bau shouldn't be here. Little golden lights glittered under my feet and I pulled the lingering feel of Constantine's spell up. The magic surged over my toes, through my legs, and up to pool in my palms. I began pushing it at the darkness.

But Neph was stretching out of my hands, toward her uncle, like she was being pulled by a rope. It was all I could do to shove myself in her way, like a linebacker working the field.

"A man with a double soul," Bau said, still talking. "He had the most interesting advice and the most pleasing gifts."

A shadow weaved behind him—like a snake fashioned into a tail. I tracked it back to an arch two circles down, where it clung with a lamprey's grip.

The golden spell in my grip cracked a section of the dark circle behind us.

"We need to get past his reach," I said. Moving Neph was like trying to push a semi with my bare hands, though. "Liv, help."

"Just look at this." Ahmed Bau touched something in the air, as if he were holding up an invisible scarf to examine. An unnerving, ebullient smile stretched his face. He looked maddened, like a junky who couldn't look away from his next hit. "Look at the control she gives away. The power. Dear Nephthys, you have always been my utmost favorite, and now, dear girl, you are transcendent."

"No," she said, strangled, and she grabbed for my magic and shoved it at him, forcing him back a few steps.

He laughed and dropped the invisible threads to grab my magic from her. "That would work on anyone except me, for I hold your cord. It has been so long. They starve us in there. Did you feel it? My deprivation?"

I fully dispelled the circle with the magic in my hands at the same time that Neph's uncle gripped the air. Neph went to her tippy toes, and I went to mine, then we were both dragged the remaining feet toward him by an invisible hand.

He laughed, but his eyes were steel as he tapped Neph on her forehead. "Don't trifle with me. I won't allow dissension, even with my favorites. We have much work to do. And I promised a few perks to a new friend."

Where were Aira and her pretty goons? Surely Elyn's pole must have sent some sort of transmission? We weren't in Outlaw Territory.

Olivia moved so fast I barely registered it. She jabbed one of Patrick's devices into Ahmed Bau's neck, thrusting it high so his chin tilted at an uncomfortable angle. "Release them."

He laughed, the lines of his throat moving against the device. "You don't even want to go there, little mage." There was an increase in power that was tangible in the air.

She shoved the device harder into the space between his jaw and throat. "Funny thing about that spell you are trying to invoke, Bau—Raphael Verisetti already used it on me once. Here's a hint"—she leaned into him —"it's not working this time."

"I know who you are." His gaze promised pain. "And I know your bitch of a mother. I'm going to have a little talk with her after this."

"Good. You *do that*. I am within my rights to put you down, I can't remember what setting is for stun and what setting is for kill on this device," she said savagely. "I was told, but it's so hard to remember these things. It would be terrible if you returned to prison in a *box*."

He narrowed his eyes at her, but released his grip on Neph, and subsequently on me. There was murder in his gaze. No way were we getting out of here without a fight.

Olivia?

Time, Ren. She swallowed, but her eyes were steady on Ahmed. *I told you.*

And then I could see what she had felt—Constantine and Axer were twenty paces away and closing in fast. The relief nearly made me limp. School officials couldn't be far behind. Ahmed must have seen them too, because suddenly he was allowing Olivia to move him more easily.

Olivia motioned him to the nearest off-campus arch, not releasing her grip on the taser-like device. "Keep walking along your *leash*. Be careful you don't slip, I might accidentally shoot something you can't regenerate."

"You see the madness of mages, Nephthys?" he called to her.

Neph rubbed her arms, not looking at him. I put my arm around her.

"The world is going to hell, dear niece, and we...we are muddling along on *leashes*, dragged along in their wake. While our brethren in the other layers fight against tyranny and oppression, we let them *chain* us. Why aren't we fighting with our kin? Why do we let the government stay our hand? Because of this." He held up a string around his neck that became visible suddenly in the air. "Because in order to have a life, our forefathers sold us into slavery."

"You are welcome to go back to the Fourth Layer," Constantine said motioning Olivia to step away.

Ahmed sneered at him. "That is exactly what you Second Layer mages always say—like your father once did—'Go back home, if you don't like it, we don't need your kind here.' And yet, you *do* need our kind. You *depend* on our kind." He jabbed a finger at the ground and a million wards lit up, each of them pulsing with the type of magic I usually associated with Neph. "You depend on us to keep you sane and comforted, to bring beauty and spirit. And yet you revile us for unsavory *possibilities*."

"No one reviles muses," Axer said.

"Lies," Bau said evenly, almost offhandedly calm once more, like a switch had been flipped. "Even a Dare can't utter that in truth."

Axer clamped his lips together. "Not everyone objects. You, however, shouldn't be here. A situation that is being rectified right this moment."

Shadows swept the landscape in the valley surrounding the mountain. Ahmed Bau's lips drew back.

"Come, Nephthys." He held out a hand. "And bring the girl."

"You can't have her," I whispered.

He narrowed his eyes on me. "She will never break free from the chains of her birth. None of us can until *all* of us are freed."

"The praetorians are here," Axer said. I could see bodies spilling over the edge of Top Circle, activating the ways that would bring them to us. The shadows of the praetorians swirled at the bottom, on the other side of the river barrier.

"They think to collect me? I've already seen their maker." Crazed eyes full of shadows shifted from one of us to another. "And I will *never* go back, but I will show the entire Second Layer the *might* of the muses as I fall."

He reached forward and I could feel the scrape of the movement in my bones. He "owned" Neph, and Neph owned me. He pulled us toward him.

* Breaking Ties *

"That's enough of this," Constantine said tightly. "The praetorians can go fishing." His palms shot downward.

Gold light pooled underneath Ahmed Bau, then with a lift and outward thrust of Constantine's palms, the muse shot backward down two levels, propelled into the off-campus arch he was attached to. Golden horses charged along the grass in his wake. One of his arms, and maybe a leg, broke on impact—it wasn't a clean exit. The golden horses dissipated as soon as he disappeared, and droplets of magic shot back into the grass.

The tail of the shadow whipped out and licked my cheek, then it too was pulled through.

Rubbing my cheek, I turned to see Constantine examining his fingernails. The last wisps of golden energy released from his fingers into the fading golden trails. "I might have lied a little about that liquid."

Olivia and Neph stared at him, while Axer bent down and examined the spot where Bau had stood.

"You hacked administration magic?" I cautiously looked behind him to see if the officials had gotten close enough to see. Now that the danger was passed, I needed to keep everyone from being expelled.

"Hacked? No, the administration was so joyful about the unity band that they connected campus magic to it. The majority of campus embraced my adjacent spell, and voila, it was set. Amazing what a few happy lights can do," he mused.

"Dammit, Leandred," Olivia said.

"Don't worry overmuch, Price," Axer said, finger tracing some magic in the grass. I hoped Neph's uncle hadn't left anything behind. "It's a protection spell against outsiders—Elias and I looked it over. It allows anyone who knows how to work the spell to guard those who accepted the spell."

Olivia narrowed her eyes at Axer. "And do you know how to work it?"

Axer hesitated and the edge of Constantine's mouth turned up.

Olivia sighed. "Dammit, Leandred."

Neph had stopped shaking, but she looked far too pale. I fished a rose from my kit. "We need to get to Medical."

"You need to get rid of that ridiculous face," Constantine said.

"Hey, blame Olivia, and it totally worked," I said, trying to channel lingering adrenaline into amusement. "Not a single person stopped to gawk at me downtown. I'm kind of surprised no one has my magic number down there."

Axer examined me. "Campus has been rather tight-lipped about you, all things considered."

"No more going down the mountain," Constantine said, looking at me through narrowed eyes.

Chapter Thirty-two

"Hey! *This* isn't even off campus. And I refuse to be cornered like—"

Something squeezed in my chest and I fell to one knee. My heart felt like it was being crushed in someone's fist.

In my mind's eye, I could see people falling everywhere I looked—like an overlay of reality; another place in time. People began wailing, writhing.

"The festival." I tried to grab Neph. "Will. Mike. The festival," I choked out. My magic was being sucked through a conduit like water dumped down a drain.

Axer, Constantine, and Olivia were all reaching for me, and I could see their free hands flying to their frequencies. And Neph...Neph's usually tan skin was bone white as she stood staring down at me in horror, all of her connections bleeding to black.

"Soul Plague," she whispered. "He unleashed the Soul Plague."

She turned and sprinted down the mountain. She was the only thing freely moving as darkness shot from her—crawling up the mountain like a blanket of drenched smoke with a clinging vapor that filled all the little voids, leaving behind an ash that was impenetrable plaque as it traveled.

It was the type of darkness that was the absence of light in the soul rather than in the sky. A soul darkening despair.

I could feel it spreading everywhere as Neph ran. It felt vile and wrong and the opposite of everything that was Neph. Joy and beauty flipped to hopelessness and slime.

Soul Plague.

Ahmed Bau's final maddened words hadn't been taunting; he had initiated a layer-wide pestilence using me as the battery and Neph as the wire.

Olivia fell to the ground beside me, and Constantine bent at the waist. I could see Constantine trying to grip the golden spell. I could see Axer looking at Neph's fleeing form and a blade flipping into his hand. Their motions were gelatinous, like they were moving through deep water.

I could see Axer throw the knife. I could see Neph almost at the arch with her own blade in hand.

She was going to die—either by Axer's knife or by successfully locating her uncle.

Black-and-white patterns flipped in my gaze, the blackness grew, and I grabbed the magic that I had accessed once before and relocated myself. I caught Neph just as she passed through the arch. I felt Axer's knife sink into my shoulder. The pain was excruciating, yet everything suddenly became a little clearer, like a bit of my control had returned.

We tumbled through the arch and into another travel henge. Neph wasted no time throwing herself into another arch with me diving after.

Even in that miniscule moment of time, darkness overtook the small

* Breaking Ties *

area between ports and people began screaming as we passed.

We tumbled out into a field of flowers. I tackled Neph. We rolled through the dying meadow—the knife embedding further, the flowers withering in a widening spread of death, magic being sucked from me, black smoke seeping from her.

"You have to let me go, Ren. I have to kill him."

I shook her shoulders. "You can't get close to him, you can't do anything. He controls you."

Tears filled her eyes and her body shook. "Killing me will just transfer you to him. There's no time, no time. There's only one thing that can be done. You must break it." She put the blade into my hand and held up the once bright connection threads between us that had turned twisted and black.

"No," I said repulsed.

She ripped the knife from my hand and angled it at the cords. Powered by the vestiges of her magic, there was suddenly something weird about the blade. Her features drew together in a pain so internal that it made me weep.

Aira's worlds rang in my ears. *Once a muse cuts a tie...*

I hit her hand off target and we struggled with the knife, our gazes locked as we fought. Long practice wrestling with a brother and battling with Axer gave me the edge, but Neph was fighting like someone with nothing and everything to lose.

Did you think I would leave you? The words of our previous conversation echoed between us.

"I never will," I said and dislocated her wrist.

I felt along the bonds. Felt my bond to Neph. I grabbed my fleeing magic and twisted.

I scrambled further through the connections, pulling along hers until I dove into the knot that made up Neph, and then to the one pulsing an angry crimson, leading out to her uncle. *There.*

Muses die without their community. It is a slow death, one of the books had said. It was the slow death that Ahmed Bau had been experiencing in prison.

A dark knowledge overtook me. I didn't know from where the knowledge came—whether it was from some reading I had done, or something I had put together with hundreds of points of intersection, but I could see a possibility there in the darkness.

The festival's despair overlaid my vision, as if I were in both places at once. Whatever Axer's knife was doing, I was more myself and less under Ahmed's control—and I realized that Axer had precognitively thrown the enchanted knife at *me*. He had seen me port like that before—to him—and had made the split second calculation.

I looked at Neph's uncle and his enraged features and the people suffocating around him. I reached further along the thin path that he had arrogantly left open, discounting an eighteen-year-old girl. Discounting two of them.

I snapped the trail.

He screamed wildly and the darkness ripped from every mage in the crowd and shot into the sky. It spiraled upward, curved, then dove downward, felling Ahmed Bau where he stood.

My gaze ripped back from the festival to the field. Magic was streaming into both of us, the flowers around us were violently blooming, then dying again as a result of too aggressive growth.

I saw shadows flying toward us. Praetorians. Stavros would have easily redirected them to come after the bigger prize instead. There's no way my magic hadn't registered.

But the magic streaming back into me was overwhelming and I couldn't move. I could only watch as the earth rumbled, and the shadows zipped eagerly closer. The praetorians weren't as menacing, and their forms weren't as *full* without Kaine's magic powering them, but they were still terrifying and they would still take us to Stavros.

"I'm sorry, Neph," I whispered. She'd be taken, too. Of course she would. She was attached to me. Like Axer, like Olivia, like Constantine, everyone attached to me was a *target*.

"You'll be sorry if you don't *move*," someone yelled.

My gaze jerked just in time to see an object flying toward me. My fingers unclenched just enough for me to catch it against my chest. The flowing magic in the air changed trajectory and all of it flew into the cube I had clasped against me.

"Let's go, you idiots," screamed Olivia, still in disguise, with her hand extended forward from where she had thrown the object. She turned and started to run.

Shadows zipped over the field, sinuously flowing around the decaying flowers, pinpointed straight for us.

Neph, also still in disguise, jerked me up under her arm with way more strength than I had thought her capable and dove through the port, dragging me with her into the intermediary travel henge. I looked up just in time to see Olivia throw something else—then we all dove through the campus arch.

Marsgrove, Greyskull, Stevens, and half a dozen other adults grabbed us when we fell through.

Someone pulled the knife from my shoulder. *Ouch.*

"You knifed me," I said to Axer. "You tackled me," I said to Neph.

"Shut up, shut up, hurry, hurry, get those faces off them," Marsgrove said, pulling us forward.

"You dislocated my hand," Neph responded. She was gripping me so tightly with her other one, I didn't know if she'd be able to let go—like one of those traumatized people who had held onto something for dear life and then couldn't get their body to release the grip.

"Yeah, okay. Fair enough."

Greyskull grabbed us both and I felt the same magic that had allowed Axer to take me to Medical when we'd been outrunning the praetorians *last* time to take us now.

I decided it was a good time to pass out.

Chapter Thirty-three

REACTIONS IN CUBES

I WOKE, then immediately pretended unconsciousness while Greyskull and Marsgrove argued somewhere in the room. I could feel Neph next to me, but she was legitimately out cold.

"—did you see the magic?" Marsgrove demanded. "Where did Axer get it? I'm telling you—"

"Yes, I saw it. Nullification cubes. Can't say that you should be surprised by anything these kids have, Phillip."

"The brightest and stupidest class of this age," he said harshly.

"And here I had thought that was us," Greyskull said calmly.

Silence fell at that, and I could only imagine their exchanged looks since I could *feel* the magic scorching between them.

"Who knows what else he has," Marsgrove said. "He's more dangerous than Maximilian ever was."

"You are misremembering your youth, or were too coddled in your family's darkness. I remember being twelve quite clearly. It wasn't a mirthful time in greater Europa."

"They were only fighting for a Bridge in that conflict. Now, it's much worse."

"And yet Stavros wanted a Bridge Mage as much then as he wants an Origin Mage now. The stakes are always high."

"I've always thought the Dares have been biding their time for another war," Marsgrove said tightly.

"Then you've always thought them dangerous. You are going in circles here."

"I know, dammit. I hate all these games."

"Tired of the webs that you, too, have spun?" Greyskull had to know that I was awake, but he continued to give no indication.

"You know I am," Marsgrove said quietly.

* Reactions in Cubes *

"I assume the Department is gone," Greyskull said, changing the subject. "Since you are here."

"Yes. The praetorians aren't happy, but they are slipping without Kaine powering them. They are calling our version of the events trickery."

"They aren't wrong. Can they pin any of it on the kids?"

"Axer's blasted baubles took care of everything *this time*. You know there will be a next time. Blasted girl can't even follow simple instructions to *stay on campus*."

"I think she thought the risk worth it." Greyskull's voice was mild.

"Oh, like one muse matters in the—"

"Phillip."

I clamped down on my instinctive anger at Marsgrove's words—spiking vitals would definitely give me away.

He blew out a breath. "I don't want *any* of my students to die, but so many more will if—" The silence grew for a beat of three breaths. "They can't grab her, not yet. They can only pin events on Ahmed Bau, who is in custody. Wrecked. No ties. And who knows how long a muse will last without them, especially one used to holding so many in his hands."

"He can talk."

"He will talk. But what is he going to tell them that they don't already know? You know he didn't think up this plot—or escape—on his own. They want to speak of trickery, how about the fact that they didn't inform the public about the escaped convict earlier today? Why? Because they *let* him escape. They were trying to get her off campus. Or to take her in a mass grab when they arrested him. Time is running out already. It's *only* a matter of time, and we grow short on it."

"You need to tell her about Omega Genesis. Miss Price may know the bare idea, but Miss Crown is going to figure it out on her own. Whether that is inside or outside the basement, whether that is with or without your aid, is up to you."

"You are saying it like *I* know."

"You know more than the rest of us."

"Not more than Rafi, I'll bet."

Silence, then—"He doesn't care about what happens to the world, only what happens to Stavros."

"The two are wrapped in the same end," Marsgrove muttered.

Greyskull sighed. "I'm tired of your cryptic bullshit. Get out of my ward, Phillip."

"You *know* it's not a trust issu—"

"*Out.*"

The door slammed, then Greyskull muttered. "Asshole. I hope someone goes through his files. Like Stavros, he relies far too much on puzzle box encryption."

I opened my eyes and saw Greyskull staring back at me, fingers tapping one arm.

"Oh, dear," he said flatly, not even attempting to feign surprise. "You are awake. Let's have a look at all my healing progress you've undone."

"You're my favorite," I said seriously.

"Yes, well I need to be *someone's*," he said.

"Grouching gains you bonus points."

"Excellent, because your roommate is ready to earn the highest score."

He wasn't wrong.

"I'm going to kill you," Olivia said, harshly shaking my shoulders fifteen minutes later after Greyskull slipped from the room. "And you." She looked over at Neph and grabbed her into a hug.

Neph hesitantly wrapped arms around her. "You aren't...?"

"I'm furious, but I know what you were trying to do. I...I get it."

They had a moment. That moment extended when they both looked at me and frowned.

"Yay?" I tried. "We won?"

Olivia crossed her arms.

"We didn't all die in despair?" I tried instead, then reached over and squeezed Neph when I felt her spike of fear.

Olivia aggressively leaned forward. "You'd be in custody right now if I hadn't nullified your presence with those stupid cubes and hadn't insisted on those stupid disguises. Stupid!"

I leaned forward. "Yeah, what were those? The cubes, I mean. I heard Marsgrove and Greyskull talking about them."

"Dare gave them to me and ordered me to throw one at you and to throw one on the ground just before we reentered campus, then in the next moment he was...elsewhere. And there were four explosions around the layer—all Origin Magic." She gave me an unreadable look. "They can't pin anything on you or on anyone specifically because of it. And the only video they got was of two pudgy boys dragging and wrestling each other around a weirdly blooming field, then a third one awkwardly waving his arms around."

"Your disguises were a great idea."

"Yes, well they won't be a second time. I'm certain the Department is already accounting for it. We're just lucky you never used one on campus. No one thought you knew how."

"Are you okay?" I asked Neph, looking at her healing wards. They were made purely of calming spells at this point, with magic specific to muses tangled in the threads.

"My uncle was a visionary once," she said, fingers pulling through the magic in tiny spirals. "And then..." She shook her head. "He returned from a trip and started to try and find ways to break free. To free us from the thumb of the Department. But mages are so scared of what we can do. And they have reason." Her gaze went distant. "You know that reason now."

I squeezed her hand. "His eyes—did you see his eyes?"

"Yes." Her gaze was steady on mine. "Whatever was done to him added to his madness, but it wasn't controlling him like you might like to believe. He made his choices."

"Raphael and Kaine, or Stavros, still pushed him to make those," I said darkly. "What were they trying to do?"

"Get you off campus—either by Bau taking you or by you following, exactly as happened," Olivia said, looking tired. "Phillip's right. Spring term is going to be a nightmare."

Greyskull tapped on the door. "Miss Bau? There are...some people here to see you."

Neph's chin lifted. "Send them in."

A quartet of muses converged on Medical. Olivia and I immediately closed ranks around Neph, but she stopped us with a hand.

It was hard to read Aira's expression as she stepped forward. But I could see the rest maintain their distance, as if uncertain what might happen if they drew too close to us.

"We all felt it," Aira said.

"Elyn?" Neph asked.

Aira swallowed. "Gone. Her campus ties cut by her own hand."

Neph looked sad. "Did anyone find out—?"

"Somewhere in the Fourth Layer. She left a note. Ahmed...he's gone?"

"His source tie has been severed," Neph confirmed. Murmurs rose from the other muses, some of whom took a step back. "The Department has him."

"And the rest of you?"

Neph kept her chin high. "My mother is now fully in charge. She contacted me through the ways immediately. We will not follow his path, but we also *will* push for better terms when things quiet down," she said firmly. "For all of us. We plan to pursue diplomatic options through the council and legislature."

Aira's gaze went to me. "And her?"

"She is my charge. That will not change."

"That may be out of your control."

"Clearly." Neph smiled, like a huge weight had been lifted from her with my ability to sever their community ties.

I frowned, but Neph sent a soothing wave to me, so I said nothing.

"She broke Ahmed's tie," Aira said.

"She did."

"The community has said nothing to the Department. We will wait to see."

Neph inclined her head.

"If she decides to break all our community ties, she can do it." Aira's voice was matter-of-fact, but I could feel her underlying fear.

"The only reason she broke my uncle's tie was because he was unleashing the Soul Plague. I was attempting to sever my own tie to her, in order to end it, but Ren took matters into her own hands."

Aira's gaze switched to me, calculation mixing with her fear. "But that she was able to do it at all...she could break *other* ties."

"Ren isn't getting involved in our politics," Neph said calmly, though there was steel in her voice.

"We all saw a new *option* today. A new chance. You can't keep her out of our politics." Aira looked between us. "It doesn't work that way just because you want it to."

"My standing increased today." Neph's voice was pure steel. "Take care of your own words."

"You aren't going to be able to keep her, Nephthys."

"I know."

I frowned at Neph and nudged her mentally.

Worry not, she responded with a mental caress.

The muses exchanged looks, then Aira bowed, gracefully walking backward to the door. "We wait to see. Do not abuse your grace period."

They disappeared through the door. Olivia didn't look pleased, and she was doing something with one of her frequencies—my guess was that Patrick, Mike, or Delia—maybe all three—were getting an earful.

"What was all that about?" I frowned at Neph.

"My uncle's schemes, though driven by increasing madness, always had a root of truth. I am free of his madness because you freed me. You freed my commune from it. What you are witnessing is a simple reorganization."

"Does that mean you'll go back to Sakkara?"

"No." Her gaze was fixed on the scarab around my neck. "My future lies here."

Chapter Thirty-four

CATS AND MICE

AS EXPECTED, the news blew wide across the magical worlds that a muse had unleashed the Soul Plague. Calls were immediate for more restrictions to be placed on their communities. Rumors that the "alleged" Origin Mage had ties to that community were gaining strength even with Bellacia's unusual media silence on the subject.

However, Neph's mother, now in charge of their commune, had swiftly gone into damage mode.

"Rogue muses are dealt with by the community. As can be seen in the memories involved, Ahmed Bau was taken down swiftly and completely from the inside. There were no Department officials involved in any of the removal procedures. If you view the memories, you will see not a *single* enforcement face among the crowd before he was cut from our community. Outside regulations on muses are nothing compared to how we regulate our own."

Like all muses, there was something beautiful just in the way that Ife Bau moved.

"Ahmed has always been outspoken about his views, but we noticed in the days since the mandatory muse call that he felt especially off, even in his distant prison. I can only speculate as to what might have caused his breakdown and his *escape*."

And lovely, vindictive Bellacia finally inserted a view of him in the newscast—one that clearly showed a shadow moving across his eyes.

It was clear as day that the insinuation was that Ahmed Bau had been infected and released by the Department. I was stunned that Bellacia, her father, and their organization had chosen to show it.

Bellacia, what are you up to?

"As a group, we value the arts and pursuit of knowledge and happiness," Neph's mother continued. "You rely on us for the balance that we bring to your communities, and we value the contracts we make."

There was a nicely veiled statement in there—that new contracts would eventually be made, and that the Second Layer better appreciate the community.

"We have had a rough past year, with the damage to the Library of Alexandria and Ahmed's decline. But the library is set to be reopened and Ahmed is no longer in control of our commune. We look forward to increasingly favorable relations with the mage community."

Neph had said that their small community had almost lost their rights to the library. The other Egyptian communities had been steadily chipping away at their power base and it had seemed like the loss of the library would be an eventual result. Neph's ejection from Sakkara finally made sense.

"Mother is...very pleased about you," she said. "Everyone has stopped grabbing at our territory and they are now watching and waiting to see what happens."

I thought about what the broadcast had implied. "Your uncle—"

She shook her head. "Couldn't have been made to do that which he hadn't already set a path for. More quickly? Yes. But whoever fed him that shadow was feeding an already ravenous beast. They just tipped him over the edge."

"Still, if I hadn't—"

"Ren." She put her hands over mine. "If you hadn't snapped the thread, all the muses in my commune, and possibly all the muses in the Second Layer, would be in chains right now. This was a play. A deliberate maneuver. We are all watching very carefully to see what happens next, for the signs point to this being the very beginning."

Olivia suddenly frowned, then touched beneath her ear. "Phillip is requesting my presence in his office."

We both turned to her. "Do you want us to come with you?"

Olivia didn't answer, and a spike of panic shot through her. Both of us were already out of our chairs as her face blanched.

"My mother's here."

"*What?*" I surged forward.

"Phillip said the spell remover is here too. They are ceding neutral ground." Her voice was steady, but I could feel the hitch in her emotions. "Today. They are going to remove the life hook today instead of tomorrow. The papers are already signed. Mother has acquiesced to everything."

No way was this not a trap. "I'm coming."

"Are you *joking?* I will chain you to this *chair.*"

Her vehemence was a living thing that forced me back into my seat. I gripped the edges of the wood with my fingernails. "But—"

She lifted a finger. "Not another word."

"I can go," Neph offered.

Olivia turned from where she had started shakily gathering her things, an expression of disbelief painting her face. "What are y—? All of you are *morons.*"

She shook her head and waved a hand over her eyes. A film of magic settled over her irises, then was gone. Abruptly, a sense of double vision overcame me. I could see Neph rapidly blinking next to me, but it took me far longer to adjust.

"Do not move from this room." Olivia pointed fingers at both of us. "Honestly, do neither of you remember *magic?*"

"But what if she takes you?" Fear gripped me.

Olivia's gaze softened. "That's why I'm taking your really irritating bondmate with me."

She opened the door and I tried to make the sudden double images of Constantine—hers and mine—form into one. He was lounging against the other side of the hall. He looked deeply bored, but I could see an underlying anticipation. He must have used the Top Track ways to arrive so quickly.

"No one wants to stay in a room with him any longer than necessary." Olivia thumbed a finger at him. "I'll be back in no time."

"I'm her lawyer," he said.

"You're my muscle," she muttered. "I'm pushing you in front of the first spell."

"I'm touched."

The door closed.

I closed my eyes against the sudden rush of moving images as Olivia began walking, her stride militant, not fluid. "How do you get used to this?" I asked Neph.

She didn't answer for a second, and I peeked open an eye to see her looking stunned. "I...I don't know. Muses aren't usually entrusted with second sight spells from mages."

I sent her feelings of love and comfort, then fumbled over, offered her a hand, and felt my way to the bed—all while my brain was telling me that I was also zooming up the mountain and walking into the administration building.

I got us both situated on my comforter, heads on my pillow, eyes closed. "Better."

It took me most of the meeting—rote as it was—to finally become accustomed to the spell. The papers were magically notarized, the inheritance spells were negated, and the life hook was removed—and I memorized everything about the removal mage that I possibly could. I also noticed that Constantine brushed past the man as he moved in the room.

Chapter Thirty-four

Constantine didn't accidentally touch anyone, ever.

"Congratulations," Helen finally said, voice bored. "You're a pauper without family."

"I'm not yours to command anymore," Olivia responded. "I don't even have to plan to rule the world any longer in an attempt to get out from under your boot. I can just rule it because I want to. Or do nothing at all." I could feel her smile and her quiet, blooming joy. "Our fight—that was catharsis. But being free of you completely—this is victory," she said quietly. "This is one of the finest days of my life."

"How twee. You always were so meek and dull and disappointing. But there are still uses for you." Helen grabbed Olivia's chin before anyone could react.

She looked through Olivia's eyes, straight into mine. "Filthy little feral. You slipped through the cracks, but so many of your brethren will be lost for it. Do you know where they are? Know that it was you who caused their demise," she whispered in Olivia's—in my—ear.

Helen was thrust backward as a beam from Olivia hit her in the chest. Magic immediately froze Helen's limbs as Marsgrove secured her.

Olivia's hands were out and shaking, magic smoking from her fingertips. "I want it noted," she said shakily. "That the other party in this dispute attacked first."

"Noted. That is a fine of one thousand munits, Councilor," the moderator, a man in tweed, said. "Any more attempts will increase the amount by a factor of 10."

"What a disappointment *you* are, *Mother*." Olivia's shaking hands formed fists. "Know that you failed at parenting, just as you've failed at so many things."

Helen's mouth pinched, but then smoothed into triumphant lines. "I've succeeded at all that I needed. It will be quite a new world soon. Goodbye, Olivia. I hope you rot during your last days."

"Goodbye, Mother. *Likewise*."

Constantine returned with Olivia to our room and he immediately sat in my chair and started fiddling with something on my desk. Olivia leaned against the inside of the door. Neph and I disabled the vision spell and ran over to envelop her in hugs.

When we finally let her go, Olivia pulled out a vial. Inside, a shadow swirled, trapped in the glass. "She put this on me when she touched my skin."

I stared at the shadow, horrified.

Olivia threw the vial to Constantine, who caught it and dropped it into whatever he was making.

"She honestly thought I wouldn't notice." Olivia laughed without humor. "I'm deeply offended."

"She sucks. You don't need her. You have us." I gripped Olivia's shoulder. "But she sucks. And I'm sorry."

Olivia looked at me with her head cocked, as if trying to figure out what drug I was on, then pulled out a small device. "I put twelve spells on her. She won't be able to brush her teeth without us knowing."

I stared at the device, started laughing, then found my legs weren't working well and sat on the floor.

"It was meant for Crown," Constantine said, pushing the vial containing the shadow away.

"Meant for me to what?"

"Be infected."

Chapter Thirty-five

MOVEMENTS FROM WITHIN

THE IDEA of it unsettled everyone. Kaine's shadows were the stuff of nightmares. It wasn't one of Kaine's, but it was a spelled likeness—something Helen or a Department scientist had created with similar properties.

"How did you know it was on you?" Will asked Olivia.

"My mother used to slip them on me when I was being deliberately disobedient," Olivia said tightly. "You learn how to recognize them worming around and separate their feelings from your own."

It made me want to get Helen Price into a room. A room that had no door.

Will started searching his skin, scanning for residue no one could see.

"Don't bother. They are invisible when they are parasitically attached," Constantine said unhelpfully. "And this is a new variant they've cooked up."

I remembered the one that had attached to me. I hadn't felt a thing. I'd *thought* I could probably identify one in the future, but a single piece of data was not a good standard to measure by.

But Kaine's shadow had provoked weird feelings—*Kaine's* feelings—feelings separate from my own, just like Olivia said.

"I think I already have one on me," I blurted out.

It would explain the *weirdness* I'd been experiencing. I'd blamed the stray wisps of thought and emotion I'd been getting, and my own weird subconscious blips, on frequency issues as I learned to use one. But the more I thought about it, the more sense it made that I'd been infected. I started vigorously rubbing my skin.

Everyone looked at me, most with horror written on their faces. Only Neph and Constantine looked calm.

"The assessor touched me. She put one on me. I need to find it," I said to them, somewhat more urgently.

Neph darted a look at Constantine, but then said to me. "When the assessor came, you already had protections on you to prevent such things from sticking."

I frowned and looked at my arms. "How do you know?"

"You've had the protections...for a while. Placed by more than one hand."

Mike nodded slowly, looking like he'd had a revelation. "Okay, so what about the rest of us?"

I tuned them out. It didn't make sense. I *had* to have a spell on me—it explained all of the weirdness that had been happening to me.

Neph's hand slipped over mine. "What you have been experiencing were likely similar spells *trying* to grab hold."

"So I could have experienced small parts of them, but they couldn't fully attach?"

"Yes."

I relaxed a measure. I could accept that explanation. The one time I'd experienced Kaine's shadow was when I'd had to leave the scarab behind. And when I'd reattached it after Kaine's shadow was in place, the scarab had been *hot*. It was cool to the touch now.

But now that the idea had been raised...where *had* all the strange feelings been coming from?

~*~

The Bandits, working with Neph, Aira, and a few of the other muses, came up with something that would identify spells, like the one Helen had put on Olivia, in the moment just before the spell attached—giving the infected mage a split second of awareness.

And it was not a day too soon.

Campus repopulated with a vengeance, and with the happily returning students for spring term came the segment that were drenched in Department magic and spells—shadow-like spells.

Olivia had long since made use of Raphael's spell to keep track of the names of the Department lackeys on campus, and Raphael's spell was used in conjunction with the identification spell, giving everyone double the advanced warning whenever a lackey was near.

"Removed another shadow, but it feels like two more have taken their place," Loudon said, shaking his head.

It didn't last a full day before Olivia went straight to Margrove with her grievances, much to the consternation of everyone who despised authority.

But shadows were illegal on campus for a reason, and simulations of such were in direct violation of the rules. The administration cracked down immediately and put a Level Five Justice Offense in place. The administration had a sudden "epiphany" regarding how to track such spells after a super sketchy meeting that included Marsgrove, Wellingham, Olivia, and a few of the others.

The shadowy spells abruptly ceased, and the new Junior Department fad became using illegal port devices. Luckily for everyone, Lifen and Greene grabbed the first one before it hit me, and reappeared in battle worn clothes four hours post-battle—though they hadn't returned to campus without making a stop for a cozy dinner on the Riviera. The combat mages outside Axer's group had taken specific interest in matters after that. Whatever Greene had told them had mobilized the squad.

With the combined powers of Will, the combat mages, and justice magic working against them, the port spells were destined for a short lifespan, but it was when Axer caught one headed for me, that the practice swiftly died on the spot.

As far as I knew, the guy who had thrown the port device was *still* in Medical three days later.

But the motive for the attacks was the real problem.

"Stavros wants you off campus. Verisetti wants you off campus. Bau would have taken you and Nephthys both, if Leandred hadn't ejected him. And you would have both gone straight to Bau, if you hadn't decided to stop and do the impossible. Even with your stop in some random field, the praetorians nearly nabbed you. And without Dare neutralizing the area—which we *still* need to discuss—you would have been sunk. There are a lot of *almosts* in there. They almost got you, Ren. They keep almost getting you. We are working with a decreasing amount of time," Olivia said grimly.

The Department's first move outside of personal attacks started with the shifts that began on the first full moon of spring term.

A large cross-section of campus was gathered at the southwest side of the mountain to watch the first shift.

"First shift is always a doozy," Will said enthusiastically. He was fully recovered from being "plagued" at the shift festival and was ecstatic with his third place finish in the competition.

Olivia kept muttering darkly about the Department wanting Will's—and my—magic, but we were trying to remain positive.

"Because the first shift is releasing the most pent up energy?" I asked.

"That and it's coming from The Belt." Will smiled and shivered in the way he did when he found something fantastic in its horror.

One of the facilities that loosened and controlled the shifts was stationed in an installation that served as both a planet wide power plant and mediation of magic in a geographic area that in the First Layer was labeled as the Bermuda Triangle. Here, it was called The Belt. And while what happened to intrepid travelers who went near it wasn't a mystery in the Second Layer, weird tales were still part of its allure.

"Gatekeeper of the first, thirteenth, twenty-fifth, etc. shifts and all around crackling energy spot," he said.

Eleven other facilities around the globe handled and controlled the other shifts. I'd heard a few of their names mentioned—Lemunia, Nu, and Aztla.

"Someday, we'll go there," he whispered.

Mike looked over, frowning. "You two are whispering. You aren't allowed to whisper."

"Everyone knows that," Delia said, eying us.

We both straightened. "Just discussing the facilities."

"Two of my recycling mates are out there right now, lucky shivits," Loudon said, angelic features only slightly forlorn.

"Shift internship?" Will asked, interested.

"Yeah, fixing recyclers, shoring up wards and security measures. One bad thing about my rap sheet—no way will they be giving me one of those jobs." Loudon smirked. "The sheet pays off in other ways, though."

"Apply next year for the valley," Olivia said, tone brooking no argument. "But go through Dean Marsgrove."

"Special projects? Yeah, maybe I will." Loudon's tone was non-committal, but he smiled.

"So you'd fix anything that goes wrong with the shifts?" I asked.

"Yes. Never quite know what a shift might do. All depends on the magic, yeah? What's been messing with things, and what magics have been produced."

I looked around us, reflecting on everything that had been changed since I had come to campus. "What about...you know, me?"

"I have fifty munits riding on you," Will said earnestly.

"Riding on me to what?"

"Blow up something."

I looked behind him to glare at Delia, who shrugged. "Told you."

The first shift started as a hum on the wind, sound growing louder with every mile that the shift grew closer to Excelsine.

Students dotted the mountainside, watching and waiting.

"And here. It. Comes!" Patrick yelled.

Energy crackled and white spikes of magic, like the foam of a giant wave breaking wildly over rocks and headed toward shore, flew over the spiked horizon and crashed toward us.

The students and faculty members in charge of the wards held their positions—mostly ceremonial—with their long banners of magic held at the ready, in case something went wrong.

Chapter Thirty-five

Most Second Layer citizens stayed inside the larger cities and moved to secured areas for shift season. Only the scientists and those actively testing stayed outside societal limits.

Excelsine was well-equipped for the layer shifts. Built under thousands of academic projects and wards that had been modified and perfected over the years, no one had been concerned about how the mountain would weather shift season in the past, but more than one eye had gazed toward me in the past week, and I'd seen money changing hands that made a lot more sense now.

The rolling wave of magic was exactly that—and each crackling dome of magic encasing the cities and towns were the tumbled rocks in its path. Each dome released a little of its own energy as the wild magic rushed over the top, adding to the wave as it rumbled forth. Most of the wild, knotted magic would be siphoned off at the other installations which dotted the globe as the wave passed them. The shift wave would keep moving until it completed its circuit.

The domes were the way the cities had figured out how to protect themselves from the overt magic at the same time that they slowly released some of their own. Magic had to work itself out. Nothing could get in the way of that without disastrous consequences.

The Second Layer had figured out an ingenious way to shake out the jumbled and knotted magic of its citizens and governments each year.

On the backs of the Third Layer, Delia said mentally.

I looked at Delia, but she said nothing more.

The Second Layer was flush with magic and opportunity. Part of that was due to the magic that had once been part of the Third Layer.

The last of the wave crashed over the mountain, hitting the wards arching over us and making everything twinkle in iridescent lights for a few moments as it sucked away the magic being offered to it and left behind an equivalent that had already shaken free from its entangled threads.

When the last of the magic passed, there was a moment of stillness, then it seemed as one, that everyone turned to look at me.

People frowned and money began exchanging hands.

I crossed my arms, disgruntled. "Fantastic. But you lost, Will, ha."

Will looked ridiculously smug. "I put my money on the whole season, not just your magic destroying things in the wake of the first shif—"

And that's when a blast of light flashed in the distance and a boom of sound shattered the silence.

Chapter Thirty-six

THE CALM BEFORE

"FREQUENCIES ARE overloading with reports. Authorities are blaming campus," Olivia said, tight-lipped.

The wards of Irsyn Fields—the largest city after Excelsine on the shifts' directional spread—had been decimated, and parts of the town looked like a tornado had hit before the shift specialists had regained control. No one had been harmed, but it had been a close thing.

The report came back immediately—Origin Magic had been found mixed in with the oily film left behind by the shift.

"We all knew this was bound to happen. Look at the Bloody Tuesday happenings," Baxter Roberts, one of the Bailey Daily reporters, said on live feed. "Vincent Godfrey unleashed hell on that campus using Origin domes, and the Department did no favors to it afterward. Bound to be some hiccups as we get through the first week of shifts. Things will get better."

They got worse.

With each new shift originating from a different location, new towns became targets—each following the Excelsine trajectory.

The fourth and fifth shifts were catastrophic—and with each new shift, the magic doubled in intensity and destruction. And death.

The same Origin Magic signature was found throughout each destructive cocktail—one that the Department said wasn't from their cache.

By the eighth shift, even Baxter Roberts looked pained. "The first round of shifts is always the most explosive, we just haven't had quite this much released in decades. I still say the terrorists are to blame. They've shown themselves to have a stash of Origin Magic. Verisetti, especially, has shown a proclivity for using it. Look at what happened in Ganymede."

His fellow panelist shook her head. "There is a lot of evidence pointing to the problem being at Excelsine itself, though. That maybe *it* was the problem that created Bloody Tuesday in the first place."

Chapter Thirty-six

A punch straight to my gut—because my presence in this world might have spurred a few things, but Bloody Tuesday likely would have happened without me—maybe without the domes, but an attack was still imminent. Godfrey hadn't even *known* about me. Raphael had joined that campaign only after I'd damaged his leash on me.

The Department was waging an easy media campaign against campus. And even with Bellacia's aid behind the scenes and slight questioning insertions into reports, public opinion was going downhill pretty fast. Even Bella's stories weren't ignoring the evidence.

Excelsine was the tipping point at which everything started to barrel out of control with the shifts—destruction spreading further and further through the layer.

The increasingly negative calls for the removal of the "cause" grew in strength with each devastating event.

"First the terrorists, now our own younger generations. What is happening to the world? Something must be done. We are good people trying to live normal lives," a woman being interviewed on the street cried. "I'm scared for my family, for my friends, for my way of life."

"I know they say that girl at Excelsine passed the test," a man said. "But everyone knows something's rotten there. I've said it before, and I'll say it again—bunch of righteous scholars on their bloody mountain top thinking they know better and are better than the rest of us. The Department is just trying to do their job—to protect all of us. What has to happen before they can step in? Cities falling? Countries collapsing? I say just take the girl, clean up that hoity-toity school, and be done with it."

There were a few naysayers. "Shift season is a nightmare that the Department has always used to control the populace," a woman stated in front of a crowd. "It is their fault things are going wrong. Put the blame where it should be placed."

But that type of argument was easily swallowed by other more bloodthirsty ones.

A man looked into the spell's lens, straight at the viewers, lips firm. "There's a simple solution. Find the mage or device responsible and kill it." He pulled a weapon from his belt.

I jerked my head back and quickly switched feeds. So much for the recent upgrade to my frequency simulator gem which included visuals now.

I looked to the sky to watch The Belt's second rotational shift—lucky number thirteen—and winced as it shuddered over the mountain.

Two unfamiliar students walking the path steered clear of me, eyes wide as they looked from the shift rippling above, to me, then back again.

I ignored them and concentrated on the feeds looping through my view as I made my way to the classroom where Mbozi, Stevens, Constantine, and

I were meeting.

It was unusual to be walking alone—a Bandit usually showed up feigning surprise that we were "going the same way." Or Axer, who never feigned surprise, showed up after I was done with class or lab and always took me somewhere pleasant for a few hours.

It warmed me that they cared, but at the same time, my guilt grew. *I* was the problem here.

I rubbed my chest.

An alarm triggered in my armband too late as a student brushed past me. Coldness seeped into my bones in the wake of her touch. I looked over my shoulder. Her pretty face flipped into one far worse. "Soon, so soon," Stavros's voice cooed from her mouth.

I swallowed and increased my pace. That type of taunting was frequent when I was alone. But they were taunts, nothing more, and I decreasingly reported them to my friends. They were already worried enough.

Mage visas were still required in order to enter campus without a student or employee contract. It was a measure that had been instituted after I had arrived on campus and brought the Ganymede destruction with me. And after the Ahmed Bau incident, restrictions had gotten even tighter.

So these face flips were *only* taunts, nothing more. Still...

I looked at the end of the shift magic in the sky as the mountain shuddered beneath my feet.

Campus had been safer before I'd arrived, and that bothered me. I might not be causing the destruction outside of it, but it *was* my magic— there was no way that the "unknown magic signature" wasn't mine. And people were being hurt because of it.

Stavros might be manipulating things to put my magic into play, but he wanted *me,* and even if it meant destroying a portion of the layer he had sworn to protect, he was slowly showing that he would do anything to get me. Throwing magical items and shadows had been lazy shots across my bow, looking to get lucky. Public opinion was an indirect first move. Direct moves would follow.

And I was hiding at Excelsine, using the mountain as my shield.

I needed to be the solution not the problem. I increased my pace again, closing in on the building.

We'd been working double and triple time on the field/shield, using all the hours that the four of us had with each other—Constantine, Stevens, and I used our vault hours, Mbozi and I used engineering hours, Constantine and Stevens used their lab hours, and Mbozi and Stevens came back from staff hours with new ideas.

Stevens was taking the slighting of Excelsine in the media *very* personally, as was Mbozi. It was a huge incentive to get the shield working before the end of shift season.

Another face flipped and smirked at me. "Time grows short."

"I will beat you," I said calmly, pushing past the crowd of Junior Department types lurking outside the main engineering building.

"You will be mine," said one of them, a single blink of their face holding the smirking features of someone else.

"It's only a matter of time," said the Stavros-flipped face of another.

~*~

If it weren't for the taunting, spells, destruction, and fear, spring term would have been extraordinary. When things occasionally went well, days and nights between the full moons slipped by in shifting wonder, and I wished I could just enjoy the season for the marvel it was, instead of the dangerous moves I could feel made with every shift.

The campus wards took the brunt of the shifts—the warding mages having spent the previous three terms leading up to this point by tweaking the old wards and putting in new fixes constantly as the shifts shuddered over the magic. The wards left the rest of us safe inside to watch from thousands of feet in the air over the valley as the magic waves traveled, leveled, smoothed, and provided a light show unparalleled anywhere.

Students in their last term were cramming in comprehensive exams, and those in pretty much every discipline that could use the shifting magic were inundated with their own mid-focus exams. As Mike had said so long ago, even the weather mages took the shifts seriously—pushing the students harder and making them test their projects or abilities.

But the continuing reports put a damper on the creative energy, and the media started freely running with news of the "Origin Mage."

"*Soon*, Ren Crown," a passing girl said, her lithe, wrapped dress figure a strange mannequin for a sixty-year-old man's face.

I rubbed my chest. "Never."

~*~

Olivia grew tenser by the day. I couldn't hide everything from her.

"It's okay, Liv, they're just taunting," I said, running my magic over a herd of pigeon-wasps that were gathered in a little grove we were passing through. The feathers and filament wings of the pigeon-wasps were droopier than they'd been before the praetorians had defiled campus with their shadowy presence. I tried to fix something around campus on every outing, adding magic wherever I walked; layering protections inside of the magic Constantine had diabolically placed.

"It's not okay, and it's not just taunting," Olivia argued. "Stavros is playing a mental game, and it's working. You look terrible."

* The Calm Before *

I looked down at my clothes. "I match for once."

"Your face, Ren."

"Well, that's hardly sporting of you. I can't change that."

"That's not funny."

The Junior Department had placed me on a list of people "recommended" for everyone to guard against in deception spells. If I used face changing or body changing enchantments everyone would see the real me through the transparent haze of my disguise. It also wouldn't pass recording spells that contained deception enchantments.

The Department had learned quickly after the Ahmed Bau incident.

I wasn't the only one on the list. Anyone I talked to was added—the public sentiment keen on knowing what we were all up to.

Patrick found the new notoriety darkly hilarious and told me so as he accompanied me to my art class—a destination I knew for a fact was way out of his way. "Can't just let you walk by, Crown, and not know who you are. You might blow us all into the Third Layer. And the rest of us...we are all holding triggers." He made exploding noises at a group of Department lackeys walking by, then cackled when they scattered.

Olivia wasn't amused.

~*~

Our project, however, was going *well*. I sent three rounds of tests to the Ophidians, and each one came back with better results. Mbozi was duplicating our outcomes with a colleague at the Third Layer university that Axer's co-champion attended. We were set to make a huge splash on the warding circuit by the end of term.

I blew past the midway point of unraveling the wards on Ori, and while my understanding of Origin Magic was still confined to piecing together a hundred other texts, my grasp of the magic was becoming stronger.

A rogue shift hit on Wednesday, and two shifts in a row were irreparably altered on Thursday, causing varying levels of destruction across four countries that were unprepared to handle the alterations. Friday began with a wave of monsters ejecting from the sky, and Saturday's forecast failed to predict the series of tornadoes dragged in the wake of the midday shift.

Axer and the rest of the combat mages were in high demand. They were being called out to do rotations in regional areas with political and community ties to Excelsine. And, if Axer and his squad were *slightly* more successful in battling everything the shifts threw, people just put it down to their battle prowess, not the extra devices Greene suddenly possessed— devices which passed through my hands in Okai first.

Bellacia returned to campus, cutting her internship short. "The real news is here, after all," she said, and firmly established herself back in the mix.

Chapter Thirty-six

We all tried to *ignore* the man-eating hamsters that ejected from purple clouds for a full four hours the next Monday, and equally ignore Will's excitement over his every result being skewed.

"I am tweaking like crazy," he said, hair going everywhere, eyes manic as we ate lunch. "Every event brings me closer to correctly designing for *all* events."

"How can you design for *all* events when man-eating hamsters fall from the sky?" Delia demanded. "How do you even program something like that in?"

"The hamsters are the result, but the symptoms and the magic—and the defense against both—are the same. This is *great*."

Hardly anyone else shared his enthusiasm, especially those scientists in their graduating term who were trying to complete their dissertations.

The shifts I could deal with. The increasingly hollow feeling in my chest each time someone brushed past me with Stavros' face was finally taking its toll.

"Poor Ren Crown, so powerless. Another feral will probably die today. Tsk, tsk," he said from the face of a passing student.

Another passing group—one that was not covered in Department spells —was arguing with each other. "What will happen to the people in the smaller towns? I'm *worried* about the Second Layer," one said.

"What about the Third Layer?" I muttered, rubbing my chest and glaring as they disappeared from view. "No one cares when world ending events happen to *them*."

I frowned at the dark emotions and shut my eyes to search for a spell— certain that one had been placed by Stavros's latest puppet.

There.

Relieved at locating it, I retrieved a container from my pocket and siphoned the spell inside. Some of the darkness clouding my thoughts instantly dissipated.

But this was the tenth one today.

Between Justice Squad, grief duties, and everything else, I was being touched repeatedly. Some times to show empathy, sometimes...not. Constantine's threats held far less sway when it came to the Department's zealots. He had silently rampaged through a slew of them, but they were *happy* to martyr themselves for their cause.

Like Inessa, whose spells were especially easy to find, but devastating in the hollowness left behind. Olivia had earned a Level Three blasting her into another level of campus the night before and Inessa had just laughed and laughed and laughed.

I scanned for new spells each day—Olivia scanned for new ones each night—but the hollow feeling continued to grow.

* The Calm Before *

And with the hollowness, campus seemed to split into a weird mix of community madness and muted fear. I had put my all into supporting the first one, making sure Sari and Bess were well funded with assistance and magic in conducting their greater campus plans. There was nothing I could do about the latter—no flag I could wave to proclaim that all of the insinuations in the press were false. They *weren't* false, not about my mage type. Complete proof was the only thing they didn't yet have.

Axer was very, *very* good at figuring out when I was at my wits end and putting one of those strange neutralization cubes in my hand, though.

No, my fellow classmates who tiptoed around me weren't *wrong* about my rare mage status, but other than the Junior Department, most kept a respectful, if somewhat fearful, distance.

"I can't believe I would ever say this, but I'm glad you are a self-sacrificing moron," Olivia said, making a note of something.

I examined my engineering homework—there was a tiny defect in the support structure, and I needed to find it—without looking over at Olivia. "I'm not even sure where to start with a response."

"I take back my derision over the thousand hours you've spent bandaging plants, animals, buildings, and other morons. Brookis Tell said publicly today in class that the only reason he didn't vote to assassinate you was because you rehabilitated his favorite orange grove two weeks ago without anyone asking you to."

I frowned. "Do I need to look for assassins tomorrow?" That would suck. I'd failed to notice one last week and Axer had scheduled me to me train with Camille in stealth tactics this weekend, and that was *not* going to be a good time, especially if he doubled it because someone else tried to kill me tomorrow.

"No. The assassination vote failed 37-23."

"Do I want to know who these sixty people—or really these 23—are?"

"No."

I shook my head and finally found the flaw in my design, tweaking the magic to fix it. "It seems like politicians should be more involved in the community circuit, then, if they want people to support them."

"Intentions, Ren. It's obvious to anyone with a spell that you are doing things without looking for recognition, you just want to help. You practically scurry away and hide whenever someone 'catches' you. Politicians can be scented for false intentions a mile away."

"I don't scurry." I rubbed my neck, which suddenly felt warm. "I just get tired of the staring."

"I know." Olivia's voice was soft, but still firm. "I would get you to embrace it normally, but this low profile gambit is working for you. It's hard to see the mouse as a threat."

Chapter Thirty-six

We both knew that mousey mien would be thrown out the window the first time my powers were captured in the media's memory.

"You look worse today. I'm worried about you," she said softly.

"The taunts are bothersome, but the spells are starting to wear me down," I admitted wearily. It had taken me a while to realize my shields hadn't worked as well ever since the shadow temporarily connecting Ahmed Bau to campus had licked my cheek. My shields *looked* the same, but there was something *off* underneath. I had only realized it with Inessa's last curse. It had been the same one she'd tried to use on me unsuccessfully weeks before.

This time, it had worked its way beneath, allowing the hollowness to grow.

"I am too," Olivia admitted. She frowned at her desk. "And...we shouldn't have to play this game on campus."

"The Junior Department has been courting the justice magic and getting burned eight times out of ten. They *are* being punished," I said. "We can't stop them from opening their own grenades."

"But we can *avoid* them," she said, fingering something on her desk— spell remnants from Raphael that she'd continuously studied from the moment she'd held the atrophying bits in her hand.

~*~

Two days later, triumph radiated from her face as she held out a new sliver of a gem for our armbands.

"What material is this?" I asked, looking over the wafer-thin gem.

"Leandred is insanely useful—*never* tell him I said that. He made enough for all of us, and helped imbue them with the spells. We included some of your magic, too. You know Leandred has a ton of it, right?" She frowned at me, but it wasn't nearly as frowny as it used to be when aimed at Constantine.

"You're going soft." I smiled.

"No, I just agree with Axer Dare—Leandred's motives are transparent at this point. Leandred would burn the world for you."

"It's not like that," I said automatically.

"No. It's way worse," she said frankly. "You are like the sole family gold nugget and the crystal on the pedestal and all the frankincense in the factory. He'd never touch you. And the world *will* burn if someone intent on harm does."

I opened my mouth to disagree with that too, but she waved me off.

"I feel the same way. We have an understanding. The good news is, between the three of us, I think we could do some serious damage to Verisetti at this point." She smiled smugly. "Verisetti really shouldn't have let the two of us live. And anyone who is part of the Department's machine is going to rue the day I turned his spell."

She wasn't wrong.

Olivia's modification to Raphael's spell diameter allowed us not only to avoid Department-laced students completely, but to target them from a distance.

And...seeing as our group had been primarily formed from delinquents and malcontents, there was a lot that could be done when you could easily find a "target" to harass with spells that were weak enough not to activate justice magic—the weak spells were just really, really *frequent*.

The tide swiftly turned on campus with Olivia's implementations and even a few of the most zealous members started to actively try and avoid us.

That didn't stop the Department outside our borders, though, or public opinion throughout the layer.

Chapter Thirty-seven

THIEVES, KILLERS, AND REPORTS

A TSUNAMIC layer shift hit the western seaboard and flooded three towns and two cities. Rogue waves far stronger than expected completely destroyed two recycling domes in Shounenvale.

Second Layer Hong Kong was devastated, and when portions of Second Layer St. Petersburg were sucked into the Third Layer, the real panic began.

When Second Layer Nigeria "flipped"—east facing west, west facing east—panic turned to terror.

"Who's worried about terrorists anymore? Our entire world is shifting. This is it, I tell you. After we've done so much to the magic here, it's moving against us now."

"It's *always* moved against us. That's why we call them layer *shifts*. Some years are worse. Everyone knows this."

"It's not the shifts, it's the system. We are overloading the *system*."

"It's not system, it's the magic."

"It's not the magic, it's the government."

"It's not the government, it's the Origin Mage."

"It's not the Origin Mage, it's the terrorists."

"It's not the terrorists, it's *society*."

"Society? Idiot, it's the ORIGIN MAGE!"

~*~

Bellacia found it all perversely delightful. She reveled in dangling the bits in front of me when we met, usually in her workroom when Inessa was decidedly *out*.

"Tomorrow is going to be a cloudy day, Ren. Better take your umbrella," Bellacia sang.

I sighed. The news had been particularly grueling earlier in the day and

I'd felt really off all evening—like constant hits were being delivered to my magic, battering at my insides. I'd turned off my communications at dinner, after fair warning to all my friends, to try for a bit of returned Zen and silence in my head.

"I'll take two," I said, and added a piece of spellwork to the field limiter I was tweaking. I'd ignored looking at the walls when I'd entered, already knowing I'd find it lit with shift gossip and Origin Mage gossip and Ren Crown gossip. The best thing about hanging out with Bellacia was that I was getting used to the madness.

"You are no fun today."

"Lies." I tugged the eastern edge of the field. The limiter would still work without the adjustment, but crafting was deliberate work.

"What are you working on?" she asked, idly—falsely idle—Bellacia Bailey was *never* idle. "Something to blow up the Noroke Region? Odds are ten to one on it not making the next Aztla shift."

"That would be quite the project." I focused on lavender shaded with hints of silver in my mind and slid a bit of the invoked magic into the shimmering outer layer of the field.

"*Fine*, I guess *I'm* doing work then."

I looked over at her and sighed. We did have an agreement. I put my work away. Next time I was out of sorts, I'd reschedule. I looked at the walls.

As usual, the feeds in Bellacia's workroom were full of emotional images and stark or baiting headlines, and the words "Origin Mage" or "Origin Magic" were all over them.

A few specific pieces had been highlighted for me, though—she was always eager to bait me into *something*. I girded myself and opened the first in my palms.

"Feral Awakenings popped up all over the First Layer at an unprecedented rate this evening," a reporter said. "Some thirteen were reported in separate sections of—"

Thirteen? I touched my armband, uncertain if I'd rather have experienced this devastation in real time one-by-one or in one lump sum due to turning off my feeds and staying away from public spaces.

I leaned in closer and pulled more of the magic toward me, opening each ball to form a magic collage.

A mage dressed in red was responding to the reporter's questions. "It happens when an Origin Mage becomes active—all of the magic changes wreak havoc on the delicate balance of the layers," he said. "Look at what is happening with the shifts. Pinpointed around Excelsine, they seem to be." The man gave a significant arch of one brow.

"But not a single feral survived today."

Chapter Thirty-seven

I clutched at the hollowness growing in my chest. Not a single one? The field was so close to being finished, and the Origin Book untethered.

"What can be done?" the reporter asked.

"We lament that these poor pre-mages self-destructed before we could reach them. Poor lambs. They just aren't ready for the magic suddenly overtaking their bodies—an even quicker occurrence than usual with the outside *push* they are getting from the pockets of magic suddenly infecting the First Layer. The only thing that can be done is to bring in the magic or *mage* responsible for the outbreak."

"The alleged Origin Mage who is on everyone's lips?"

"Precisely. Piotr, whether the Crown girl has gotten access to a stash of magic or is an actual Origin Mage, it is for the safety of everyone, especially these poor feral children,"—he said, with a sad shake of his head—"to bring her in."

"Some of them are hardly children. One was reportedly twenty-five."

"They are *all* children, Piotr," he said with false gentleness. "Playing with forces they don't understand. Poor lambs."

A picture of the devastation caused by a feral mage superimposed itself over a First Layer news report. The incidents had all been blamed on something First Layer sensibilities could grasp—a gas main, a natural disaster, a disgruntled person—whatever popular current event the Second Layer spinners wanted to use.

As the magic dropped, though, there was something about the first image, then the second, that made my throat seal. I could smell electricity, rain...death.

I could see the faces of...

I grabbed the magic back into my hands, manipulating and replaying the threads of the pictures.

There was a man in the background, looking over his shoulder as he walked away from the scene of destruction. The second image held the same man.

The features of the man connected in points in my mind, like the first draft of a portrait. Eyes, nose, cheekbones, ears...a facial recognition in my mind.

I grabbed Bellacia. "Who is this? Where is this?"

She looked at my grasping fingers with her eyebrows raised, but intrigued by the intensity in my voice, she looked at what I was viewing. "Oh, you read the article. I was wonde—"

"*Who is this?*" I demanded.

She narrowed her eyes at me, then at the image.

I pointed, rippling the magic in a wave around his face. "*This* man."

She flicked her fingers around him and pulled him from the frame of the magic into a sphere in her hand. She pulled outside streams from the walls into the ball, then smoothed them out until a dossier on the man hung starkly in the air.

It all blurred together around the edges for me, but Bellacia, familiar with this type of report, was studying it with quick calculation. "A number of very large red flags in his history. How do you know him?" she asked sharply, sensing something important.

The world spun. "He should... He should not be... That man should not be free."

But there he was, his current whereabouts listed, living in a city somewhere in the vicinity of Second Layer New York.

Christian's killer. One of them, at least.

I knew him from a day long ago—associated him with the smell of burning dea—

I bent over and vomited.

Just as quickly as the bile spilled, rage rolled through me, and it took every ounce of control I had learned not to let it free. I took deep breaths and focused on the image of Axer's cloth beneath my cuff, instead of in its current location in my room. Control flowed through me.

Bellacia was speaking in the background, but I couldn't make out the words she was saying. I threw a rote cleaning enchantment somewhere on the floor, hoping that it hit the mess I had made, but I couldn't concentrate on anything but the man's cruel face and the remembrance of his voice telling me to "get away from the boy."

I wiped a shaking hand across my mouth and strode from the room. Ashes, electricity, and blood. I scrubbed my hand across my face again, this time with magic, trying to sterilize all senses in my mouth, in my nose, in my mind.

Magic sharpened my senses to a self-preservative edge, and I could immediately tell that Constantine was out, but Axer was in his room.

He strode toward me as soon as I entered.

I batted his outstretched hand away. "Why?" I said hoarsely.

"What happened?"

He tried to reach out to me again, but I scooted back. His fingers curled into a fist, and taking the hint, he didn't try again. He took a step back and crossed his arms. It was a position used for shielding, and the least threatening for someone who could kill with a flick of a finger.

"Tell me," he urged.

"He's out. He committed *murder*—committed murder *again*—and he's free. *Why?*"

Axer wasn't slow. He processed my mental state and words, and reached the correct conclusion. "Which one?"

Chapter Thirty-seven

I threw the magic I was still carrying at the wall, and a picture of the murderer's face appeared.

My brain kept issuing half-formed cries. "I thought... But it's not... Is it just a slap on the wrist? Ferals aren't important? We only count as reptiles, second class citizens?" My voice was getting hysterical. "Why didn't you lock him up?"

Why hadn't I made *sure*? All this time... I put a hand over my mouth as I looked at the number of dead ferals and tried not to throw up again. Bellacia's media dossier said the man had been living at his current residence for three months. That meant that, at most, he had spent five months in prison.

Why hadn't I made sure? Why hadn't I looked? I *knew* why I hadn't looked. Even now, the nausea was halfway up my throat again. I didn't want to have anything to do with those men. I didn't want to think about them, didn't want to spend an iota of time pretending they were even human.

But I *sure as hell wasn't going to let one walk free.*

"We delivered all of them for processing." Even though Axer's attention and gaze were on me, I could see that he was contacting someone. Perhaps questioning Julian or asking the men in the white coats to come give me a lift.

"He is not in prison," I said. "Maybe...maybe *none* of them are."

Axer's eyes narrowed and he looked to the place where I had thrown the magic. "A puzzle."

"A p...pu... it's not a puzzle!"

And then Neph was suddenly next to me, my head in the crook of her throat, soft nonsensical murmurs running over me.

Voices were speaking in the background—Olivia and Dare, maybe Mike?—then Constantine's strident tones filled the spaces.

"Well done," he said cuttingly.

Thoughts whirled in disconnected patterns, but I grabbed the edges, unwilling to let the spiral take me down with it. *Breathe.* I closed my eyes.

"That man did it. He killed that mage," I said. "That feral. Killed both of those ferals. Maybe *all* of them."

All conversation stopped and everyone turned to me.

"Ren—" Mike started.

"He did." Nausea made me swallow painfully again. "I bet if Bellacia pulls up every event today and in the last few weeks, we'll find him at more than those two scenes."

No one waited to ask Bellacia. Magic flew around the room; reports were pulled up and combined.

"There."

"There too."

"She's right," came a grim response. "Blurred, but he was present in at least four of them."

"Could be that he was trying to collect the magic edges?"

"Scavenger? Maybe, if he wasn't supposed to be in prison."

"Prison for what? Rehab enchantment?"

"Murder," I whispered.

Mike looked my way at my words. "So, wait, what is the Department doing? Killing ferals? Why? It's not like they are all going to pop up as Origin Mages. I mean, yeah, the magic when Origin Mages start to manipulate the world starts getting all screwy—sorry, Ren. But these people, they'll probably just be regular ferals."

"Awakening magic is powerful," Will said, shrugging helplessly. "You can use it for a lot of things."

"The primary goal of those men *is* to steal magic," I said, voice no longer a whisper. "He's an Awakening thief. You said so." I turned to Axer. "Back when you saved me, Julian said you needed to report that the thieves had a new tool to identify and hide an Awakening."

The fact that Alexander Dare had saved me in the First Layer was news to more than one person in the room, which was very obvious by the reactions.

"Yes," Axer confirmed. "Though Julian was given a different task soon after we turned those men in. A suspicious occurrence when this is taken into account."

"Because you weren't supposed to find us," I confirmed.

"You got lucky with that sudden trace that popped from nowhere."

"Or maybe I'm just that good."

The whispers of the past. Unaware that my brother was gone, my confused thought had been that my savior sounded hot.

"No," he said quietly. "We likely weren't supposed to find anyone. We were hunting for something else that night. I only found you because of luck. Fortune and fate," he added softly.

The tie between us pulsed and I couldn't look away. I had made paint the exact shade of his eyes—paint that could break or remake a world—and my initial savior crush had turned from starry eyes to vexing irritant to friendship, to a far deeper emotion.

Mike cleared his throat.

Axer jerked, then looked away from me. "I'll...check numbers with Julian." He disappeared into his workroom.

Mike looked at me with a clear facial expression pointing to some idiocy of mine. I frowned and Mike pulled a disbelieving hand over his face.

"You think it was the Department, all this time?" Olivia demanded.

Chapter Thirty-seven

I looked back to the reports, letting grim reality seep back in. "Yes." Helen had even made it a final taunt. The grim set to Olivia's mouth said she recalled it too.

"So, the Department spin is not to cover up their inability to save them, it's to cover up the use of their magic?"

I frowned. There was something else sliding around the edges of my mind. Helen's taunt had been...odd—worded oddly. She had asked me if I knew where the ferals *were*.

"Uh, guys?" Will was staring hard at one of the holograms. "Look at that one, in the background."

"Bit morbid, Will," Mike said from the side of his mouth.

"No, *look*. They are reporting her dead, but..."

We all stared, and sure enough, the body twitched in the background.

My gasp joined Mike's. "Not dead. What if they *aren't dead*—they are just reporting that they are to the media? Where are the bodies going? What are they using them for?"

No one had any answer for that that was good.

~*~

Bellacia hadn't waited to ask questions. She had done exactly what we had done and run through the recordings of the events, connecting images of the man to multiple scenes.

A headline ran that night with his picture attached. "Scavenger or Provocateur?"

The man was picked up before Julian got to him, and he disappeared into the system. Shelle Fanning held a conference to report that the scavenger was being "severely dealt with." However, she also maintained that the Awakenings were still a result of the magic disequilibrium.

"He's gone," I said to Bellacia, arms crossed, looking at the headlines she'd written.

"He's being held in Spartine Prison, or so my sources say."

A quick reference search indicated that it was not a place I could easily enter—Department run and maximum security. I'd do just as well to ask for a key to the Department's basement.

"You didn't wait to question him first," I said. "You've lost your lead." And I had lost mine.

Bellacia smiled. "No, dear. You are my lead. My answers will come from you."

That pronouncement brought me little relief. Nor did Axer's report.

"Julian checked the graves. Not every feral was buried, but those that were have empty graves."

I sharply turned to him. "Empty?"

"No bodies. Thin traces of magic only."

"They have them," I said, grimly certain. "All the ferals, they *have* them."

"It doesn't mean they are alive, Ren," his voice held a combination of soothing, warning, and command. "They could be studying the bodies, looking for—"

"But they *could* be alive." Energy whipped through me. "They *could* be."

"Ren."

Thoughts and plans whirled in a maelstrom inside my head. *Alive.* I could *save* them like I hadn't been able to save Christian.

"Whether they are holding them to see what they manifest as, or to steal their magic over and over, or to taunt me—those individuals are dead to the outside world. The Department can do whatever they want with them. And that edict they are trying to put in place will make it all legal. Bellacia is always going on about brainwashing ferals to Second Layer ideals and—"

"Ren." He took me by the shoulders. "We'll figure it out. Leaving campus is exactly what Stavros wants. He wants you to look for them. He wants you out in the open."

"I can't *leave* them there."

He pulled me into a hug. "We won't, Ren," he whispered into my hair. "I promise you, we won't. Just...give me some time to figure this out. This was never part of the plan."

Chapter Thirty-eight

SPINNING IN PLACE

"WE ARE DOING everything in our power to determine what is going wrong with the shifts, Awakenings, and world magic," Shelle Fanning reported, as I squeezed the stress ball Olivia had made for me and sat on Olivia's bed with her, watching the news feeds together. *"It is all pointing quite deliberately in a single direction, but Excelsine is certain that they can handle any issue there, and we would like that to be true."*

"Right," Olivia muttered.

"We are currently abiding by Excelsine's decision to handle their own security and jurisdiction regarding students."

"That's because you have to." Olivia started folding another little hummingbird paper. She had taken to origami as a stress reliever with surprising force.

Hummingbirds were associated with purification, energy, life, and creation—messengers of the gods, bringers of spiritual balance. We'd started adding the little birds to the flower rotation after Olivia had seen the tattoo Greyskull had gifted to me.

Something inside of me was still unnaturally unnerved by it.

"Of course, if it is determined that a student threatens the security of the entire layer, I think it is reasonable by anyone's standards that we neutralize that threat."

"Totally reasonable. Use excessive force even," Olivia replied.

A reporter's raised magic flipped the visual feed to their desk as they questioned the Department spokeswoman—*"Critics are saying that this is just a strategy to get a potential Origin Mage under the control of the Department."*

Olivia issued a rough huff. "Nooooo, you don't say?"

I poked her and lifted one of the finished hummingbirds, letting a little magic flow through its wings. "You are becoming really sarcastic, you know that, right?"

A papered beak jabbed me in the arm.

I caught the other bird absently, magicking it as well, and watched Shelle Fanning return verbal fire.

"There is a dark history of what happens when Origin Mages are left to their own devices. I don't think anyone wants one running around without checks in place. When our entire existence is predicated on the goodwill and good judgment of a single person, we risk much, for what if that person falls to the dark?"

I shifted my back against the wall and rubbed my chest. I decided to switch feeds.

Shelle Fanning was in this new one, too, doing something at a shift festival, participating in fun and clever ways with the scientists. Joining activities, having a jolly laugh with the regular folks, reminding people that the Department folks were just like every mage.

I switched to another broadcast—another of Fanning's, but this one about the terrorists.

"It's a new era in an ongoing fight. We have made mistakes, but we have only your safety and security in mind."

"They are separating out the public face of the Department from the far more subtle terror of the Praetorian Guard," Olivia said, looking over, expression jaded. "A well-used tactic, and one that will not benefit us."

Fanning laughed when a man asked if a praetorian might show at his door one day. *"No, of course not. We are a dynamic organization comprised of hardworking mages whose primary goal is to safely guard the Second Layer. But we do have to use an elite corps to manage those mages who are improper citizens. Only those who are against what this layer stands for should fear the praetorians."*

"If you aren't doing anything wrong, it doesn't matter if you have no freedom, blah, blah," Olivia muttered.

I looked at Shelle Fanning again. As much as I hated her party lines, she seemed...genuine. Genuine in her desire to help, though not necessarily in her desire to see past her own workplace and the people she served.

Politics class had been filled with examples of people who'd started out determined to do the best for their country and layer, then slowly gone down a different path.

And I had my own examples to draw from—Ahmed Bau. Godfrey.

How did a leader who became a leader in order to better his people get lost? Or corrupted, even?

How did an Origin Mage go bad?

I put my head back against the wall and stared at the ceiling.

"You're being too quiet."

I looked over at Olivia. "Just thinking," I said.

"About?"

"Good and evil. How good people go bad."

That finally got her to look up. I could feel the tug on our threads as she examined me visually and magically. I could feel the tumultuous emotions from her in them.

"The same way anything happens," she said softly. "The same way bad people turn good. Choices. They make choices."

"One bad choice?" I asked lightly.

"Or one good one," she said quietly, looking at me. "But, no, it's not one choice. It's a string of them." She looked at the wall opposite us. "A tube you can't stop sliding down."

"A tube of doom?"

"Sometimes it's the tube of...love or happiness or some other positive emotion."

"But if it's doom?"

"Then," she said quietly. "Sometimes you just need to find the hand hold that breaks your slide."

Chapter Thirty-nine

WHAT ALMOST WAS

WITH THE FIRM commands from everyone to stay focused and *"On campus, Ren!"* I did so, making certain to dedicate even my free hours to either freeing the book—more often in the company of Axer instead of Delia, after Mike and she had had a rather strange argument about it—or working on the field.

If I could find the ferals before the Department and protect them, all the better for *everyone*.

And we were so *close*.

Constantine and I collapsed into chairs in their living room, exhausted in all ways. He lifted the edge of his shirt and grimaced at the scorch marks.

"You had to try the extinguisher," he said.

"Your mixture melted the *desk*."

"I wouldn't have added that second drop of anisia if you hadn't given me the idea."

"All I said was that it was *sunny* outside."

"And we can *use* that power."

"Not if we're part of the *pavement*."

He waved a hand. "I had it under control."

"Right. Congratulations. I'm no longer threat #1 on Mbozi's radar."

He closed his eyes and leaned back in his chair. "You spelled me."

"Sure." A second later, though, I started giggling. "His *face*."

A half smile cracked his mouth. "I thought Stevens was going to legitimately beat you this time for tinkering with the power sponge."

"Whatever, they love it, the field is *working* and I've never seen either of them so excited. Stevens *smiled*."

"Don't let it go to your head."

I pulled my armband from my bag and checked to make sure everything was still there. I had learned the first time we tested the field to remove all my stray bits of magic—putting everything in my armband made that the easiest thing to remove. I checked the scarab first, then the communication gem, then the Third Layer marble. I lifted the dragon figurine next.

I examined the little dragon fondly, then started to tuck him back inside as well.

Long fingers reached out and grabbed it before I could.

Constantine turned the dragon over in his hands, then looked at me through the strands of hair that had fallen into his eyes when he'd stretched forward. There was a quietly banked, furious fire in his gaze. "What is this?"

"A dragon figurine." I let my armband drop to the table and tried to grab the figurine from him, but he held it out of reach. "Give it here."

"Do you hold this to you as you sleep each night?"

Blushing furiously, I tried to grab it again. "None of your business."

He gripped it more tightly, his gaze far away—I could almost see the thoughts whirling through his mind. I made another grab.

His other hand held me back. "He didn't mean me," Constantine whispered.

"What?" I let my hand drop, unease running through me at his tone.

"Your dream. Son of a... Verisetti meant—"

Anguish and fury combined in his expression. "I trusted him," he hissed. "I actually trusted his word on this." Things in the room started to lift into the air—a loss of control that I had never seen in Constantine.

I lurched forward and grabbed his wrist. The furniture dropped, but the air was still swirling with rage.

"I can't believe I trusted him. You've *infected* me, Crown."

Whoa, none of that was good.

"What do you mean? Trusted whom? What's wrong?"

He grabbed me in return, forcing us into a locked position. "I made a vow."

"Y'okay," I said, slurring words together, trying to find the right one.

"To protect you. And he assured me that I could trust him with you. Right in that dream, too, shiving bastard, probably right after he—"

"Why would you trust Raph—"

"Verisetti?" He gave a dark laugh and let me go. "No. Alexander's magic is all over this, and he's the only one who inspires that dopey look in you. You won't convince me anyone else gave this to you. This is a *leech*, Ren."

The room tilted. My hand froze in midair. "He wouldn't—"

"He's leeching you at night." The quietly banked fire became one that was fully stoked. "I *knew* he couldn't be trusted, and I fell into the trap anyway. But this time, this time I'll *deal with him*."

His rage became corporeal as darkness gathered in a swirling circular shadow around him.

"No, no, let's take a moment. I'm sure there's been some misunderstanding. There must—"

He gripped my chin. "Do you feel like you are being leeched?" he demanded. "Search your magic. You know the feeling."

I did. And...I did. There had been a slight tugging for a while—not a malicious one, more of a gentle pull. "He can't mean anything bad by it. Maybe it's for—"

"Orphans and children? Little mages of the poor?" He sneered and let go of me.

"It lets us talk at night. Maybe that is its purpose—it has to pull some of my magic to let us talk," I said, grasping at an answer.

"It's a dreamshare device, but that's not what this resonance is." He pointed to a tiny network of filaments on the surface. "This is the crystal structure of a dream leash."

I rubbed my temples. "No."

But there was something deep within me that was perking up in excited agreement. *Yes, this is exactly what has been happening*, the voice that sounded like Christian said. *I tried to tell you.*

"Ren, how long have you had this?"

"Since Wednesday? Bloody Tuesday's Wednesday?"

He swore and flung the dragon like a throwing star, embedding it by its tail in the opposite wall. "Don't touch it," he said as my feet started to move. I froze. He paced back-and-forth, whipping his ribbon in agitation.

Evil, evil, he's using you, Christian's voice was saying. *They are all using you.*

I pushed the voice down. Christian was dead.

"I'm sure that he had—"

"I swear to every hell that there is that I will *send* you to one if you complete that thought," Constantine warned.

I scrubbed my hand through my hair. "I trust him."

"I *know* you do. He's *trustworthy*. That's the whole point of the gambit."

"What did he do?" I asked softly. "To you? Why are you enemies?"

"What did he do? Everything. *Nothing*. He did everything and nothing at all."

"What—"

"It doesn't matter." His hand cut through the air. "What matters is that you give too much of yourself. You even trust *me* and I am *not trustworthy*."

"You came with me to the Third Layer and risked your life. You tried to save me from that shift, tried to get me to leave you behind. You chose to attack Kaine instead of Raphael. You chose to save Axer instead of yourself. You made a potion to reinforce and increase a community atmosphere. You helped Olivia. You kept me safe. You—"

He put two fingers against my neck and dragged away the magic that had been there for weeks. "I never removed this from you."

Something in the back of my mind perked up with excitement. *All gone, all gone! It's time!* The voice said.

I curled my fingers around his. "I knew that you didn't."

"And yet, aside from a little joking, you never made me *remove it*. And I just keep adding things to it! Find a shadow, add a guard! You didn't even know! You let everyone put spells all over you," he yelled, throwing the magic. It turned into its own ribbon and fluttered softly to the ground. "All the scavengers around the mountain are pulling and grabbing your magic. Your roses *drip* with it. How do you think Stavros is getting your magic— it's *everywhere*. You gift it, you practically *exude* it. I had to do *something*."

My breath caught. "It's a leech to *you*. That's what Mike meant. What does it leech?"

His fingers tightened into a fist. "Protection. Deep family protections. My mother was...she had a specialty. The only ones she forgot to protect against were other family. It seems we do make the same *mistakes*. But this one can be recti—"

Axer took that moment to enter the room. He had to have felt it— Constantine's darkness, my panic. I couldn't be surprised by him showing up so quickly. His gaze took in the two of us, my armband and the ribbon on the ground, the dragon embedded in the wall, and the wards pulsing furiously.

His gaze was focused, battle-ready, when he looked back, focused on Constantine.

"The prodigal mage returns," Constantine said, darkness reaching out long spikes. "Before I deal with you, tell Ren what you were doing with that thing." He swept a hand toward the dragon embedded in the wall.

"I was leeching her," Axer said calmly.

Being dropped out of an airplane must feel like this. My stomach flipped into my chest.

"And that isn't the only time I've done it," he said just as calmly.

The dark spikes from Constantine *tripled*. "I *trusted* you in this. You said you would protect her. Just one more *oops* for you. I didn't think it was possible for me to detest you more." Constantine's eyes darkened. "I hereby revok—"

"Stop." Axer grabbed his arm and Constantine abruptly stopped speaking. It looked like he was being held by something, some thread of magic. Constantine's expression was heartbreaking—the countenance of a person who had been betrayed all over again.

"I would never," Axer said gravely, responding to something I couldn't hear. "I won't. Look. *Look*."

It was another moment before Constantine stopped struggling and the two of them stared at each other in silent conversation. "Your secrets *kill*," Constantine growled.

"I know," Axer said quietly.

"I won't let it happen again," Constantine said.

"Neither will I."

"I'll be checking her for spells after this. *All* spells."

"Good."

Constantine took one last look at me, still furious, then strode into his workshop and slammed the door.

Axer's expression was complicated, but I could see regret as well as a firming of resolve.

"I did exactly what he said." Axer looked at me. "You were boiling over with magic. I took the extra. Bottled it." His fisted fingers uncoiled and I could see one of the beautiful orbs from the pond in his palm. He flipped his wrist, and in the orb's place was a cube. "Neutralized it."

I stared at the cube. "The Neutralizer Squad will be very jealous."

"Ren."

I looked up at him and swallowed. "Why?"

"Because I'm too accustomed to large-scale strategies and secrets." He stared steadily at me for a long period of time. "And some actions have more than one purpose."

"What is one of those purposes?"

"Stavros has been trying to capture my mother for twenty years. My entire life has been built around making certain that he doesn't succeed, and in the process, to position myself so that one day I'd take him down."

If I wasn't going to vilify Constantine for his retaliation against Raphael, I wasn't going to vilify Axer for his family goals. However—

"That doesn't seem fair for your family to put that on you."

"It is a role I chose. And one I will continue to choose, even more strongly. I've never second-guessed my father's choices, but I understand them even more so now. I saw the way Stavros looked at you."

"Stavros hasn't succeeded in taking your mother, and she is a declared Bridge."

"But not for lack of trying, and not without a war. That's the upside to a defensible island and staying out of the public's eye. Even when they malign you—you can hide. You can keep others away, and keep what you are doing locked inside."

I thought about what Julian had said back in the Midlands, about taking me. I thought about all the dreams where we'd visited some part of their island. "Were you, are you—?"

"I saw the way he looked at you," he repeated grimly. "You are now the keystone of his plan. Stavros isn't going to let anything stand in the way,

Chapter Thirty-nine

even us. I will do everything in my power to make sure that never happens, though. Preparation." He pressed an opalescent orb into my hand. I lifted it and the crystal light swirled with the cream.

"You made them for me?"

"Everything."

Emotion filled me.

"And the other purpose for all of these things?" I whispered.

The pads of his fingers slipped up my neck, thumbs brushed my jaw, and his eyes connected to mine. Electricity thrummed along my skin, down my throat, spreading into my chest like ink dropped into water—the finger coils of sensation hooking into me.

Throat working, his lips parted and I could feel an increased beat in the feel of his skin—like his pulse had picked up its pace and was beating into mine. I blinked to see if it cleared with my vision. No, he looked *nervous*. My world upended a fraction. When was Alexander Dare ever nervous? He almost looked like I was going to curse him and he was preparing for it.

As far as I knew, he had faced every beast known to man and come out the victor. I had seen him surprised—rarely, but a few times it had occurred —but nervous?

Something that someone—more than one someone—had said dragged through my thoughts, as if they were suddenly molasses. Like I was thick syrup and revelation had been dragging along in the tar of my brain, trying to reach a firing neuron. Alongside those words were his own statements on my obliviousness.

Axer never dated. Not a single person, if gossip was to be believed.

Oh. *Oh.*

Wow. *Wow.*

The molasses cleared in a burst of emotion, cascading the lot of memories, images, and exasperation on friends' faces into a sudden, coalescing piece of *art*, with Greene's whole shovel talk weirdness as a too-obvious caption card in its corner.

"I felt a connection to you the moment I saw you on the street trying to crawl to your brother. The series of events after that were...*singular*. It was very odd to have the same mage doing something *interesting* over and over. I knew I wanted you when you were standing in line to leave campus Fall term... I knew that feeling was not going to wither, that it would only grow stronger, after that first day together in the Midlands."

My heart was nearly beating out of my chest. "Not when I threw Ambrosia all over your lap?"

I was kind of an idiot. But that could be *rectified*. I was *all over* this.

My lips pulled between my teeth, then bloomed into a smile that was both painful and hopelessly wide—trembling with my rabbiting heart and

348

my stomach, my body caught somewhere between flight and *everything* but flight. The thread between us felt stretched, like a rubber band pulled too far away and needing to rejoin its other end, even though our chests were now only a foot apart.

"And now?"

My voice had gone breathy, like I couldn't get the words out around the violent fluttering in my chest and midsection, and I couldn't even imagine what sort of cocktail of emotion and magic I was suddenly sending out.

A nearly aching expression of relief crashed over his face—like he'd been half-certain of rejection—and the smile that curved his mouth was unsteady, even as it was incandescent and warm.

That smile—I had seen it without its shakiness before. That smile was for *me*.

His hand wrapped around the back of my neck, right where it always itched these days, rubbing over the spot.

He touched his forehead to mine, our bodies closing the distance between us.

A weird, foreign feeling was overtaking me.

I tilted my head up. Ultramarine eyes, so blue.

Impossible anger bloomed, physically overcoming me.

And that's when my hand pulled back without permission and a shadow exploded from my palm right into Axer's chest.

Constantine burst from his room, horror written all over his face, and his eyes fell to the ribbon and my armband still lying discarded on the table and floor. One finger flipped the air around the ribbon and sent it winging toward me.

"Too late, boy," came the voice from my mouth.

I wrapped a shadowed hand around Axer's neck and we fell through the floor.

Chapter Forty

SHADOWS ON THE SOUL

THERE WAS A strange grinding sound I recognized as unnatural Origin Magic, and it provided just enough of a jolt for me to catch and yank us back from wherever we were about to be taken. We jerked and landed in the dirt.

"*No,*" said the voice, that I realized—horrified—was coming from me. "Stupid girl!"

Axer was already casting magic, but my hand gripped his neck harder and pressed something against it—my quick moment of recovery was gone.

"Those nullifying cubes are quite the thing, aren't they?" the voice said. "Clever, but merely a delay in the inevitable."

I saw the surprise on Axer's face—and I examined the phenomenon for the millisecond it took for my hand to complete the motion.

The magic split and dually twisted around his neck like two beefy hands wringing a flimsy t-shirt.

He immediately gripped the magic and twisted it, throwing it to the side.

My hands flew out again, wrapping crushing magic around his windpipe.

I was in my own body, but not *of* my body. Like my consciousness existed within myself but wasn't fully filling out my frame. Like it had been constricted inward, layered with something else—a shield, a frame, a shell.

Like I was a ghost within my own shell. I fought for control. It felt like trying to grab smoke.

"I can kill him here just as easily, girl," my mouth said. "Wouldn't you rather be together? I can give you that. All the lovely tests we can run together before I wipe your will..."

I scrabbled for control of my own shell, but I existed only as a wind, a memory trapped inside.

The Midlands echoed strangely. The levels were always strange, but today it was almost eerie, the lack of noise. Usually there were creatures shrieking, wind whistling through tree branches, magic crackling. Today, there was a ghostly silence, like the spirits of the dead were silently watching, waiting. A barrier rose around us—sickly green magic rising from the edges of the tile we had landed on.

I watched my hands slowly murder Dare. It took a lot longer for Axer to work his way free the second time. He had to connect to me and overpower my magic while keeping the tainted magic away from himself.

He worked free enough to twist my hands between our chests. The magic broke, leaving me shaking. But it was *me* shaking. I could feel the outer part of my body again, though I couldn't feel my magic.

"What, why—I can't," I stuttered.

His hands trailed from my wrists, up my arms, and up into my hair. I could see him dart a look around, could feel the sickly magic entombing us. He gripped my cheeks between his palms. "Ren. Breathe."

"No." Why was he letting go of my hands? I was *dangerous*. I couldn't feel my magic, but *Stavros* could. My breath was coming in pants, my shoulders heaving with the effort. My chest *throbbed*. That hollow feeling...all those spells carving out a nice little spot for—

"Ren."

I jerked backwards, scuttling like a crab. My breath was coming too quickly. "The paper."

"What?" He tried to touch me again.

"Here." I pressed a hand against my throbbing chest. "Replicator, reader, riveter, recorder, and ratchets. Those were what the assessor brought with her. Tools she didn't need inside Medical, but on the way to Top Circle...especially the riveter...what do you use that for?"

"You think she put a link to Stavros inside." He was calm. Too calm. I had just wrapped magic around his *throat,* and he looked like he was going to pull me into his arms.

No one knew exactly how Stavros's magic worked—I had asked Bellacia specifically. The party line was that it was a simple viewing enchantment mixed with a permission spell—that each face-flipped minion had permitted the attachment. But it was ludicrous to think someone like Stavros needed to ask *permission*.

Why wasn't Axer taking my magic?

Yes, dear girl, do get him to do that, came a silky mental reply.

I stumbled, trying to maintain the distance Axer kept closing. "Stay back." Some sort of link back to Stavros, or his own version of a shadow, had been put into my storage paper, and as the paper was my own creation, when I had gotten it back, I had connected to it and invited the magic inside.

"The seed waited. Grew. Whispered," I murmured.

Chapter Forty

I put my hand over my mouth. Everyone had seen the golem with my brother's face—Patrick had used a memory of it as part of our diversion to get out of the Magiaduct after Bloody Tuesday. Bellacia had seen the picture of my brother on my nightstand—others must have too—*Inessa* must have. Would it have been hard to get a recording of his voice?

No, not with the murderers who had *killed* him working for Stavros. All they would have needed was a memory of his face.

I shook my head.

And the seed? Neph's uncle had damaged my shield set and the Junior Department had started feeding it, making it bloom. That same seed could be passed to Axer if he used his abilities, because the way he used them invited the magic inside *him*.

"Please, go," I pleaded with Axer.

"I can't go, and I can't connect to anything other than the basest of spells. Stavros neutralized me with your magic." Axer pulled two fingers calmly along his neck, healing the bruising with the barest wisp of magic. He crouched and shoved his fingers in the dirt—tiny spurts of magic trying to push into the ground. There was a resigned set to his features. "If you can hold him here for five minutes..."

"You could...knock me unconscious?"

"No. He'll just take complete control. Even death won't stop him for the first thirty seconds—plenty long enough when he has you. Right now, you are still fighting him." His gaze held mine. "You can do it."

The only thing that had been holding Stavros back before had been whatever magics my friends had laced upon me. Neph's scarab, Constantine's spell—the spell only removed when Constantine had been so angry.

The weird feeling was returning, shadows were zipping along the edges of my sight, the sickly green magic was flowing again, and Axer was far too still. "It's coming back." My thoughts muddled, as if they were the first thing the entity was trying to take from me. I needed to get *away*. I grabbed for the core of my magic, locked behind an iron fist.

Axer reached for me, face set. "I know."

He touched me and feeling ripped away, like a film had been ripped from my soul, my consciousness.

Axer fell to the ground and *arched*. Magic fled from his fingers as he scrabbled for something. I could see the magic sealing his windpipe between two clawed fists.

The film of my soul bunched up in the corner of my mind. I scraped mental fingers for it, but they passed straight through.

"Here's the thing, dear boy," my mouth said. "You guard against everything else. So *confident*. But all those attachments and feelings you have for her have given me the one thing I can use against you. Something you didn't even know you needed to guard against. So many of you make the same mistake. I've long waited for you to make this one."

My body moved. It wasn't like Raphael or Constantine leeching me, or even Godfrey controlling me. This was something far more alien—a magic that made me someone *else*. I tried to gather the emotional component just out of reach.

Axer's last reserves of magic, called upon as his body died, flew toward me and my body simply sidestepped it. The forces that were being called upon—forces that I had never wielded so casually—made it ridiculously easy to sidestep each move. I could see the external magic streaking into my body in kaleidoscopic bows. In battle or in time of stress, I had wielded this type of power, but this held an unnatural feel of my talents.

"Poor Mr. Dare." The voice came from my mouth, but they weren't my words. "So useless, here in the end."

I tried to grab my own throat, to rip out my own heart, but ghostly fingers passed through both. My body was moving, far more naturally than any marionette on strings.

The left hand of my shell twisted the ultramarine thread streaking outward from my chest into a fist and Axer arched again, his shields compressing underneath the force of the magic.

"It's truly lovely, the bond you share, the nascent love. It allows for such...finesse."

"Stop," I choked out between the other words I was, and wasn't, uttering.

"You have given him such access to you, Ren Crown. But in the taking, he has given his to you as well. We have never had opportunity this good. The others he has gathered around him are all politically untouchable. But you? Well, most people will welcome you being under the control of the government. It only requires a slight further push. And Alexander Dare thinks himself above such petty things as control. He wins and he wins and he never loses unless he wants to lose. But you? You are his utmost *liability*. Losing the Leandred boy was a blow, but he knew how to guard that attachment. This one has no guard. I've been waiting a long time for this."

My body moved in a deliberate fashion that it had never postured before.

"His mother is out of my reach and dear Alexander has kept himself free far too well," my lips said. "He thinks he can keep control of you like he can everything else, it's obvious and pathetic. Except you...you can snuff his life force. I was going to do this all properly, in the lab. But when you kill him here in full view? Well, we'll just take his corpse with us and call this whole production a wrap."

Chapter Forty

My shell laughed, then nudged Axer's arching body with the toe of my boot.

"Oh, Mr. Dare, we'll reanimate you, don't you worry. Are you trying to call your friends? Again, I had meant for the both of you to come straight to me—and in such a nice display of teenage emotion, too, all three of you failed your protections—but the Midlands are a fine set of levels to traverse when you have the type of power that Miss Crown has."

For the first time, I noticed the tiles shifting rapidly around us. Axer's group appeared, then they were gone. Then two of them, then one at a time as they split up to try and gain better access. Their strikes at me across the tile barrier were always a half moment too slow, the tiles shifting them before their strikes could land.

I could see Constantine. Marsgrove. Greyskull. I could see Olivia and Neph and the others, faces drawn and terrified as they, too, tried to gain access. I heard Constantine yell something at Olivia that sounded like, "She's in that meatsack too, it doesn't work on—," then I saw Constantine grab Olivia, Neph, and Will and push them toward something.

"I've always been interested in these levels," Stavros continued. "During a rather *creative* session between the two of us, Kinsky hinted at it being one of the spots on the fabled Origin Circuit. I couldn't really understand him well though sometimes—when his mouth was so full of blood. And he had to go kill himself a day later, alas."

I gained enough control to use our momentum to withdraw the knife from my pocket. I tried to stab myself, but Stavros anticipated the motion and the knife flew into the dirt instead.

The vine was gone, but maybe... I flayed open the underside of my arm on the edge of my belt buckle through sheer determination and force. Blood dripped to the ground.

"Now, now, none of that." My skin knit back together. "Just a few minutes more while your magic finishes connecting, then we'll be off. I approve of your pain tolerance, though. It will benefit you, dear girl."

The vine didn't show, and nothing flew out of the ground to devour me. The Midlands continued to flicker around us, unchanged by my offer of blood. The connection that Stavros was talking about was forming faster now, almost there... I sent out a mental plea, a last effort.

"Yes, *there* you go," another voice, a familiar voice said. "A lovely appeal, Butterfly, and it *is* time."

My face sneered at Raphael as he stepped from the shadows. No, not from them—with them, parting them, trailing them in his wake. They traveled with him, a cape of smoking tendrils lapping his limbs.

I felt Stavros's trepidation, like *nectar*, and for a sliver of a moment, his control wavered. The green smoke thinned. Axer rolled unsteadily and dove

354

from the tile. Relief that he had escaped crashed through me so hard that I staggered a pace before Stavros regained control.

Stavros was livid, but he said, "Don't worry, girl, I'll get him back, along with everyone who has a connection to you. I'm certain that you will be far more *malleable* with a few friendly faces tormented by pain. Emotional manipulation is my specialty."

"He does love pain, Butterfly," Raphael said, anticipation in every movement.

"Come to return home?" Stavros asked him.

Raphael smiled. "Come to die."

"I could have handled that cleanly, if you'd just stopped in for a *visit.*"

Raphael reached out and gripped my arm. "I was planning on it, but it's a funny thing, in order to control her, I can *see* you. You are extending far too much of yourself, Enton."

I tried to think about what that could mean about his type of magic.

He bared my teeth. "And what, you are going to kill her? Take me down? Destroy the mountain and yourself? You don't have the *balls.*"

"You did a *pathetic* job trying to take them." Raphael twisted my arm and pulled out a knife. "I had anticipated this going down in your lovely laboratory. The explosion would have sated every bit of bloodlust you've fed within me. I will weep for the few souls on this mountain whose love you couldn't kill from me completely, and for my Butterfly, of course. She didn't get to fully bloom, but she was always special."

He raised the knife. I closed my mental eyes.

"No." Olivia was gripping the edge of the tile, teeth grinding together. Will, Neph, and Constantine had their hands pressed against her, as did Camille. Patrick, Delia, Asafa, Mike, Loudon, Dagfinn, Adrabi, and the others were all hanging off of the chain. Axer's combat mage squad was all hand-clasped with Camille. Axer crouched near them, battle cloak firmly in place, fingers in the dirt—a trail of crystal magic zipping outward.

"You don't touch her," Olivia hissed and held out her hand. In one motion, Constantine flung his ribbon into a sword that Olivia snatched from the air. She ran Raphael through.

Shadows burst from him and he dropped to the grass.

The lot of them flew from the tile's edge.

"Ah, friendship," Stavros said, once more in control. He reached out and physically pulled Axer through the chaos magic to land at my feet. He toed Raphael's form and looked at where the shadows were reforming into the silhouette of Kaine. "What a *lovely* gift for me. My four favorites in one spot, all bundled up for me to take home. Friendship really is something. But do not fret, I will make quick work of all your attachments once we are gone. As I said, emotional manipulation is my specialty."

Chapter Forty

Shadows flowed from me and from Raphael—Kaine's shadows—ones I hadn't realized I had been holding dormant inside of me—likely ever since Raphael had spelled me in the dream, hiding them beneath Stavros's hibernating presence, which he had definitely sensed.

If only I had understood at the time what he was saying in that dream.

The shadows were forming into Kaine. And once he formed...between my magic and Kaine's, Stavros would take us immediately.

The Midlands were growing hazier—like darkness had slipped in and filled the void left behind by Raphael. I stared at Axer's bent head.

Olivia should have stabbed me. Should have let Raphael do it. I fought for control.

"Now, now, girl. Just another moment. One moment for me to take back what is mine. Dear Mr. Dare, weakened by you, need not be alive. I can revive him in his cell. One moment for me to see all that you've learned."

But there was something weird about Axer just crouching there—especially since he had his battle cloak on—and I saw him look up with the edge of a smile.

Something small flitted over the ground, like a maple leaf skittering in the wind. Another shadow in the Midlands, jumping from tile to tile, but this one navigating like it was possessed of a magic not bound by any other. It lifted, flipping through the air.

Weight landed on my shoulder and pain bloomed suddenly at the junction of my neck and clavicle. A surge of natural magic burst from my core, overtaking everything else. Axer threw a full blast of magic at Kaine's forming shadows, tearing Kaine apart, and Stavros roared. My hand, still under Stavros' control, threw the weight from my shoulder. The small being tumbled through the air.

But it was the last movement Stavros could perform as my puppet master.

I looked at my hands, and at the hummingbird flying around my skin.

"The goal or the game," I whispered. "I'll show you what I've learned."

And I let my magic fly.

Chapter Forty-one

THE UNLEASHING OF REN CROWN

THE MIDLANDS STOPPED—every tile and person stilling in unreality—as patterns of magic and electric colors zipped from me in every direction, flipping my sight so that I was seeing lines, designs, and fractals everywhere magic touched.

My magic expelled the piece of Stavros from the hollow in my chest, and the ghostly tendrils of his magic shot from me like the twisting branches of an electrical burn. His clinging claws latched onto the breaking form of Kaine.

Lights in motion, my magic revealed the fractals of spells overlapping each other in the Midlands—its twisting, repeating, chaotic patterns—and beneath them, the tight magic that made up the very layers around us.

It also revealed the spells that laced every inch of me.

"You let everyone put spells all over you! How do you think Stavros is getting your magic?"

Constantine was right.

The magic flowing outward from me curled back around in a wave not unlike that of a layer shift.

Break it. Break them all.

I looked at Neph, whose eyes were closed and whose hands were out, wrists exposed. Sacrifice.

I hesitated.

Break it. Break them all.

The voices sounded like a mixture of Christian and Raphael. But those were false voices.

"Are they false voices?" Stavros' voice said, face half-formed, dripping like a Dali, within a remnant of Kaine's broken shadow. He was somehow existing outside of the paused tableaux forced upon the others. "You will never be free."

Chapter Forty-one

I let my magic hover and lifted the strong and unbroken community spell that traveled through the mountain. The threads—thousands of them now, all of different thicknesses, colors, and vibrations—arced into and out of my hand as different tethers pulled and pushed, requested and demanded.

With my other hand, I gathered my own ties.

Raphael's spells overlapped all of mine, and Stavros and Kaine's dispersing shadows were insidiously twined throughout. Marsgrove, Stevens, Greyskull, Axer, Constantine, Neph, Olivia, my parents, the rocks, the Bandits, campus, *everything* I had ever created—hooks were everywhere; some wanted, some not.

I lifted the community spell in front of my face, then looked over the top of it to the shadow shard of Stavros—only a tiny piece of the man—that was growing more menacing, and gaining strength with each partial moment that passed.

I wondered what would happen, if I chose to throw the spell at the shard. Greyskull's tattoo of love and unbreakable friendship had made Kaine scream. What would a spell full of the community spirit of an entire campus do to Stavros parasitically attached to Kaine?

I let the spell fall. He'd likely disappear, flee his host. But I wasn't going to risk inflicting his spirit on campus. I called one of the opalescent orbs so carefully collected by Axer.

I crushed it in my palm.

Community and Origin Magic burst outward like shattering glass, throwing each shard of magic and each person into an asteroid field orbiting me.

My bonds gleamed in the light—the dozens of thick ropes connecting me to the people in the circle, the hundreds, the thousands that were streaming beyond. Those thousands were slimmer, but we'd come together as a community on this mountain—joined in blood and ash.

I let the hovering magic form into a knifepoint and I started with the smaller threads first.

Each of Axer's team jerked, their backward thrust pushing them farther from orbit as time achingly began to crawl for them now that their strings were cut. The Bandits, still frozen in orbit, were next. Only I moved in real time—the motion of every other person in the circle dragging—each successive person only the most miniscule of moments behind the previous person as they all began shooting backward in a long chain, screams in formation upon their successive lips. And I kept cutting.

Neph's body was frozen like the others who had yet to be cut, but her gaze was the single anomaly as she tracked my movements, watching as I sliced each thread.

Her face said so many things, so many things I couldn't parse.

I didn't understand her expression, but suddenly *I was Nephthys*—standing in her soft-slippered shoes, watching the world's magic swirl around Ren and lift her hair, like a vast tornado of creation twining around its eye. I watched all of the connections diving into Ren, pulsing with life and acceptance. Watched her cut each one.

Brown eyes specifically took in the pulsing strands of chocolate and sand, pulling long, graceful fingers over those connected to her own face and chest. There had been no other connection as valued as this one, and there never would be again. And Ren needed to be released. She needed to be free.

Deep, tearing regret punctured me—no, not me, *Neph*. And it wasn't regret. It was sorrow, understanding, an ache—a soft sort of yearning.

I had this for a little while, her voice said. *I had this and it was worth everything. And she will be more powerful. A gift. Always a gift.*

Her eyes closed in acceptance, closing my view and shooting me back into my own consciousness. I looked at Neph, her eyes closed, palms up, waiting, all her magic available for use. Understanding and acceptance.

I looked at the magic I had whipped up, and at what it was telling me to do. Giving me the ability and understanding to break free of my bonds—the ones that would be used against me again. The ones that would be used against *them*, as Stavros had said.

But...choice. There was a choice. Always a choice. I could make a choice—like Olivia, like Constantine, like Neph, like everyone on campus—I could make a choice. And I could give it as well.

I held the chocolate and sand threads to Neph in my hand, and I cut them. And Neph, with a look of acceptance on her face, fell backward.

Olivia, Constantine, Axer, my parents, cut, cut, cut. The last frozen bodies in the circle were released.

There was only one tie remaining. The box from my Awakening. I felt that one keenly—the most keenly of them all because it was part of me. It contained Christian's magic, my magic, and Raphael's magic inside.

I looked at Raphael, slowly rising, and alongside him, Kaine, Stavros, and Axer, who were moving a fraction faster than everyone else's slowed suspension of time.

I could see it very clearly and dispassionately for a moment. The unreality of it, the break from humanity. What I could do in order to gain the exact mechanical resolution that would resolve the problem.

Connections. Connections kept me human.

I snipped the last thread.

Stavros's shard moved slowly, but somehow he was still able to communicate in my real-time reality, shadowed and without moving his lips. "And now, you are attached to no one. You will have no one. You can rule all."

I tilted my head at him, emotion completely removed from me in this temporary state between destruction and creation. "You understand nothing."

I held out my hands and the cut threads flew into my palms. Carefully discarding only those that I could be certain were impossible to keep, the rest, I held—hundreds of them, thousands, vibrating with distress—roses, storage papers, paint, rocks, dye, metal, creations, contracts, and all of the personal and community attachments I had formed.

Bodies continued to thrust backward in their slowed, domino pattern, no one yet reaching the ground.

I gathered the threads.

Stavros' gaze moved infinitely slowly between my hands and my face, shadow still in a suspended animation. "You seek subservience then." I didn't have to look to know that the smile that would break upon his face would be in its beginning stages of forming.

"No." I looked at Neph, the resignation and acceptance in her features that would shatter me, when I was capable of feeling normal emotion again. "That is the problem with not thinking outside of what is. You must contemplate what could be."

"I was *born* to think about what could—"

"You aren't going to take my community away," I said to him, uncaring what he was going to say.

I brought my hands together, pulling the community spell and my concentrated Origin Magic screaming back together, like a shattered window reassembling with the threads in my palms, and did what I had started in Medical with Olivia, what I had done with Neph, what I had sought with the enchantments I had been playing with on campus, and the forces in the shield project.

I changed the spell.

Not subservience, not like Raphael wanted, or Stavros, or Ahmed Bau. No leashes or domination or unequal distributions.

Unity.

It was a subtle shift—just the *feeling* of some of the spells, really—to change from subservience to unity. And more than one of them—far more than one—of the inequalities were solely on *my* side of the spell. I had always chosen to give more.

I tilted my head in contemplation—emotion not a part of my decisions here in this emotionless state—and fixed those connections too, resetting them to a balanced state. Unity. The desire of both parties to give, and together to be part of something more.

* The Unleashing of Ren Crown *

Some needed no tweaking at all—most of those with the people I already loved—and others, like with some of my more insane projects, with Raphael, Stavros, and even Marsgrove, I changed the nature of the leash or discarded them completely.

Until there was only one remaining. The box. The tie stretched far—the box likely in another layer. I held the broken tethers and links that connected me to my Awakening box—the one that Raphael had used to unleash terror and destruction on the Second Layer. I considered it, then considered him, my logic and puzzle solving centers working over plans and seeds. And instead of destroying the box completely, I *changed* it.

I let the cut threads drop, and the magic dropped with it, as did everyone around me. I saw Greyskull reach out with quick fingers in the sudden chaos and touch something to Raphael's forehead.

"There is nowhere you can go where I won't find you," Stavros said to me, voice cold. "This was nothing. A game. When next we meet, it will be face to face, and your magic will be mine."

"Until next time, then." I thrust my hands outward like Constantine had done. "You don't belong here."

Stavros roared and fled as his borrowed shadow shard burst from the gold spell. Kaine's body ruptured completely, curling and flipping, tendrils fleeing into the air. Raphael smiled, then his campus-banned form was propelled backward like Ahmed Bau's had been. He angled himself like a skydiver, though, and shot through the nearest arch. Greyskull, Marsgrove, and Stevens ran after him.

Emotion burst back into me. Horror, conflict, fear, relief, understanding, resolve.

Stavros wasn't done. He had just started.

I watched my friends as they regained their feet—and I wanted to go to each and every one, help them to their feet, apologize in the most hysterical way—but there were too many directions to turn, to step, so I ended up just standing there, frozen, while I checked all of the threads brightly connecting us still. Threads that, in some cases, were far brighter, cleaner, and in others—

"Those were my last clean pair of pants," Will said regretfully, as he brushed himself off.

—other threads felt exactly the same.

A sound emerged from my throat—something between a laugh and a sob.

Axer's arms were around me.

"I'm sorry, I'm so sorry," I sobbed.

Olivia's and Neph's arms joined his.

With my head turned, I looked at the object sticking out of me. A pencil, stabbed into the meat of my neck joint was dripping paint down my shirt. Movement on the ground made me look there. Guard Rock toddled over and motioned.

I dropped to a crouch on the ground, the others still closed in around me.

Guard Rock hopped up, gripped the pencil, then pulled it out. He tumbled back to the ground, but regained his feet quickly. A small piece of his rock was missing—torn from him when Stavros batted him to the ground—and I could see it gripped in his other hand.

"Thank you," I said, tears dripping from both eyes.

He nodded and stamped his pencil against the dirt. The earth gave a little shake at the connection of the painted tip. Guard Rock looked at the tip, then reached over and wiped it against the hem of Axer's cloak, cleaning it off like one would a battle sword.

"Thanks," Axer said, voice far more rueful as the paint seeped into the threads, probably changing the nature of at least one of the spells.

I gathered the rock to me and smoothed his missing piece into place with magic, then put him in a protected position sticking out of my pocket. Axer must have called him—he'd done something to Guard Rock in Okai when I'd joked about him enchanting my friends.

Stavros was gone from me—a presence that I hadn't sensed until he was absent. The voices in my head were silent. I could only mourn the loss of Christian's a little. It hadn't been him.

"I'm still me." My uncertainty and guilt made me sure of it. Though, those both were a little lighter. A little less...potent.

The cut threads squirming on the ground told me so.

A blaze set the threads on fire, and Constantine very casually ground them into the dirt with his boot.

"I'm still me," I repeated. Axer pulled me tightly against his chest again, like he knew I might start crying.

"Which, frankly, is *still* terrifying, Crown," I heard Patrick say.

"Seriously horrible," Loudon added eagerly. "Can you just snap your fingers and end the world now?"

I turned my head from Axer's chest and blinked at him. "No?"

He sighed, disappointment painting his features. "Not to be my light show, then. Alas. I thought for sure we were getting a front row seat."

I looked around at the rest of the Bandits, who seemed to have similar questions on their faces.

"I didn't absorb the knowledge of the universe?" I said questioningly.

More than one face drooped. Perversely, this made me feel far better.

"I just remade the connections." The idea of it, of what I had done, hit me all at once and I hurried to explain. "I made them so they can be accepted or rejected by anyone at any time. On either side. And so that both sides—especially you guys—you can remove your connection to me. At any time."

Nothing happened. No one discarded their threads. I had expected at least *one* to do so.

I checked my threads in unease, what if I had accidentally bound them all to me? I started to panic.

"Sometimes, Crown, you are an idiot."

My head whipped up and I stared at Patrick. "But—"

Patrick shook his head. "You didn't change mine to anything negative, and I'll bet it's the same for the rest of this lot." He motioned around him. "These are connection threads that can be fed. And they can, conversely, wither. It's the choice of both parties. Choice, Crown." He smiled in a somewhat tragic manner, gaze almost distant. "It's not something all of us get."

I opened my mouth.

"Stop talking, Crown." He rubbed a hand along his forehead. "I need to go play a video game. Something where I can blow up some authority figures, turn off the game having learned nothing, and go to bed. Saf."

Saf sent reassuring vibes through our...community.

Because that's what the threads were now—a complicated, yet simple, bundle of zipping magic nestled together willingly—not tangled or wild.

Well, maybe a little wild, but the kind of wild that bumped pleasantly with its neighboring threads, jostling them into motion or easing them to stillness. Even Axer's group was tied in.

The Midlands flashed around us and presented an exit to the Ninth Circle.

No one looked surprised.

"I'm still going to put in my bid on these being the scariest levels on the mountain," Mike said.

"Agreed." Delia pulled an unsteady hand through her bobbed hair.

"Chaos, kids. We all need a little more of... What is that?"

I followed Loudon's gaze to the sky. Dark clouds were rolling toward us like *The Great Wave Off Kanagawa* mixed with *The Scream*.

"We aren't supposed to be getting another shift today."

"That's not a shift," I murmured. I could feel the magic—the oily corruption of my own. "It's Stavros's first piece of revenge. He's going to make campus pay."

Chapter Forty-two

UNITY IN DESTRUCTION

"HE WILL BE outed," Olivia said sharply.

"Not if he already has someone lined up to take the fall," Camille said, eyes fierce as she looked at the crazed storm heading our way. "And he always does."

Olivia looked sharply at her.

The rogue shift brimming with corrupted Origin Magic—*my* corrupted, collected magic—was heading straight for us. Towns in the way were *lifting*, pulled up into the roiling chaos.

"Where is it *from?*"

"How can he do this?"

"He means to do far worse," Axer said, tone distant, likely speaking to someone mentally at the same time. "He has no more patience now that the opening gambit has been lost. He needs Ren off campus. He'll destroy the mountain to do it. And it will be spun as the Origin Mage destroying her own home by accident or by fury."

Raphael's voice whispered on the wind, "*Allies, Butterfly. How will you save them?*"

"I'll take care of it," I murmured, walking forward.

"*You* will be outed," Neph said softly, sticking to my side like glue.

"Bit late for that after that display, don't you thi—ow!" Loudon finished on a yell.

"It's Origin Magic. It has to be me," I whispered.

"No it doesn't," Constantine said. He firmed his lips. "There are others positioned for this fight."

The professors and staff were all gathering at the top of the mountain, pooling their magic together with the administration wards. I was very familiar with a number of the magical signatures I could feel gathering there. The adults had abandoned their Raphael hunt to protect their home.

"I'm being called to Top Circle," Neph said.

"Everyone, please remain calm. Exits are available from all the normal arches." The administrative voice droned on, filtering down campus.

"Portents of doom," Inessa yelled, suddenly appearing from who knew where, pointing at me in crazed mania. "She has brought this upon us!"

"*No.*" Olivia sprinted over and punched her in the face, then followed her to the ground, not stopping her blows. "You do not get to do this now."

Mike and Will ran over to grab her. Delia followed at a much slower pace, mouth quirked.

"Really, Price. In our last minute before sudden death, you are going to turn puerile?" Bellacia said, appearing next to them but not looking down—attention fully on her recording orb, which was focused on the oncoming destruction. There was a weird mixture of emotion in her gaze. She was not happy about what was about to happen, but she was resigned to it as well.

An argument broke out between the gathering groups—Junior Department types, my friends, and people on all ends of the community spectrum—as people fled.

The little dragons shrieked and dove into the Midlands behind us. Students were fleeing to the arches. Some had already abandoned ship, not sticking around to go down in united...

Constantine's gaze fell to meet mine.

I lunged forward, snagging Axer's cloak as I held out my other hand for my armband. "That's it."

I didn't wait to converse. My armband hit my palm and I ran, knowing Constantine, Axer, Neph, and the others would follow in my wake.

"What is she doing?" I heard more than one person say. "Ren, what are you doing?"

"Gather everyone." I threw the words over my shoulder and through every frequency and communication I had collected—I sent the packet of information *streaming.* "Everyone who wants to save campus. Grab them all."

I jumped the Midlands using one of the arches for that very purpose—the idea of stepping into the Midlands felt like a bad one—and ran for the closest arch to the Eighteenth Circle. I could hear people yelling behind me and in my head, but people were streaming in my wake. I ran for my position, Guard Rock clutching the edge of my pocket as I bounded.

Mbozi and Stevens were somewhere very near—closing in on us quickly.

"Whatever position is closest! Quickly!" Wellingham's magnified voice yelled.

It said something to the power of the community we'd been building that so many people showed. That the professors left their positions on Top Circle on the word of a few key colleagues and the community. Even people who were streaming off campus down the mountain, stopped, turned, then started zipping back toward us.

I pressed my hands to the ground. "The magic seeks to destroy us," I said to the spell, to the mountain—always sentient in my mind. Then I funneled my magic inside. I saw all the people around me dropping to press their hands to the dirt. The golden threads spread, connecting from one person to another, faster and faster.

"Ren!"

I looked over at Professor Mbozi, who tossed me the device we'd been working on as if we'd made it for this exact purpose, this exact moment. I caught it and shoved it into the ground. It was a personal shield, still so small in our specs. But Constantine's hook—the extra addition to the unity band—was an attachment to me, and that could make it so much *more*.

It was just a matter of scale, and the connection between the mountain and my magic could provide that. Trust and resolve filtered through the connected mages—a unity of mind.

"Only grab the magic that seeks to destroy," I whispered to the device, to the mountain, and to myself as the focal point of the spell. There was a flipside to this magic—one that I *didn't* want to engage.

I grabbed the tip of the device and whipped out the fibril canopy like only something that Constantine made could flow, a banner that flew, rippling left, then right, down, then up. It became a rippling liquid of silver, a net of shimmering stardust, that burst over the mountain—connecting to every person crouching beneath in solidarity. The gold from the ground reached up through each mage toward the silver and the silver reached down to the gold. A last push of magic connected everything into sparkling lights of silver and gold, and a gleaming dome zipped along all sides to encase the entire mountain.

The wave of corruption crested the final mile and crashed against it.

I could hear the screams. I could hear the thoughts of the people, now part of the net. Even if the magic didn't crush us, it would spring off the shield to wreak untold havoc elsewhere. This was country-ending magic that Stavros had unleashed.

"Steady!" Wellingham yelled, and it occurred to me that he must know —from Mbozi or Stevens—what was about to occur.

The magic hit like a pounding fist, trying to break the barrier. Spray from the blast burst over the top. But the hit took the momentum from the corrupted magic, and the magic of the canopy became a swirling vortex of gold and silver satin—sucking the magic in a downward spiral right into the box. The end of a long satin ribbon skimmed the top of the vortex, gleaming gold and silver in the sun. It swirled downward like a thread called violently back to a spool as it followed the swallowed magic inside.

Schwoop. Gone—like the hunter who'd fallen into my sketch so long ago.

There was dead silence, not even a breath of wind, as particles of silver and gold fluttered down to settle in the grass.

As soon as the motes touched, the mountain pulsed, and the little dragons chittered and chirped then flew up into a suddenly existent breeze, spiraling around Top Circle once more.

People were looking at me in horror or awe.

Marsgrove pivoted and disappeared toward Top Circle like a three-headed dog was nipping his heels.

"The Legion is demanding immediate entry. They can't get onto campus and are saying they'll use force," Olivia whispered, obviously hearing it mentally.

"What are they going to do? Attack us again?" Loudon asked aggressively.

More than one person exchanged loaded glances—not all of them part of our group.

Mbozi straightened his suit jacket and waved a discreet hand. I nodded and tucked the box into my pocket while trying not to look too conspicuous as I did. Stevens was staring at me, her expression a sad mixture of pride and resignation.

"Well, Crown." Patrick clasped his hands together. "I'll buy one of those devices from you for a penny. In early on the Munit Exchange, at least, yes? For your old pal?"

The Layer Equilibrium Society, resplendent in their black robes, bent their heads to me, hands extended palms up in a gesture of supplication. I swallowed and looked away. I didn't know what to do with that.

I turned to Constantine instead. "Did you know?"

"Know what precisely?" He was fiddling with modifications to a black ribbon. My ribbon. I wasn't sure what he was doing with it, but it had been the thin veil protecting me from Stavros taking over all along. "That this is entirely my fault? Yes. I never should have remov—"

"Hey," I said, putting a reassuring hand on his arm. "Stavros was going to get through eventually. That spell kept me safe for *months. Thank* you. You were right about everything."

"Of course I was," he said gruffly.

He held out the ribbon to me and I looked at the threads. There was a small opening clasp that could be activated by either of us. "You can remove it at any time." His voice was gentle.

I clasped it in my hand and closed my eyes against the wave of emotion. "Thank you," I said softly.

Chapter Forty-two

I looked down at the glittering gold and silver dust still sparking among the grass and tried my question again. "Did you know?"

"This exact thing—that a rogue shift would be thrown our way?" He cocked his head arrogantly, apparently done with feelings. "You gift me with the appropriate amount of insight."

"Con—"

"I knew it would be something," he said quietly. "There will always be something, with you. And the unity spell provided an avenue to use. That you chose to spend my gift on saving campus instead of saving your own skin is so *you*." He grimaced.

I hugged him and he held me with the usual combination of fondness and resignation. He, Olivia, and Stevens were so alike in some regards.

"Which part was weird?" I could hear Dagfinn say to someone. "The whipping us into an unbeatable force, repelling the attack, recycling the shift, or trapping it inside something? Okay, yeah, that last part was weird, Lou."

I looked to where the combat mages were congregated. Axer looked over and smiled, the edges of his eyes creasing. My heart flipped a little. Because it had only been about an hour since I'd realized that my crush turned friendship had maybe turned into the start of a relationship while I wasn't paying attention.

That hour hadn't gone well. But the *possibilities* now...

The happiness of the people around me, campus, magic itself, enveloped me in a sudden sense of beauty. Like a magic spell, making everything possible, euphoric, *utopic*.

Bellacia stood to the side, contemplating all of us.

"I suppose I have half a story." She clicked off a little device. "I'll want the other half soon—when you find it or are captured."

My breath caught and my stomach dropped into my shoes. Then I saw it, over the valley, the shadows slipping toward the mountain, an abnormal occurrence for a cloudless sky.

"You can't do this, Bailey," Saf said, frowning. "Ren just *saved* campus."

"She saved it, and now I'm going to report it." Bellacia turned to me, her gaze softening the smallest of measures. "There's nothing to be done. Your little spat in the Midlands? Dear, it was captured by more than one memory. And though I have Cam assuring me that it wasn't *you* in your own body, that isn't what the memories show. No one could hear, and did you take my recording device?" She looked down her perfect nose. "No, you did not."

It hadn't even been an option. I hadn't even had my *scarab* on me, no less anything else I regularly stuffed in my armband.

Our group was slowly gathering behind me.

Constantine started moving toward Bellacia but I stopped him, my gaze

368

on the shadows growing closer. Axer magically appeared on his other side. I could feel the campus wards lock. The Legion had done something, overpowered Marsgrove's or Johnson's authority. Most people seemed unaware of it, though I felt Axer and Constantine stiffen beside me, and saw horror dawn on Olivia's face.

"Bella—"

She toed the sparkles still glistening under our feet. "Ren, it's over. They called for another Origin Mage test the minute you broke the travel wards within the Magiaduct. Even if it wasn't *you* who was driving your body when you did it, it was your magic that registered, and Stavros made certain it showed. The Department sent the evidence and request through the council and got a complete set of signatures fifteen minutes ago. Stavros is thorough. He had at least four plans in play that were waiting for an inciting incident. He is going to get you one way or the other, we've just been marking pleasurable time."

"They can call for a test all they want—" Mike said.

"My demographics show they *will* gain enough public support to issue a test for her regardless of her consent. And you won't pass, Ren. The Department has had samples of your magic for weeks, waiting for the moment to release the knowledge to the public, building up fear and concern. It's been a very interesting few weeks. Daddy is displeased with some of my questions." She smiled. "But we have been waiting for the moment to release the revelation of your mage type, and we will do so before the Department does. Right now, in fact."

"Bella—" I pleaded.

"Ren," her voice was almost gentle. "You really want me releasing it first." She pressed a button. "You have thirty seconds to say your goodbyes. Do make sure the praetorians don't get you right away."

She turned to where an orb appeared in the air. "I'm Bellacia Bailey, reporting live from Excelsine University, where—"

Neph waved her hand and the air shimmered, then firmed into a curtain between Bellacia's broadcast and our group. It curved around, enclosing us in a privacy field.

"The Legion has legal signatures claiming marshal authority on campus for the sole purposes of securing the student named Ren Crown," Dagfinn said grimly, repeating something he was hearing. "They closed all off-campus arches. No one who is registered as a student can leave until they are done searching."

Everyone exchanged small, significant looks, then piled in for a hug.

"Thank you," I said, reluctantly stepping away after far too short a moment. I looked at the greater group—twenty-strong—and swallowed. "Thank you. Thank you for—"

Chapter Forty-two

"Crown, that woman is mad if she thinks this is goodbye."

"Campus can't—"

"Oh, you are leaving, for sure," Patrick said with a deadpan expression, interrupting me. "But goodbye, it isn't."

"They are coming," Neph said distantly.

And I could feel it too, the Legion and praetorians streaming onto campus grounds from opposite directions.

Constantine toed the glimmering spell beneath our feet, sending a pulse of gold through it. "Let them come."

Olivia nodded fiercely, pulling magic into her palms.

"No." I put a hand on her arm and sent a thought on the wind to the administration building. *Will you take care of them?*

They won't get a single one, came back the promise, the reply. I felt the loosening of the magic connecting me to campus as Marsgrove did whatever was needed to free me.

"No." I let my fingers slip from Olivia's skin, then threw my arms around her neck. "Don't let them give you someone dull," I whispered into her hair.

I stepped away, quickly dodging her horrified fingers trying to grab me back. Neph wrapped arms around her and Olivia immediately started to struggle. "Ren!"

I backed away and avoided her gaze as I felt the magic slipping free, campus reluctantly disengaging tentacles that had clung to me so fiercely moments prior. An unsanctioned tear slipped down my cheek. "It's...okay. It's time."

I looked at Axer, who looked nothing short of deadly as he ripped his gaze from the praetorian shadows at the base of the mountain beginning their ascent. He narrowed his eyes and nodded.

I swallowed, and before the contract magic released me completely, I gave a tug at one of my changed threads. I reached through the connection and wrapped the wards that remained around the book's consciousness— including the travel ward—over the pedestal instead, overlapping the stone like drooping petals over a stem.

It didn't matter, now, if I used my powers.

Be free.

I backed away. Axer looked over at Constantine and Olivia, and they both nodded jerkily, though Olivia looked like she might throw up at any moment. A backpack appeared in Constantine's hand and he threw it toward me. *Don't do anything stupid until I find you,* he sent grimly. I caught the pack and pulled it on. I could feel the mass of magic inside—things created by all of my friends, little pieces of campus, my personal items.

One of them—or all of them—must have gone through and tagged items to be collected with a spell. Just in case.

The campus tie released completely. I touched all the vibrant connections still streaming from me, though, and gave them a soft strum, like a harpist starting a beautiful tune. "Thank you. For everything."

A wave of returned strums shivered over me and Neph's curtain fell.

Soldiers spilled down the mountain and shadows flew up. The shadows screeched in pain every time they touched the community spell lacing the entirety of campus, but they kept coming. I could hear Stavros's voice on the wind—*there is nowhere you can go where I won't find you.* I watched them come, then tilted my head to the sky.

Wings of black-and-white came soaring through the air, darting between the dragons.

Magic streamed from its binding—knowledge, destruction, creation, design, secrets, and danger. The book dipped into a sharp dive.

Guard Rock launched himself onto my shoulder, wrapping his arm through the pack's strap.

I stroked his head, then opened my arms and let the pages take me.

About the Author

Anne Zoelle is the pseudonym of a USA Today Bestselling author. Anne is currently working on the next book in the Ren Crown series.

Find Anne online at http://www.annezoelle.com.

If you'd like to contact Anne directly, you can reach her at anne.zoelle@gmail.com.